RECKLESS LIES

Vikki Holstein

PRESS

Published by Vulpine Press in the United Kingdom in 2021

ISBN: 978-1-83919-371-2

Cover by Claire Wood

www.vulpine-press.com

Always and forever, to my rock, my hero, my Superman, Craig.

Dear Reader,

The fictional town of White Wattle Creek and its inhabitants have been my constant companions for the last seven years. Over that time, the characters within these pages grew into people who fight for what they believe in, and for each other.

The White Wattle Creek series follows a group of friends who each have to face the after-effects of abuse, be it rape, emotional abuse, sexual abuse, or domestic abuse. As they learn what family and friendship truly means, they learn about self-forgiveness, trust, and love.

Although the White Wattle Creek stories deal with abuse, they don't romanticise it or go into minute detail. They simply tell of the struggles so many survivors face every day of their lives, and show that survivors not only deserve a happy ending, but can have that and so much more.

For the survivors reading this, I see you, I am you. For everyone else, I hope my stories set you on a path to understanding.

Thank you, and I hope you enjoy *Reckless Lies*, the second book in the White Wattle Creek series.

Vikki Holstein

WHITE WATTLE CREEK

RECKLESS

LIES

Carol's Playlist

'You Need to Calm Down' – Taylor Swift
'Slow and Steady' – Of Monsters and Men
'Skyscraper' – Demi Lovato
'We Are the Champions' – Queen
'Return to Sender' – Elvis Presley
'Let You Love Me' – Rita Ora
'The Archer' – Taylor Swift
'Sanctuary' – Welshy Arms
'Thinking Out Loud' – Ed Sheeran
'Whatcha Gonna Do About It' – Sex Pistols
'Chasing Cars' – Snow Patrol
'Truly Madly Deeply' – Savage Garden

CHAPTER 1

Rain lashed the floor-to-ceiling windows of the clubrooms. It smudged the bright lights surrounding the oval outside and turned the football players training in the winter downpour into ghostly streaks of colour.

From behind the bar, Carol mentally composed how she might paint the scene. Maybe with bleeding watercolours or thick oils. Acrylics would allow her to play with the colours but would dry quick enough to make a large piece doable in the time she'd have.

As streaks shifted and distorted the scene outside, Carol tilted her head and frowned. Inks. That's what would catch the fluidity of the disjointed world beyond the glass. She'd use the inks Mr Arden, her former art teacher, had given her for Christmas. They'd been sitting on her desk for six months, waiting to be used, along with the roll of good paper he'd given her the year before. He'd gifted the items to her without flourish. Must have wanted to see what she'd produce with them. To see what his encouragement, his time, his belief in her would spark.

She'd let him down the last few years, had needed to smother the thrill a clean line or the perfect mix of colour could give her. Repressing the need to lose herself in the creative process had become easier than fighting with Paul, so she'd hidden her sketchbooks under her bed, had swallowed the urge to hum along to songs, and had forgotten about one day using her art to change the world. Paul had made sure *that* stupid notion died along with every other dream she'd had. Even now, two years after she'd promised herself that she was done with him, that nothing he'd ever said or done mattered, he still invaded her every decision, her every thought.

1

Turning away from the window and the itch to capture the clash of light, movement and Mother Nature, she took a deep breath. Tonight, she'd intended to banish the demons Paul had left behind, not summon them. It was time to start her life again, so that she could pick up a pencil for more than scribbling a note, or sing at the top of her lungs when her favourite song came on the radio. She wanted to enjoy her gigs at the pub with Jex without hearing Paul's voice in her head telling her that people only clapped so she wouldn't feel bad. Even Jex's assurances that her voice had the power to move souls couldn't stomp out Paul's words.

No one had been able to dull her memories of his constant insults. He didn't have to be right there, shaking his head at her voice, her body, her thoughts, for her to second-guess everything she did. He didn't have to be standing beside her, sighing at the dress she wore, for her to look in the mirror and cringe.

But it wasn't up to anyone else to make her forget, make her change. She'd let him into her life and convinced herself she'd meant something to him, so she'd deal with the aftermath of that mistake. Tonight, she'd sing in front of the crowd she hadn't been able to face last year, and she'd stop thinking about Paul. She wouldn't waste any more energy on him. He didn't deserve the space he took up in her life.

Change happened with effort, as Gran had always said, so she'd put the effort in and get her life back. Starting tonight. And tomorrow she'd pull out those inks and that paper. She'd chip away the rust from her muscle memory by sketching perfect lines and mixing as many colours as she knew. Carol mulled over what her first subject would be as she lined pitchers of water along the polished red-gum bar, smiled as she ducked under the bar flap into the main clubroom.

Here, the air vibrated with energy and warmth as a dozen people put last-minute touches to the room. In the centre of it all, Rita Morell offered encouragement and suggestions, her navy dress matching those of the half a dozen Blue Ladies working among the volunteers. They reminded Carol of older versions of the Beauxbatons girls from *Harry Potter*, in both dress and decorum. Each woman personalised her blue uniform with either a broach, a button, or a bow pinned to her collar. And tonight, each woman's usually sedate hat overflowed with feathers and flowers.

Crazy Hat Night was an annual event run by the Blue Ladies to raise funds for cancer research. And for those who'd either battled cancer, still fought it, or had lost someone to it, the event had grown into a celebration of love and laughter. White Wattle Creek might not be a big town, but when someone needed help, people pitched in. Carol had witnessed it time and again; had done what she could, when she could. Donating her time to work the bar would be her contribution, as it had been in other years. Except last year.

As guilt smeared a cold blob over her heart, Carol gripped the last water jug against her chest and fought memories of last year's event.

Rita held up a hand, beckoning her fellow volunteers to gather around.

Was Carol delusional to wish she'd one day be as confident as Rita? The woman organised her volunteers as she did Ethan's office—with a steady hand, a cool head and enough compassion to put the most distressed person at ease.

As the last Blue Lady joined the group, her smile quick as she straightened the hat of the woman beside her, Rita checked the small fob watch pinned to her lapel.

'First of all, ladies, thank you for your beautiful work with the decorations. I know Lou and Lisa need to get going now.' She smiled at the two women. 'Thank you for giving what time you could tonight. The rest of us will now head to the kitchen and help out the CWA ladies with the finger food and sweets.'

As the two who were leaving exchanged hugs and goodbyes with the others, Carol set the water jug on a table and walked to where Rita turned in a circle, nodding at the final product.

She smiled at Carol. 'We're nearly ready to open the doors.'

'I don't know how you get this done every year.' Carol stood with her hands on her hips and took in the mermaids swimming across the windows, the unicorns prancing across the brick walls, the toadstools and fairies nestled in flowerpots. 'I'm getting magical vibes this year.'

3

Rita nodded. 'Everyone needs a touch of magic in their lives, don't you think? Especially those faced with the stark realities of life. And as for getting it done each year, I have a lot of help.' She patted Carol's shoulder. 'Are you ready?'

Swallowing the *no* on the tip of her tongue, Carol glanced at the bar. 'Zoe's not here yet, but I can handle serving the drinks alone for now.'

Rita checked her watch again. 'I hope she's not too far away. I'll go and make sure Marley and his art students are ready, then I'll open the doors. A few will come early, but I don't think it'll get busy just yet.'

Trusting Rita's prediction, Carol made her way to the bar, waving to Jex as he set up a microphone on the square patch of lino that would act as a stage for the night. He had soft music playing over the speakers set throughout the room, and she smiled as Taylor Swift's 'You Need to Calm Down' started playing.

Taking a breath, she hummed as she double-checked the stocked drinks and ice. As she turned back to the bar to check the straw holder, a bright flash blinded her.

Putting one steadying hand on the bar, she rubbed her eyes. 'Is that you, Lilli?'

As the photographer for the local paper, Lilli would cover the night, capturing candid shots of the laughter and tears, the triumphs and the pain. She'd put them together with an article, an homage to those she captured, that would warm hearts and give hope.

Lilli grimaced. 'I'm sorry. I'd taken photos of the players and forgot to switch the flash off. I wanted to snap a picture before you saw me because that green hat goes fantastically with your pink hair. Combined with that broody look, it makes for a strong shot.' Lilli turned the camera to show Carol. 'You have such presence, on and off camera.'

Carol huffed out a laugh. 'I think it's more the photographer's skill than the subject matter.'

Lilli shrugged, snapped another shot of the room. 'This must all remind you of your gran.' She seemed to realise what she'd said and frowned. 'Sorry, I should have said that better.'

But Lilli's words and how she'd delivered them didn't matter. Because the ache Carol felt at having lost her grandmother to cancer was constant.

'It's okay, Lil. I do wish Gran was here to see it all, though. She'd love the clash of colours.' And, if she'd still been alive, Gran would have seen through Paul. *She* would have listened to and believed Carol.

Then again, if Gran were still alive, Carol would never have gotten involved with Paul in the first place. Not that Carol could bring herself to blame Gran for Paul being part of her life. Only for dying and leaving her alone in a world that insisted on taking everything from her.

'I'm sorry I wasn't there for you when she died.' In a rare gesture, Lilli reached out and squeezed Carol's hand. 'We all seemed to have things happen that year.'

Carol nodded. 'We did. But we all survived, so that's a bonus.'

One corner of Lilli's mouth lifted. 'Yeah, we did.'

Carol scanned the room for a new topic of conversation. When Rita opened the door, Mark stepped in, his police cap soaked and his high-vis vest bright over his dark uniform. He turned a circle, taking in the room's transformation. When he caught sight of Carol and Lilli, he gave them a nod, but then, holding up a finger, he tilted his head to the radio clipped on his vest. Carol sighed; with his attention on whatever job he'd just been given, Mark strode to the door and out into the freezing night without looking back.

'One of these days he'll actually get to stay and enjoy the party instead of being called away to make sure everyone's safe,' Carol said.

Lilli tapped the camera. 'I wonder who makes sure he's safe.'

Carol frowned at that. 'I guess he looks out for himself.' Glancing from the clock above the drinks fridge to the door behind her, she blew out a breath. 'Is Zoe still coming in to work tonight?'

Not that Lilli and her twin were close, but as they both still lived with their parents, Carol figured Lilli would have some idea where her sister might be, whether she was still coming into help behind the bar as she'd promised.

Aiming her camera at the cluster of disco balls throwing rainbows against the walls and the floor, Lilli snapped a photo. 'As far as I know. When I left, she was in the bathroom doing her hair and stuff, getting ready to come in.'

'Well, I hope she gets here soon or I'll be run off my feet.'

5

'If you get stuck, I can help.'

Lilli's simple offer pushed aside some of Carol's tension, and she smiled. 'Thanks, I know you would, but Zoe promised she'd be here.'

Lilli held up her camera. 'Well, I'll be around, so let me know.'

As Lilli walked away, Mrs Glade hurried up to the bar, one hand holding her wide-brimmed multi-feathered glitter-laden hat, the other clasped to her full bosom, which was barely contained by her low-cut dress. As the event's MC and founding member of the Crazy Hat Night committee, Carol's former English teacher and now neighbour revelled in her role as costume influencer.

She leaned as close as her hat and bosom would allow and winked. 'I'm running late. Mr Glade insisted I model my hat for him before I left.'

Carol closed her eyes and shook her head. 'I don't want to imagine that.'

With a huff, Mrs Glade tapped the bar. 'Why do young people think they have the monopoly on sex?'

Instead of getting into *that* discussion, Carol opened her eyes and smiled. 'What can I get for you?'

'That wine I like. The white, I can't remember what it's called. The wolf one?'

Carol reached for the bottle and poured Mrs Glade a glass. To keep the conversation off sex, she nodded at the room. 'Looks like it's going to be another fantastic night.'

Mrs Glade accepted the glass, took a sip and nodded. 'It is. I'm sorry you were sick last year. Not only did we miss you, but we felt the gap in our entertainment schedule for the night.'

Guilt sat like a hot rock in her stomach. She'd told them she'd been sick, and though she had been, she hadn't caught a sudden bug. Instead, she'd been curled on her bathroom floor, wallowing in self-pity and shame while Mrs Glade, Jex, and everyone else she'd promised to help, had been forced to cover for her.

'I know,' she mumbled. 'I'll make up for it this year.'

Mrs Glade patted Carol's hand. 'You don't need to make up for anything. You made the right choice, staying home instead of infecting everyone. We just missed you.'

Giving Carol's hand a final squeeze, Mrs Glade turned, managed to hold her hat, bosom and wine glass, and hurried over to where Jex tuned one of his guitars. She took the microphone from the stand and blew into it.

'Is this working?' When half a dozen volunteers stopped to nod, Mrs Glade risked letting go of her dress to lift her glass in a salute. 'Are we ready for another fun-filled fundraising night?'

Receiving a few mumbled responses, Mrs Glade frowned, which had everyone standing to attention and answering, *'Yes, Mrs Glade!'* as though they were back in school.

With a nod of approval, Mrs Glade turned to Jex and spoke into the microphone, even though he squatted right next to her. 'Are you set up and ready to go?'

Jex grinned and leaned towards the microphone. 'I'm ready to go.' He glanced over at Carol and lifted his chin. 'Are you?'

Carol managed a smile. Would she ever truly be ready to sing in front of a crowd again? Their pub gigs were often spontaneous, so her nerves didn't have time to take hold. But tonight, with the memory of last year festering like a splinter under her skin and Paul's voice a ghost in her psyche, her nerves dug in deep.

Frowning, Jex set his guitar aside and made his way over to her. 'Are you getting sick? You've gone pale.'

Carol handed him a bottle of water. 'No, I'm fine. Just looking forward to getting the first song done.'

'Okay.' Jex hesitated, his eyes on hers, then he uncapped the bottle and took a long drink. 'See if you can talk Kelsey into doing a duet with you. I got Pipa onto it the last week, so you shouldn't have much trouble.'

Carol gave a genuine smile. 'That's fighting dirty. But clever. She'd do just about anything for Pipa.'

'Who wouldn't? That kid is adorable and just as smart as me.' Jex grinned. 'Isn't Zoe supposed to be here too?'

Carol glanced over her shoulder as the outside access door slammed. 'And here she is, finally.'

'Sorry, got caught up.' Tall, blonde and beautiful, Zoe wore flustered like she wore everything. Perfectly.

'I'll be ready.' Carol waved Jex off, then turned to Zoe. 'Everything okay?'

'Sure, just lost track of time catching up with friends in the car park.' Her blush said it all.

Carol ignored it. Listening to Zoe's sexcapades—as Carol had for the three years they'd been working together at the McKinley Hotel—only highlighted the lack of her own. Zoe flirted enough for the both of them; Carol had lost count of the times her friend returned from a break all flushed and grinning, whereas Carol had only ever returned itchy and bothered after meeting Paul outside.

But she didn't have to worry about that now.

'I've stocked the fridges and ice buckets, so the first rush should go smoothly.'

Zoe pulled her hair back into a perfect ponytail. 'Excellent, because here they come.' She nodded towards the open doors, where Rita was welcoming the first shivering group.

As the room filled with chatter and laughter and warmth from exchanged hugs, Carol fell into the familiar rhythm of serving drinks, chatting with locals, and generally getting everyone in the mood for the coming fun and frivolity.

Turning to serve the last person in line, Carol grinned at her best friend. 'Kelsey Ryder, how goes it?'

She could ask that now without Kelsey clamming up to avoid letting secrets slip as she had six months ago. Not that Carol could blame her. Kelsey had spent five years running from a drug-crazed killer with her daughter, Pipa. Out of options and hope, she'd finally come home, had found protection with her friends and family with Ethan.

Now, Kelsey's smile radiated happiness. 'It goes well. And would you believe it still gives me a thrill when people call me Kelsey Ryder.' Ethan came to stand beside her and she wrapped her arms around him. 'Just like it does to call this one *my husband*.'

They both radiated happiness, the likes of which Carol would never know; she'd never let herself get that close to someone again.

Shoving her demons aside, she leaned her elbows on the bar and tilted her head. 'Somehow, I don't see either of you losing that thrill. And speaking of thrills, Jex tells me I'm doing a duet with you.' She shot a finger at Kelsey.

'That's my exit cue.' Ethan dropped a kiss on Kelsey's head. 'I'll get us a table.'

Kelsey watched him walk away. 'He's said his piece about it, and he's right.' She turned back to Carol. 'Jex got Pipa excited for me to say yes.' Kelsey glanced towards Jex. 'I just don't know if I'm up to it.'

Carol couldn't let Kelsey flounder in self-doubt. Not after she'd spent five years in hiding with Pipa before coming home and finding that innate inner strength Carol had always admired, managing to free herself from a drug-crazed stalker. Now, she wanted Kelsey to remember the times they'd performed together, before everything had changed.

'Have you forgotten how to sing?'

'No, but I haven't done more than sing to Pipa for the last five and a half years.' Kelsey twisted her wedding ring around her finger.

Carol straightened. 'You have no reason to hide anymore, but if you really don't want to do this, I understand.' More than Kelsey knew. 'Just remember, you run a horse therapy business that's becoming known across the country. You have support, both here and in Melbourne. You have people who would fight not only *for* you but right beside you. Most importantly, remember that you're safe now.'

Kelsey's chin jutted. 'You're absolutely right. I will sing with you.' She met Carol's gaze. 'I'll do it tonight, first up, because there's no reason not to.'

'Exactly.' Carol picked up two glasses and the bottle of wine Kelsey and Ethan favoured. 'You're a fighter. Pipa sees that with everything you do.'

Kelsey reached out and tugged Carol in for a hug, nearly pulling her over the bar. 'Thank you for the reminder.' She let go. 'And we're all fighters, so we all need to remember that.'

Carol's history told a different story, but she smiled. 'I'd be happy to give you a kick whenever you need a reminder.'

Laughing, Kelsey took the glasses of wine and went to join Ethan and their group at a table near the windows.

Mrs Glade waved as she hurried over and held out her nearly empty glass to Carol. 'Better top this up before I get the night started.'

Carol refilled the glass and handed Mrs Glade a bottle of water as well.

'You'll need to keep hydrated,' she said in response to Mrs Glade's raised eyebrows.

No one wanted a repeat of Mrs Glade's wine-induced strip tease from the first Crazy Hat Night, even though she'd raised a quick thousand dollars from people wanting her to stop. The second event had seen her graphically performing 'I Touch Myself' by the Divinyls.

Last year, Carol had missed the experience of seeing a drunk Mrs Glade reciting a few not-appropriate-for-work limericks as the night wound down. This year, Carol would keep an eye on her and hopefully stop her doing anything she might regret tomorrow.

Taking both the water and the wine, Mrs Glade raised the glass in a salute. 'You're a good girl for looking after me.'

The easy praise warmed Carol. A soft and comforting thread wound through her, relaxing her shoulders. It sparked the hope that she'd be ready for whatever life threw at her next. That she'd take whatever it was and make the most of it. But as she clapped along with the crowd after Mrs Glade opened the night with the list of sponsors and supporters, the hairs on her arms stood up. She frowned at the spreading goose bumps, and when nausea burned a path up her throat, she turned to the doorway where Mr Arden greeted the stragglers.

Paul.

The room tilted. The air in her lungs froze. The noise in the room fell away under the throb of blood in her head, and time collapsed. She was seventeen again and desperate to matter, to mean something to someone. He'd seen that and had used it to bend her, break her. He'd made her hate herself for hoarding every little scrap of attention he'd given her.

He'd rolled his eyes at every dream, every wish she'd ever mentioned until she'd given up on them. He'd made her feel worthless, hopeless. And every time she'd fallen as far as she could into the black hole he'd dug for her, he'd throw her a smile, a look, and she'd fall at his feet, let him do anything, say anything, as long as he didn't ignore her again. But as soon as he'd used her, the cycle would start again.

She'd crawled her way out of that humiliation, had sworn again and again that she'd never go back. Yet here she was, hating him even as her heart screamed for him to turn his head a fraction and send her that look. She wouldn't fall again, though. Not after last time. Paul took everything but only ever gave misery in return.

She couldn't stay here now. Couldn't face him or the memories his presence dredged up. She stumbled towards the back door, her hand shaking as she pushed it open and stepped out into the cold, spitting night. Doubling over, she clutched her chest. How could she survive this? How could she survive the humiliation and shame Paul always buried her in. How could she move on when he had everything and everyone, and she had nothing and no one?

'Are you okay?'

Carol's knees gave way, so she squatted against the brick wall of the clubrooms. 'What are you doing out here?'

He held out a hand as though to help her up. 'Am I not supposed to be out here?'

Sucking in air to stop the ground tilting, Carol squinted at the man who stood frowning at her. 'You're not him.' She pressed a hand to her galloping heart. 'You're not him.'

'I don't know who you think I am, but I'm Blake Sender.' He didn't offer his hand again.

He looked like Paul—the same dark hair, the same strong jaw line, the same dark eyes—but his mouth didn't have that hard edge to it.

Still, she straightened slowly, ready to escape if necessary. 'If you're here for Crazy Hat Night, you're running late.'

'I'm always running late these days.' He thumbed his ute. 'I have an auction piece I need to get to the kitchen.'

'You want that door.' Carol nodded further up the building.

'Right.' He scratched his chin. 'Is there someone who can help me? It's more awkward than heavy.'

She rubbed her arms. 'I can give you a hand.'

11

He eyed her. 'You're freezing.'

'So the exercise will warm me up.' And would keep her from facing Paul.

Maybe she could leave, get word to Jex that she *was* sick. Except she'd told him she was fine, had promised him she'd be there for him.

She ran through possible excuses as she hefted her end of the package and helped Blake carry it to the clubroom's kitchen. Nodding when he thanked her, she wiped her hands over her hips, then crossed to the door and peeked out into the clubrooms, swallowing back the nausea.

Paul sat two tables down from Kelsey's, his easy smile attracting everyone as he talked. She'd bet everything she had that he'd planned this. Just as he had a year ago. And he'd expect the same outcome.

About to take a step back, her heart telling her to bolt, she froze when Kelsey stood and made her way to Jex.

Carol deliberated. She could still leave, could save herself the humiliation and pain of failing in front of Paul and everyone else. Because she would fail; singing when her breath rasped through her throat into locked lungs would be impossible.

But Kelsey glanced over, tilted her head and frowned. She deviated from Jex and came to stand in front of Carol, just out of sight of the audience.

'Why do you look like you're about to run? And before you lie to me, remember that I saw that same look in the mirror every day for four years.'

Carol loved Kelsey, but she had an inner strength Carol didn't possess. 'I don't know if I can do this.'

'So you're going to let Paul think he's won? That he can still affect you after leaving you the way he did?'

He hadn't left her. At least not in the way Kelsey and everyone else believed. And no one knew how easily she'd fallen for the look he'd given her last year. Would they figure it out if she went out there and stammered her way through the first song? Would they all laugh and shake their heads? Or worse, boo her off the stage for being the pathetic touch-starved girl she was.

Coughing, she patted her chest. 'I think I'm coming down with something.'

Kelsey lifted her chin. 'Bullshit. We're doing this, because like you said, there's no reason not to.' She grabbed Carol's hand and pulled her out in front of the crowd.

Instantly, the cheering and clapping started. Paul sat at his table, with one elbow propped on it as he kept chatting with one of his friends.

She was nothing but a toy he enjoyed playing with. Her life, her future, meant nothing to him. Why couldn't she move on? Why did she let him have such a hold on her?

Jex strummed the first few cords of 'Slow and Steady' by Of Monsters And Men and quietly counted them in. Carol closed her eyes against the truth of the lyrics.

Her shadow would be the only thing she'd let hold her now. And no matter how much time passed, she'd never show anyone her true self. Not while the monsters in her head drowned everything else out, or while Paul sat at the table and ignored her. She'd be forever alone, moving slow and steady on her own.

#

Blake stood in the doorway, hands in his pockets, fiddling with the stubby pencil he had in one and the small notepad in the other. Behind him, a dozen people worked to prepare plates of finger foods. Before him, the woman with bright pink hair and haunted eyes sang with Kelsey, his new friend and neighbour.

Kelsey had many talents. She could gentle a horse with nothing more than confidence and a keen eye. She baked an awesome welcome-to-the-neighbourhood chocolate cake and could pick the weeds from the flowers struggling to survive in the jungle that was his garden.

Her husband, Ethan, was the conveyancer Blake had hired when he'd bought the old McGrath place, as the locals called it, a month ago. In the past three weeks, Ethan and Kelsey had gone from being acquaintances to friends, and Blake had come to rely on Kelsey and her whirlwind daughter coming around for their weekly drop-off of home-cooked stew and cakes.

13

Pipa's enthusiastic commentary on his work gave him an ego boost and made the loneliness at three in the morning easier to handle. He'd never really thought about having kids but watching the Ryder family together tickled something in him. Then again, it could just be that he'd gone from living in an apartment in a city full of people to what most would consider a cabin in the woods. Birdsong filled his mornings instead of the sounds of traffic, and stars, millions of them, lit his nights. And he loved it. Loved that he could walk outside, naked if he wanted, and have magpies warble to him or kooka-burras laugh at him. It made the quiet nights bearable.

Would having the soul-touching voices of Kelsey and her friend spilling from his music system scatter the quiet of his house? And although Kelsey could sing, it was her friend—with her sexy, husky pitch, who spiked his skin. Her voice could inspire him, with that tumble of emotion wrapped around him, to make some magnificent works. But though his body reacted to her, he mentally shook his head. A relationship was the last thing he wanted right now, but her voice and that guarded way she held herself, sparked an instinct in him. One that wanted to protect.

When Kelsey and her friend each stood and took a bow, he clapped along with everyone else. He'd never believed in having a muse to keep artistic blocks away. You worked and creativity flowed, simple as that.

Still, the things he could make if she modelled for him …

With his gaze on the pink-haired pixie, he pulled out his pencil and note-book and flipped to a clean page. Then he let the sketches spill, rough and raw.

He could make a whole series centred around her. In wire, a sculpture of her as an impish faerie, whispering in a horse's ear. Or a moulded mesh piece of her leading a puppy on an adventure through tall trees. A life-size sheet-metal cut-out, with wings and wild hair. All of them would set him apart from the competition, and using one of their own as a model could help him fit into the community he now called home.

Home.

For years, it had been an empty word. After moving to a distant city with his father, he'd grown up in a house filled with uncertainty and strain. And even once he'd moved in with Tish and she'd filled their beachfront apartment with light and love, he'd never found the heart to call it *home*.

The only place that came close was his mother's bush cottage, but as much as he loved and missed her, he didn't want to live with her. He'd left everything behind to live his life *his* way; moving in with his mother would have defeated his purpose.

The moment he'd seen the real estate advertisement for the run-down house on twenty-four acres and surrounded by bush and pine plantations, a spark had leapt in his heart. He'd bought the place as soon as he'd walked through the front door and had spent the last three weeks trying to turn the house into a home. And whenever he'd needed a break, he'd gone into town and walked through the streets with the eyes of a local, rather than a tourist, taking reference photos for art pieces and travelling the back roads and tracks. He'd talked to the locals too, and it was clear they thought they already knew everything about him. Questions weren't so much asked of him as facts relayed—he was a city boy wanting a tree change; he'd chucked in a successful career in real estate for life on a farm out in the sticks.

Stories of the founding settlers—the Todds—met him at every stop. The locals loved their town's history, so he'd tried to capture some of it in his sculpture by featuring the paddock with the white wattle tree around which the town had grown. The response from the people gathered here tonight would tell him if he'd hit the mark.

As with muses, he didn't believe in make-or-break moments, but tonight's reception of his work would either help him establish himself in the town as an artist, or it wouldn't. There was nothing he could do about it now. He'd scrambled to complete the piece between fixing his leaking roof and renovating the house to pull it from dump to something at least partly liveable.

As Mrs Glade, who he both admired and feared as he had his own high school English teacher, stepped up to the microphone and adjusted its height, he slipped his notepad and pencil into his pocket.

Mrs Glade tapped the microphone, successfully quietening the chatter around the room. 'Now that we have the evening under way, I would like to point out those of you with bare heads and give you a minute to remedy your oversight.' Her gaze travelled the room and landed on Blake.

15

He nodded and smiled as he made his way through the room to the ticket table.

'Welcome to our annual Crazy Hat Night.' A man with a biker's build and beard shook Blake's hand heartily. 'I see you don't have a crazy hat, so you have two choices. You can buy one decorated by our wonderful creatives'—he pointed to where four teenagers sat behind a table spread with cheap glitter hats—'or you can pay the fine.'

Blake considered the hats, the reason for the night. The kids had turned them into works of art that called to his soul. 'Can I do both?'

'Well,' Biker Beard scratched his head, 'I guess. I mean, I'm not going to say no.'

'How much is the fine?' Blake pulled out his wallet.

'Twenty dollars.'

'And the hat?'

'Also twenty.' Biker Beard grinned. 'People usually grab a hat seeing as they're paying the fine. Plus, the kids have put a lot of work into them.'

'They have.' Blake pulled a fifty from his wallet and handed it over. 'The rest is a donation. And if you have any hats left over at the end of the night, then I'd like to buy them.'

'Well, that's something, isn't it?' Biker Beard scratched his cheek. 'The kids will be tickled about that.'

'I hope it's a statement of the school's art program.'

'It is.' Biker Beard puffed his chest out. 'My art students are the best around.'

Blake smiled. 'I wish my art teacher had been half as good as you then. I might not have wasted the past seven years doing something else.'

'An artist?' Biker Beard tilted his head. 'Not a painter, you don't have the look. Not a sculptor, or not exactly.' He nodded. 'A metalworker.'

Blake laughed. 'I'm worried you're psychic and will tell me everything I've done wrong up until now.'

'No fear there, mate. My wife's the psychic. I can just smell the welding on you.' He grinned again. 'Don't worry, most people will think it's a new sort of cologne.'

16

'Thanks.' Blake resisted sniffing himself; he'd become desensitised to it anyway. 'I better grab the hat I want before someone else does.'

'You do that, and we'll catch up at some point. Get you into the local art group. We could do with spicing up all the paint and pencils.'

'Sounds interesting.' He left Biker Beard and headed for the hat table.

Once he'd settled on a hat, he turned to find a table and bumped into Kelsey. Putting a hand on her arm to steady her, he smiled. 'Kelsey Ryder. That was a great performance.'

Kelsey's green eyes lit up. 'Thanks. It's been a while since I've sung in front of a crowd. I'd forgotten how much fun it can be once the nerves clear away. It definitely gets the blood going.' She fanned her face with her hands. 'Do you have a table yet?'

He glanced around the room at the groups sitting and chatting. 'Ah, no. I haven't got that far yet.'

'Come and join us.'

'Thanks, that would be great.' He followed her to a table where Ethan and a few others sat, shook hands and tried to commit names to memory, then took the empty seat next to Kelsey.

She poured him a glass of water. 'You got your piece done for tonight?'

'Just.' He toasted her. 'And thank you for putting me in touch with Rita and Mrs Glade.' The schoolboy in him couldn't call the teacher by her first name. 'I wasn't sure I'd be accepted so easily.'

Kelsey leaned against Ethan as his arm came around her. 'I know what you mean, but they know it can only help raise more money, so it's a win-win, I think. Plus, Ethan put in a good word for you.' She smiled and, turning her head, kissed her husband's jaw.

They were a couple completely in love, in sync, and best of all, happy. Blake hadn't been in the company of many couples who'd forged their relationship purely out of the need and want to be together. Love had played a part in the relationships of some people he knew, but in high society, many married for power, money or convenience rather than wanting to wake up with someone for the rest of your life.

Tish had wanted that, had tried to give him what he wanted. Their break-up had been his failing. He'd tried to live yet another lie, had hoped it would work. But, just as with all the other lies he'd been living, their relationship had crumbled, and he'd hurt the one person he'd never wanted to cause pain.

'Hey.' Kelsey touched his hand. 'Are you okay?'

'Yeah.' He picked up the glass of water and downed it. 'You'll have to bring Pipa out again now that I have some flowers to pick among the weeds. And I have a couple of dog sculptures ready to go now too.' He pulled out his phone to find the photos he'd taken. 'Here they are.'

Kelsey tilted her head to see the screen. 'They're adorable. I'm guessing she'll pick this one.' She pointed to the fat dog he'd made out of a shovel head, rusted wire and the fuel tank of an old PeeWee 50.

He'd guessed the same. 'I'll make sure it's within easy reach then.'

He slipped his phone back into his pocket as an itch tickled his neck. Scanning the room, he blinked at the frown Kelsey's pink-haired friend aimed at him from behind the bar.

He leaned closer to Kelsey. 'Your friend doesn't seem to like me.'

Kelsey glanced at her friend. 'That's Carol, and I don't think it's you, exactly.' She pointed to a table further down. 'The dark-haired guy is Paul, her ex. You look a lot like him.'

At least his earlier encounter with Carol made more sense. She'd mistaken him for her ex. As he and Tish were only just back on speaking terms, the last thing Blake wanted was to be caught in the on-again off-again dance some couples engaged in—and something was definitely still humming between Carol and Paul.

Before Blake could dwell on the reason for the odd twist in his gut, Mrs Glade gave her familiar tap on the microphone.

'If I could have Blake Sender to the front, please.' She smiled and started clapping, encouraged the crowd to join in as two people carried in his art piece. 'I can't thank Mr Sender enough for this generous donation. This piece, I believe, is called *Home* and will be displayed in the town hall until its auction next weekend as part of the Wattle Yard Art Group's cancer appeal. I also believe that once tonight's event has concluded, Mr Sender will be happy to answer all your questions about this piece and the other works that will soon be displayed in the town hall.'

Blake nodded. 'That's correct. I'm excited to be a part of the community's efforts in supporting cancer research, as well as the community in general. I named this particular piece *Home* because that's what this town is to all of you, and I hope it will become that for me, too.'

A man wearing a neon orange top hat raised his hand. 'What's it made from?'

Walking over to the piece, Blake pointed out its features. 'The base is corrugated iron, the hills are bike chain and wire, the trees are links from a chainsaw, and the cattle are nuts and washers.'

A woman from the front table called out, 'When do we get to bid on it?'

Ethan stood up. 'Can I buy it now?'

'Do you have more of them?' was yelled from the back of the room.

It was a better response than he'd expected. The tension he'd held since loading the piece into his ute eased. Perhaps he wouldn't be run out of town as an impostor, which was something he'd feared would happen since he'd arrived. He had big dreams and an even bigger longing to fit in, but he'd spent most of his time working, creating stock to launch his business, or had been knee-deep in renovations.

But as he stood before the crowded room still erupting with questions despite Mrs Glade's best effort to quell them, he had to face the truth. He'd hidden himself away. Because to try and fail at launching a career—his *chosen* career—as an artist would prove he should have kept living the lie.

And that, he couldn't do again.

CHAPTER 2

With her feet aching and eyes gritty, Carol changed into her leathers. Glad she hadn't left her bike at home to walk the ten minutes from her house to the clubrooms, she stuffed her uniform into her backpack, fished her keys from her pocket and grabbed her helmet from under the bar.

'Before you go, Carol,' Rita waved an envelope as she crossed the nearly empty room, 'I just want to make sure you're still donating your services tonight. The committee are happy to pay you, of course.'

Carol nodded, though her empty fridge came to mind. 'I am. I'd rather the money be donated to the cause instead.'

Rita smiled. 'Thank you. That's very sweet and generous of you.'

Tapping her fingers on her helmet, Carol glanced at the door. 'It's not that generous.'

'When a person has very little but gives what they can, that's generous.'

Carol shook her head; arguing the use of words like sweet and generous to describe her would be a waste of time. All she wanted was to get home, snuggle down in her bed and forget that Paul had ruined her night.

She'd gotten through it by remembering how her hand had stung the day she'd slapped him—after he'd jumped out of her bed and off the red head he'd been fucking. His apology had been in the form of *I'm sorry, but this is all your fault.*

She'd burned the bed after he'd left last year. And tonight, as she'd sung Demi Lovato's 'Skyscraper', she'd recalled the way the flames had engulfed it. It made her believe she could be that strong again, that she would wake up and be able to untangle herself from his hold. She'd even managed to over-look the game he'd played tonight of *ignore her and she'll come crawling back to me*. She'd had a year to break that cycle, and she believed she had.

Still, she couldn't help being angry that he hadn't even said hello. Though she hadn't wanted to talk to him, or even look at him, he'd chatted to the people around him while she'd sung, as if she'd been nothing but background entertainment. As if the three years they'd lived together had meant nothing to him. It still shamed her that she'd stayed with him. Shamed her more that he acted as if she'd play her part.

He didn't know her now, though. She could ignore her need for his at-tention and still function. She could acknowledge all he'd conditioned her to think and feel without acting on it. No one would have guessed the effort it had taken her to serve drinks and smile while the memories of everything he'd ever said to her, and everything he hadn't, swirled through her. But she'd pulled through, hadn't fallen in a heap.

Banishing thoughts of Paul from her mind, she glanced around the room. Some people had stayed to help with the clean-up, and Mrs Glade was slow dancing by herself in the middle of the room.

Carol nodded in her direction. 'Does Mrs Glade have a ride home?'

Rita turned, and her mouth fell open in a silent *oh*. 'I hope so.'

Mrs Glade began to unbutton her dress.

Leaving her helmet on the bar, Carol hurried over to still the woman's hands. 'Mrs Glade, is Mr Glade picking you up?'

Mrs Glade giggled and pulled Carol into a waltz. 'Mr Glade likes it when I strip for him.'

'Oh, wow, okay.' Carol glanced at Rita and mouthed *help*. 'Is he picking you up? Or do you have a ride home?'

'You could take me home on your motorbike. That would give us all a thrill, wouldn't it?' Turning the waltz into a dance, Mrs Glade spun Carol with surprising strength, then, when she yanked her back in, nearly sat them both on the floor.

'I only have one helmet.' Though if it stopped the spinning and jerking, Carol would gladly give it to Mrs Glade and cop a fine if she got caught without one. 'Besides, it's too cold to ride on a motorbike in a dress.'

Mrs Glade winked. 'I could always take it off.'

'Now, Milly,' cutting in smoothly, Mr Glade hugged his wife close, 'we leave our clothes on until we get home, remember?'

'I do love it when you scold me.' She grinned over his shoulder at Carol. 'And when he spanks me.'

Carol groaned. 'I really didn't need that visual.' Turning away to collect her helmet before Mrs Glade spilled any more secrets, Carol froze. Blake leaned against the bar with his hands in his pockets.

'Blake. We're closed, I'm sorry.'

He removed his hat and sat it on the bar. 'I'm after something better than beer.'

She zipped her jacket to her chin. 'What could be better than beer?'

His gaze met hers. 'Your songs.'

She waited for the punchline. When none came, she tilted her head. 'I'm not sure I understand.'

'Have you and the guy on the guitar recorded any songs together? Your rhythm and voices mesh so well. The sound you produce together is inspiring.'

Alarm bells sounded. Had Paul found this guy and put him up to this? Was it a new type of manipulation technique?

'You want a CD of our music?'

'CD, digital, whatever. Of you singing, mainly.' He glanced across the room to where Jex pulled down the last of the streamers. 'But I figure ... Jex is a big part of your music.'

She crossed her arms over her chest. If Blake had an aversion to Jex because of his sexuality, she'd put a stop to his enquiry right now. Paul had nearly destroyed her friendship with Jex once, and she wouldn't put it at risk again.

'He's a huge part of it,' she said, 'and he's a good friend.'

Blake nodded. 'I figured. There's an easiness between you. My guess is you've known each other since childhood, though he's a couple of years older than you.'

She narrowed her eyes. 'Are you some kind of psychic?' It was either that or he'd been fed the information.

A smile softened his eyes. 'I asked the art teacher the same thing.'

Unlike Paul's shark-like smirk, Blake's smile nearly pulled an answering one from Carol.

'You asked Mr Arden if you were psychic? I thought you'd be the one to answer that.'

'Up until six weeks ago, I didn't know what I was, only that I wasn't who I am.' He frowned. 'And that made no sense.'

'Unbelievably, it did.' Because she'd carried the burden of a false life inside her as well. 'Who you were wasn't who you wanted to be.'

'Yeah.' He nodded. 'Thanks.'

'You're welcome.' She waved to a group of people heading out into the cold. 'I'll warn you, if you stay much longer, you'll be roped into cleaning up.'

He gave a shrug. 'If it means you'll answer my question, I don't mind.'

Carol eyed him. Something about him beckoned her to relax. She wouldn't, couldn't, until she figured out who he was underneath the confidence and charm. Not that she'd be getting to know him. She had enough men in her life, and the drama and pain a relationship caused wasn't worth a sexy smile and curious conversation.

'Well, you didn't answer my question either.'

He pointed at her. 'I asked first.'

Sighing, she shook her head. Blake was like her dog, Snow, when she gave him a bone. Snow would gnaw and growl and chew, then he'd bury what was left of the treat only to dig it up again the next day, ready to gnaw, growl, chew and bury again. Finally, once he'd finished it, he would sit and stare at her until she gave him another. She had a feeling that if she didn't give Blake an answer to chew on, he'd keep asking.

'We've never recorded anything,' she said. 'I've never been interested.'

Blake tilted his head, much like Snow did when she told him no.

'I don't believe you,' he said. 'Your eyes flickered when you said that. Besides, I doubt someone who sings with such passion can honestly say they've never wanted to record music.'

Carol jutted her chin. 'I don't like people telling me what I should think or feel. If I say I don't want to record, it means I don't want to record.'

23

Serious now, he leaned closer. 'I'm not pushing you to do anything, Carol. And I'm trying to work out why you think I would.'

Instinctively, she wanted to step back, but she stood her ground. 'You don't need to figure me out.'

A person waving from the doorway caught her eye. Glancing over, she saw Jex raise his eyebrows questioningly.

Carol shook her head, letting him know she was fine, but he strode over anyway and stood beside her. 'Everything okay?'

'I'm Blake Sender.' Blake shot out a hand, and Jex shook it.

'You're Alex's brother? Annie's son?'

Blake inclined his head. 'I am. I was just asking Carol if you two have ever recorded together, or if you would consider recording some songs for me to purchase.'

Carol snorted a laugh. She couldn't help it. 'Do you always get posh when you're trying to get what you want?'

He ignored her, addressing Jex instead. 'She said she has no interest in recording, but I don't believe her.'

She'd kick Jex later, for his moment of silence and the telling glance he threw at her.

Yes, she was lying, but to everyone else her reasons didn't matter. They thought they knew where her reluctance stemmed from.

Jex opened his mouth, but she shook her head and dragged in a breath. Bloody Paul. He still dictated what she did and how she felt.

'You know what? Stuff it.' She turned to Jex. 'If you want to, we can record some songs.'

Jex gave a whoop, lifted her off her feet and swung her around. 'Finally!' He grinned at Blake. 'Thank you. This is the first time she's even come close to saying yes.' Then, singing Queen's 'We Are The Champions', Jex danced to the door and, with one last wave, left.

Blake rubbed his hands together. 'Seems it's a night of firsts for both of us. Rita Morell has commissioned me to do a piece for her.'

Carol softened. 'It's your first local commission?'

Blake's merriment disappeared and a weird kind of horror darkened his eyes. 'First commission ever. I've made pieces for friends as presents, and I've sold a couple of things over the years, but since quitting my job and going out on my own …' He shrugged. 'I don't even have a business name yet. I didn't want to jinx anything.'

His blank stare pulled at her.

She'd been there, lost in the brutal wonder of jumping into a life she desperately wanted but that scared the absolute shit out of her. Closing her eyes and taking that leap, not knowing if the fall would kill or create her, was one of the hardest things she'd ever done.

Both she and Blake had taken that leap, but it seemed they were both still flailing through the freefall. She hoped they'd both land on their feet.

To pull them both out of the terror-filled spiral, she touched his arm. 'What job did you quit to become a full-time artist? Maybe you can incorporate it into your business name?'

He blinked at her, frowned, then gave a lopsided smile. 'I was in real estate. One of the most secure jobs there is.'

Real estate? He might as well have tasered her. Did he know Paul? Was she being played by them both?

Stiff and cold, she fisted her hands and jammed them under her arms. 'Okay, well, good luck with it all. I have to go now.' She took two steps, then remembered her helmet, stalked back, grabbed it, and left without looking back.

She wanted to get home, needed the oblivion of sleep. Only then could she forget that Paul was back in town, and that Blake not only looked like him but had moved in the same circles as him.

Did they know each other?

It didn't matter; she'd avoid them both. She had nothing in common with Blake, and they had no reason to be more than passing acquaintances. Paul, though, she knew, would follow his pattern of making sure he was seen to be giving her room, while he played mind games with her until she cracked and had sex with him. Once he'd humiliated her, he'd leave, but the price to make that happen was soul-destroying.

Shivering as much from the cold as her thoughts as she hurried through the car park, she stopped five feet from her Triumph when the flare of a match glowed against a cigarette and lit Paul's smile as he took a drag.

25

He breathed out a grey stream of smoke. 'Aren't you going to say hello?'

Saying anything while nausea balled in her stomach would be a mistake. She'd either puke or scream. Or cry. None of which she wanted to do in front of Paul.

He flicked the unfinished cigarette away and walked to stand in front of her. 'This is why I left. All the silent treatment, the sulking, you blaming me for your shortcomings. How could I, or anyone, have put up with that yet still love you? But I tried, I really tried. You know that. But even the sex couldn't make up for everything else.'

His words hit their mark, ripping open old wounds and causing her insecurities to spill at her feet. Still, when he moved closer and his chest bumped against hers, his scent settled in her lungs and made her pulse throb.

Mortified that her body automatically responded to him, she lowered her head and squeezed her eyes closed. Then, taking a deep breath, she tried to turn away, but his hand closed over her shoulder, stopping her escape.

'Don't be like this, Carol. We can put the past behind us. You need me. Look what's happened since I left.' He flicked a finger at her hair and tapped the piercing in her eyebrow. 'You aren't looking after yourself. You've obviously stopped jogging'—he sniffed—'and you've forsaken basic hygiene. Without me, babe, you're doing nothing and going nowhere.'

'I'm doing what I want,' she said, sounding as sullen as she felt.

What gave him the right to come back and throw her world into chaos whenever he got bored? Why did he have to cut her down just when she'd started to pick herself up again? And why couldn't she just tell him to get fucked. If it were anyone else, she'd say it with no qualms at all, but with Paul, the words got stuck. He was the giant to her mouse. A big scary man to her lost little girl. The monster in her nightmare.

Paul flicked a glance at the clubrooms and sighed. 'You've always done whatever you wanted, which is what got us into this mess in the first place. I guess I can take some of the blame, though, not that you'll ever forgive me. Because that's just not you, is it, Give-No-Quarter Carol?' He mock saluted her. 'Well, I'll be around for a while this time, so I hope we can at least be civil to each other, if nothing else.' He leaned in. 'Besides, we both know you don't have the will to resist me. I'll get what I want eventually.'

He stepped back when orange lights flashed and the soft clunk of car doors unlocking signalled someone's arrival.

'Sorry.' Blake jangled his keys. 'Didn't mean to interrupt.'

All smiles now, Paul stepped forward with his hand held out. 'Blake, isn't it? You made an impression tonight. The town needs a decent artist.'

Carol moved a step closer to Blake. Though she didn't want to align herself with either of them, in this case, the devil she knew was not the better choice. Paul would only ever dig at her confidence and remind her that she would never be good enough.

Blake leaned against his ute, resting the toe of one boot on the ground so that his heel was lifted, reminding Carol of the way horses often stood. 'I'd say the town already has a few, but I'm glad to be counted as one of them.'

It was as if they were twins; Paul rubbed a hand over his chin and mirrored Blake's stance. 'I hear you bought the old McGrath property. If I'd been your agent, I would've advised you to bulldoze the house and start again.'

Carol started. 'What?' A harpoon to the heart would have hurt less.

Paul just smirked, so she turned on Blake.

'That was my grandparents' place. I grew up there. You can't bulldoze it!'

Blake held up a hand. 'I'm not bulldozing anything. I love the house.' He rubbed a thumb along his jaw. 'Maybe you can help me. I've been renovating but keep hitting walls, no pun intended. How would you feel about coming out and telling me about the place sometime? Maybe that will give me some inspiration.'

Could she tell him about her life with her grandparents? The wounds were still so raw, fragile. And her memories were precious; she held them close whenever her life crumbled around her. 'I'm not sure you'd be interested in my memories of the place.'

He shrugged. 'I get the feeling there's a lot of history there and I'd like to know it. Besides, if you come out, I might be able to talk you into posing for me. You'd make the perfect model for an impish fairy.'

Paul barked out a laugh, then covered his mouth. 'Sorry, I just imagined you as Cinderella's fairy godmother.'

Blake frowned. 'No, nothing like that.' He squinted at her. 'I'd make the wings like you. Tough, a little dark and full of mystery.'

27

Paul leaned close. 'Will you tell him the truth, or shall I?'

To anyone else, it would sound like a joke. But Carol knew it was a veiled threat. The same one he'd made four years ago in order to drive a gap between her and her friends. Blake would never be close enough to her to matter, but her stomach churned at the thought of what Paul might tell him just to hurt her.

Blake kept his gaze on her. 'I tend to think that the only one who can tell your truth is you. Others only tell what they want known.'

Feeling understood, Carol flashed a smile before she could stop it. Without knowing it, Blake had blown up Paul's attempt to control her. For that, she would tell him anything he wanted to know about his new home.

Paul cleared his throat. 'Well, I guess it's time to call it a night. At least you live close, Carol. Probably not much chance of having to blow into a breathalyser between here and home.' He finger-gunned her. 'You don't want another run-in with the local police.'

He walked away, whistling.

Carol sighed. She wouldn't have to worry about avoiding Blake for long; Paul would make sure that Blake avoided her.

Not that she cared.

Blake pushed away from his ute. 'You're right to get home?'

She wouldn't let his assumption hurt. 'I don't drink and ride.'

'I didn't mean to insinuate you would, but you look tired and ... upset. My mother would be disappointed if I left without making sure you could get home okay.'

She rubbed her forehead. 'You're a confusing guy, Blake.'

He tossed his keys and caught them. 'Not really. And I have to wonder why you'd think I am.'

The answer to that was too complicated, so she shrugged. 'Doesn't matter.'

Turning for the safety of her bike, she stopped. She had to know. 'Are you and Paul friends?'

His eyebrows shot up. 'No. And I doubt we ever will be. Why?'

She shook her head. 'No reason.'

His words played over in her mind as she showered and crawled into bed. As she drifted off to sleep, the answer came.

He wasn't confusing, but he did confuse her. And she didn't know what to do with that.

#

Two Pauls stood side by side, like a twisted Tweedledee and Tweedledum duo. Carol held a water gun filled with pink liquid; if she shot one of the Pauls, the other would reveal his true identity, but if she chose wrong, the real Paul would lock her in the metal cage of his heart.

She'd been there before, that cold, dark, crushing place. She'd lost herself in there. It would destroy her to go back to the void where nothing she did or said mattered, where everything was her fault, and where she'd believed that not existing at all was better than the ghost life she lived. And Paul knew it.

The Tweedles grinned. 'You have to choose one of us.'

Carol shook her head and turned the water gun in her hands. Pink liquid leaked from it, staining her skin. 'No, I don't. I'm enough on my own.'

Tweedledee Paul cocked his head. 'Are you?'

Tweedledum Paul frowned. 'But what about being lonely?'

She lifted the gun and shot Tweedledee Paul. The facade fell away from Tweedledum Paul, leaving Blake standing before her.

The gun in her hands melted. As it dripped and congealed into a heart, she shook her hands to dislodge it.

Blake reached out and trapped the heart in her grip. 'It's a lie.'

Panicking, Carol jerked away from him. 'Everything is a lie. Why do you think I don't want this?' She shoved the heart at him. 'Take it. You take it and deal with it.'

He shifted, locking his gaze on hers. 'It's yours. You need to deal with it, then let it go. He'll follow you forever otherwise.'

The heart in her hands started to pump, while the heart in her chest galloped. 'He won't let me forget him.'

29

Blake gave a half-smile. 'Forgetting and letting go are two different things, you know that.'

Highlights of her childhood flashed around them. Most images were of her and Kelsey laughing, though they were interspersed with the two of them riding with Zoe and Lilli, or camping in paddocks, with Gran dropping off homemade lemonade and cakes.

But then Kelsey had left, and Carol had forced herself to let go of love and trust, had severed her connection to her friends. Their absence had left a hole in her she'd never been able to fill, and she shied away from getting too close now the pain of losing them again would be too much.

Then Paul had come along. He'd offered her none of the things she'd craved, had given her everything she'd never wanted. Loneliness, humiliation, despair, and a blackness so deep she'd only just started to dig herself out of it.

'What if I can't let go?'

Blake took a deep breath and stepped back. 'Then he'll always control the part of you that wants to live.'

The heart buzzed and vibrated in her hands. It turned to goo and dripped onto her bare feet. The heart in her chest threatened to do the same.

'What's happening? Am I dying?'

'Maybe.' Blake flashed a smile. 'Or maybe you're waking up.' He reached out and tapped her nose. 'Better do it soon. Life is waiting.' He turned and walked away, his feet buzzing with each step.

Jerking awake, Carol sat up in bed, her heart—the one she'd thought had turned to mush—bashing against her ribs.

Her phone vibrated and beeped on her bedside table. Who would ring her at—she checked the time—two in the morning? Zoe's name and number flashed on the screen.

Carol swiped to answer. 'Zoe? What's wrong?'

Nothing. She glanced at her phone, now sitting still and silent in her hand.

Was she still dreaming? Was this another subconscious reckoning of her brain? A sign that she should take notice of her friends or she'd lose what little connection she had left?

She knuckled her eyes and yawned, started to stretch, then froze. Great friend she was; Zoe had called her at two a.m. and had either hung up or dropped out, and all *she* had done was wonder if she was still dreaming! What if Zoe had been in an accident? What if she'd been hurt? Or worse?

Carol flicked on the bedside light, pulled the blankets around her, and hit Zoe's number. The call rang out. Wide awake now, Carol mumbled as she dialled again.

After three rings, Zoe answered. 'Carol? What's wrong? It's two a.m., so there better be something wrong.'

Carol's jaw dropped. 'What's wrong with me? What's wrong with you!'

'What? You're not making sense. Are you drunk?'

Carol clenched her teeth. 'I never get drunk. *You* called *me*, Zo, a few minutes ago. I thought you were hurt.'

'How could I call you when I was sleeping?'

Rubbing at the headache beginning to thump behind her eyes, Carol relaxed her jaw. 'Check your phone log.'

Silence, then, 'I'm—I must have butt-dialled you.'

Carol frowned. 'I thought you were asleep.'

'It's a figure of speech, Carol.' Zoe's snarky reply came clear through the phone. 'If you're done playing the caring friend, I've got things to do.'

'Sure, sorry. Goodnight.' Carol stared at her phone until the screen blanked.

Was that the lie Blake had spoken of in her dream? Instead of protecting herself against heartbreak was she instead just pretending to be friends with Zoe and the others?

Rubbing cold knuckles along her sternum, she winced. She loved Kelsey. And Pipa, of course. Who wouldn't? Ethan, Jex and Mark were her substitute brothers, each one playing a different role in her life. She might not be a big hugger or drop in for a cup of tea or coffee all the time, but that didn't mean she was a bad friend, did it? She saw people when she did, talked to them about whatever, listened to their problems; people didn't have to be in each other's back pockets to be real friends, did they?

She closed her eyes, squeezing her eyelids tight against the sting. Crying only ever made her headaches worse, and she was done shedding tears that only dehydrated her soul.

Two years ago, she'd wasted energy and tears on Paul. He'd heard her, ignored her, then waited until she'd thought she'd been over what he'd done. Then he'd started his games all over again.

Now that she was fully awake, she recalled all the times he'd ignored her, all the times he'd told her she would be pretty "if only". *If you smiled instead of frowning. You could get away with wearing that if your hips weren't so big. If you didn't whine so much, I might actually spend some time with you.* And then there'd been the long periods of time spent living with him in the same house but having no contact, no communication. He'd go months without looking or smiling at her, or even acknowledging that she actually existed.

Sometimes, in the dead of night, she'd woken with a jolt, her chest tight, her breath sticking in her throat, convinced that she was a ghost or some type of spirit that annoyed people enough that they saw her. Had she died at some point and didn't know it? Had she died when Gran had, and that's why her grandfather hadn't held on? Was it the reason her parents had never come home?

Clutching her phone to her chest, Carol wriggled down and pulled the blankets up around her ears. She'd lived through the pain of being abandoned by her parents and Kelsey, and of losing her grandparents, but she'd tried to be there for the friends she'd had left, hadn't she?

Kelsey disappearing had broken them all apart for a while. Mark and Ethan had suddenly become adults, especially seeing as Mark had returned from the police academy to become one of the local officers. He'd lost his smile somewhere, though. Maybe they'd all lost their smiles to a point. And maybe she hadn't been able to help anyone because she'd been so lost.

Zoe was wrong. Carol didn't pretend to be a caring friend; what she'd done was worse. She'd been so caught up in her own life that she'd let her friends flounder on their own. No wonder Zoe was often distant or curt. Carol would be too if she'd been treated as she'd treated everyone the last few years.

As sleep crept up on her, slowing her breathing, it invited her subconscious to play. Just as Zoe grew claws and swiped at Carol's face, her phone buzzed again. But by the time she'd struggled out of the dream and her blankets, the call had gone to voicemail. It'd been from a private number, not Zoe, and no message was left.

Putting her phone on the other pillow, she closed her eyes again. Snippets of conversations she'd had and regretted flittered through her brain. All the times Zoe or Ethan or Mark had rolled their eyes at her, or worse, shaken their heads as they walked away. All her failures, disappointments and humiliations crushed down on her chest.

She'd spent too many nights like this, fighting to breathe through panic so thick and heavy that she wished it would smother her, just so the feeling would end.

She needed to think of one thing, she reminded herself—just one, instead of the volcano of screenshots that threatened to erupt and sweep her away. Her and Kelsey exploring tracks, collapsing in laughter when they fell off their horses. Gran's smile. Pop working in his shed. Her parents leaving, while she cried and begged them to stay. Paul pretending that she didn't exist. His smile when he wanted her. His face as he came, while she lay under him aching inside and out.

Turning her head, she screamed into her pillow, tried to focus on something or someone other than Paul. But he invaded everything. Even Crazy Hat Night.

Like the rain that had dribbled down the clubroom windows, distorting the reality outside, Paul created a kaleidoscope of her life. He split the truth into manageable lies. He made everyone believe he was generous and lovable, reserving the real version of himself just for her. He took everything, gave nothing, made her feel worthless and hopeless, all while telling the world he had her best interests at heart.

Carol punched the pillow. 'Stop. Just stop.'

If she could stand to see his face staring back at her from the page, she'd draw him as she saw him—hard, selfish, a monster in the shape of a man. She'd show his eyes as they truly were, turning cold and lifeless as soon as he'd gotten what he wanted and was done with her.

Her phone buzzed again, and this time she kept her eyes closed. 'Hello?'

Nothing. Not a disconnected call but a deliberate silence.

'I'm hanging up now.' If she could convince herself it was stupid kids who had nothing better to do that were calling, then she could sleep until the next time her phone buzzed.

Every hour, on the hour, someone rang. By six, with sunrise still an hour away, Carol sat waiting for the phone to ring. She'd stopped answering it. What was the point? And why give whoever was on the other end the pleasure of hearing her getting pissed off? Besides, she had her suspicions on who would be prank calling her.

Paul had arrived last night with a plan to repeat what had happened last year, but not only had she silently refused him, Blake had stood up for her without even knowing he'd done so.

Blake, who still confused her.

Her phone buzzed, sending the hot stones in her belly skittering and clacking against each other. Picking up the phone, she eyed a spot on the wall and cocked her arm. But then let it drop to the bed. She wouldn't be up for a new one because of Paul.

Instead, she shoved the blankets aside, stretched her stiff limbs as she stood, then pulled on trackpants and a thick jumper. Shivering as she made her way outside, she went to let Snow out of his cage. Appearing as a black blob in his kennel, Snow morphed into a gangly, white-bibbed, boof-headed dog as he stood and stretched before bulleting from the enclosure.

He could make her smile, even when her head throbbed and all she wanted was to curl up and let the earth cover her. His bounding laps around the yard caused her to tire, pushed her to dig deep and find enough energy to throw the stick he pulled from one of the bushes lining the fence.

'I should hire you out as a gardening service.'

He ignored the stick she threw and grabbed a pebble. Trotting back to her, his white-tipped tail wagging, his eyes bright and happy, he dodged and ducked, daring her to catch him. The chill air filling her lungs and pinching her cheeks combined with Snow's boundless joy wiped away some of the aggravation that had racked up over the past twelve hours.

'Good morning, Carol,' Mrs Glade sang and waved over their adjoining fence.

Carol smothered a yawn. 'Morning. How are you today?'

Smiling, Mrs Glade patted Snow's head when he rested his front paws at the top of the four-foot fence. 'Oh, I'm fine, thank you for asking. He's grown, hasn't he?'

Carol frowned. 'He has. I might need to watch that.'

Mrs Glade rubbed his jaw. 'He's a good boy, he won't jump out. And he can't go far from our place. Unless he jumps the extensions Barry put up against next door.' She nodded across her yard to the shade mesh that turned the original six-foot fence into an eight-foot barrier.

As both their back fences hit six foot, as did Carol's other boundary fence, she nodded. 'No, he won't go far, but he does love to prune bushes.'

Mrs Glade lifted Snow's muzzle and gave him an air kiss. 'Ah, well, we'll have none of that if you come to visit, will we?' She tilted her head and gave Carol a coy smile. 'That new young man Blake seems nice.'

Carol didn't know him well enough to make that call. 'He's talented.'

Giving Snow's head one last pat, Mrs Glade pushed at his chest until his front paws dropped back to the ground. 'Very talented. And speaking of talented, I hear you're going to finally record some songs with Jex.'

It jolted her, to hear someone else say it. It made it seem real, not just a maybe thing that she'd get around to one day. Why had she agreed to something she'd sworn she'd never do?

Because it was a dream that lit a fire in her soul. She'd always wanted to share the deep emotion she felt while singing. To put the love, healing and heartbreak she felt into songs that could hit people right in the solar plexus.

Mrs Glade put a hand on Carol's arm, perhaps sensing her conflict. 'I know that you're probably still kicking yourself for rejecting the opportunity Paul gave you, but you weren't ready then. You have another chance now, though. Don't throw it away because you're caught up in regretting the past.'

She regretted ever being connected to a man who lied as easily as he breathed. But everyone else trusted him; why would they listen to her side, the true side, of the story?

'You're talking about the recording contract Paul said he got me. Are you suggesting I start things up with him again?'

'Maybe if you two talked things through. I know he hurt you when he left, and that it upset you when he came back last year and didn't visit you, but you need to let it go, honey. For your own sake.'

Carol's silent scream started in her head, fell to her heart and stayed there, thudding against her ribs. Mrs Glade, like everyone else who thought they knew the story, meant well. But they didn't know the truth, because *she* hadn't told them. Couldn't without sounding like a jilted ex-lover out for revenge.

'I want to move on'—she gritted her teeth, then faced Mrs Glade—'but he won't let me. He cornered me last night about getting together again, then called me multiple times throughout the night. He didn't say anything, but I know it was him. And whatever he's saying about us, it isn't true. I don't want anything to do with him.'

Mrs Glade frowned. 'What? Why would he do any of that?'

Carol's shoulders sagged and she stepped back. 'I don't know. Forget it, it doesn't matter.'

If she told Mrs Glade the truth and she let it slip to someone and it got back to Paul ... well, he'd find a discreet way to make her life hell. He'd do as he'd done before—use anything and anyone against her—and if he somehow involved Kelsey or Pipa this time, Carol would never forgive herself.

So instead of purging her secrets, she shook her head. 'I'm tired. It was probably just kids prank calling.'

Mrs Glade's frown deepened the lines on her forehead. 'The Todds developed this town from the settler days, you know that.'

'I do.' It was how Paul got away with everything. He was too well bred and wealthy; he had no need to manipulate young girls into having sex with him.

Mrs Glade opened her mouth, closed it, then checked over her shoulder. 'You need to watch what you say about the Todds.'

Or as Paul would say, *'Keep your mouth shut because no one will believe you anyway.'*

Keeping her gaze on the fence between them, Carol shrugged. 'I've got nothing to say.' She shouldn't have said anything but had needed to know, one way or another, if anyone would listen to her. 'But'—she jerked a thumb over her shoulder to the house—'I've got things to do.'

Mrs Glade hesitated, then patted the top of the fence. 'Okay. Take care.'

'You too.'

Snow leaned against Carol's leg as she turned and walked back to the house, rested his head against hers as she wiped his paws.

'You'd believe me, wouldn't you?'

Snow nuzzled her cheek. He was the only one she told everything to, because he listened without judgement, didn't pose a threat or cause her fear that her words would come back to hurt her. He was the only one who'd seen her shaking and holding on by a thread. And he was the only one who'd stepped in and anchored her when she fell apart.

Except Blake had stepped in last night.

And as much as it scared her to let him even an inch into her life, she owed him a proper thank you.

CHAPTER 3

The colour didn't work. Taking another backwards step to observe his efforts, Blake jammed his paint-splattered hands on his hips and scowled.

The golden-yellow he'd picked, hoping to turn the small bedroom into a bright and airy space, made the surrounding grey walls muddy and dull. It should have worked. Should have popped like it did in his mind's eye.

Disgusted, he dropped the roller into the bucket of water. He'd be sleeping on a mattress in the spare room for another week now while he found the right colour and waited for the fumes to fade. Not that sleeping rough worried him, but after three weeks, he should have at least finished this one room. He liked the grey, the almost corrugated-iron tone of it, so the yellow would have to be painted over. Maybe a strong rose colour. Not pink, he scrunched his nose, but something deeper that would complement the grey. He stood hipshot, scratching his chin as he imagined a dusky pink on the wall. Not the hot pink his brain kept conjuring, or the woman that went with it.

She'd been on his mind all night, tripping through his dreams as the impish elf he wanted to recreate her as, but she'd stayed just out of reach as he'd tried to catch her, and he'd woken frustrated and antsy. It could only mean one thing. He was attracted to her, intrigued by her. But aside from the fact that he and Tish were only just back on speaking terms, he had a business to build and a house to fix. And he was still trying to find himself. Adding lust or whatever this was to the mix would be a mistake.

Except that Carol got to him. On a few levels, the top one being his instinct to protect.

When he'd first seen her, he'd wanted to give her his jacket, buy her a hot drink and ask what had put that panic-stricken look on her face. He had an idea now what it had been, but knowing only heightened his desire to wrap her in something soft and warm, and ask her what was wrong and what he could do.

Not that he thought she'd let him do anything. Besides, he had plenty to keep him occupied and his mind off creating wings for Carol and turning her into the imp he imagined.

Palms as itchy as his mind, he turned from the wall and stalked from the room. It was time to work.

In his shed, where old tools hung on pegboards next to shiny new ones, where the concrete floor was free from tripping hazards, and where his table was set up and ready for his next project, he laid out the napkins he'd drawn on last night for Rita Morell.

He'd liked the older woman as soon as he'd met her a week ago, and having her commission the commemorative sign for her late husband had been the boost he'd needed. Listening to her talk about life during the merino wool boom, the years of drought that had ravaged their land and bank accounts, and the heartbreak they'd experienced when the bottom fell out of the industry had given him great insight into the community's history.

Rita's life, along with many others, had evolved when they'd turned to beef farming twenty years ago. Her husband, she'd said with a smile, had found working with cattle involved less swearing than working with sheep. Her husband, though, had missed his sheep and had mourned the loss until the day he'd collapsed in the paddock, the gate he'd been hanging left unhinged. Blake would use that somehow. That visual of the open, unfinished gateway.

As he rummaged through the oversized wooden crate that held a wonderland of metal offcuts, ideas began to flow for how he might infuse love and grief into welded metal and twisted wire. How he might bind it all together to represent the love and life Rita had shared with her husband on their land.

Choosing a piece of metal for the base of the sign, Blake placed it on the work table, staring at it as he thought about what he wanted for the second layer. He'd have to cut and shape as he went with this one, because even though he had a clear vision for the end product, nothing would bring it to life without some manipulation.

39

This would be a challenge he could sink his teeth into. It would keep his mind occupied, meaning he'd have less time to think about Carol and whatever might have gone on between her and Paul. Because something had definitely gone on between them. If a woman came face to face with her ex after a normal break-up—if there was such a thing—she didn't usually look as if a monster had picked up her scent.

Blake had broken up with a few girls over the years and had been broken up with, and yeah, it hurt. You avoided the other person if you could. If you couldn't, you greeted each other as if you were strangers and hoped no one pointed out you used to be together.

Paul had seemed at ease, though maybe a little careless, in the car park, while Carol had changed from being the sharp sassy woman he'd talked to about music. And though Jex said Paul had left Carol behind for bigger and better things, to Blake, she hadn't acted like the jilted lover or lovelorn girl Jex seemed to think she was.

Shaking his head, Blake attached the sanding disk to his angle grinder, fitted a mask over his nose and mouth and slid safety goggles on. Carol's relationship with Paul, past or present, was none of his business. He took a moment to breathe in, out, then, flicking the power tool on, let the vibrations travelling up his arms be his only stimulus and his vision for the sign be his sole focus. He soon lost himself in the wonder of creating something beautiful out of what most would consider rubbish.

For an hour he sanded, ground, shaped and slowly brought his vision to life. Standing back with his head tilted and his hands tingling from the tools, he nodded to himself. Maybe it wouldn't take weeks as he'd first thought but only days, especially if he kept this momentum up.

On another bench, his phone screamed. Glancing at it as he slipped of the protective gear, he smiled at the caller ID, then swiped to answer. 'Mum. How's everything?'

'Oh, I thought you'd be working, so I was prepared to leave a message.'

He smiled as he grabbed a bottle of water from the bar fridge tucked under the bench. 'I can hang up if you want.'

'You are a devil of a child.' But she laughed. 'And speaking of devil children, I thought that seeing as your brother will be coming home for a while, we could all have dinner together.'

Blake blinked. 'Alex is coming home?'

His mother sighed. 'Don't you two ever talk?'

'Of course we do.' He'd accidentally dialled Alex's number a few weeks ago. They'd made small talk, then had run out of things to say.

Alex had stayed with their mum after the divorce, whereas Blake had left with their dad, thinking he'd been helping everyone. He'd thought a lot of things at the time that had turned out to be false.

'Seeing as you've moved back here, I thought that the two of you could spend a bit of time together when he's home. Get to know each other again.'

'We know each other.' Maybe too well. They each knew what buttons to push, what triggers the other had.

They'd loved each other once, had grown closer in the knowledge that neither of them was their father's favourite. Blake had looked after Alex through the shouting matches between their parents, then had left him with their mother so she only had one of them to worry about. But all Alex seemed to remember was that Blake had left, and nothing Blake had said or done since had bridged the gap that stretched between them.

'Hmm.' His mother sounded doubtful, then, 'How about when he gets here on Friday night? I'll cook a roast.'

Sitting at the table trying to make conversation with Alex without wanting to reach over and shake him? Or without Alex punching him? That wasn't a night Blake wanted to endure.

'Why don't I take us all out to the pub?'

'That's sweet of you, but I don't want to drive if the weather is as bad as it has been.'

Because she couldn't see him, he rolled his eyes. 'Why can't Alex bring you?'

'I think he's seeing someone, so I doubt he'll come straight to my place or stay for long when he does. A meal at the pub would suit everyone, I think.'

So it would be a quick meal for his brother again.

'Okay, I'll pick you up and drop you off. Easy.'

A beat of silence. 'Okay, that would be lovely. Thank you.'

'Excellent. I'll see you before Friday anyway, but I'm looking forward to taking you out to dinner.'

All the talk of food had his stomach rumbling as he hung up, so Blake went to sit outside the shed on an upturned bucket, a sandwich in one hand and his phone in the other. Taking a photo of his dirty boots, he sent it to his mate Drew and got a comparison photo back five seconds later.

Drew's boots had dirt ingrained from months of stomping wet earth, digging mud, concreting fence posts and pergola footings, but he'd been doing his own thing, living his own life since he'd started his landscaping business fresh out of high school. Blake had always envied him the freedom to choose what he'd wanted to do. Looking back, he realised he could have chosen too. If he had, though, would he be here, where it seemed he was supposed to be?

Drew's next photo showed a bright blue sky dotted with seagulls. The birds' wings were spread wide to catch the breeze as they hung over the sparkling surf. Blake trained his phone's camera on a lonely yellow flower with rain drops hanging from its petals, snapped a photo and sent it.

A flash of light along the track that turned into his driveway had him standing for a better look. The only people who drove out this far were usually lost. The track went no further as there was nothing but bush beyond his property.

He angled his head as the car—a white four-wheel drive—turned to start the long, windy trek along his driveway. Finishing his sandwich and wiping his hands on his jeans, he wandered around to the front of the house and waited. Only when the vehicle stopped at his gate did he see the red and blue lights on the roof, and the chequered blue-and-white line up the side with *Police* in bold under it.

Blake had seen the officer before, walking around White Wattle Creek, and had been stopped by him at a breath test site the day he'd moved to the town.

'Mr Sender?' The officer walked towards him.

Blake's heart jumped. 'Is there something wrong?'

His thoughts immediately went to his dad. He was the only one he hadn't talked to recently. He should have called him already, checked in. Why hadn't he?

The officer held up a hand. 'No, nothing's wrong. I'm Leading Senior Constable Mark Jones. I'm just paying a courtesy call.'

Breathing easier, Blake held out his hand. 'Blake's fine. Mr Sender is my dad.' Who he'd call as soon as he could. He kicked himself for neglecting the man who'd raised him. Though he'd done so in his own fashion, he'd given Blake everything he could.

'I get that.' His handshake firm and eyes direct, Mark glanced around the overgrown garden and at the piles of metal and old wood stacked at the side of the house before meeting Blake's gaze again. 'We sometimes get reports of thefts out here. Sheds broken into, equipment stolen. Not often but enough for me to drop in and let you know to keep an eye out.'

Maybe Blake should get a security system, after all. He'd hoped not to need one out here. 'I guess nowhere is safe from crime. Though I guess there'd be less here than in the city.'

'You'd think.' Mark gestured towards the back of the house. 'Do you mind? I haven't been out here for a few years.'

'Sure.' Blake led the way. 'I haven't been able to do much yet.'

'Not exactly the right time of year to get much done.' Mark nodded his head at a pile of rusted steel droppers and miscellaneous lengths of metal. 'I saw your … creations in the town hall this morning. They're good.'

'Thanks.' Blake shoved his hands in his pockets. Would he always find it hard to take praise? 'The people I bought this place off didn't do anything with it, other than let a few cows run wild. Before that, it was the McGraths'.'

'It was.' Mark glanced back at Blake. 'I hear you met a few of the locals last night. And that you talked Carol into recording some songs.'

'Yeah, at the Crazy Hat Night.' He followed as Mark wandered toward the shed. 'She's a friend of yours?'

'I know her.' Mark stopped at the open double doors and rested his hands on his hips. 'Nice.'

Blake tore his gaze from Mark's belt, which sported an impressive array of things, to glance around his workspace. 'I've found I can sleep on a mattress on the floor and cook in a mostly gutted kitchen, but I can't work in a half-finished shed.'

Mark turned and didn't hide the full-length study he gave Blake. 'Fair enough. You've got a thick chain and padlock for those?' He thumbed the doors.

Blake pointed to the chain hanging just inside the door. 'I do. Locked up each night and when I'm not here.'

'Good.' Mark made his way back to the front of the house, stopped when he got to the police vehicle and looked at Blake over his shoulder. 'I'll see you around, no doubt.'

'No doubt.' Because, Blake realised, the local policeman hadn't made up his mind about the new guy yet. 'Thanks for dropping in.'

He waited until Mark drove away before heading back to his shed. He couldn't brood on the dynamics between Leading Senior Constable Mark Jones and Carol when he still had work to do. Besides, he didn't have a reason to brood.

#

Carol tried to jog her fatigue away, thoughts of last night running through her head. Did she really look as if she hadn't exercised during the last year? Because she had, especially once Snow had grown and needed the energy outlet. But even if she hadn't, was it any of Paul's business?

No, of course it wasn't. He could take his opinion and shove it.

She glanced over her shoulder, just in case he'd somehow managed to sneak up on her. What did it say about her, that she could only ever think of brave comebacks like that once it was too late? Why couldn't she force the words out when he stood in front of her?

Her sneakers slapped against the wet road like the beat of a drum, creating a rhythm with her thoughts. Stumbling to a stop and lifting her face to the sky, she felt tempted to let out a scream. Instead, she turned for home. And cursed Paul for making her feel like a quitter.

Oblivious to her mood, Snow danced beside her, his abundance of energy making her frown. When had she lost that youthful verve for life? She'd had

44

it once. Gran used to laugh at her whenever she ran around the garden chasing butterflies or as she sprinted across the paddocks because she wanted to catch and play with a lamb. She'd had it during her adventures with Kelsey, Lilli and Zoe, but after Kelsey had left town, they'd all lost their innocence.

Could Carol lay the blame for that on Kelsey, though? No, she'd been the one to let her life slip, not Kelsey. She'd been the one to let Paul treat her like a toy he either played with or didn't. And she'd been the one to let her friendships crack. Sure, it went both ways, but she could have done something before now.

She started jogging again, her breath rasping from her throat faster than it should.

Paul had been right whenever he used to say she neglected things, though some, like not shaving her legs or pits, had started as a passive aggressive protest at his week-long silences. She'd considered herself victorious whenever he'd screwed up his nose as she walked from the bathroom to her bedroom wrapped in a towel.

But that was before he'd broken her with constant comments about her clothes being a bit snug, or by mentioning she looked ragged, or by rolling his eyes at whatever she chose to wear. After three months of living with him, she'd taken to covering herself in baggy shirts and jumpers and obsessing over every hair on her body.

At that point, she'd avoided her friends, because she'd thought that if Paul could see all the things wrong with her, they must too. Was that why she still kept some of that distance? Because deep down she believed they must see all her flaws as clearly as she did, and one day, someone would surely point them out?

She stopped at her front door, doubling over to catch her breath. Snow sat staring up at her, then bunted the door wide as soon as she turned the handle, his nails clacking on the kitchen lino a moment later. After toeing her sneakers off just inside the door, she followed him but doubled back to pick them up and throw them in the basket so Snow didn't take one and hide it.

'You don't think I'm a bad person, do you?'

Snow sat by his food bowl and smiled at her.

She shook her head. 'Of course you don't. Well, eat up then.'

She tipped food into his bowl and got herself a small tub of yogurt. When Snow finished and stared at her, she sighed and held out the tub for him to lick clean. As she dumped the spoon in the sink, her phone rang.

After glancing at the screen, she closed her eyes and swallowed a scream.

He'd skipped an hour, teasing her into relaxing.

'Enough.' With her belly jumping, she tapped her thigh for Snow to follow her out to his enclosure. Kneeling, she gave him a rub and a hug before closing the cage door.

He bowed his head and still managed to look up at her.

'Not gonna work today, buddy.' But she wiggled her fingers through the mesh and scratched his muzzle. 'I'll be back later.'

Kelsey would have answers. She'd dealt with the shitty side of people before, but unlike Carol, she'd mended whatever had been broken, or had at least tried. Carol needed to try too.

As far as Paul went, she wanted never to see him again, to forget he existed. That would be impossible, of course, but she had to do something, otherwise she'd drown in the river of lies he continued to spew out about her. So, pulling on her leathers, she tucked her phone in her bike's saddlebag and set off for Kelsey and Ethan's.

Ten minutes later, pulling up next to Kelsey's white Hyundai, Carol grinned as Pipa, dressed in her bright pink coat, purple boots and yellow hat, created a wild rainbow as she twirled and splashed in the puddles. Ethan and Kelsey stood under the verandah, their smiles full of love and happiness as they watched their daughter.

Had her own parents ever watched her that way? They must have at some point, before she became more of an annoyance than a novelty. But no matter how far back she searched her memory, she couldn't find a picture of either her mother or father smiling at her as if they would stand before a speeding bus to save her.

Despite knowing that her parents had never loved her enough to stay, Carol pushed away the ache, took off her helmet and ran a hand through her hair. It didn't matter now. Her parents had chosen what was important to them, and she had to live with it or go mad.

As Carol settled her helmet on the handlebars, Pipa ran over, hopping from foot to foot, waiting. When Carol swung her leg over the bike and stood, Pipa clapped, then threw her hands up and leapt at Carol.

'I missed you, and I miss Snow. Can you bring him next time? Will he fit on the bike?'

Carol swung the whirlwind up into her arms. 'Good morning, Pipa. I missed you, too.' Though it had only been yesterday when they'd last seen each other. 'But, no, I don't think Snow will fit on the bike, and I can't slip him inside my jacket anymore.'

Pipa wiggled and clutched Carol's shoulders. 'I could fit in your jacket.' She slipped freezing hands down the collar of Carol's leathers. 'I be small enough.'

With a shiver, Carol bent and set Pipa back on her feet. 'I think you've grown too. And just like Snow, you have a lot of energy today.'

'It was May's birthday and Billy ate too much and puked up all the lollies and May cried, and Billy cried so they called his dad and he went home.'

'Sounds like a normal party.' Carol slid her phone from the saddlebag to her pocket, hoping it would stay silent for a while, then took Pipa's hand and led her towards the verandah before the next grey cloud dumped rain on them. 'Was that this morning?'

'Nope, we had a sleepover, only not everyone slept over because they missed their beds and their mummies and daddies had to come and pick them up.'

Carol tapped a finger to Pipa's nose. 'But I bet you stayed.'

Ethan grinned, confirming Carol's suspicion before Pipa did.

'Yes, May's mummy droppeded me off before beckfast.'

Kelsey laughed and shook her head. 'It was about half an hour ago. She claims she's starving, even after listing everything they ate at the party.'

Carol patted Pipa's yellow hat. 'That also sounds normal. You look like you're dressed to do something.'

'We were just going out to feed the chooks and horses.' Ethan pulled a coat and hat on, then kissed Kelsey.

Pipa grinned. 'Then we make mucky eggs for beckfast.'

'Sounds like I came at the right time then. Give the horses a pat for me.'

'I will.' Pipa raced out into the light drizzle that had started to fall, spinning in circles and dancing in the puddles as she waited for Ethan to pull on his boots.

Carol toed hers off, slipped her neck warmer onto her head to warm her ears and peeled off her leather jacket before hanging it on a hook beside the door. 'She's such a little whirlwind. I don't know how people manage multiple kids.'

Kelsey bit her lip. 'Well, we'll be finding out in about seven months' time.'

Carol stopped and stared at her.

Pregnant? Kelsey was pregnant? That meant there'd be a baby, one whose life would solely depend on the people around it.

Kelsey was a braver person than Carol could ever be. She'd decided early in life that having children wasn't her thing. How could she raise a child when she'd basically raised herself, and look how that had turned out!

Taking a deep breath, she followed Kelsey into the house and closed the door. 'So, you're having a baby.' Her gaze automatically went to Kelsey's stomach.

Kelsey pulled up her shirt. 'I've got a little bump.'

Carol squinted. Was there a bump? Either way, it didn't matter. And neither did her own worries about having babies. Kelsey radiated happiness, and there was no way Carol would dim that. Pulling Kelsey in for a hug, she took a moment to steady herself.

'Congratulations. I'm really happy for you guys.' And she was. It worked for Kelsey, being married and having kids. 'I'm glad you found what you have with Ethan.'

She let Kelsey go and stepped back.

'You'll find it too.'

Carol shook her head. 'I don't know if I want to. I don't think I'm marriage material.'

'Stop that shit.' Kelsey frowned. 'You aren't a piece of fabric to be cut and sown to someone else's specifications.'

Carol blinked. 'Is that a pregnancy thing, the swearing? I've never heard you talk like that.' She followed Kelsey into the kitchen.

48

Kelsey slammed two cups on the bench, then turned, her hands on her hips and her eyes narrowed. 'Pipa came home from kindergarten crying because one of the kids told her she was stupid for saying she wanted to marry one of the other girls in a make-believe game.'

Carol pulled the neck warmer from her head and slapped it on the bench. 'Oh.'

The kettle shivered and boiled as though it fed off Kelsey's fury.

'Yes. And she cried when she asked me if she was stupid for maybe wanting to marry another girl when she was older.'

Carol sighed. Pipa crying under normal circumstances broke her heart, but witnessing such innocence being crushed would have brought Carol to her knees, as it had obviously done to Kelsey. 'What did you say?'

Kelsey rubbed her forehead, her shoulders sagging. 'Once she'd calmed down, I told her that when she was an adult, she could marry whatever person she wanted, as long as she loved them and they loved her.'

She added a tea bag to each cup and filled them with hot water from the kettle.

'Ethan and I went and talked to Miss Finn. Have you met her? She's lovely, and so good with the kids. Anyway, she said she'd keep a closer eye on the kid in question. I thought I was over it,' she said as she handed Carol her cup. 'I guess I wasn't.'

Carol shrugged. 'Someone hurt your kid.'

Would her life have turned out differently if her parents had been more like Kelsey? If they'd stepped in as soon as they'd noticed a change in their daughter? Then again, if her parents had stayed when she'd begged them to, she wouldn't have been living with Paul in the first place.

Kelsey led the way to the lounge room. Carol loved Ethan's home, though it wasn't just his now. Changes showed in the little things, like the *My Little Pony* books on the shelf and the toy horses peeking out from between the couch cushions. Then there were the photos on the mantle above the fireplace that showed the expanding Ryder clan, the childish artworks hanging proudly on the fridge, and the lingering energy of youth in the air.

Sitting on the couch, Carol took a sip from her cup and sighed, then froze when her phone rang. She fumbled it out of her pants' pocket and swiped decline, then considered turning it off, but no doubt she'd miss a call from work. Or one of her friends.

Kelsey raised an eyebrow. 'Speaking of someone I love getting hurt, you never told me what happened between you and Paul. It was more than him leaving you behind, wasn't it?'

Carol sat her cup on the coffee table. 'I wanted him to go. I wanted to be free. He suffocated me, made me feel helpless and hopeless.'

Kelsey gasped and covered her belly, as if to protect her unborn baby.

Carol swallowed her words. How selfish could she be, thinking she could unload her woes on Kelsey when she still carried her own trauma? And now that Kelsey was pregnant, Carol wouldn't share anything upsetting in case it hurt her or the baby.

'It wasn't like things were for you before you came home.' She shrugged. 'He just put me down a lot and cheated on me.'

Still pale, Kelsey raised an unsteady hand to her mouth. 'You never told me.'

And Carol wouldn't tell her the rest now, either. 'It didn't matter, because in the end he left town.'

Kelsey leaned forward. 'But now he's back.'

'Not for long.' Please let it not be for long.

Kelsey opened her mouth but closed it when the back door slid open and Pipa ran in, an egg held high in each hand.

'We have mucky eggs for beckfast.' She launched herself at Kelsey, who grabbed the eggs before they smashed against her chest.

'What have I told you about running inside, Pip?'

'Sorry, Mummy, but I wanted Carol to stay for mucky eggs.'

Carol was a sucker for those big blue eyes that seemed to see into the soul, so she shrugged. 'I've always wanted mucky eggs for second breakfast.'

Ethan laughed as he came inside, carrying the rest of the eggs in a bucket, and followed Pipa into the kitchen. He grinned at Carol through the open space over the breakfast bar. 'Pipa has it for second and third breakfast sometimes.'

'Only because you let her sucker you into cooking it.' With her colour now back to normal, Kelsey joined her family in the kitchen where she exchanged a not so chaste kiss with Ethan while Pipa giggled and danced around them.

'Do they always do that?' Carol pulled a face as Pipa laughed and skipped over to the couch before she climbed up next to her.

'Do *you* kiss someone 'cos you love them?'

Carol frowned. Other than her grandparents, had she ever kissed anyone because she loved them? 'I don't kiss anyone.'

Pipa frowned. 'Oh. You not love anyone?'

Carol squirmed under Pipa's level stare. 'I love people. It's just not the kissing kind of love.'

'Oh.' Pipa leaned against Carol as she watched her parents working in tandem to make breakfast. 'I might kiss a girl one day.'

Carol stroked Pipa's hair. 'There's nothing wrong with that.'

Pipa grinned up at her. 'Maybe you find someone and they make you happy.'

Carol couldn't dull Pipa's happiness with the truth, so she tapped her nose. 'Maybe.'

'I think maybe you should come for a ride with us,' Kelsey said while whisking eggs. 'It's been a long time since we did that.'

It had been too long, and the itch to feel a horse moving beneath her, to experience the sheer thrill of riding settled between Carol's shoulders.

'It *has* been too long.' She nodded at Kelsey. 'But I'm not exactly dressed for riding today.'

Kelsey sighed and shot her a look. 'That never stopped us before.'

'True.' Carol smiled. 'I remember we used to sneak out and ride no matter what.'

Pipa bounced on the couch. 'I ride too? Please, Mummy?'

Kelsey raised a questioning eyebrow at Carol. Did they need privacy to talk?

Carol tugged on one of Pipa's pigtails. 'Better eat up so we can get saddled and go before it rains again.'

51

Pipa neighed and jumped from the couch to take the plates from Kelsey and put them on the table. Getting up to do her part, Carol shook her head at Kelsey's silent question. No, there was nothing to talk about, with or without Pipa.

By the time they'd finished their mucky eggs, saddled the horses and Pipa's adorable pony, a long-forgotten excitement tingled in Carol's belly. Maybe losing herself in the scent of warm horse and the heady rush of riding through the bush again might help her find the spark she hadn't been able to grasp since Paul had come into her life.

Maybe getting back to who and what she had been before Paul would teach her who she could be now.

Or maybe she'd grab at anything that made her life seem better.

On her pony, Pipa smiled and reached out to pat Dusty's neck. 'Dusty like you,' she told Carol. 'She used to be scared, but Mummy showed her people not so bad.'

'Your mum has done a wonderful job.' Carol scratched the chestnut's cheek. 'I remember when no one else could get near her.'

'You'll be the first person to ride her other than me.' Kelsey led her own horse, a big black gelding, out of his stable. 'I've been secretly hoping it would be you.'

'Me? Why?' She followed Kelsey out into the yard, the chill of the wind stinging her ears.

Kelsey smiled over her shoulder at Carol as she checked her girth. 'Because I believe she's meant for you.'

Carol stepped back, holding her hands up. 'I can't own a horse!'

Just like having a baby, how could she take on a horse without ruining it? They needed love and attention.

'Why not?' Kelsey swung up into the saddle and frowned down at Carol. 'She can stay here and you can ride her whenever you visit.'

'I can't pay for feed and her upkeep. I can barely afford rent and dog food.'

'Am I asking you for money?' Kelsey tilted her head. 'You know, if you need help, you only have to ask.'

'I'm not asking because I can look after myself.' She wouldn't destroy her relationships further by begging money from her friends. 'Now, are we riding, or not?'

'You're the only one not on your horse.' Kelsey turned hers towards the track that would lead them out beside the house and down the driveway. 'Come on, Snot.' She patted the black horse's neck, then tilted her head at her daughter. 'Come on, Pip.'

'Come on, Pop. Come on, Dusty.' Pipa giggled and waved at Carol as she followed Kelsey, her pony living up to his name as he lifted his tail and popped out wind with each step.

Carol would have laughed if her chest hadn't been so tight. Owning a horse again was right up there on the list of things she wanted to accomplish to show Paul how wrong he'd been about her.

Everything else on that list mocked her now. She wanted a place of her own, so that she didn't have to live in the dated, cheap house Paul's parents let her rent, but she had more hope of flying to the moon than earning enough money to do that. And now that her childhood home had found a new owner, she could cross that pipe dream off the list too.

Ethan came to stand beside her and let the filly smell him from foot to head. 'You aren't riding?'

She pushed a breath out and dropped her shoulders. 'Yeah, I am.'

'But?'

If he yelled at her, she'd take it. She deserved it. 'I upset her.'

Ethan tapped a finger on her helmet. 'You think she's going to snob you now?'

She lifted a shoulder. 'Wouldn't blame her if she did.'

'One,' he said, checking her girth, 'Kelsey doesn't work like that and you know it. And two, you don't work like this.'

'No, she doesn't.' She sighed. 'And no, I don't.'

'So what's going on?' He gathered up her reins. 'Is it Paul?'

'Kind of.'

'I know he hurt you, and I know how it can feel when someone, who you thought you were through with, comes back.'

'He cheated on me, Ethan. More than once. He cheated and lied and …' She shook her head, too ashamed to say the rest. 'Everyone thinks I'm unhappy because I'm still in love with him. But I'm not. I'm pissed because he's an arsehole and no one will believe me.' She took a breath. 'I don't want to tell Kelsey because she's still working through her own shit, and now she's pregnant. I'm not doing or saying anything to upset her.'

'She'll understand.'

Carol shook her head, stuck her foot in the stirrup and huffed out a breath as she scrambled into the saddle. 'Maybe I'm not ready for this.'

Ethan looked up at her. 'Riding, or working through your own shit?'

'Both, I guess.'

'We're here for you. You know that, right?' His phone dinged in his pocket, and pulling it out, he held it up for her to see.

I'm waiting at the end of the driveway. Please get her to come.

'For now, just go for a ride and enjoy it like you used to.' He patted Dusty's neck, then stepped back.

With his words replaying in her head, she turned Dusty and followed the hoof prints made in the soft, muddy track.

She found Kelsey and Pipa waiting for her, and she stopped beside Kelsey. 'I'm sorry I snapped at you. I know you're here for me.'

'Don't forget it.' Kelsey leaned over and gave her a one-armed hug. 'Now, come on, we've got an adventure waiting.'

CHAPTER 4

Blake cruised the aisles, pausing in the confectionery section to debate which box of chocolates he should get for his mother. She liked both Roses and Favourites, and he and Alex always bought her some when they visited. Alex usually grabbed a box of Roses, so Blake would get Favourites, but sometimes Alex arrived with Favourites, just to annoy Blake.

'Bloody Alex.' Blake grabbed a box of each. He could always take one home with him.

Adding a bag of chips to his shopping basket, he doubled back and grabbed another, because it was a two for one deal. If he got a couple of beers, he could have himself a party. A lonely party for one, in the house that refused to become a home.

He'd been serious when he'd asked Carol to visit and tell him the history of the place. All the work he'd done on it so far had been wrong—he'd bought so many sample tins of paint that he could build a fort with them, yet he still felt as if he were squatting in a house that had cost him a fortune—and he thought that if he learned what the house had been like in its heyday, he might be able to find its soul again.

And, he thought, as the fourth woman to smile suggestively at him today passed by, having somewhere to hide away from unwanted attention would be good. He might not be looking for a relationship just yet, but that didn't mean he was going to fill his nights with empty sex just to chase the loneliness away.

Rounding the corner into the next aisle, he stopped. At the other end, Carol stood in front of the pasta. Pipa stood beside her, talking rapid fire with a packet of pasta in each hand.

Although Carol hadn't made him uncomfortable like some of the other women in town, she'd settled in his mind, and thoughts of her took up too much of his time. If he went near her, he'd want to stop and talk to her, to try to convince her to model for him when instead he should be working. And as much as he wanted to quiz her about his place to help with the renovations, he didn't have the energy to be caught up in her today, so he detoured to the next aisle. It wasn't his usual style, but neither was having a woman he barely knew take up every waking moment, not to mention every dream. By the time his basket overflowed with mostly junk, he'd avoided bumping into her three times, and she hadn't seen him once.

At the check-out though, his luck crumbled. She was already there, chatting to the guy serving her with one hand clamped firmly to a dancing Pipa's shirt. She happened to glance his way, frowned, then turned her back to him.

Shit. She *had* seen him then.

It shouldn't matter that he had two strikes against him as far as she was concerned, but it did, and not only because he wanted her to model for him and tell him about the house. His feelings went into territory he'd never explored, not even with Tish, and that scared the crap out of him.

He could leave it, let her walk away and not have to worry about talking to her ever again, but at least she was someone not looking to hook up with the new guy—she'd made it clear last night that she wasn't interested.

Besides, damn it, he couldn't let her think whatever it was she was thinking, so he stepped in line behind her.

Pipa spun in a circle, then clapped when she saw him. 'Bake!'

The way she said his name made him laugh. 'Hey, Pip. How are you?'

'I'm good. I went to May's party and ate lots but I didn't get sick like Billy. Mummy says I have a iron stomach.' She patted her belly.

'My mum says the same about me.'

Her eyes went huge. 'You have a mummy?'

He laughed again. 'I do. You might even know her. Her name is Annie Sender.'

Pipa screwed her nose up. 'Ann-ee.'

Carol hefted three shopping bags of groceries in one hand and held the other out to Pipa. 'She made your mum the earrings and necklace for her wedding, Pip.'

'I like Mrs Bake's mum. She pretty.'

Carol kept her gaze on Pipa. 'She is, but we need to go.'

Kicking himself for hurting her, he sat his basket on the check-out's conveyor belt. 'Can I talk to you for a minute, Carol?'

Her gaze met his, and yeah, under the pissed-off heat lay the dark bruise of pain.

'Why?'

The woman who'd passed him in the aisle earlier unloaded her groceries behind his basket. She smiled at him and winked.

Good manners had him smiling back, the exchange taking only seconds, but when he turned back to Carol, he found she was already walking away. Pipa toddled backwards, waving with her free hand as Carol led her through the exit.

Blake shoved his basket at the check-out guy. 'Can you hold that for me, please? I'll be back.'

He strode outside and scanned the parking lot for her motorbike before remembering she had Pipa and groceries with her. A familiar white Hyundai, Kelsey's, started backing out of a space three cars away.

Jogging to the corner of the building, he stepped out in front of her as she took the turn that led to the road. She stopped, stared at him and raised a pierced eyebrow as she tapped a finger on the steering wheel.

He raised his own eyebrow. She rolled her eyes. He did the same. At the hint of a smile, he dipped his head and slipped his hands into the back pockets of his jeans. She shook her head, then pointed to a parking space behind him. He held her gaze a moment longer before stepping aside and letting her park.

Hunching his shoulders against the chill breeze, he followed after her and squatted beside the car as she wound down the window.

'I was being childish. I'm sorry.'

Not smiling now, she stared at him. 'I'm used to people avoiding me.'

He bowed his head, shook it. 'Not avoiding, as such, just trying to lessen the distraction.'

She snorted a laugh. 'What was such a distraction?'

He met her gaze. 'You are. And I don't have the tools I need to cast you in bronze or iron, or whatever, and it's driving me nuts.'

She frowned and leaned back, just a little.

It made him want to laugh—at himself, at her, at everything. When he threw his head back and let it out, she sat wide-eyed, her mouth open as if she didn't know what to say.

He rubbed at the ache gathering on the tips of his ears—a sign that he hadn't let go enough lately—and calmed the chuckle still tickling his throat. 'I'm sorry. I think I needed that.'

She tapped a finger to her forehead in a salute. 'Glad I could help.'

He sighed. 'Look, I'm sorry I hurt you. I didn't mean to. It's just that everyone I've bumped into so far has wanted to talk or—' He glanced at Pipa in the back seat, watching them. 'I just want to get home and keep working.'

She nodded. 'You're a popular subject at the moment. But I'm fine with saying hi and moving on, just so you know.'

She proved just how fine she was with casual greetings when he bumped into her in the bakery the next day, then the bank the day after. He missed her on his trip into town on Thursday. He'd been hoping to see that smiling eye roll she'd taken to giving him, the deliberately sarcastic *hi* as she passed. The curry pie from the bakery lacked the bite he usually enjoyed, and though the sun shone in a clear blue winter sky, it didn't reach into his soul and tickle the creative juices that usually flowed.

She'd snared him without even trying. He'd driven around for an extra five minutes, hoping just to catch a glimpse of her, and now he was sitting outside his shed on a glorious day, munching a mouth-watering curry pie but not enjoying either because he couldn't get his mind off her.

He needed to work, to focus on his business, on the reason he'd turned his back on the life he'd had up until two months ago. Doing so, deciding to live not just exist, had been both the best and scariest moment of his life—apart from when he'd told his father of his plans.

They'd worked through it, with his father giving encouragement in his own gruff and blunt way. But Blake wouldn't get any creating done if he went down that particular memory lane, so he brushed the crumbs from his fingers, stood and stretched.

He needed a few hours with the scream of tools and the scent of hot metal. He needed to twist, bend and melt the materials he used into forms unrecognisable.

And as he ate his hot chips for dinner that night, he did his best to think of anything but the pink-haired pixie leading him astray.

But by the time he picked his mother up on Friday night, he'd given up on trying not to think about Carol. He'd find her tomorrow and remind her that she'd promised to come out and see her childhood home, to share her memories of the life the house used to hold. And if he could convince her to sit for him, just for a few quick sketches, then maybe he'd be able to think about her less.

He opened the passenger door of his ute to help his mother out.

'Thank you.' She smiled at him as she shifted the box of Roses to the floor and took his hand. 'You seem distracted tonight. Is there anything else you need to tell me?'

He'd finally confessed to her how living a false life had slowly been killing him. Like his father, she'd been upset, but also like his father, she'd hugged him and told him she'd always be there for him.

Locking the car, he hooked her arm through his as they walked to the Mckinley Hotel. 'No, just thinking about a project.'

Annie pulled the cloak she wore tighter around her shoulders. 'A work project, or a more personal one?'

He glanced down at her. 'Meaning?'

She inclined her head as he opened the hotel door for her. 'I'm not suggesting you jump into another relationship straight away, but I wonder if you have your eye on anyone. You haven't said much about how you've been spending your time, and with you, that's usually an indication that you've met someone.'

He may have only spent holidays with her for the last seventeen years, but his mother knew him. 'It's just a work project, Mum. I'm happy being single for now.'

'For now.' She smiled at him.

He laughed as he followed her into the warmth of the hotel, and there was Carol, her bright pink hair held back from her pale face with a glaringly green headband. Why did she look so pale? Why did she look as if she'd been sick? Was that why he hadn't seen her the last couple of days?

Blake caught sight of Alex, waving to them from a table in the dining area, but Blake waited, willing Carol to look up and see him.

She did, and shock widened her eyes, then she blinked, gave him a slight nod and went back to serving the line of patrons who were sitting and standing along the sleek curve of the bar.

When Blake and Annie joined Alex, Alex stood, kissed their mother on the cheek and grinned at Blake as he handed Annie a box of Favourites. 'Good to see you, Mum.'

She patted his arm. 'Good to finally see you, too. I have your room set up for you.'

Blake offered his hand, glad he'd been right for once about his brother's choice of chocolate. 'It's been a while.'

His brother grinned. 'I've been too busy to notice.'

The table Alex had chosen sat against the window, the streetlight outside making the cars look as if they'd just rolled off the showroom floor.

Blake fiddled with one of the menus propped against the salt and pepper shakers. 'I'll order if you both tell me what you want.'

Alex made a show of looking over his shoulder to the bar. 'Well, I know it's not Jex you want to talk to, so it must be Carol.'

Blake resisted rolling his eyes. 'I'm hungry and want to order.'

'Sure.' Alex ran a finger down the menu, chewed on his lip and mumbled to himself. 'Hmm, do I feel like carbonara or the reef and beef?'

Annie handed Blake her menu. 'I'll have the house special, thanks.'

Alex continued sliding a finger down the menu and reading out each option.

Just as Blake considered punching his brother and ordering him the kid's meal, something crashed. Blake stood just as Alex did, but he beat his brother to the bar by a few long strides. Carol stood frozen, her hands thrown in the air. Her cheeks were bright and her eyes shiny, and a broken pitcher lay at her feet, beer spreading in a puddle around her.

Beside her, Jex put a hand on her shoulder and made her step back. 'It's okay, honey. Grab the mop bucket while I pick up the glass.'

Carol turned and, walking stiffly to the bar flap, let herself through. While Alex leaned on the bar and pointed out shards of glass to Jex, Blake followed Carol out into the breezeway behind the hotel.

Somewhere between hearing the glass smash and seeing her so pale, Blake had given in and admitted to himself that there was more to his feelings for Carol than simply needing to sketch her. His protective instincts ran deep and hot whenever he was around her, and right now he wanted to comfort her. Maybe, instead of spending energy trying to bury what she bought out in him, he should just go with it. Surely they could be friends without it getting complicated.

She stopped and pressed her hands to her face.

He cleared his throat. 'Are you okay?'

When she whirled, he stepped back and put his hands in the air. 'I'm sorry, I didn't mean to startle you. I'm not here to hassle you, but something's wrong, isn't it?'

At her blank stare he lowered his hands. Friends helped each other, so that's where he'd start.

'Are you okay?' he asked again. 'Have you been sick?'

She didn't move, didn't speak.

How could he help her if he didn't know what was wrong?

'Do you need to see someone? Talk to someone?'

Carol laughed. Laughed so much that she doubled over and braced her hands on her thighs. As she gasped for breath, coughing as tears ran down her cheeks, he realised she was no longer laughing, and his blood ran cold.

#

Carol rubbed the tears from her cheeks and chin while Blake stood watching her, his face impassive, though he must be questioning her sanity.

She shook her head. 'I'm sorry.'

He tilted his head. 'Why, exactly?'

61

It was a good question. Was she sorry for the sketches of him that filled her notebooks and now hid under her bed? For deliberately avoiding him in town yesterday? Her reasons were complicated and selfish, but they also protected him against Paul.

Paul, who'd taken to being silent for hours on end, only to then call her every five minutes for the next. She hadn't slept since Monday, couldn't eat because her throat snapped shut every time her phone vibrated, or someone else's did, which was why a pitcher of beer currently covered the floor behind the bar. The one time she'd turned her phone off for the night, Lilly had left half a dozen messages, each one increasingly worried, until she'd finally knocked on Carol's door.

And besides the prank calls, she was now receiving texts. They weren't lewd or anything she could report as harassment. But there were photos, too—of her house, her motorbike, her jogging with Snow. It was enough to give her chills and make her look over her shoulder constantly, but she never saw him.

Why he would go to so much trouble when there were plenty of women who wanted him bewildered her. Especially when he'd told the whole town he no longer wanted anything to do with her. Every second person at the pub told her to move on and stop pining for him, to let the poor man be. Even when she told them she didn't want anything to do with him, they rolled their eyes as if they could see her desperation a mile away.

She had no response to that behaviour. None that didn't involve screaming and punching anyway.

Now, Blake stood waiting for her to speak, his frown deepening as the silence stretched. She'd drawn his varying smiles, from the confident one he often flashed to the slightly embarrassed and bewildered one he'd let slip when questions about his work had flooded the room at Crazy Hat Night. His vulnerability in that moment had set him apart from Paul; and it had scared her. Because if he wasn't like Paul, who was he?

'I'm tired,' she told him. 'I didn't mean for you to witness my mini-meltdown.' She ducked into the storeroom to get the mop and bucket.

He was standing in the same spot when she came back out, his hands tucked in his pockets. 'You didn't answer my question.'

She shook her head; answering would be dangerous. 'I'm okay. Like I said, I'm tired.'

He shifted his weight, stopping her retreat without moving. 'Have you been sick?'

She frowned. What was with him?

'No, I'm just not sleeping.'

'Why not?'

Starting to get pissed off, she sighed. 'If you're thinking it's because I'm dreaming about you, you're sadly mistaken.'

She wished it was thoughts of him keeping her awake. At least she could scratch that itch herself and get on with life.

'Well,' he said with a grin, 'you aren't keeping me awake, either.'

Surprised to be smiling back, Carol shook her head. 'You're a bad influence.'

His grin widened, brightening his eyes to the colour of dark smoke. 'No, I'm not. You're just scared I might actually be worth knowing.'

He'd pegged her, of course, but she couldn't afford to wait and see if her gut feeling about him was right. 'I need to get back to work.'

He stepped out of her way. 'You haven't come out to see the house yet. Or to pose for me.'

Carol paused at the door and looked back at him over her shoulder. Was the shimmer of vulnerability she saw real, or was it just something he'd perfected to get what he wanted?

She chewed her lip, trying to stifle a yawn. Would losing herself for an hour in the only place she'd ever felt whole shift this dragging fatigue? Or would it just add to it when she saw all the changes he'd made, noticed all the memories he'd altered. But then again, at least Paul wouldn't be hiding out there, ready to snap a picture of her. That, more than anything, had her nodding.

'Are you home tomorrow?'

His eyebrows rose. 'Sure. All day.'

'I'll see you tomorrow, then.'

Shouldering the door open, she stumbled a step when she saw that Paul leaned on the bar, his smile indulgent as he talked to someone, his back strategically to Jex.

He hadn't seen her yet, so she could turn and walk away. And probably get fired.

She let a breath out. If she didn't work, she didn't get paid. No pay meant she wouldn't have money for rent or to buy food for Snow, let alone herself. Her dream of buying her grandparents' old house might not be possible, but she still wanted a place of her own one day. For now, though, she just needed to survive, and that meant ignoring the thump of her heart and the oily roll of her stomach so she could do her job.

So, chin lifted, she gripped the mop and bucket and strode behind the bar. Giving her a meaningful look, Jex inclined his head towards Paul.

She gritted out a smile. Yeah, she'd be fine. She'd rather die than give Paul the satisfaction of seeing her lose her shit in front of everyone. Because that was what he wanted; to stand back as an innocent bystander while she got labelled too emotional or unhinged or petulant. Then he could step in, apologise on her behalf and look like the hero.

She'd lived that life before. When she'd skipped parties because he'd rolled his eyes at her choice of clothing, commented on her waistline, or belittled her attempt to look like an adult, he'd told everyone she'd thrown a tantrum. But it had been easier to stay at home rather than face the knowing smiles or see Paul receive pats on the back for looking after her through her tumultuous teenage years. Would they have been so congratulatory if they'd known exactly how he'd *looked after* her?

Gritting her teeth, she mopped the beer off the floor and smothered the urge to dump the dirty bucket water over his head. He glanced her way, and traitor that it was, her whole body clenched. She was Pavlov's dog, reacting to the slightest show of interest from him. With her heart hammering, she turned and hurried to the kitchen, hiding when she wanted to run, wanted to go home and burrow under the covers.

If she had run, she wouldn't have to curse herself for being able to pinpoint exactly where Paul sat or stood every second of the night. That she could also sense when Blake sat at his table, played pool or pulled his mother up for a quick laughing dance was slightly less upsetting.

At midnight, with her feet aching and eyes stinging, she walked out into the icy, moonless night. A figure stood in the wash of the hotel's floodlight, the collar of his jacket flipped up and his hands deep in his pockets.

Carol didn't even bother sighing. She stood out of reach and crossed her arms over her chest, even though her leathers and undergarments kept her torso warm. She pulled her neck warmer up over her ears and tried to jut out her chin.

'I don't want anything to do with you. And I don't care what you want from me, you're not getting it.'

He took a step towards her.

She took one back.

He arched a brow and pointed at her. 'Stay.'

Like a well-trained dog, she did, her breath visible as short puffs of air rising between them.

Standing in front of her, he leaned close enough to almost touch her. Close enough for her to smell the beer he'd had. Close enough to pull her into memories she'd rather forget. She squeezed her eyes closed against the images, pressed her thighs together to stop the conditioned response of his breath on her cheek.

'You can throw empty words at me, but I know that you dream of me. You want me.' His shark smile appeared. 'So I'm willing to be gracious and take you back.'

'Take *me* back?'

She'd walked away from *him*, because finding him in her bed with someone else had been the last straw.

With a sigh, Paul stepped back and slid his hands into his jacket pockets. 'Look, I'm offering you what you'll never get from anyone else. You won't have to work or worry about money. Being with me will open doors for you, create opportunities you could only dream about.'

'Why do you want me back?' Paul Todd didn't do anything for anyone unless it benefitted him.

His face tightened. 'Because girls like you exist.'

'I don't understand.'

'You don't need to.'

She opened her mouth, but at his glare, the familiar clutch in her belly had her closing it again. Cocky Paul scared her, but an angry Paul terrified her.

Now he smiled. 'Get some sleep. You look like crap.'

Pushing past her fear, she lifted her chin. 'Stop calling me and I will.'

'Me? Calling *you*? You really are delusional.'

Turning, he walked to the last car left in the lot.

She stayed in the same spot until he'd driven away, then she squatted, cradled her head in her hands and let the shudder run through her. Mortified by the sting of tears, she held her breath until the feeling passed.

Would she ever be free of Paul? And just what lengths would he go to now that he'd decided he wanted her back?

CHAPTER 5

Carol pushed herself to keep up her pace as she jogged. She should be enjoying the slowly waking day, be inspired by the glittering leaves of the red gums dipping their toes in the river. But even the steam rising from the backs of the cows munching hay in their paddocks didn't tickle a smile.

Beside her, Snow leapt and bounded, his tongue flopping from the side of his mouth. At least he was enjoying their new early morning routine. She'd rather have stayed in bed for another hour, but as she still couldn't sleep, even though her phone stayed silent, she'd decided to let Snow have some fun.

She followed the curve of the trail as it hugged the river until the paddocks gave way to houses on double blocks, their yards filled with gardens and kids play equipment. Most had dogs that delighted in announcing her passing with high-pitched yaps. So instead of staying on the trail and waking the other side of town, Carol turned at the bridge and jogged along the main street, glancing in the darkened pub windows as she passed.

In the brightness of the rising sun, she could nearly convince herself that she'd dreamed last night's events. Because none of it made sense. Why would Paul want to get back together with her when he'd told everyone in town that he wanted nothing to do with her? And why did he want her back anyway? She didn't believe for a second that it was only because he could easily manipulate her, and aside from that, they had nothing. She wanted nothing from him, either—nothing he could offer would convince her to go back to him. It would kill her to spend any amount of time with him, let alone be emotionally hooked to him again.

She shuddered and stretched out her stride.

A shower would help. The water had run cold last night, and though it hadn't washed the shame and humiliation from her skin or the sickness from her mouth, it had given her a chance to think of nothing but the gurgle of the drain swallowing everything.

Snow had loved the treat of sleeping on her bed; his big body sprawled across hers should have stopped the shivers rippling through her, should have made her feel safe, but it had done neither.

Would Paul always be the ghost who haunted her, the shadow behind the door that made her jump?

He'd laugh at her if she said anything. To him, every complaint she'd made had been irrational. He hadn't been ignoring her; he'd been busy the last few weeks working his way towards manager. The women he took out for lunch and dinner were clients.

Hysterical and juvenile had been his favourite labels for her.

After he'd given his calm explanations and had counter-blamed, Carol would fall silent and avoid his gaze and touch. Paul would then drag up every shitty thing she'd ever said and done to anyone. She'd lie awake at night, convinced everyone should and must hate her, until she finally spiralled into a hole so deep and dark, she couldn't see a way out.

Then, just when she would give up trying to find a reason to live, he'd give her *that* look, and her heart would race. He'd make her a cup of tea, and the elation that she was worthy of him once more shifted the sun, let her see the world waiting outside. But by the time he'd creep into her room and slide into her bed, she'd be gasping for air, her body vibrating with need. He'd still make her cry, make her beg to be used, and she'd do it just so she could feel something; she'd do anything just to keep the feeling of being buried in misery at bay.

Recognising that the familiar spiral into depression threatened to pull her under now, Carol sprinted the last block. Snow took it as a challenge and nearly pulled her over as he took off on long powerful legs.

She kept pace with him until, stomach churning, ribs aching and legs shaking, she stumbled up the steps to her front door. Using it as a prop, she kicked off her shoes, then leaned against the cold wood, eyes squeezed closed against the urge to beat her fists against it and scream.

Nothing that'd happened in the past could be changed. She'd been reckless, had made mistakes and would have to learn to live with them. But she *could* change the course her life was on now, so that's where she'd put her energy. Paul would only be in town for as long as it took for city life to call him back. All she had to do was wait him out. Once he left, she could go back to living her normal life, seeing her friends every day, going outside without worrying he was hiding somewhere, watching.

Shuddering, she scanned the empty street. Not that she'd been aware of him when he'd taken the photos he'd already sent her. After letting Snow in and closing the door against the world, she leaned against it.

What did she do now? Why hadn't she done something back then? Why had she let him use her, lie about their relationship, about her?

Because he'd made it impossible to do otherwise.

How could she have spoken up, told his friends and hers about the thing he did to her, and what he didn't do, when they believed he was the dreamiest housemate and boyfriend anyone could have? They'd believed he loved her, saw him treat her with respect when they were out. Saw him treat her like a human being instead of a well-trained dog.

Sit, stay, roll over, suck my dick, beg me to fuck you. And she'd done it all, so desperate was she to have someone, *any*one, who wanted and needed her.

Neither of her parents had been the type who hugged their child, nor had they given in to her begging for a dog or cat each birthday and Christmas. Their habitual travelling would have made having a pet difficult, so Carol had chased lambs and butterflies, and had hugged Gran and Pop whenever she could.

Until the last time …

Wiping her cheek on her shoulder, she hugged herself but found no comfort, and when her phone buzzed, she swallowed a sob. Crying wouldn't stop the phone buzzing and neither would a scream, though either reaction might keep her sane. Instead, she pried the phone from her leggings pocket and swiped decline before registering the caller readout.

She hit redial.

Kelsey answered on the second ring. 'You hung up on me?'

The week since Carol had last seen Kelsey had dragged, but she wouldn't give Paul any reason to pull her friend into his elaborate games.

'No, I … sorry, I thought you were … telemarketers.'

'Telemarketers?' Kelsey's voice pitched low. 'Why would you think I was a telemarketer? What's going on? I've been leaving you messages and you haven't called me back.'

Carol tapped a fist against her temple. 'I was jogging.'

'For the last week? Why are you avoiding me? Is it because I'm pregnant?' Kelsey's voice cracked.

'What? No. Why would you even think that?'

'Because you haven't talked to me since I told you about the baby.' She sniffed. 'You're my best friend, and I want to share this with you. I want to have you with me.'

Carol sat on the floor. Sensing her mood, Snow tried to curl up in her lap.

'Are you okay,' she asked, clutching her phone. 'Is something wrong?'

Kelsey sighed. 'I'm fine. Nothing's wrong, but I miss you. I thought we were going riding again.'

If Carol could go back and change things, worrying Kelsey would be the first mistake she'd eliminate. Letting Paul into her life would be next.

'We were. We *are*. I can come out this afternoon.' And she could do the two birds with one stone thing.

She hadn't given Blake a time, but she had given him her word that she'd drop in. All she had to do was say hi, have a look around, appease his ego that he'd done a brilliant job so far, then leave. If he pushed her to stay longer, she could claim that Kelsey was expecting her.

Did that make her even more of a shitty friend?

'And you'll tell me what's going on with you?' asked Kelsey. 'Because I know something is. Jex said you've been dead on your feet, and it's not like you to stay so quiet. I'm worried about this baby and about Pipa, and now I'm worried about you.' Her voice broke.

Carol doubled over and rested her head against Snow's. 'You don't need to worry about me, Kel. I'm fine. I'm just … taking some me time.'

Kelsey blew out a breath. 'Are you painting again?'

70

Carol's sketchbook lay open on the table where she'd left it before her jog. She imagined Blake's eyes as she'd drawn them, staring up from the page, his gaze serious yet soft. The pages before that were filled with him too; she might as well label it her Blake book. She'd have to make sure she locked it away once she'd gotten him out of her system—her artistic system, that was. She wouldn't let him in anywhere else.

'I'm getting there,' she lied.

'You're sketching then?' Kelsey's voice warmed.

Carol would say anything if it meant keeping Kelsey happy. 'Yeah, I am. I'm practising portraits, so I can do you, Pipa, Ethan and the new one when it's born.'

Kelsey's sigh was full of wonder. 'That's perfect. Thank you.'

Carol sat straight again and stretched her back. 'It's no biggie.'

'You know it is.' Kelsey cleared her throat. 'So, I'll have the kettle on at one. I expect you to be in my kitchen by the time I've made cuppas.'

Carol forced a smile into her voice. 'You've got that mummy thing down pat, don't you? And, yeah, I'll be there.'

'Good. Don't be a stranger.'

Don't be a stranger.

The words played over in Carol's head as she gave Snow his breakfast and had her own. Who *really* knew her, enough for her not to be considered a stranger? It used to be Kelsey, before they'd both been forced to grow up too quickly. Her parents had no clue who she was, had never known her well enough to even pick an appropriate birthday card.

She'd learned to not expect surprises, but she had once dreamed of receiving flowers picked because someone had seen them and thought of her. Or chocolates just because. But dreams only ever distorted reality and gave a false sense of hope for the future; she didn't bother with them now.

Don't be a stranger. The words plagued her as she locked Snow in his cage, then dressed in her leathers. They vibrated through her as she rode her motorbike towards her grandparents'—no, *Blake's* property. Was she truly a stranger to her friends? Each of them knew a version of her, depending on what she'd shown them or what Paul had told them.

71

To some people in town, she was someone they could have a laugh with. To the kids in Mr Arden's art class, who she helped out with once a month, she was a rule-breaker and a little scary. To most of the older people in town, she was a troublemaker, a drama queen, and poor little Carol who'd been abandoned by her parents, had lost her grandmother and had found her grandfather dead. *Hence the attitude*, they'd whisper.

Carol slowed and came to a stop at the end of the long driveway she'd ridden, walked and driven down countless times right up until her grandparents had died. Once she'd spent that week repainting before her mother had sold the place, she'd no longer had the right, or the heart, to come back.

Rubbing her gloved knuckles to her chest, she breathed in the damp pine scent from the nearby plantations. Featuring the bright cream of newly laid limestone instead of the weathered old brown, the long winding driveway cut down through the bowl of magnificent grazing land and into the house yard tucked among the gum-surrounded gardens.

Carol's heart was already telling her she couldn't come back after today. Even if Blake kept the bones of the house, it wouldn't be the place of joy and love it had once been, the sanctuary she'd always craved. He'd change it, and rightly so, to infuse his own personality, his own style. He'd mark the house and gardens, and the land surrounding it, as his own. But she'd promised to visit, just this once, and so, taking a deep breath and hoping the pain in her heart would clear once she finally said goodbye to her grandmother, she accelerated, turning her bike into the driveway and making her way to what she had to remind herself again was now Blake's place.

She pulled up in front of the house where paint cracked liked spiderwebs across the old weatherboards, the poles of the verandah slanted like broken fingers, and where the garden beds her grandmother had once loved were now more weeds than flowers. Piles of neatly stacked junk dotted the path along the side of the house and down to the big shed where her grandfather had tinkered with this and that. She'd loved sitting in the doorway watching him, the smell of grease and freshly sawed wood always in the air.

Something banged in the shed and cursing followed. Carol took a deep breath and glanced over her shoulder at her bike. But she'd promised, damn it. Prepared for the stab to her heart, she walked to the huge double sliding doors of the shed she'd always remember as her Pop's—and stopped.

Blake *had* stamped the space as his, with shiny new tools hanging on the old pegboard her grandfather had hung, and in the big new vice bolted to the bench her grandfather had scarred and singed while building things for Carol and her grandmother. Blake had done what Pop had always said he would do; he'd pulled a few sheets of corrugated iron off the roof and had replaced them with clear polycarbonate sheets. Even with the fat grey clouds rolling across the sky, the area was flooded with light.

Moving to the side wall, Carol traced a finger over the date neatly printed in her grandfather's no-nonsense writing. He'd written it there, or so he'd told Carol, the day the shed had been built, while her grandmother, pregnant with their first child, had done her best to make their temporary home as cosy and love-filled as she could. The second date, marking their son's birthday, had been added three months later, and the third marked his death, just six weeks after that.

When her grandfather had finished building the house, they'd welcomed their second baby, a little girl, whom her grandmother had always spoken of with such affection. Carol had wished she'd been that baby, because then she would have known what it was to have parents who loved and wanted her. But that baby, though loved and cherished, had lived only eight months; the selfishness of Carol's juvenile wish clogged her throat.

As she walked slowly along the wall, hearing her grandfather's voice in her head, she touched each date, each record of how many head of sheep or cattle had been sold, or, in the hard years, how many had been lost. Three more babies' names and birth dates were there too. Only one child, Beth, had lived beyond two years and into adulthood. And as that adult, she'd sold her father's property, her mother's haven and her daughter's dream without hesitation.

Blake had framed the timeline of her grandparents' life at Lone Wattle Park with strips of thin steel. He'd hung hooks under it to display the old rabbit traps and other bric-a-brac that had been left behind. He'd kept the history and, for her, the stories that went with it.

'I can guess most of the dates and notes,' Blake said from behind her, 'but this one'—he tapped the only note written in cursive—'I can't quite decipher.'

Carol put her hands in her pockets. Shaky, and not sure she could blame it all on her memories, she stayed facing the wall. 'Gran wrote that one. She'd made a bet with Pop that she could crutch more sheep than him in twenty minutes. She won, by three sheep, and wrote the date on his timeline so he'd never forget it.'

Blake chuckled. 'I doubt he'd forget it anyway. From what I've heard, they loved each other very much.'

She swallowed the lump in her throat. 'They did. He died a month after she did, and I know it was because he'd given up. He couldn't live without her.'

'Shit, I'm sorry.'

She shrugged it off. 'Wherever they are now, they're together again and happy. That's all that matters.'

And it mattered that Blake had kept it all, but she locked those words down. He was already too close to becoming someone she not only admired for his talent but respected for his heart. And she couldn't do that and keep her distance.

So she turned and looked up at him. 'Thanks for last night. And the other night. And for this.' She nodded towards the wall. 'Pop would love that you've kept what he put blood, sweat and tears into. No doubt you'll add your own.'

He held up a thumb to show the thin line of drying blood trailing from the tip to his first knuckle. 'Hard not to leave some behind when you work with your hands.'

Carol frowned, more at the kick of concern to her stomach than the minor cut. 'You should clean it so it doesn't get infected.'

He shrugged. 'When I take a break.'

Carol fisted her hands in her pockets so she didn't reach for his hand and tend to the wound herself.

#

Blake held his breath. Carol smelt of leather and wild weather, and the scent overrode the greasy fumes of his morning's work—in the same way her presence in his space pushed away thoughts of finishing his current project and starting something else. If he could just get her to sit on the bench with her legs dangling, her hands braced either side of her thighs, he could attach wings to her back and turn her into the impish fae that haunted him.

But she'd come into the shed braced, her shoulders bearing an invisible weight, and he'd swallowed the curse his throbbing thumb demanded. She hadn't told him what time she'd visit, which he suspected had been deliberate, so he'd fallen into work instead of watching the clock. Then she'd been there, standing at his door, the tips of her boots butted up against the edge of the concrete floor.

He'd nearly said hello, but Carol hadn't been aware of him as she stepped over that line and tentatively explored a space that must have been so familiar yet was now so different. He'd waited, as if to see if he'd passed a test on what he'd done so far. He'd had to stop himself pacing as she'd made her way along the wall, her fingers tracing each notation that held a history he'd never dream of removing or covering.

Did Carol know he could read pain, loss, surprise and the beginning of gratitude in those winter blue eyes? Did she know that hint of softness made him want to dig deeper to see exactly what he was up against?

He'd told himself he wasn't ready for the entanglement or the distraction of a relationship, yet he wanted to spend all his spare time with her, just talking or coaxing a laugh out of her so that her dimple flashed. If he could get near the scar tissue she protected, he'd break it up into smaller pieces so she'd be able to let go of it easier, then maybe her smile would stay.

Now, as she stared at the cut on his thumb, he wanted to enfold her and give her back some of that softness she tried so hard to hide. But his timing was wrong; she wasn't ready for the implications of friendship, so he shifted to a safer topic.

'Did you know the people who owned this place before me never lived here?'

She turned her head to stare out the door. 'Yeah. They snapped it up cheap and figured they could make big money growing beef. I guess they didn't realise they actually had to look after the cows.'

Now that he could breathe, he stepped back. 'The cattle were wild when I first looked at the place.'

Her gaze cut to his. 'You looked at it before you bought it?'

He wouldn't get any work done now until she left, so he began turning everything off and packing his tools away. 'Of course. I had a few days off, so I flew down.'

'From where?'

He glanced at her. 'Queensland.'

Her pierced eyebrow lifted, as if she were offended that he could fly interstate at the drop of a hat. 'Of course.'

With all traces of softness and concern now gone, she walked past him to his work table, which dominated the centre of the space. 'This is Rita's?'

'Yeah. It's rough, but it'll turn out well.'

'It's already beautiful.' Her hand hovered over the heart he'd made from horseshoe halves, then she nodded to the board that held his rough plans. 'You sketch it all beforehand?'

'I do.' Leaning a hip against the workbench, he gave her room to explore, though her last *of course* niggled at him. 'Can I ask you something?'

When her face blanked and her gaze dipped to the floor, he mentally kicked himself. Clearly, she'd assumed his question would be too personal, too probing, because, like all small towns, the people of White Wattle Creek loved to tell stories about the more colourful characters among them. And Carol was a popular subject; most whispers covered her non-conformity to anything society considered ladylike, as well as her connection to Paul. But the woman who stood before him didn't resemble the person in the stories he'd heard. Her skin wasn't as thick as everyone presumed, and the *I don't care* attitude sat about as deep.

So instead of potentially bruising the vulnerability she'd exposed by asking who'd put that chip on her shoulder, he changed tack. 'What do you think of Metal As Anything for a business name?'

The look she shot him wasn't quite pitiful. 'I think there'd already be a few with that name.'

He scratched his chin. 'True. I guess Scrap Art and Metal Mania would be the same.'

Her dimple flashed for a second. 'You can be more creative than that.'

He pulled the scrap of paper from his pocket and handed it to her. 'This is as creative as I can be.'

She took the paper, smoothed it out, then held it up, her lips moving as she read through the list of names. 'Blakesmith's Rusty Recycled Sculptures. That one is a bit of a mouthful. Return to Sender.' She lifted her gaze to his. 'I'm going to have that stuck in my head now.' Focusing on the names again, she hummed the song, giving her hips a distinctive Elvis shake before she cleared her throat and crossed her ankles. 'Rustic Beauty isn't bad, but unless you're only ever going to create beautiful stuff, then it could be a bit misleading.'

'I had considered that, though if you pose for me, I could make a whole line of fae-inspired sculptures from all sorts of scrap metal.'

Then it hit him.

'Rip the list up.'

Carol held it away as he reached for it. 'I haven't finished reading them.'

'You don't need to. Daily Grind could be mistaken for an adult shop, Milling Memories only covers part of what I do, and though I love Rustic Wattle, I've just come up with the perfect name.' He held his hands up to frame the imaginary words. 'Scrap-2-Sculpture, where discarded metal is given one more chance to shine.'

Carol nodded. 'Now *that* is a unique name. And it gives hope that not everything thrown away is junk.'

'Exactly.' Energised, he grabbed a carpenter's pencil and a scrap piece of board. 'Do me a favour. Brace your hands on the bench behind your back, lift your shoulders and look outside.'

She lifted her eyebrows instead. 'Why?'

'You're smarter than that.' But he waited her out. If she refused, he'd let it go. For now.

As she took a deep breath, then stood how he'd asked, he wasted no time in sketching thick lines. She stood stiffly, and though her frown was aimed out the door, he'd rather she relaxed.

'Tell me, what colour is the kitchen meant to be? I've tried the typical white and blue, but it just doesn't work.'

She glanced at him. 'Gran wasn't a typical decorator. She'd see a paint colour she liked, would get it, then paint whatever piece of furniture or fixture called to her. The cupboard doors were every colour of purple you can imagine, from soft lilac to screaming magenta.' Her whole body softened with the memory, then snapped tight. 'But I had to paint everything white before my parents put it on the market. Mum was afraid it wouldn't sell.' She pursed her lips. 'Anyway, it's your kitchen now, so whatever colour you pick should suit it.'

'Nothing has so far, though. The house has'—he circled the pencil in the air—'feelings, I guess. It lets me know if the colour isn't right.' He cocked his head. 'You know what I mean?'

She stared at him. 'Yeah, I do.'

He'd never regretted having only rough drawing skills—he didn't need anything more than that to get the basic shapes of his work down—but in that moment, he would have loved to sketch the finer details of her face, the shock of understanding and the glint of what she was trying to hide. He wanted more time to capture all of her, especially the parts she kept locked away.

'I could use your help,' he said. 'If you go through the rooms with me and tell me what you remember about them, it might inspire me to finish renovating. Then I can stop sleeping on the floor and actually live in the place.'

She chewed her bottom lip. 'But you won't want it exactly as my grandparents had it. You'll want to make it yours.'

He set his sketch of her aside. 'The thing is, I love this place. The rain on the tin roof reminds me of spending holidays at Mum's. As I watch the shadows grow long across the paddocks, the sun shines through the trees and I know that everything the light touches is mine. Even walking out here only to be faced with a massive 'roo ready to box my head in is exhilarating. I'm used to the deafening riot the cockies make morning and night, but the house hasn't accepted me yet.'

Carol studied him, then shook her head and raised her pierced eyebrow. 'Fine. I can take a look and give you some ideas. But I don't know about this posing stuff. It feels weird.'

Biting the inside of his cheek to stop a smile and ignoring the need to argue about the work he could do with her as his model, he gestured at the shed doors. 'Now? I'm going into town later, so I can pick up more paint and get started. Again.'

She walked beside him towards the house but stopped at what had once been the kitchen garden. Weeds choked everything now, while patches of mud linked up to make a sad sort of maze through the rows.

Carol squatted and touched the leaf of one struggling plant. 'You'll get the garden going again?'

'Not me.' This time he did smile when her gaze shot to his. 'I'm not sure what colour my thumb is or how much time I can dedicate to it before spring, so I'm trying to spark a friend's interest in tackling it for me. He runs a land-scaping business in Moffat Beach.'

She stood and surveyed the tangled clumps and bare patches, then shrugged. 'Fair enough. But what do you mean by "spark his interest"?'

He let their elbows bump as they turned and walked up the steps to the verandah. 'He's finishing up a big community garden project at the moment, but I've sent him a couple of photos, hoping they'll make him want to visit.'

'So you don't push people to do what you want?'

'Pushing usually creates friction, which either puts a stop to what needs to happen or at least makes things more difficult. I'd rather find the right approach and get a better result.'

'Some people think pushing is the only way.'

'I'm not some people.' Sensing an opportunity, he angled his head to better see her face. 'I want to ask this, not to pry or upset you, but is this about Paul and how he treated you when you were together?'

'Why do you want to know?'

'Because I look like him. Because he's in real estate and you walked away from me when I said I'd been in the industry. Because he obviously has money

79

and so do I.' He nodded at her scowl. 'I know you don't like the similarities between us, but I'm not him. When I say something or ask a question, I'm not hiding anything in my words.' He held his arms wide. 'What you see is what you get.'

Carol frowned, then bent to unbuckle her boots. 'I see a human, and humans can be selfish without even meaning to be. I'll help you because I believe you have good intentions. I believe you want to be a good neighbour, a good artist and a good guy, which I think you are.'

She stood and met his gaze. 'But Paul did hurt me, in more ways than I want to talk about, and I do keep expecting you to act like him and talk like him, but you don't, and I have to get used to that.'

Setting her boots aside, she faced the door like she expected it to slap her.

Blake said nothing as she reached out and opened it, and when she stepped inside, he stayed out in the chill wind, his hands jammed in his pockets. Damned if his protective instincts hadn't lit every cell of his body at her words.

As a boy he'd learned to protect his heart and head against criticism and rejection, because his father hadn't been able to help hating his sons and wife—he'd never been the same after his accident. Therapy had helped his dad control his anger, but Blake could never forget hugging Alex to his chest as they'd hid from the glares, the words, the threats.

He had better memories, too, of course. He recalled the first hug he'd received from his father in ten years, and the first time in twelve that his father had told him that he loved him. He remembered the day he'd sat down with his father, terrified of what his reaction would be as he told him that life was slowly killing him, and the staggering relief when his dad merely smiled and told him to chase his dreams.

Carol hid her terror well, but it leaked out in the way she held herself, always ready to defend or deflect. He wanted her to do neither with him. If she could see him as a friend, someone she could relax with or talk to without having to choose her words or hide them behind half-truths, then he could help her uncover the confidence to live life and chase the happiness she deserved.

But even if she couldn't see him as a friend right now, he'd still be one to her. And eventually, hopefully, she'd see that he wanted nothing more than to see her happy.

CHAPTER 6

Carol sipped her cup of tea as she sat across from Blake at his chunky-legged, scarred and stained kitchen table. 'This is a great find. It suits you and the house perfectly.'

'I haggled for it at a garage sale,' he said, then squinted as he regarded her over his coffee. 'Are you saying the house, my table and I are all tough and ugly?'

She huffed out a laugh. He had a way of doing that, of saying things that made her want to smile.

'You got the tough part right,' she said, 'but I meant it's not flashy and new, with no stories to tell.' She traced her finger over the *D* and *P* someone had scratched into the surface. 'It has history, so does the house, and it's clearly something you want for yourself. To build a history of your own here.'

He inclined his head in a salute. 'Very astute of you.'

This time she snorted into her mug. 'Very posh of you.'

His grin flashed, quick and full, and Carol had to concentrate on holding her cup. She forgot to be cautious around him. Not once, as they'd walked from room to room, had he belittled her memories or rolled his eyes at her suggestions like Paul would have done. He'd listened and asked questions.

When she was with Blake, Carol felt as though the outside world no longer existed. Or was it being here, in this house? Either way, she wanted *more*. More quiet time, more freedom to sit and talk with someone who appreciated her mind instead of constantly making her feel dumb. Someone she could spend hours with and enjoy every minute.

Not that she would let herself. One afternoon in this strange alternate universe would have to do, because as much as she was enjoying her time with him, the pain of losing another friend—and she would—would destroy her.

Blake leaned forward and gestured to the notebook he'd given her to scribble ideas and memories in for him. 'Tell me what part of this is posh, other than your brilliant sketching skills.'

She'd already fobbed off his compliments about her drawings, so she simply shrugged. 'None of it.'

He tapped the picture she'd drawn of Gran sitting by the fire. 'But no comment about the skills?'

She'd been told so often that her skill was merely a lucky gift, not a hard-earned ability. Taking credit for it had always felt awkward and wrong, so she shrugged off Blake's comment. 'When Gran and Pop died, things got rough. Mr Arden made me promise that I'd keep drawing and painting, no matter what. For a long time, I broke that promise. And although I've pulled pencils and paper out in the last week or so, I don't have room to paint.'

'You would've had plenty of inspiration and room out here.'

'An abundance of it.' She smiled. 'When I was five, Pop made me an easel and Gran gave me some of her leftover paints. In the summer, they'd set me up outside and hose me down at the end of the day. In winter, Gran would lay some newspaper in a corner of the lounge room and put the easel in there for me.'

It had been too long since she'd thought of them like that. All of them happy.

Blake sat back with a laugh. 'Hose you down?'

She shrugged. 'I never stood still for long. I'd play in the paddocks with the lambs or roll around in the dirt with the dog or chase the chickens. I disappeared once. Gran said she only looked away for a few seconds and I was gone. Scared the life out of them.' She bit her lip as her heart ached all over again. 'They found me down near the billabong, which is part of the reason it's fenced off now. At least I guess it's still fenced off.'

He'd propped his chin on his hand, his eyes steady on hers as he listened to her. 'I haven't explored much of the property yet.'

'You'll want to do it before summer.'

'In case of fires?'

'In case of snakes.'

When he grew pale, she laughed. 'Don't tell me you're scared of snakes.'

He held out a shaking hand. 'No, not scared. Petrified.'

Seeing the raw terror in his eyes, she reached out and touched his hand. 'Get a dog and a cat and keep some stock close to the house. They'll keep them away.'

He gulped down the rest of his coffee. 'Will a horse do the same?'

She sat up. 'You have a horse?'

He shrugged and some of his colour came back. 'Of course.'

She rolled her eyes at that. 'Why didn't you tell me? I would have dropped in sooner.'

'Hmm, so you *do* have a weakness.' Standing, he held a steadier hand out for her cup. 'Come and meet Felix, then maybe when I ask you to come back tomorrow to tell me what you think of the paint I plan on buying this afternoon, you'll say yes.'

Smiling, she drained the last of her tea. Maybe it wouldn't hurt so much to come out again. What harm could it do to explore lingering memories while being entertained by Blake's wit and humour?

Her phone buzzed in her pocket, and she fumbled the cup. Struggling to keep the dregs from running onto the table, she pulled out her phone.

When she saw it was Kelsey's name flashing on the screen, relief made her vision waver. Then she registered the time.

Swearing under her breath, she swiped to answer. 'Shit, I'm sorry, Kel. I lost track of time.'

'Better than you being unconscious on the side of the road somewhere, I guess.'

Carol closed her eyes and rubbed her forehead. She couldn't blame Kelsey for being angry. 'I'm only five minutes away. I'll be there soon.'

Blake touched her shoulder and she jumped. A frown darkened his eyes. 'Everything okay?'

'Is that Blake? You're at Blake's?'

'I am. I'm leaving now.'

Should have left ages ago, before she'd forgotten the outside world. Before she'd relaxed so much that she would now have to snap her bones back into the armour she needed to survive.

'Don't rush.' Kelsey sighed. 'I thought you'd forgotten, that's all. Or that you were avoiding me.'

Could she be a worse friend?

'I'm not avoiding you. I just lost track of time.'

'It tends to slip away out there, doesn't it?' Though Kelsey no longer sounded angry, her voice still held a trace of hurt at being ignored. 'It was the same when we were kids. But I'm glad you're getting to see the place again. Stay as long as you need.'

Carol eyed Blake. 'I'm about to meet Felix, then apparently, I'm coming back out tomorrow to look at some paint.'

Blake grinned at her, and she could see him as a little boy, charming Annie with those dark eyes that danced with mischief. She bet his charm was second nature now, that he got what he wanted more often than not.

Kelsey chuckled. 'You'll love Felix. He's a real charmer.'

Carol bared her teeth in a smile at Blake. 'I bet he is.'

'Okay, send me a text when you're leaving, and I'll put the kettle on.'

'I will. See you soon.' She hung up and slipped her phone back in her pocket.

Blake's smile was gone now; he regarded her with a frown. 'You were expecting a call, and not a pleasant one, from someone else.'

She shrugged. 'Telemarketers.'

He shook his head. 'You know Alex is my brother, right? That I grew up dealing with his stubborn-arse shit?'

It was the first time he'd mentioned his family. She'd heard rumours, of course, but that's all they'd been, and she wasn't one for taking everything she heard as truth.

'Yeah,' she said. 'Alex was part of our group the last two years of high school. He and—' She bit her lip, unsure how much she should say.

'Jex, I'm guessing, and they're having some sort of relationship at the moment?'

Carol frowned. 'You don't approve?'

Blake sighed and leaned a hip against the table. 'Alex isn't one for long-term anything. I love him, he's my brother, but I know his pattern. He stays as long as the thrill lasts, then he moves on. I don't want to see your friend get hurt, that's all.'

'Neither do I, but Alex and Jex are both adults.'

Blake pointed at her. 'You're good at deflecting. Who did you think was calling you?'

If he wasn't going to let it go, it'd be easier to give him something, so she lifted her hands, palms up. 'I don't know.'

He stared at her. 'You don't know, or you don't want to say?'

'I've had a few calls from a private number. Probably kids being idiots.' She went to the door and looked back over her shoulder. 'Are you going to introduce me to your horse?'

He stayed where he was. 'It's not going to work. I've felt the kind of terror I saw on your face just now, and after you dropped the jug at the pub last night. You looked the same way the first night I met you at Crazy Hat Night, too. It adds up to something, Carol, and that's without even considering you're as pale as a ghost and look like you haven't slept in a week.'

She rolled her eyes. 'Gee, thanks for the glowing flattery about my looks.'

'It's nothing to do with your looks, and you know it. Has Kelsey seen you lately? Are you going to fob her off as well?'

'She doesn't need to worry about any of this, and if you mention it to her, I'll ...'

'You'll what? And why would you need to do anything if all you're getting is calls from telemarketers?' He shook his head. 'You're not a very good liar, Carol.'

Carol blinked away the sting of tears. She'd been accused of lying when she'd been telling the truth so many times that she'd given up trying to defend herself, yet Blake had managed to strip her soul bare before handing the quivering, quaking mess back to her.

Afraid she'd lay everything at his feet, she yanked the door open. 'I'll meet Felix another time.'

Outside, with her nose running and her ears stinging, she pulled on her boots.

Blake stepped out beside her, curling his sock-covered toes against the cold. 'I'm worried about you.'

She wiped her nose on her sleeve. 'You don't need to be.'

'Need to be or not, I am. You're hiding something, and it's going to make you sick.'

She jammed her foot in her other boot, then stood to face him. 'There's a reason I'm keeping it to myself.'

'What's that?'

'That's my business and no one else's.'

He opened his mouth, closed it and ran a hand through his hair. 'I get that it's hard to ask for help and to let people know what's going on inside you, but if Kelsey had a problem,' he said softly, 'would you want her to come to you? If I had a problem, could I ask you for help?'

How could that look of understanding be anything but genuine? He made her want to spill everything, to stamp it into mush and bury it—and she was tempted to let him help. Instead, she gripped handfuls of her hair. 'You're complicating everything.'

'No, I'm not.' He eased her fingers from her hair. 'What's going on?'

She stomped the length of the verandah and back again. 'I'm getting prank calls, okay? I never know when, and I don't know who they're from.'

Stroking his chin, Blake leaned against a wooden post. 'Did you know that Paul is telling everyone you're stalking him?'

A jumble of words pushed up her throat, but she swallowed them and let only one out. 'What?'

'Last night at the pub, I heard him tell a few people you couldn't let go of the past and kept calling him.'

Her world tilted. 'I'm not. I don't want anything to do with him.'

His gaze searched hers. 'I believe there's *something* going on between you two, but I don't think it's you stalking him.'

She couldn't drag enough air into her lungs. 'You're the only one who would believe that.'

'I never grew up believing he was the town's golden boy.'

She covered her mouth to stop the hysterical laugh from bubbling up inside her. He'd already witnessed her losing it once and had stayed. What did that mean?

When he stepped closer, she held her hands up and shook her head. She'd fall apart if he offered her warmth and refuge. 'I don't know what to do with this. With you.'

He reached out and sandwiched her hands between his. 'Try this. You come out tomorrow morning and forget about phones and exes for a bit. If you feel comfortable, you can pose for me again, and I can show you the mixed-media fantasy designs I have in mind. Then you can tell me more about the place and your grandparents.'

'Why do you want me here? You must have heard more rumours about me than Paul's latest lies.'

Raising their hands, he pressed a thumb to her chin. 'I told you that first night, only you can tell your story. I hope one day you trust me enough to do that, but in the meantime, we can be friends, can't we?'

It wasn't what she wanted, yet his words warmed more than just her hands. And maybe, just maybe, doing something other than counting the seconds until her phone rang again might allow her to build up some strength. She'd need it to face Paul in the flesh again, as she knew she would. And it looked as if she'd need strength to make sure Blake featured only as sketches in her notebooks and not as a permanent fixture in her life.

#

Carol gave a cursory knock before letting herself into the house—it had only taken once to learn that when Pipa was at kindergarten, Kelsey and Ethan took advantage of their time alone.

Kelsey smiled and waved from the kitchen with her phone pressed to her ear. 'Thank you for this. I'll have everything ready.'

She pointed to the mug on the kitchen table and the plate of biscuits sitting beside it. 'Okay, I'll see you then. Bye.' Dumping her phone on the table, she grabbed a biscuit and bit into it. 'Mmm, you have to try one. Ethan and Pipa have been baking up a storm.'

Carol took one and studied it. 'Who breaks the eggs?'

Kelsey laughed. 'If he lets Pipa do it, Ethan checks for shell.'

With a nod, Carol took a bite and moaned. 'Why can't I have someone cook biscuits and cakes for me?'

Kelsey pulled a chair out and sat down. 'Well, I don't know what sort of cook he is, but from what I hear, you could have Blake baking anything you desire.'

Carol paused, then dropped into a chair. 'I didn't think you were one for gossip.'

'Well, when my best friend goes silent for a week then gives me a flimsy excuse, I know she's hiding something. And I don't have much to go on, do I?' She brushed the crumbs from her fingers as she held Carol's gaze. 'So if I've misunderstood, are you going to tell me what's going on?'

Carol glanced at Kelsey's belly and tried to swallow the last of the biscuit that was stuck to the roof of her mouth. She'd keep Paul's nauseating offer to herself, and though talking and thinking about Blake made her stomach tremble, she'd suffer that and more to protect Kelsey.

'Blake had some questions about the house. And he wants to be friends.'

Kelsey stopped chewing. 'And you said?'

'I answered all his questions and gave him some ideas. As far as friendship goes, he seems like a nice enough guy.' She narrowed her eyes. 'How much of this do you already know?'

With a shrug, Kelsey shoved the rest of the biscuit in her mouth. 'None of it. He stays surprisingly quiet when it comes to you.'

'That's because he'd have nothing to say. We've barely spoken since Crazy Hat Night.'

Kelsey took another biscuit and pointed it at Carol. 'Except that he abandoned his shopping and ran out of Foodworks to talk to you.'

Carol rubbed her chest. 'He just wanted me to know he had good reason for ignoring me.'

Kelsey leaned forward and took Carol's hand. 'Does your reluctance to be around Blake have anything to do with what happened with Paul? Because if it does, I get it. I know when I came back everything was upside down for a while.'

'That was different. You'd always loved Ethan, and he never stopped loving you.'

Kelsey's face fell, as if she were confused. 'You never loved Paul? Not even in the beginning?'

Carol fisted her free hand against her stomach. 'It's not that. We needed each other then. I'd rather he ignored me now.'

Kelsey sat back and studied her. 'I get the feeling there's more to it than that.'

Carol shrugged and traced a finger through the crumbs she'd scattered on the table. 'Not really.'

Nothing she'd clutter Kelsey's heart with, at least. Time to change the subject. 'Blake is picking up some paint this afternoon, so I'll head out again tomorrow to see what he got.'

Smiling again, Kelsey took another biscuit. 'He's a good guy, Caz.'

'I'm only telling you because I'll be out this way again, so maybe I can drop in and ride Dusty.'

Kelsey fidgeted with her hair, hanging in a long ponytail over her shoulder. 'I wasn't going to say anything yet.'

'About what?' Ice settled in Carol's belly. 'You've changed your mind, haven't you? I knew this would happen!' She shot to her feet and, pacing to the fireplace, stared at the frames of the happy family smiling down at her. 'You got me excited about having a horse again, but now you've realised that you can't give her away.'

Kelsey put a hand on her shoulder and turned her around. 'I hope you don't seriously think I would sell her to someone else when I've told you she's yours. I've just asked a friend to take her for a couple of days so she knows that going in the horse float isn't a reason to panic. It's part of her rehabilitation.'

Carol let out a shaky breath. She needed sleep, even just a few hours; then her brain and emotions could chill. 'I'm sorry. I didn't mean to snap at you.'

Pulling Carol in for a hug, Kelsey stroked a soothing hand up and down her back. 'It answers my question, though. You really do want her.'

Carol wrapped her arms around Kelsey and hung on. 'I do.' So much that it wobbled her knees. 'Can we still ride now?'

Kelsey gave one last squeeze, then held Carol at arms-length. 'I was hoping you'd still want to ride. I've got some barrels and poles set up, along with some other play equipment. Would you mind being the crash test dummy?'

Carol sniffed and laughed. 'I knew there was a reason you wanted me out here.' She looped her arm through Kelsey's. 'But I know you wouldn't let me on Dusty if you thought she'd get scared or I'd be hurt.'

When they stepped outside, where the sun was drying the puddles scattered across the paddocks, Kelsey handed Carol a pair of riding boots.

'I'm putting you on her,' she said, 'because she's yours, so you should do the work. I know you can handle it, and besides, she trusts you.'

Carol had no faith that she wouldn't destroy that trust, because, really, what did she know about good relationships, good friendships? Nothing, that's what. Her parents were happy being half a world away from her; the only guy she'd had sex with only lured her into bed because she was a weak-willed idiot; and she lied to her friends.

'I don't know why she trusts me. I've only ridden her a couple of times.'

Maybe she should let Dusty stay with whoever she was going to visit. She'd be looked after and loved; Kelsey wouldn't let her go otherwise. Carol gritted her teeth against the need to know who'd be feeding Dusty apples and scratching her favourite spot behind her ear. She wouldn't ask, because it would prove Kelsey's point—that she really did want the filly, needed her even though she knew she'd ruin her like she ruined everything.

Kelsey stopped and tilted her head at Carol. 'You look like you just swallowed something bad.'

Carol rubbed her eyes. 'I'm tired and everything is blurring into one big ball of bad. What if I do something to ruin Dusty? What if I do something that pisses Blake off and he tells me not to come back? What if I cave and—'

She snapped her mouth closed. Out of all the hypothetical possibilities she'd considered, *that* she wouldn't do. She'd given in before, had been worn down by Paul and his games. This time, she wouldn't. He could play any game he wanted, but she wouldn't cave. Wouldn't let him think he could keep coming back and make her beg every time he wanted sex.

Kelsey touched Carol's arm. 'If you cave and what?'

Defer and deflect.

'Start enjoying Blake's company.'

Smiling, Kelsey slung an arm around Carol's shoulders. 'I can think of worse things for you to do.'

Carol huffed at that. 'Yeah. Me too.'

While Kelsey went to the paddock to catch Dusty, Carol slid out of her leather pants; she'd ride in her leggings. After stomping her borrowed boots on, she went to the tack room and collected Dusty's saddle and riding halter, then doubled back and grabbed a grooming tote when Kelsey led the mud-caked filly past.

'I guess she's been having fun.'

Kelsey glanced over her shoulder at Carol. 'Maybe you can learn something from her.'

Maybe, thought Carol, she could learn something from Kelsey, too. Both she and Dusty had been shown the darker side of what humans could do, yet both had learned to trust and love. And *were* loved, too. And they thrived on that love.

Could Carol find some semblance of that as well?

Would she have a future where Paul didn't call her at all hours of the day and night, when she no longer had to hide the truth from everyone? Would she ever find a fraction of the happiness Kelsey had?

Carol didn't dare to contemplate the answers to those questions. Not when her whole body ached and her mind fuzzed with fatigue. And not while Dusty cocked an ear her way, waiting, her soft brown eyes full of the love and trust Carol longed to feel.

Because wasting time hoping for, wishing and dreaming of a time that might not come would crumple her, Carol stepped closer to Dusty, *her* filly, and anchored herself in the moment by reaching out and stroking her velvet nose.

'So soft.'

Even after the tough life she'd had, Dusty had so many soft parts.

Carol rested her forehead against the horse's. 'Maybe I *can* learn from you.'

She took her time saddling up, stopping every now and then to give Dusty a scratch on the cheek or her neck, and talked nonsense the whole time. It helped keep the filly calm *and* levelled Carol's pulse rate.

By the time she led Dusty out to the yard behind the stables and mounted up, Kelsey had set up a grid of poles, lined up some cones to weave around, hung balloons around the fence line, and put a bucket on an upturned forty-four–gallon drum.

Kelsey grinned at Carol. 'So, what are your colours going to be?'

Carol frowned down at her black leggings. 'Colours?'

'Every horse-crazy girl gets gear in their favourite colours. You know, matching saddle pad, bandages and bridle, as well as boots, shirts and jodhpurs for you.'

Carol lifted an eyebrow. 'Guess.'

Laughing, Kelsey walked over to stroke Dusty's forehead. 'Pink it is, then. Now that's settled, take five minutes to warm up and get her soft, then we'll see what she thinks of everything.'

Twenty minutes later, Carol had Dusty standing alongside the fluttering balloons, one leg cocked, ears listening but steady. 'Have you done this with her before?'

Kelsey snapped a photo on her phone. 'Nope. Like I said, she trusts you.'

Leaning forward to stroke Dusty's neck, Carol shook her head. 'I don't know why she would, but I'm glad she does.'

'It's a good feeling, isn't it?'

It was an alien feeling, but one Carol wanted to hold onto, so when Ethan arrived home with Pipa, Carol waited while Pop the pony was brushed and saddled, and Pipa, snugged up in her bright orange jacket and purple jodhpurs, trotted into the yard. By the time they'd played tag, bending races and had each won a game of stepping stones using bucket lids, Carol's sides hurt from joining in with Pipa's infectious laughter.

Bracing her hands on her knees, she winked at Pipa. 'You and Pop make an awesome team.'

'I love him.' Pipa kissed the pony's nose, then threw her arms around Carol's neck and smacked a kiss on her cheek. 'And I love you.'

'Right back at you. And we'll have to do this more often.' But she waited until Pipa had turned away before wiping the transferred pony hair from her cheek.

Kelsey grinned over her shoulder as she walked to the stables with Pipa. 'Definitely.'

Ethan stroked Dusty's neck. 'It makes Kelsey happy to see you happy.'

Carol removed her helmet and ran a hand through her damp hair. 'And I like seeing her happy.'

Ethan tilted his head a fraction. 'She's worried about you. So am I.'

If Carol dwelt on the real world, she'd lose the flutter in her stomach and the energy pumping through her veins, so she gave Ethan the same excuse as she'd given Kelsey.

'I'm taking some me time.'

He held her gaze, his eyes searching hers. 'You aren't preoccupied by trying to run into Paul? I get it if you are. Paul hurt you, and it's hard to let that go and move on. But I have to say, you're heading into stalker territory and it worries me.'

She lifted her chin, her stomach now churning. 'I'm kind of sick of everyone thinking I'm the obnoxious brat in all of this. Have I made a scene? Run my mouth about him? Done anything at all to make people think I'm making things hard for him? And what about me? Not one person has asked how I am. They only tell me I'm being selfish. They think I'm either avoiding him or chasing after him because I want him back. Well I don't, okay! And if I never have anything to do with him ever again, I'd be ecstatic.'

Shaking, she braced her hands on her thighs. This time the pain was thick and heavy with regret and shame. 'I'm sorry, I shouldn't have taken my frustration out on you.'

Ethan squatted and rested a hand over hers. 'Maybe not, but it sounds like you need to talk to someone. Holding onto resentment like that only eats away at you and makes you reckless. You know that.'

She closed her eyes against the tears. How could she forget one of the biggest lies Paul had ever told? A lie her friends believed but hardly ever mentioned.

Meeting Ethan's gaze again, she swallowed. 'So if the bakery gets broken into again, you'd all believe it was me acting out against Paul?'

His shoulders dropped. 'You were young and lost, you—'

'Didn't do it.' She stood straight and stared down at him. 'I didn't break in and carelessly leave an earring behind to incriminate myself. Paul did it and set me up.'

Ethan stood slowly, his face blank. 'That's a serious accusation, Carol.'

And her heart broke. 'Forget it.'

On shaking legs, she walked to the stables. If she could hold it together until she got home, she could turn off her phone for a couple of hours and hopefully fall into the oblivion of sleep. She'd let Snow on her bed again, and she'd gratefully accept his silent support while she fought her way through the nightmare Paul had created.

Ethan stood near the tack room door when she put her saddle away. She ignored him as she pulled her leather pants back on, buckled her boots and left the borrowed riding boots near Dusty's saddle. She'd have kept on ignoring him, but he fell into step beside her.

'Kelsey and Pipa are getting cuppas and biscuits ready.'

She shook her head. 'I need to get going.'

He put a hand on her arm. 'If what you're telling me is true, you need to say something.'

'If?' She gave a sad smile. 'And who would I tell? Who would believe me if you don't?'

'It's not that I don't believe you, but I need to know more.'

He had no reason to believe her, and she had no evidence to give, but God, it gutted her that she should have to prove herself to him.

'Forget it. Tell Kelsey thanks and I'll see her later.'

'You won't come in and say goodbye?'

Not without falling apart.

'No. I think I'm coming down with something. I'm going home to bed.'

He stood there with his hands in his pockets as she got on her bike and drove away.

At the end of the dirt road, she stopped. Turning right would take her back to town and her home, where the only warmth would be Snow's body pressed against hers. If she turned left, then took a right just up the road, she'd be at Blake's within minutes.

She shook her head and turned right. Sooner or later, he'd hear all the rumours and decide he'd be better off keeping his distance. Heading back so soon wasn't an option, but she'd spend whatever time she could with Blake, knowing the end would come, and would soak up the peace she felt whenever she visited the only place she'd ever been truly loved and welcomed.

Pulling up in her driveway, she tipped her face to the sky, where the sun dipped low on the horizon and sent long shadows across the yard. If the sky stayed clear, there'd be a frost in the morning. Imagining the crunch of frozen grass and the tracks she and Snow would leave behind on their run, Carol pushed her bike through the gate and into the backyard.

Snow jumped and yapped a bark, his tail swinging in a wide arc and tapping his ribs on either side. He ran to the gate of his cage as she walked towards him, crouched as she flipped the latch, then bulleted out when she swung the door open.

'You'll always be glad to see me, won't you.' She patted his head as he bounced beside her into the house.

She changed into old jeans, a thick jumper and a pair of hot-pink fluffy socks. She didn't bother chasing Snow when he grabbed one of her discarded socks and took off into the lounge room ahead of her. Instead, she walked to the kitchen and boiled the kettle, the mundane movements helping to settle her.

When she made her way to the lounge room, blowing the steam from her mug, she shook her head at Snow sprawled out on the couch.

'Shove over, buddy.'

When nothing but the tip of his tail moved, she put her mug on the coffee table.

'You wanna play?'

His tongue lolled from the side of his mouth when he smiled at her.

Carol lunged for him; he shot off the couch and, after doing a lap of the room, skidded and crashed near the front door. Carol laughed when he stood up and did a full body shake, but then she caught sight of the folded piece of paper that had been slipped under her door.

She knew immediately that it would be from Paul, another snapshot of her to let her know he was watching, waiting.

She knelt down and picked it up, and when Snow pushed his head under her arm, she hugged him close. Creased from Snow's foot, one corner of the paper had folded back on itself, so it showed only part of the picture—the sky and the edge of a brick building. The town hall, perhaps? Only she hadn't been there recently …

Her heart thumped when she unfolded the picture.

It showed not her face but Blake's. Not the town hall but Foodworks.

Shaking, she dropped the picture and hugged Snow closer.

'He saw it. Paul saw Blake follow me out of Foodworks.' She closed her eyes. 'And now he's warning me to stay away.'

CHAPTER 7

Blake ignored the passing of the morning sun across the dappled sky, but when his stomach grumbled, he downed his tools and sat on the bucket to eat his lunch in a patch of sunshine.

The ham and salad sandwich he'd made for Carol sat in the bar fridge alongside the slice he'd bought—the same slice she'd ordered when he'd run into her at the bakery the other day, just before she'd given him her promised smile and greeting. He wished she'd show her sass and quick wit more often, along with that dimple-popping smile. And if she could just forget about comparing him to Paul and relax, her dark humour would shine through too. He looked forward to that happening as they became friends. Looked forward to being seen as himself, not cast in the shadow of another man. One who'd obviously hurt her deeply.

He and Carol had a lot in common, though she'd roll her eyes if he told her that. While she saw the differences between them, he saw the common ground they could build on—like their creative souls. She drew and painted and sang. He twisted metal, reshaped junk and gave it purpose.

They both loved the town and the countryside, and they both rode horses—something he hoped they could do together now, thanks to Kelsey's suggestion. Glancing over to where Carol's filly stood next to his gelding at the gateway, he smiled. He hadn't hesitated to take the horse for a few days, especially when Kelsey told him that Carol would be more than happy to ride the property with him. If they did, if she showed him where she used to ride and dream of her future, maybe she'd open up to him again. After all, she'd shared a few stories of her life when she'd seen the house.

After finishing his sandwich and starting on his slice, he snapped a photo of an ant carrying a butterfly wing and sent it to Drew. Their friendship had taken a while to form as well. He and Drew had been the new kids in school, and though they'd both come from broken families, they hadn't clicked—at least not until the class bully had tried to start a fight with Blake. Drew had stepped in, using his size to make the bully back off. Later, when he and Blake had been laughing off their nerves, Drew had confessed he'd been scared. But his grandfather had taught him their native *haka*, and though he hadn't stomped or shouted at the bully, he'd been doing it in his head. They'd been friends ever since. Something Blake had been grateful for over the years. Drew had realised just how unhappy Blake had become, and he'd been the one to point out to Blake that marrying Tish when he wasn't in love with her wasn't fair to either of them. Blake had known it, of course, deep down, but Drew pointing it out had given Blake the confidence to take action.

After spending time with Carol yesterday and seeing what a bad break-up could do to a person, he'd called Tish last night, just to make sure he hadn't made her wary of starting another relationship. In her easy way, she'd laughed at him, and assured him that she and her new boyfriend didn't have any ghosts to evict. His relief had outweighed his embarrassment at her teasing, and now, as he took a deep breath of cool, clean country air, he closed another door to his past.

With his lunchbreak and daily contemplation time over, Blake got back to work. Shaping Rita's and her husband's initials in barbed wire and weaving them through the horseshoe heart had been a pain but worth the effort. Sheep made from bike chain links stood in a flock to one side and a miniature unfinished gate on the other.

Now he set about bending and twisting wire to shape a tree that would wind through the whole sign, the roots flowing into a river here, the branches reaching up to catch the wind there, then lifting into clouds on the other side. Energy cascaded from one element to the next, pulling it all together and capturing the love Rita still held for her late husband.

When he twisted the last strand into shape, manipulated it into place and clamped it for welding, sweat ran down his forehead and into his eyes. Grabbing the cleanest rag that he could find, he wiped his face and walked out into the light drizzle. Cocking his head, he heard the rumble of Carol's motorbike echoing in the gully.

Perfect timing, he grinned. Rubbing most of the grease from his hands, he strode back into the shed to turn off the power and stow away his tools. Detouring to the bar fridge, he grabbed the sandwich and slice. If she'd already had lunch, she could eat while he saddled the horses.

Outside, he frowned as she walked towards him, dragging her feet with her head bowed, her shoulders hunched and her hands in her pockets. What had happened to put that sad defeat on her face? What weighed her down so much that she couldn't lift her gaze to his? About to call out, he stopped when Dusty let out a quick grunting neigh.

Carol's head whipped up, her wide-eyed shock almost comical until she turned to him. 'You? You're the one who took her?'

'Kelsey didn't tell you?' he said as he closed the gap between them.

Her eyes narrowed as she glared at him. 'Tell me what, exactly? And whose idea was this? Yours or hers? Because if this is some sort of coercion—'

'Kelsey wanted her to experience a short trip and stay to boost her confidence, that's all. And she thought you might like to go for a ride out here, for old time's sake. Besides, making you food is about the extent of any coercion you'll get from me.' He held out the sandwich and slice.

She stared at him, then at the food. 'You made me lunch?'

He lifted the sandwich. 'I made this, bought the slice.'

'And you have Dusty here as a favour to Kelsey?'

'Yes. I really thought you would have known about it. It's fine if you don't want to go for a ride.'

She took the sandwich and unwrapped it. 'I'm sorry I jumped to the wrong conclusion. Though I think I need to have words with Kelsey.'

'Don't be too hard on her.' He shrugged at her raised eyebrow. 'She wants you to be happy.'

'I threw her a party when she came home, you know. I didn't ask her, but I wanted her to see that people supported her.' She glanced past him to the horses. 'She brought Dusty here for me to ride'—her gaze came back to him—'and you made me a sandwich.'

Something he vowed he'd do more often now that he knew it touched her so deeply.

As she ate, they wandered over to the fence to pat the horses. Blake smiled as Carol gave each of them a piece of crust from her sandwich, and when he handed her the slice, he had to push Felix's inquisitive muzzle out of the way.

'Would you like to go for a ride with me?' he asked. 'Tell me more about your life here?'

Tipping her face to the fleeting sunshine, Carol closed her eyes; when she opened them again, her frown had disappeared. 'I do.'

'Okay, then. Kelsey left some clothes in a bag on the couch. You can get changed while I saddle up.'

She put her hand on his arm as he turned away. 'Thank you. For thinking of me. For taking Dusty. I just …' She gave a helpless shrug. 'I'm not used to it.'

Once they'd set out, Blake thought about those five words as he let Felix pick the path through the bracken fern. He had questions but kept them to himself, because Carol's silence held a weight that only the kookaburras and magpies dared interrupt.

When the track widened, he nudged Felix forward until he rode beside Carol. 'I haven't explored this area.'

She glanced at him, her cheeks and nose nearly as pink as the hair poking out from under her helmet. 'I used to know every ditch, every rabbit hole, every kangaroo track. It's only been four years since I was last out here, but everything has changed so much that I feel like I'm a stranger here. Does that make sense?'

'It does,' he said, leaning forward to scratch Felix's neck, then Dusty's. 'Maybe talking about what you used to do out here, your favourite memories, that sort of thing, will help you reconnect.'

She lifted her face to the sun. 'I could always tell the season by the smell. Days, months, years meant nothing to me as a kid. Hot weather meant swimming and snakes. When it was cold, we wore gumboots and collected firewood. Spring and autumn brought lambs and calves, and we worked in the garden. But no matter what time of year it was, or what the weather was like,

101

we were always riding. We'd explore every kangaroo track, every river crossing, every cave. Scared ourselves witless once when we found a tin shed in the bush and thought drug dealers would know we'd poked around.'

'You found drugs?'

She grinned and her dimple flashed. 'No. But we were thirteen and naive as hell. Kelsey let it slip to Ethan that we'd found the shed, so he and Mark had a look.'

Intrigued by the merriment in her eyes and wanting to keep it there, he tipped his head. 'And then what happened?'

She chuckled. 'Turned out we'd crossed a downed fence onto someone's property, and it was just a shed.' Her leg bumped against his as she turned Dusty, leaving the track to cut through the overgrown fog grass.

The confusion and heartbreak she'd started the ride with lifted from her shoulders with every step the horses took. Where before she'd sat hunched, her movements stiff, she now sat tall in the saddle, her hips moving fluidly with Dusty's gait. And she was talking without reservation, without weighing each word.

She met his gaze, jutted her chin out to his right. 'You've got about three kilometres of river winding through these outer paddocks.'

He'd been so focused on her that he had to blink and force his head to move. Until that moment, he'd missed the fact they'd stopped at the river, *his* river, or at least the part of it that flowed through his land. It twisted through the trees from the west and dog-legged in front of them, the far bank a sheer wall of rock that rose up a hundred feet or more.

Carol pointed to the first sharp bend of the dogleg where the water rushed and gurgled around a logjam. 'I fell in there once. Kelsey and I were exploring and found a tree that had fallen across the river. We left the horses and argued about who would cross first, but while she was coming up with all these good reasons that it should be her, I just ran and jumped on.' Her grin shot to her eyes. 'She was pretty upset with me, but when I fell in, she was happy it was me and not her.'

The image of Carol as a girl flailing against the sucking water jolted him. 'Were you hurt?'

'No. Too young and full of myself to be anything other than annoyed. And it was summer, so there wasn't as much water flowing as there is now.'

She turned Dusty away from the river, as though it meant nothing that she could have drowned or been seriously hurt. As though she wouldn't have left a gap in so many people's lives. Chilled by the thought, he let Felix follow her through the swaying grass.

'That's the billabong paddock,' she said, pointing to a fenced riot of bush-land that dipped down a hill. 'And this track is where Kelsey and I set up a cross-country course once. Took us days to drag branches and logs from the billabong paddock, but it was worth it. Mr Davidson, Kelsey's dad, caught us hitching them up higher and tying some to the trees with binder twine. He nearly had a heart attack. Between him and Ethan watching us like hawks, we didn't get to have much fun for a month after that.' She fiddled with a lock of Dusty's mane. 'Six months later Mr Davidson died and everything fell apart.'

'Kelsey said she left town after she lost her dad.'

'Yeah. His death hit her hard. Hit us all hard.'

'And your parents?' He'd been wondering why Carol had spent so much time with her grandparents.

She shrugged but her face blanked. 'They were too busy landing gigs on cruise ships to worry about me.'

'Kelsey said you used to sing with them,' he said softly, hoping she'd open up to him.

'I did, and they didn't mind taking me with them when they performed. But I loved it out here. I loved Gran and Pop and my friends. So I told them, the week everything went to shit, that I wanted to stay and finish high school with my friends. I begged them to stay, too, to be there for me.'

She lifted her gaze to where the sun shone through the patch of blue in the low, rolling clouds. 'They left the next day and haven't been back since. Not for Gran's funeral or Pop's. Not for Christmas or birthdays.'

She shook her head. 'They sent money when I needed it, and they call every few months, but I hate that they left me like that. I hate that I had to go through the worst parts of my life without them.'

103

Dusty snorted and started jogging sideways, her ears flicking back and forth as she searched for danger. Sighing, Carol leaned forward and stroked the filly's neck. 'Sorry, girl. It's okay. It'll be okay.'

Desperate to wipe the misery from her eyes, Blake reached over and touched her shoulder. 'I'm not one to give advice, because I'm only just sorting out my relationship with my dad, but I'll say this. Your parents neglected you, and that's on them. You've done nothing wrong, and you don't deserve to be treated the way they've treated you.

'And, yeah, it *will* be okay. You're a strong, independent woman with a heart and mind many would envy.'

She laughed at that, but without joy. 'You don't even know me.'

He shook his head. 'Not true. I know that you helped me, a stranger who ask for a hand. You look after your former English teacher when she gets drunk. You're there for your friends, and you have the patience and heart to take on a horse who still thinks most humans are monsters. And,' he pointed at her as she rolled her eyes, 'I know I'm looking forward to riding out here with you again, maybe when you're not helping me renovate my house'—he rushed to get his point across before she could object—'because I know you cherish the history of this place and can help me turn it into a home.'

After a moment of silence, she scratched her chin. 'You want me to help you paint and restore the house?'

'I do,' he said.

She played with Dusty's mane. 'I was going to tell you today that I wouldn't be coming out anymore. There are so many reasons ...' She met his gaze. 'I need to think about it.'

He hoped that one day she'd feel comfortable enough around him not to hesitate to visit, so she could be where her heart needed to be, but for now, he'd take it as a good sign that she'd consider not only continuing to see him but to help him, so he smiled.

'Of course,' he said, 'take as much time as you need.'

Because no matter how long it took, he'd wait for her.

#

Carol rode in silence until they reached the house paddock. She slipped off Dusty's back and gave her neck a good scratch. She opened the gate, holding it wide for both horses to walk through while questions circled her head.

Why did Blake want her help? Could she ignore Paul's warning and keep spending time here with Blake? Did she want to? That one was both easy and hard to answer. Her kneejerk reaction was to say no, but under that, her heart whispered yes. How could she not want to be with someone who made her sandwiches and encouraged her to talk about her life before …

Before she'd been abandoned by uncaring parents. Before she'd had to mourn the two people who'd loved her. Before Paul had broken her.

Did she feel a connection with Blake because he'd experienced a similar loss with his father? She'd heard the rumours, of course, about Blake and Alex's dad. Alex had always scowled and changed the subject whenever people asked about his father, and though Carol had visited Annie's little stone house a few times over the years, she'd never dared ask about her ex-husband. But Blake had opened the door to find out more when he'd mentioned his dad.

She glanced at him now as he unsaddled Felix, his movements quick and steady. 'Can I ask you about your dad?'

He glanced at her as he lifted the stock saddle from Felix's back and slung it on the fence rail. 'What do you want to know?'

Though he appeared relaxed, she trod carefully. 'I don't trust rumours. And Alex never talked about your dad, but he mentioned once that you went and lived with him when you were ten.'

Blake bowed his head and took a deep breath. 'He had an accident. Got hit in the head and ended up with an acquired brain injury.'

After slipping off Dusty's saddle and bridle, Carol rested her head against the filly's. Like hers, Blake's wound still healed. 'I'm sorry. It's okay if you'd rather not talk about it.'

He opened the gate into the yard and waited for her to walk through, then lifting his saddle from the fence, he led Carol to the old single cow shed, where her grandmother used to milk her house cow by hand. Blake had turned it into a tack room of sorts.

He slid his saddle onto a makeshift rack, then turned and took hers. 'I was seven when it happened and couldn't understand why he didn't want me around anymore. Alex was four but, even then, was hell-bent on making life as difficult as possible. The doctors said Dad's anger and hostility towards us might get better over time, or it might not.'

Standing in the small space, where the scent of damp earth mixed with the smell of leather, Carol's heart ached for the little boy he'd been.

'Did he get better?'

'To an extent, but only after years of therapy and hard work. Mum tried to help him in the beginning, but she had to protect us, too. He never hit us but came close a few times. And the fights they'd have …'

He closed his eyes, and Carol could see his pain. She'd opened this wound in him, so she'd soothe it as best she could. Stepping closer, she wound her arms around his waist, and pressed her forehead to his chest. Could you miss something you'd never had? Had never wanted until it was within your grasp and made your soul sigh? If she were a cat she'd curl up under his chin and purr. As a woman, she wanted to burrow in and savour the feeling of having her arms around him. Even as it scared her to feel so much from such a simple action, she couldn't step away.

As though he felt it too, he sighed, and his arms came around her. 'A couple of weeks before they split, they had a huge argument. We lived in a part of town where screaming matches were the norm and dogs barked at all hours. I hated it there, but not as much as I hated having to escape to the neighbours with Alex when things got bad. We were there that day, but I'd forgotten his blanket, so I was sneaking back into the house when I heard Mum ask Dad why he stayed if he was so unhappy. When he answered, it was with so much hate in his voice. He said that he regretted getting Mum pregnant with me in the first place, that he'd had to stay right from the start because of me. And I know it was said in the heat of it all, and that he'd only wanted to hurt her, but I made a vow that day never to make him regret anything about me ever again.'

Carol held her breath to keep the tears at bay. The last thing Blake needed was to comfort her when the pain of that memory vibrated through him. She could say she knew how he felt, but it would be a lie. She might question if her parents had ever truly loved her, but she'd never been faced with outright hate and regret at her existence.

106

Blake rubbed a hand up and down her back. 'Alex was such a handful by then that Mum spent most of her time at the school trying to convince them to give him another chance, so when Dad said he was leaving, I knew I had to go with him. I could look after him and give Mum one less person to worry about, so I said I was going too.'

Carol lifted her head so her chin rested on his chest. 'You know that he didn't really hate you. Some part of him, however deeply buried, loved you. And your mother must have known it, too.'

One side of his mouth tipped up. 'And how do you come by that conclusion?'

She loosened her grip and stepped back. 'Because he took you with him, and she let him.'

Blake shook his head. 'It's not that simple.'

'It is. Why would he have taken you with him if he hated you, or if you were a burden? And why would Annie let you go if she thought he'd harm you?'

He opened his mouth, then closed it. 'I don't know what to do with that.'

'Let it sink in,' she said. 'In the meantime, I should get going. I only meant to drop in and look at the paint you'd bought.' She shivered and hugged herself. 'And about the renovations, I don't know how much help I can give you at the moment.'

The printed picture of him shoved under her door had kept her awake until sunrise. Only then, with Snow snoring beside her and the new day making the dust motes dance near her window, had she slept. She'd woken four hours later to Snow's cold nose pressed to her ear. It had been a battle to make it to Blake's before noon, and then there'd been Dusty and the food, and she hadn't been able to walk away.

Blake shifted and slid his hands in his pockets. 'Why is that?'

As she tried to find the right words, she realised that Paul's warning had rattled her, and she was doing exactly what he wanted—withdrawing. But why the hell should she? She wasn't Paul's to dictate. He no longer said who she could associate with. He'd retaliate, of course, but whatever he did to her, it wouldn't change the way Blake made her feel or how her heart calmed when she was out here.

107

Looking for strength, she stepped from the tack room into the drizzle that greyed everything, and it fell like a soft hand upon her face. Her heart ached for her grandmother's gentle touch; no one else had ever made her feel so loved and valued with just a touch.

Running numb fingers through her hair, she straightened her shoulders, determined to take her life back. 'There's a lot I'm not ready to get into, so don't ask, but you need to understand that when Paul and I were together, he would go weeks without acknowledging me if I said or did the wrong thing. He didn't yell or hit me, he'd just pretend I didn't exist until he wanted me again.'

When he opened his mouth, his eyes hard, she held up a hand.

'You don't need to tell me you aren't him. I know you aren't, but I still can't help comparing the two of you.' She lifted her chin, kept her gaze on his. 'Paul and I were never friends. He paid attention to me when I was feeling raw after Kelsey and my parents left. He let me stay with him when I had nowhere else to go. Looking back, I can see that he manipulated me and made me dependent on him. When he suggested we be more than friends, it seemed the right thing to do.'

'He groomed you.'

It punched the breath out of her, that Blake believed her, that he so easily connected the dots it had taken her three years to see.

'Yes. And although I'm friendly to people, because in my job I have to be, I don't make friends easily.'

'I can understand that.'

'Maybe you can, but I'm telling you this because I'm floundering right now. One minute, things are great. I'm out here, riding, remembering the happy days, then the next I'm battling old demons. In between, I'm trying to patch up my life.'

'From what I can see, you have people around you who are trying to help, but I'm guessing they don't know half of what you've told me.'

She rubbed at the droplets running down her cheeks. 'They wouldn't believe me if I told them.'

'Have you tried?'

'Yes. But unlike you, Paul uses his charm for evil not good. He skews the truth and makes up outrageous lies to make himself look virtuous, while ruining any respect people have for me. He's convinced everyone that I'm a spoilt brat, so anything I do or say to anyone is coloured by that.'

'It's not for me.'

She shook her head. 'See, that's why you confuse me. You give me room and it makes me want to be closer, you listen and believe and it makes me want to tell you more. I came here to say that I won't visit anymore, yet I know I'll be back. I'm going to help you bring this place back to life and make it yours.' She sucked in a breath. 'You make me want. Just want.'

He moved towards her, and when he stood toe to toe with her, she held her breath, steadying herself for a kiss she wasn't ready for. Instead, he trailed a fingertip from her temple to her chin.

'You've lost so much in your life. Not only people, but trust, choices and I'd say a part of yourself.'

'Yes.'

'Have you found it again? That part he stole from you?'

She swallowed. 'I thought I had.'

He rested his hands on her shoulders, then slipped them around her back and—as she'd done for him—held her while the inferno blazed through her soul.

Denying that she wanted what he offered—sanctuary and friendship— would be a reckless lie; it would hurt them both. So she wound her arms around his waist, let herself lean into him and took his comfort.

CHAPTER 8

Carol had the wood fire roaring, her thick bed socks warming her toes and her dog snoring with his head on her lap. She ached all over, her muscles unaccustomed to time in the saddle, but she didn't mind, because it meant that after a few more rides, she'd only have the muscles and not the aches.

With nothing on TV, she balanced her sketchbook on Snow's head, and though horses weren't her forte, she sketched Felix with his soft eyes and the small snip on his nose, and Dusty, with her distinctive *Cat in The Hat* blaze. Annoyed that none of the eyes sat right, Carol flipped the page and did a few studies.

When the last one turned out human, she stared hard at the challenging glint gazing back at her. After adding the other eye, then the face and the tiny scar on his chin that she hadn't had the courage to ask about, she took her time detailing everything that made Blake's face nothing like Paul's; especially the curve of the mouth, with the hint of a smile that Blake's carried. He used that mouth, that smile, to put people at ease, and whenever he spoke, his words did the same. His eyes shone encouragement and praise. They mesmerised her, with their shape, their shade of deep blue-grey, and the way they went from amused to concerned in a blink.

And he did worry about her, though she wished he wouldn't. But when he looked at her with those eyes and talked to her with that mouth, she wanted to touch his face, just to see if it was as warm and real as he projected. She wanted to stay and talk to him about his life before they met and what he wanted from life now. She wanted to be the one to always put that laughing spark in his eyes.

She thought about how it had felt to have him hold her today. Why had slipping her arms around his waist felt so natural and right? *Was* it that he looked like Paul that made her react to him? Should she be ashamed that she had reacted to him? Unlike with Paul, though, her body had warmed from the core, relaxed, then had hummed with an energy she couldn't name. But she'd hid it all, because giving anyone that kind of power over her, when she'd only just scratched back some independence for herself, would mean blurring her identity again..

Blake had been right; Paul had stolen part of her, even before she'd found him in bed with someone else. Initially, her parents had put the crack in her self-worth when they'd walked away, but Paul had ripped it from her body and the echoes still vibrated through her.

She couldn't expect Blake to close the gaping hole within her—it was her responsibility to rebuild—but what she could thank him for, if she ever worked up the courage to tell him everything, was that he'd changed the tenor of that echo. He'd given it a voice that didn't tear her to shreds. He'd offered her comfort with no strings attached, understanding without reservation, and friendship without the expectation of sex.

Her subconscious spilled onto her sketch pad and filled the page with Blake. In one image, he sat in his seat at Crazy Hat Night wearing his dark suit and tie. In another, he was bent over his work, his hair dishevelled and his jeans ripped. She'd drawn him, too, as he'd stood at the gate earlier, with hands in his pockets and his gaze direct as she'd kick-started her bike to leave. Another three were projections of a future her heart shied away from—a future where they sat together, laughing, then embracing, then—

She slapped the sketchbook closed and sat staring at the flames leaping behind the glass door of the wood heater. Imagination was all well and good, and she'd use hers to scratch the itch that twitched between her thighs, but in reality? No, she wouldn't go there.

Huffing, Snow shook his head and dislodged the sketchbook, then flicked an ear towards the door as headlights flashed through the windows.

Carol shivered, put her pad and pencil aside and stood. Snow growled, and Carol glanced at her phone. Who would be pulling into her driveway at eight o'clock on a Sunday night, especially with the wind blowing a gale and hail threatening?

Only one person came to mind.

She wanted to run to her room and hide under the doona with Snow, like a child in a horror movie, but her feet refused to move. Her heart galloped, sending blood rushing to her ears and causing her pulse to thud at her throat. Could she lock the door to keep him out? Could she fight her way out of this debilitating spell and tell him to leave her alone?

Before she could force her feet to move, the door opened and Paul stepped inside. Warmth fled the room as he stood staring at her.

With a huge sigh, he shook his head. 'You're determined to make this difficult, aren't you?'

She stepped backwards, his clenched jaw twisting her stomach. 'Make what difficult?'

Paul lifted a clenched hand and pointed at her. 'I came back to town, ready to forgive you and take you back, yet you slap me down at every turn. I've given you time to see how it is. I'm the best thing you're ever going to have, and I'm done waiting. I'm done watching you slobber over the artist. He's never going to be anything to you but a fantasy.'

She stared at him, her chest aching and her heart thumping as she screamed in her head, words overlapping. She shouted four above the rest—*Get the hell out!*—only she couldn't force them past the burning breath rasping in her throat.

Paul left the door wide open as he stalked over to her. 'Nothing? You have nothing to say to me? No apology? No thank you?' He sneered down at her. 'You're pathetic, Carol. Worthless, and everyone knows it. Even your so-called *friends* talk behind your back, and all of them say you'll never be worth anything without me.'

Each word tore her down and smashed what little confidence she had into sharp shards that sliced her heart. He was right. She *was* pathetic and worthless, but she'd rather be those things on her own than be the empty shell she'd be if she were with him.

Paul grabbed her by the shoulder. 'Stop the charade. We both know how this ends. Accept it, and I won't take things any further.'

112

Take things further, how? Afraid to hear the answer to that, she swallowed.

'Accept what?'

He cupped his hands to her face, pressed cold thumbs to her cheek. 'That you're destined to be with me.'

Frozen to the spot, she stared up at him. 'Why do you want me to accept that?'

His smile was a flash of teeth as he slid one hand to her neck and pressed his cheek to hers. 'Because I'm sick of little girls thinking they can go up against me and win. Having you by my side will show everyone who I am and what I can do.'

A pulse beat at the base of her skull as she considered her options. Calling for help would only make things worse; he'd trapped her in a web that she'd helped weave by staying silent. Now that she wanted to break away from him, she was stuck in the false reality she'd let everyone believe was true.

Then it hit her. 'There are other girls?'

His hand on her throat tightened a fraction. 'You weren't the first.' He pressed his thumb over her jerking pulse. 'And you won't be the last, but you'll always be mine. Always.'

Carol pulled away only to cry out when his hand clamped on the back of her neck.

Snow growled.

'Tell your dog to back off,' Paul snarled, 'or I'll make sure it does.'

Carol had to swallow the lump in her throat. 'Go to bed, Snow.'

But the dog whined and growled again.

'If you can't control your dog, you shouldn't have it.'

'He's protecting me.'

Paul raised a sardonic eyebrow. 'From what? The pub is full of people who know I'm here because, despite everything, I'm worried about you. What does your mutt need to protect you from?' He eyed the dog over her shoulder, baring his teeth.

In answer, Snow barked, ran towards them and away again. Shoving Carol away, Paul lunged for Snow, who tucked his tail and ran through the open door and into the night. Not caring about the consequences, Carol dodged Paul and raced after Snow.

She sprinted under the orange glow of the streetlights, with her socks now soaking and her breath burning her lungs, and screamed as a ute skidded to a stop only metres from her, barely avoiding hitting Snow as he ran down middle of the road.

'Snow!'

Snow stopped and stood shivering, his feet planted as the driver stepped from the ute.

Carol ran to Snow and, dropping to her knees beside him, threw her arms around his neck. It took a moment for her to realise the shiver rippling through him was a growl.

Rubbing her cheek to his, she stroked a hand over him. 'It's okay, boy. We're okay.'

The ute's headlights winked as the driver walked around the vehicle. 'I don't think I hit him.'

Carol squeezed her eyes closed at Blake's voice. Why did it have to be him finding her like this?

Fighting to pull herself together, she swiped a hand across her cheeks and hoped he'd blame their wetness on the rain. When she stood, it was only the hand she kept on Snow's collar that shook.

'What are you doing, driving around town on a night like this?'

His gaze swept over her, and it was as if he could see everything she was trying to hide. 'Taking the back way home from having dinner at Mum's.'

With her heartbeat slowing, she scratched the side of her nose. 'Wouldn't the back way be the Old School Road?'

He smiled. 'I'm not that adventurous.'

In this weather, she didn't blame him. 'Fair point. Well, you'll want to be getting home so you can get warm and dry.'

He nodded at her as he held out a hand for Snow to sniff. 'Not until I know you're home safe, so jump in.'

She shivered; the sensation started in her shoulders and travelled down her back to her knees, and it had nothing to do with the icy wet shirt sticking to her skin. As he did every time he was near, Blake calmed the storm crashing inside her. Right now, she needed that energy to hold her up until she could crumble in private, but she might not make it home before breaking down and she didn't want Blake as a witness.

'Snow's wet. And so am I.'

Blake opened the back door of his ute for Snow to jump in. 'I don't care. And I'm not leaving you both to freeze.' He held out a work-roughened hand and gently wrapped it around hers. 'Which you already are.'

She stared, transfixed, at a fresh scratch across his knuckle. Could his hands—hands that manipulated metal—give pleasure instead of pain? Paul's had often purpled her skin. He'd never hit her, but he'd been rough and selfish, and had always left her cold and crying while her body still craved release.

Lifting her gaze from their joined hands to Blake's face, she slowly shook her head. Blake would never get off on hurting her, physically or mentally. If she told him *no*, he'd respect her boundaries.

Blake sighed, his eyes darkening. 'You're thinking about him.'

'Only because I'm thinking of you and how you're nothing like him.'

He rested his forehead on hers. 'Okay.'

After a moment, he pulled back, his lips quirked. 'You do realise we're standing in the middle of the street in the rain, don't you?'

No, she'd barely registered the fact. All she knew was that she stood in a bubble of comfort where nothing mattered but his warmth on her skin, his words in her ears and his scent in her lungs. If she could stay here, right here, with no past or future, no pressures or expectations, she would. Then she wouldn't have to go back to a cold house and search under the bed, in the wardrobe and in every dark corner for the monster who wouldn't leave her alone. She wouldn't have to sit up all night, too terrified to close her eyes in case he still hid somewhere.

Or feel petrified that he was right about her.

Blake pressed his lips to her forehead. 'I'm losing you to him again.'

Was it fair to Blake, to have these moments with him, if she couldn't stop comparing them?

Too tired to think, she stepped back from him and put a hand on Snow's head. 'It'd be better if you just went home.'

Blake opened his mouth, but before he could speak, a set of headlights swung around the corner. The approaching car rolled to a stop beside her and Paul wound down the window a few inches.

'I closed your front door for you,' he said, then glanced at Blake. 'She'd forget her head if it wasn't screwed on.'

Blake slid his hands into his pockets. 'That hasn't been my experience.'

Gripping Snow's collar, Carol stared at Paul's thumb as it tapped on the steering wheel. The same thumb he'd pressed against her throat as he'd threatened her.

His sigh made her shudder.

'Don't let her fool you. She's a mess ninety-five percent of the time.' He gave her a look that spoke volumes. 'I hope you accept my offer soon. We both know it's in your best interest.'

When she didn't answer, he glanced at Blake. 'We should have a talk.'

Blake huffed out a breath. 'No, thanks.'

Paul clenched his jaw but still managed a smile. 'You'll find out the hard way then. I'm just trying to save you the trouble.'

After winding the window up, he drove away.

Too cold to shiver, Carol glanced at Blake. 'Thank you for stopping and making sure we were okay.'

Blake rocked back on his heels, his frown deepened by the darkness. 'You keep saying I'm not him, yet you still treat me like I am.'

Carol bowed her head. 'I just …'

'You should let me take you home before we all freeze out here.'

Snow stared up at her, his tongue hanging from the side of his mouth. Blake seemed to have the same effect on the dog as he had on her.

'Okay, thank you. I'd like that.' Maybe on the short trip she'd stop shaking enough to function.

With her throat still hurting, she spoke only to give directions until he pulled up in her driveway. Truthfully, everything ached, and once she got inside, she feared she'd collapse and not move again.

Sick of letting Paul shatter her, she stared through the windscreen. 'He'll be pissed at you for sticking up for me. And he'll blame you because I'm not falling at his feet this time.'

Blake lifted an eyebrow at that. 'You mean I'm not even partly responsible?'

She owed him the truth.

'You are, because without even trying you've shown me how one person should treat another. I could easily get used to being around you, being close to you, and that terrifies me.'

But not in the same way Paul's offer—if it could be called that—had. Instead, the thought of being close to Blake made her belly jump with anticipation.

Earlier, she'd wanted nothing more than for Paul to leave, but Blake?

'Do you want to come in, have a cuppa and dry off a bit before you go home, because I'm still shaking and would appreciate the company.'

It was definitely dangerous to want him for comfort as well as company, but she wouldn't take it back.

He studied her a moment. 'I'd love to.'

After letting Snow out, Blake crossed in front of the car and opened her door. She took his hand and had to push Snow out of the way to jump down. The dog pressed against her leg as they walked to the house.

When she pushed her front door open to let Blake in, he raised an eyebrow. 'You don't lock it?'

She didn't have the energy to explain, so she shrugged. 'I was in a hurry.'

Tugging her soaked socks from her feet, she dropped them by the front door, then headed to the hallway cupboard for towels. When she returned, she found that Blake had wandered over to the dining room wall where dozens of photos hung. Some she'd framed, most she'd stuck up with adhesive.

He took the towel when she handed it to him, though his attention was still on the pictures. 'Who's the photographer?'

Carol rubbed her towel over her hair. 'Lilli. Zoe's twin sister.'

At his raised eyebrows, she waved a hand in the air. 'Zoe's the blonde who worked the bar with me on Crazy Hat Night. Lilli was taking photos.'

He nodded his understanding, then went back to studying the pictures.

Carol forced herself to go to the kitchen to make the hot drinks she'd promised, but she stopped with a cup in each hand to study him. She'd nailed his profile—his nose, his lips, the slant of his cheek, the way his eyelashes

117

defined his eye—but if she had paper and pencil right now, she'd get a much better likeness of him down.

Not wanting him to catch her staring, she turned and concentrated on making their drinks and small talk.

'Zoe is the extrovert,' she said, 'and is always in front of the camera, while Lilli is introverted and would rather see the world through a lens.'

'She's good.'

'She is. How do you have your hot chocolate?'

He came to lean on the breakfast bar. 'There's only one way to have hot chocolate, isn't there?'

Trusting that he'd tell her if she was doing it wrong, she heaped spoonfuls of chocolate powder into each mug and added sugar.

Blake rested his elbows on the countertop. 'Do you think Lilli would be interested in taking photos of my place throughout the renovations? Maybe even some shots of my work? It'd be good to show examples to prospective customers.'

Carol poured boiling water into the mugs. 'I don't know. I can ask her.'

'Where's your phone?'

She frowned. 'Why?'

'So I can put my number in it'—he winked—'so you can give it to her if she's interested.'

How was it possible that he could make her laugh when her insides still shook?

'See now, *that's* smooth.' She unlocked her phone and slid it to him.

When he merely added himself as a contact then put her phone down, she raised her eyebrows. 'You're not going to ask for my number?'

'You'll give it to me when you're ready.' He took the mug she handed him, blowing across the top as he studied her. 'I'm not going to take anything unless you give it to me, Carol. And I'm not going to ask for anything if I don't think you're ready.'

She trusted he wouldn't do either of those things, because—apart from being nothing like Paul—he was a good guy. He was someone she could learn to trust, lean on and rely on.

But could she take what he offered? Could she risk losing herself again?

118

He'd been the only one to tempt her since Paul had come into her life, and that, more than anything, scared her. Because where Paul had gutted her, broken her and destroyed her trust, Blake could do far worse damage.

If she let him, he could break her heart.

#

Taking his mug, Blake wandered through Carol's living space. Despite the crackling fire, the room held an odd chill. Not as odd or as worrying as the icy pallor that clung to Carol's skin. Or the way her dog followed her every move, as if he were determined to protect her.

Blake had kept his panic under wraps as he'd driven her home, though his relief at her invitation to stay had blown through him so hard he'd taken a moment to answer. Sticking to small talk, he'd faked interest in the pictures on the wall, sensing she needed time to recover from whatever had sent her and Snow running through the night. Now, he moved back to study the photos, giving her the space she hadn't asked for but needed.

Lilli had captured images of Carol laughing and posing with Kelsey, comparing muscles with Ethan, playing with Pipa and the dogs. There was even one of Carol with Mark, both of them staring off into the distance. In another, she ran, grim-faced with a thick hose in her hands. But the picture that gripped him the most was of her with her eyes closed, a fist to her heart and holding a microphone while she sang.

He'd had those hands on him today; she'd wound her arms tightly around him, giving comfort, and later, taking it from him. Instinct told him she'd skitter away if he tried to create that level of intimacy now. Perhaps, she'd let him take her hands to warm them, but anything more than that and he feared he'd lose her.

He wanted to sit her down and find out what had happened before he'd found her and Snow in the middle of the street. Had Paul attempted to gaslight her again?

Clenching his jaw, Blake breathed in through his nose. The bastard had actually thought that Blake would believe him and turn his back on Carol.

119

Blake had wanted to reach through the window and wipe the smug look off the guy's face. He wouldn't have punched him; only a man would deserve that, and Paul was nothing more than a slug.

But until Carol instigated that conversation, Blake would wait. For now, he'd stick to safe topics, like the photos on the wall.

'Even the pictures without you in them say something about you,' he said and leaned closer to one that looked out over the town in full spring bloom. 'Where was this one taken?'

She stood beside him, and Blake noted that her dog was right behind her.

'The lookout,' she told him. 'I bought that one off Lilli as soon as I saw it.' She angled her head to look at him. 'You haven't been to the lookout?'

He gave her a wry smile. 'I didn't know there was one.'

Her gaze dipped to his mouth before bouncing back to the photos, then she cleared her throat and tapped a picture. 'That's Bailey's Rocks. If you ever need a place to think, or need inspiration, go there.'

How often had she visited and lost herself in that place? Asking would most likely wipe away the colour she'd gained back, so he sipped his drink instead.

'What are you doing here?' He pointed to the one of her running with a hose in her hands.

'Fire running.'

Was that a smile she hid behind her cup? He waited a beat. 'Fire running?'

It *was* a smile.

'It's a competition, or a season of competitions, for rural fire brigade teams. We start training in February and state championships are in April.' She gave him a quick once-over. 'You look like you'd have a bit of speed and might.'

Puffing out his chest, he flexed an arm. 'I surfed nearly every day since I was ten until I moved here, if that counts.'

That made her eyebrows lift. 'You surf?'

He grinned at her. 'You don't?'

'No.' Smiling, she turned away from the photo wall and headed for the couch. The dog followed, sat in front of her when she sat on the couch, and whined a yawn.

Blake sat next to her, leaving space between them. 'He loves you.'

She set the dog's back leg kicking when she scratched behind his ears. 'Yeah, and he shows it by chewing my boots, stealing my clothes to make a nest, and taking a run down the road in the middle of the night.'

Snow's tail whipped from side to side as he grinned at her, but Carol only shook her head. 'You aren't cute, so quit it.'

Blake sat back but shot forward when something jabbed him in the hip. He pulled a sketchbook from between the cushions. 'Can I look?'

Carol sat frozen, her eyes widening before she grabbed it out of his hands and shoved it under the couch, nearly up-ending her mug and headbutting Snow. 'It's nothing.'

'Looks like an important nothing.' Did her reaction have something to do with Paul?

Carol pressed her lips together and stared at Snow as though daring him to tell her secrets.

The dog whined another yawn, and with a sigh, Carol patted her knee. 'Come here.'

Snow stood, gave a full body shake, then wiggled his way up onto her lap. Or at least he tried; he overflowed onto the couch and into Blake's lap.

Patting the dog's muscled rump, Blake grinned. 'How long since he's been able to curl up on your lap?'

She stroked the dog's head as he huffed a big sigh, closed his eyes and started snoring. 'A while.'

Something in her eyes and the way her hands moved over the dog worried Blake. What had happened earlier to make Snow take a mad sprint down the road? And how did Blake prove that she could trust him enough to confide in him? He didn't know, only that he couldn't push her.

'But you'll never stop letting him try, right?'

She smiled a little. 'Why would I?'

He wouldn't ask the hard questions, but he'd be open with his thoughts and feelings. 'I like when you smile. Your dimple pops and your eyes go bright.'

She raised her eyebrows at that. 'My eye tooth is crooked.' She tapped a fingernail against it.

He'd noticed, of course. 'It's cute.' Throwing his arm across the back of the couch, he flicked a finger at the ends of her short hair. 'Why pink?'

She flashed a fake smile. 'Why not?'

When he kept staring at her, she sighed. 'Fine. If people are going to talk about me, I want them to talk about *me*, and not in the context of my parents or Kelsey or Paul.'

'You know they still do that, don't you?'

She waved a hand in the air. 'Of course. Especially now that Paul is back and everyone thinks I'm losing my mind over him.'

He'd heard the stories, but the woman who'd comforted him today, who'd leaned on him in turn and now sat beside him, absently soothing a dog big enough to take down a kangaroo, wasn't the same girl whispered about in the bakery and the cereal aisle.

'Why don't you tell them the truth?'

She laughed, tapped a fist to his shoulder as though he'd told a brilliant joke. 'Yeah, good one. I should have thought of that.'

He frowned. 'I'm serious.'

Her jaw tightened. 'So am I. But like I said, I've tried. And if I even hint that he's not the person everyone thinks he is, I'm automatically labelled as bitter and ungrateful. Or I'm jealous and want him back.' Shrugging, she gave a twisted smile. 'Either way, he's told the believable history between us. Now all I want is for him to leave so I can get on with my life without his shadow hanging over me.'

Maybe, thought Blake, he should have that talk with Paul. Not that Paul would get to say much. Blake would make sure he got the first, middle and last words in—*leave Carol alone.* He knew Carol wouldn't appreciate him interfering, but he didn't know how much longer he could stand back while the bastard hammered at her and got the whole town backing him?

Blake shifted, earning himself a kick from the sleeping dog, but he managed to hook his leg up and face her. 'You have support, though, from your friends.'

And from him, even if she wasn't ready to accept it.

But her face fell, and tears gathered before she blinked them away.

'Paul has always been more convincing than me.' She rubbed the back of her hand across her cheeks. 'It doesn't matter. The fact is, he left once, and eventually, he will again. Once he does, this won't be such a big deal. Life will go back to normal.'

'And what is normal for Carol McGrath?'

Her quick frown scrunched her eyebrows. 'I work and jog with Snow.' She shrugged. 'Compared to your life, mine is pretty pathetic, really.'

He rested his fingers under her chin and ran the pad of his thumb across her cheekbone. 'You're a bartender. You listen to people's problems, congratulate them for their wins and commiserate their losses. You know people, you look out for them, and you help them.'

She shook her head minutely as she stared at him. 'I just do my job.'

With the dog between them, Blake leaned closer, his fingers gentle on her face. 'No. You look out for people because you know what it's like to not have that. But mostly, you look out for them because you, Carol, care about people, even when you think they don't care about you.'

'I'm a shitty friend, and an even shittier person.'

Pulling her forward an inch, he pressed his lips to her forehead. 'I doubt that, but the person who needs to believe it is you.' Letting her go, he rose from the couch. 'Thanks for the cuppa and the company.'

She stared up at him with a mixture of confusion and misery, and when he held his hand out to her, she frowned before taking it, then followed him silently to the door.

Blake lifted her hand and kissed her knuckles. 'Good night, Carol.'

'Good night,' she said after clearing her throat. 'Drive safe. The road can get slippery.'

'I will.' He touched her cheek because he needed to. 'If you feel up to it, come out early tomorrow. We can go for another ride, then maybe you can help me tackle the kitchen.'

He winked to let her know there was no pressure, then left out without waiting for an answer. He knew he was being persistent about the renovations, which wasn't his style, but he also knew that spending time at her grandparents' old property would help her heal, so he'd keep putting it out there.

He stood for a moment, trying to rein in his emotions with the closed door at his back and the streetlights turning the wet road orange before him.

He'd found Carol cold and alone, but he'd left her pink-cheeked and confused. He didn't like doing it, but if she spent the rest of the night thinking about him instead of Paul, then he couldn't be sorry. Paul would be though, if he kept putting that look on Carol's face.

As Blake walked to his ute, he spun the keys on his finger. Paul wasn't the only one with Carol's future in mind. Blake was involved now, and he wanted to make sure her smile flashed more than her frown.

In his ute, with the heat blasting, he took one last look at her house.

Her friends didn't understand the reality of Paul's influence, but Blake did, and he was going to make damn sure Paul stayed as far away from Carol as possible.

CHAPTER 9

After Blake left, Carol had crawled into bed and dreamed of them talking and laughing together, their limbs and mouths entwined. Waking with her body throbbing, she'd thought of him as she brought herself to peak, then had lain with her eyes squeezed closed against the shame of wanting more. More of *him*.

But of all the things she wasn't good at, sex was at the top of the list. Never—no matter what she'd let Paul do to her—had she orgasmed during intercourse. Paul had blamed her. He'd told her she was too emotionally cold, too deviant to satisfy. She'd learned to bring herself to orgasm, but the fear of being an inadequate partner had stopped her from wanting to try with anyone else.

And yet, as futile as it was to dream of Blake, as stupid as it was to entertain the idea of letting him kiss her, she'd drawn pages and pages of him doing just that. And more. Sick of her head and heart warring over him, and whether she should spend more time with him or cut ties, she pulled on her sneakers.

Patting her leg as she headed for the door, she sent Snow into a spin. 'Let's go for a run.'

He bounced beside her the first block, his tongue lolling. By the time he settled and trotted beside her, Carol had come up with a dozen reasons to stay away from Blake.

Paul's warning hit the top of the list. He'd find more ways to punish her for ignoring him, and he could potentially try to hurt Blake, too, but as Blake had already stood up to him twice, she doubted Paul would be game enough to try. And besides, despite her exhaustive list of reasons to stay away, she had one overwhelming reason to ignore her doubts.

She wanted to. She wanted to spend time with the guy who pulled her out of herself, who saw past the self-depreciation, the sarcasm and the fear, and gave her time to just be. How could she not want to experience more of that?

Turning for home, she sprinted for a block, delighting Snow, then slowed, her breath sawing in and out as she jogged the rest of the way.

She'd visit Blake. They'd go for a ride, then she'd help him with the kitchen, the painting and whatever else he had in mind. And for that small amount of time, she'd feel normal.

But was it right to use Blake like that?

As she showered, she refused to let the guilt creep in. It suited them both, didn't it? Besides, if he didn't want her around, he wouldn't have offered. Still, she had to work the unease out of her system, even as she arrived at Blake's.

He stepped out under the straightened roof of the verandah with a steaming mug in his hand and his long legs clad in worn and ripped jeans. A jumper, equally worn and ripped, was his only defence against the chill in the air.

As she climbed the steps to join him, he smiled.

'Good morning.'

She shivered, even though her leathers kept her warm. 'Morning. I see you fixed the verandah.'

He opened the door and waved her inside. 'It looked sad. I got the flue cleaned too, and the fire's lit, so at least it's warm in here now.'

Unzipping her jacket, she moved past him and wandered along the hallway to the open-plan living area. He'd cleaned up a bit since she'd last walked through. The naked walls and floors had been cleaned and were ready to be dressed with colour and texture. The windows were bare and waiting for curtains. It should have felt depressing but didn't.

'It doesn't feel sad,' she said.

Leaning against the wall, watching her, he sipped his coffee. 'Just empty.'

She shook her head. 'No, it's not. You've filled the space with your intentions.'

Looking around again, she frowned. 'I mean, it's your place, it just needs your'—she waved a hand in the air—'commitment.' But that wasn't right either. 'No, you *are* committed, anyone can see that. I think you just need the confidence to let it go in here.'

When he just stared at her, she shook her head. 'I'm sorry, I'm out of line.'

'Not at all. I'd say you're spot on.' He pushed away from the wall and held up his mug. 'Coffee?'

'Thanks.' She followed him to the kitchen where he'd sandwiched a toaster oven, a microwave and a kettle on the bench to the right of the old wood stove. Nostalgia hit her like a sucker punch, and she cleared her throat to hide it. 'Will you get a new oven?'

He pressed a sock-covered toe against the bottom grill. 'I like this style, though I think I'd rather the simplicity of using electricity.'

Carol hummed. 'You'd be better off with gas. At least then, when the power goes off, you can still use the burners.'

He glanced over his shoulder at her as the kettle boiled. 'That happens often?'

She had to smile at his sceptical frown. 'Yeah, it does. What will you do with the old one?'

He cocked his head as he looked at the oven; its colour had long since rusted away, and the firebox door was hanging on one hinge. 'I could fix it up and move it down to the shed.' His gaze came back to hers. 'Why?'

She lifted a shoulder. 'If you were going to throw it out, I'd take it.'

'But you rent, don't you?'

'I'd find somewhere to store it. I just don't want it thrown.'

Turning now, he grinned at her. 'You have an oven fetish?'

She huffed a laugh, her shoulders relaxing. 'I always teased Gran when she stood there. She looked like a witch, stirring whatever she had bubbling away in her huge pots as the fire crackled under the plate. My mother hated that oven. She burned everything she put in it.'

'And you?'

127

'Gran taught me how to cook in it. To go by smell rather than time.' She stepped closer and ran a finger along the top. 'It used to be blue. A bright bold blue. I've already mentioned the cupboard doors were different shades of purple, but the trim around them was an earthy green and the walls a light orange. The splashback was bright yellow.'

'She loved colour.'

'She *was* colour.' Carol sighed and turned in a slow circle. The memories didn't hurt as much with Blake listening. 'It killed me to cover it all. But I didn't want anyone else doing it, either. I owed it to Gran.'

Blake touched a finger to her cheek, the gesture a sweet comfort. 'I think whatever she taught you or gave you, she did it because she loved you, not for you to repay her.'

Most of the memories Blake teased out of her eased the ache of losing what she'd had, but some of them still twisted her heart, and those, she couldn't deal with yet. So re-boiling the kettle herself, she put half a teaspoon of coffee in the cup he'd set out for her and changed the subject.

'So while you're replacing the stove, I'd suggest doing the floor at the same time. That's if you're planning to replace the lino.'

He studied her carefully before glancing at the floor. 'Do you know what's under it?'

'Slate, I think. Pop used to complain that he'd laid a beautiful floor for Gran but she'd covered it all up. She'd just laugh and say she was protecting it for future generations.'

Not that Carol would be continuing the family line. Not while Paul still shadowed her.

Blake rested a hand on her shoulder. 'Hey, what's wrong?'

She stepped back, had to, or she'd break the promise she'd made and lean on him again.

'Tell me what you want me to do in here after our ride,' she said. 'Where do you want to start?'

Grimacing, he dropped his hand. 'I have to take a raincheck on our ride. I need to drive to Melbourne later to pick up Drew from the airport. He's bringing too much gear with him to get the train. Besides, he wants to call into some nurseries on the way back, so we'll stay the night in a hotel some-where and drive home tomorrow.'

Carol wrapped cold fingers around her mug and sipped her coffee. It scalded her tongue but stopped her from pouting. Of course he had other things to do. His life didn't revolve around her, but she had been excited about riding with him again.

'I guess you'll need to get as much work done as you can then.'

Leaning against the bench, with one ankle crossed over the other, he sipped his coffee. 'I will. But I'll admit, I'm going to miss seeing you pull up in the morning. It's getting harder and harder not to tell you how much it drives me crazy to watch you unzip that leather jacket.'

Carol chewed her lip. Unzipping her leather's drove him crazy? Why?

Shaking her head, she chose to ignore him. 'We can ride on Wednesday. And tomorrow, I can drop in, check on the horses and spend a few hours here before my lunchtime shift at the pub. If you're okay with that.'

When he smiled, his eyes softened. 'I think I'd like knowing that you're here, singing while you fill the space with your energy. It lingers, did you know?'

The hairs on her arms stood up at the intensity of his words, of his gaze, so she finger-gunned him. 'Like a bad smell?'

Blake sighed. 'Okay. Moving on. I'm thinking the cupboard doors need to be stripped. They'd have a few layers of paint on them.'

Carol hugged her mug to her chest. 'They do. It'll be hard work to lift it all.'

Since walking in his door, she'd ignored his concern, diminished his feel-ings and deliberately kept him at arms-length. How long would he put up with her insecurities and attempts at self-preservation before he gave her up as a bad joke? And why did she care that he would?

'I'm not afraid of work and neither are you. I've got a sanding disk for the grinder, but the heat gun might work better.' He moved as he spoke, tidying up the bench and kitchen table. 'I hope you'll give me a chance to help you one day.'

While her nerves jumped at the dark storm firing in his eyes, she sipped her coffee. 'If you take off the higher cupboard doors, I can start stripping. The doors,' she added when he shot her a glance.

'I guess the daily dose of watching you unzip your jacket will have to do.' He rubbed a hand over his mouth. 'But if you want to go further than that, I won't complain.'

Was he grinning behind that hand? He was flirting with her, she was sure of it. And it wasn't the harmless grin-and-wink some of the pub patrons gave her either. This heat between them meant something, and it froze every sardonic comeback she had.

'Just the doors,' she whispered.

With a wink, Blake sat his mug in the sink and walked through the side door. In his absence, Carol drew in a deep breath, regretting it when his scent filled her lungs and made her skin tingle.

He walked back in a few minutes later, a screwdriver in one hand and a cordless drill in the other. 'The heat gun is out on the verandah. It's out of the wind, but it's still cold, so you might need something thicker than what you're wearing. There's a clean jumper at the top of a pile of clothes in the laundry.'

'Thanks.'

He opened a cupboard door, gave it a few testing swings, then set to work on the first screw. Leaning hard into the screwdriver, he braced his hip against the bench, his jumper and shirt rising enough for a finger-width of smooth skin to show.

Forcing her gaze to her coffee, Carol finished what was left and put the cup next to his in the sink, then escaped to find the jumper and get her erratic hormones under control.

Lifting the jumper from the pile, she smiled at the decal across the front, then laughed when she pulled it over her head and it hung to her knees. Rolling the sleeves until her hands peeked out, she made her way back to the kitchen where Blake stood at the sink, holding his hand under running water.

She rushed over, her stomach turning at the sight of bloody water gurgling down the plug hole. 'What happened?'

He hissed between gritted teeth. 'Screwdriver slipped.'

'Let me see.' She took his hand and turned it under the tap. The puncture wound was in the fleshy part of his palm just under his pinkie finger.

'It's deep, but not too deep. I don't think it'll need stitches, but it'll ache for a while. Do you have painkillers?' In his silence, she glanced up to find him staring down at her. 'Blake?'

His gaze dipped to her mouth. 'I want to kiss you.'

Instinctively, she licked her lips. 'Why?'

He made an impatient sound. 'Because this is hurting like a bitch and kissing makes everything better.'

His words, the way he looked at her, set fire to her blood and made her insides shake with anticipation. Without even trying, Blake had proven Paul wrong—her body could react to other men. But she clamped down on her desire, because while her body might be ready and willing, her heart screamed that it wasn't.

'It makes everything better,' she said, 'when it's the hurt that's kissed away.'

'This'll take the pain away.' He took her by the shoulders and moved so their bodies bumped close.

She held her breath as he stared down at her, waited for the rush of heat, the crush of lips … and the hollowness that would surely follow.

When he did nothing, she frowned up at him. 'What's wrong?'

The muscle in his jaw jumped. 'I want to kiss you, but unless you want to kiss me, it doesn't happen.'

She hesitated, searching his face for the hint of a lie. 'I don't understand.'

'Do you think I'd kiss you if you didn't want me to?' His blue eyes stormed, crackling grey and flashing, as if with lightning. He stared at her, waiting.

'It happens.'

His shoulders sagged. 'How many times?'

She frowned, trying to remember if she'd ever been kissed, properly kissed, with full consent before. Did being made to beg count? She'd never wanted Paul to kiss her the way he always had, with anger and dominance. But that wasn't a confession to make now.

'Jex asked if he could kiss me once.'

'Jex?' Blake tilted his head, the storm easing. 'You and Jex?'

She managed a smile. 'Only once. We were talking about our poor choices in partners, and thought, hey, maybe we're the friends-to-lovers trope in real life. We aren't.'

His jaw tightened. 'But Paul never asked if he could kiss you?'

She eased back a step, in self-preservation. 'No. And I can't let you kiss me, but not because I'm comparing the two of you. I didn't want to be friends with you because you are so different to him. And now, we can't be more for the same reason.'

When he opened his mouth to speak, she held her hands up. 'You're making a life here, the sort of life my grandmother imagined this place supporting. It's what you deserve, and you deserve someone who can give you their all. I'm not that person. I don't have the kind of past that bodes well for a good future.'

#

Heartsore that Carol thought so little of herself and what she deserved, Blake pressed the oozing wound to a cleaner part of his jumper and addressed the falsehood that was easiest to conquer.

'Didn't? You *didn't* want to be friends. That's past tense.'

She pressed her lips together and held out her hand. 'You need to clean that and cover it or it'll get infected.'

He let her inspect the wound, her hands half the size of his, her fingers cool against his skin. Soothing. 'Is it really easier to deal with blood and gore than it is relationships?'

'Yes.' She reached for his other hand, held them together to compare them. She had no trouble touching him, being close to him when she called the shots. Only when he took control did she freeze up. Then, she seemed to wait for things to happen *to* her, as if she were a passenger in a speeding car rather than a fully involved partner.

What exactly had Paul done to her? Until he knew that, he couldn't fully combat the fear she carried.

'He was more than just an arsehole, wasn't he?'

She sighed. 'Much more. But I played my part, too.'

That infuriated him.

'So you're to blame as much as he is? He manipulated you when you were vulnerable, but it's your fault? How does that work?' He had to take a breath. 'Carol, he controlled your life then, and he's controlling it now. He's making you think you don't deserve happiness or a good future. You might not be worried about a physical blow, but bloody hell, you're ready for your heart to be torn apart.'

She braced her hands on the edge of the sink. 'I don't like that you see and say things other people don't.'

'I see them because I see you, and I say them because I care.' He leaned against the bench so he didn't pull her close again. 'He's the reason you think you're a shitty friend and a shitty person, isn't he? What happened?'

She lifted her gaze to his. 'Do you have a secret that shames you? One that grabs your throat every time you try to form the words to talk about it?'

Tish's face flashed in his mind. 'Yes.'

'What is it?' She nodded at his hesitation. 'It's hard spilling those secrets, isn't it?'

He bent and pulled his meagre first aid kit from the cupboard under the sink. 'It is. But I want to tell you.'

Crossing her arms, she jutted her chin at him. 'Because you want me to tell you mine?'

He gritted back his frustration. 'Because I want you in my life, so you need to know. Up until six weeks ago, I was engaged.'

Her mouth fell open, then snapped shut as she stared at him. When she said nothing, he ran his hand under the tap again.

'We'd been engaged for nearly two years, but we'd known each other since high school. Our dads were golfing buddies as well as business partners. Getting engaged seemed the logical thing to do.'

'Getting engaged is supposed to be logical?

He smiled at her over his shoulder. At least she'd snapped out of her shocked silence.

'Every other major decision I'd made in my life was based on logic. Moved with my father across two states so he'd have someone to look after him, finished school planning to follow in his career footsteps. It made sense to marry a woman with similar tastes and expectations, so we could raise a family and continue the cycle.'

Carol tilted her head, as if hoping his words would make more sense if she considered them at a different angle. 'I don't mean to be rude, but that sounds so cold. Did you love her? Did she love you?'

He'd asked himself the same questions until the words had no longer made sense. But with Carol, the truth came easily.

'In our way, yes, we loved each other. We had fun, laughed together, and we did have similar tastes in things, but neither of us were *in* love.' He frowned. 'Does that make sense?'

She rummaged around in the first aid kit and pulled out a crinkled tube of antiseptic cream. 'It does. So are you both okay now? You're friends?'

He smiled, then hissed when she rubbed the cream into the wound.

'Yeah. Though it was rocky for a while.'

With a wince, she dabbed the excess cream away. 'Sorry.'

'Not your fault.' Just like a lot of burdens she carried weren't her fault. 'Can I ask you one more personal thing?'

She held a square of gauze over the wound while she wrapped a small bandage around his hand. 'Okay.'

'When we met, you didn't want to be friends, but we are now, tentatively, right?'

She tucked in the end of the bandage, smoothed it down and let go of his hand. 'I guess.'

'Don't guess.'

Frowning, she crossed her arms over her chest. 'Okay. Yes, we're tentatively friends.'

'So things changed, right? People can change their minds about things.'

Wary, she tilted her head. 'People change their minds all the time.'

'Do you think there might come a time, then, when you'll want me to kiss you?'

Her eyebrow twitched. Did she already want him to kiss her? It gave him the confidence to continue.

'Because if you can honestly say that there's no chance anything will ever happen between us, then tell me now, and this is where it stops. But if you think you might change your mind, then I'll keep showing you I'm interested. And it'll be up to you.'

Sceptical, she eyed him. 'You'd do that? Leave things as they are and back off if I said that's what I wanted?'

'Yes. I'd rather spend time with you as a friend, a good friend, than have you walk away.' He waited a moment. 'You aren't telling me there's no hope.'

She stared up at him, her eyes flickering as she studied his face. 'I could lie, but I won't. But I honestly can't tell you the truth yet, because I don't know it.'

He touched her chin. 'That's okay. We've got time.'

'Can I ask you something?'

'Anything.'

She pulled at the front of the jumper he'd lent her, the bright yellow words *the only man for me is Mothman* shaped jaggedly on the black material.

'If I decide that I want you to kiss me,' she said, glancing up at him, 'am I going to have to compete with Mothman?'

Laughter burst out of him, and when she gave that half smile, he held an arm out in invitation. She stepped closer, and he wrapped it around her shoulders, sighed when she rested her cheek against his chest.

'This is good. I can live with this.'

#

Carol hopped from foot to foot and rubbed her numb hands up and down her arms. Deciding to take Snow for a late afternoon run to Jex's had been a good idea while she'd been antsy after leaving Blake's. Now, being home in front of the fire with Snow curled on her lap seemed a better option, but that could be her nerves talking.

The time she'd spent with Blake had blinked past, because he'd done as he'd said and playfully flirted with her but nothing more. He hadn't cornered her or rolled his eyes when she didn't flirt back; it had been an odd experience but one that she secretly hoped she'd get used to.

Even the hour he'd spent working in his shed had made her smile. The clash of metal against metal and the scream of the grinder had been the back-beat to her playlist, and she'd sung without restraint as she'd stripped the cupboard doors.

She was excited for tomorrow because, while Blake drove home from Melbourne, she'd be repainting the doors, and she planned to surprise Blake with the different shades of yellow and orange creating a brilliant sunset across them all. The trims between would frame each panel in a crisp, clean blue. It looked perfect in her mind; she just hoped Blake would like it.

Beside her, Snow lifted one paw off the cold concrete step and whined, so Carol knocked again.

A few seconds later, Jex answered with a smile, and when he saw Snow, he dropped to his knees and gave the happy dog a good scratch. Then, standing, he took the lead from Carol and beckoned her in.

'I was just about to message you.'

The thought of her phone chiming made her shudder. 'Glad I could save you the time.' And her own sanity.

Jex led her into the kitchen with Snow prancing at his heels. 'Can I make you a cuppa or anything?'

'Actually, I was hoping we could get a recording done.'

He stopped the boisterous play with Snow and looked at her. 'Really?'

She guessed she could add him to the list of people she'd disappointed but who patiently waited for her to pick herself up and do something with her life.

'Yeah, really. I've been dodging your hints for a couple of years, and I'm sorry I did it, but I'm ready now.'

Ready as she'd ever be, anyway.

He cocked his head. 'If you really don't want to do this ...'

She took a deep breath. 'No, I do. Blake was right, I've wanted to for a while, and ...'

And as Jex had been the one to encourage her to sing when giving up had been easier than trying to prove Paul wrong, she now owed him the truth. Or

136

at least as much as she could stomach telling him. He'd been there for her after the bakery scandal, too; he'd been the only one to ask about what had really happened. Too rattled and confused at the time, she hadn't been able to answer him.

Because her legs shook, she pulled a chair out at the table and sat. 'You heard about the deal Paul struck with that producer?'

Pouring himself a coffee, Jex leaned against the bench. 'I heard about it. People were saying you got cold feet, which is understandable.'

Sweaty now, she spread her hands on the table. 'I didn't. There never was a deal. He made it all up in order to get what he wanted from me.'

Jex frowned as he came to sit with her. 'What did he get from you?'

It made her sick, even now. 'You. He didn't like how much time I spent with you. He didn't like you.'

With his fingertips, Jex turned his cup around and around on the tabletop. 'I got the second part. Got it loud and clear in high school.'

She swallowed the lump lodged in her throat. 'I know, and I told him when I first moved in with him that I didn't like the way he'd treated you back then. He said I didn't understand the dynamics of being a guy in his position.'

Jex huffed a breath. 'That's one way to justify it.'

Carol shook her head. 'No, it wasn't. Nothing justifies making your life hell when you'd done nothing wrong. And I told him that, too. He waited until he had me hooked, then showed me exactly what his position in this town could do for me ... and take from me.'

Needing some time, she rose, grabbed a glass of water and drank it all before turning to face him again. 'I didn't know anything about the supposed contract, because there never was one. He'd told a few key people about it and asked them to keep it quiet, then when the bakery was broken into, he put forward the theory that I'd snapped and acted out because of the pressure. Of course, the non-existent contract was then pulled, and instead of being the town's new sweetheart, people started crossing the road to avoid me.'

When she sat back down, Jex reached out and took her hand. 'And so you started avoiding everyone. And still do, to an extent. You work the bar and get up on stage to sing, but you don't often put yourself in a position that calls for one-on-one contact. You don't talk about yourself, and you don't let us in on what's happening in your life anymore.'

Wishing that anger would override her pain, she jutted her chin to keep it steady. 'I tried to talk to people. I tried to tell them I wasn't responsible for the break-in, but no one listened.'

He came to squat beside her chair. 'I knew you didn't do it. I kept hoping you'd open up to me one day and tell me what really happened.'

'I couldn't. Not while Paul still had such a hold on my life.'

Jex scowled. 'What exactly does that mean? What hold did he have? And why?'

'I was young and weak, and I let him manipulate me. Eventually, I believed every negative thought he planted in my head. I wasn't good enough to be seen with him. I wasn't good enough to breathe the same air as everyone else. I was stupid and annoying and boring and whiny. I was too short, too chubby. I smiled too much, sung off key, drew like a five-year-old. I wasn't worth anyone's time, especially not Paul's ... unless he was in the mood for sex.'

She put her hands to her throbbing head and squeezed. Why hadn't she gotten over it yet? Why did she still let it eat at her? Why did she let Paul's narrative on her life override her own?

Jex cupped her elbows and lifted her to her feet. 'There's a lot I want to say and ask, but it can wait. What I will say, though, is you didn't let Paul manipulate you.'

She opened her mouth to object, but he shook his head. 'No, you need to listen now. The very definition of manipulation is to control or influence cleverly or unscrupulously.' He wrapped his arms around her. 'It was never your fault. So how about you give that young grieving girl a break. You know what he is now. You've beaten him and thrown him aside.' He held her away from him, his eyes dark with the questions he held back. 'And I'll add this for you to think about. You have this life now. You have opportunities. And it's up to you what you do with them. No one's pulling your strings now but you, Carol.'

Taking a deep breath, she let it out slowly. He'd said the words that lacked strength and clarity in her own voice. Now, they held promise and possibility.

She let her fear and doubt skitter over her skin and away but caught and held the tremble of relief that followed.

'Okay, then,' she said. 'This is my choice, my wish. I want to record the songs that make me *feel*, and I want to share them with whoever needs to hear them.'

Jex grinned and, taking her hand, led her down the hallway. 'You've got a playlist picked out, then?'

Carol pulled a crumpled piece of paper out of her pocket and handed it to him. 'I feel selfish for refusing for so long, and now that I'm ready, you're dropping everything to record.'

He stopped at the end of the hallway and turned to her. 'Do you know how many cartwheels I'm doing in my head right now?'

She bit back a smile. 'Thank God they're only in your head.'

With a huff, he moved her aside and perfectly executed two cartwheels along the hallway and flourished a bow.

Laughing, she gave him a round of applause. 'I might need to give you a massage after that.' She nodded to the room on her left, where a massage table, stacked with bright towels, waited for tomorrow's clients.

'After last time? No, thanks.' But he grinned.

'You told me to get deep into the muscle.' Putting her nose in the air, Carol strode through the opposite door and into his home recording studio.

He rolled his eyes. 'Your fingers nearly came out the other side. If I did that, I'd never have gotten my diploma in myotherapy or kept any clients.'

Carol just poked out her tongue.

Jex laughed. 'See, that's the Carol I've missed. But'—he pointed at her—'sass like that won't get you a massage later.'

Taking the stool near the microphone, Carol sat on her hands to keep from touching all the electronics and instruments. 'You've come a long way from the music room in high school.'

Jex glanced at her before adjusting some knobs. 'We all have. Some of us are just taking longer to realise it.'

Hunching forward, Carol shook her head. 'I know that's supposed to be one of your encouraging bits of wisdom, but my feet are stuck in the same mud they were five years ago. I don't know if I can pull them out without losing my footing.'

Jex came to squat in front of her, pulled one of her hands free and turned it palm up. 'What you don't realise is that you've already pulled your feet out. You may have lost your boots in the process, and now you're walking around barefoot, feeling every stone, every stick. But your feet are getting tougher. One day soon, you'll realise you don't need those boots, that you're fine, and always have been, just as you are.'

Her heart thudded against her ribs. 'I want to believe that, but history tells a different story.'

'Whose story? Yours or Paul's? Because this is what he wants, you second-guessing yourself, convinced that you're in the wrong, that you deserve people looking down on you. So let me tell you this. It was all a lie. Everything he ever said to you. You aren't in the wrong, and the people who know you love you because of who and what you are.'

She stared at their hands, his big with long fingers, hers small. Could she be the person he described? Would she be strong enough one day not to care what people thought of her? Or whether people—namely her parents—cared about her or not?

With one last pointed look at her, Jex went back to his seat.

Carol pulled her phone from her pocket and put it on silent. 'You said you were going to message me?'

Jex looked up from her playlist. 'Oh, yeah. I was wondering if I could borrow your bike tomorrow. You can take my car for the day.'

Determined to inject some levity into their conversation, she smiled and wiggled her eyebrows. 'Hot date?'

His grin flashed. 'Maybe.'

'Then of course.' Finding her smile came easier now, she donned the headphones and flicked one earpiece off.

Jex swivelled to face her, his gaze direct. 'I have to ask, Carol, why now? Why did you knock on my door about this today?'

She could swallow the truth, keep her answer light and flippant, but she'd come this far.

'Because it's time. My life is mine, and I regret not doing it sooner.' She met his gaze. 'I want to be proud of who I am and what I accomplish. I want others to be proud of me too.'

'We are.' Jex reached over and rubbed her knee. 'Pick the first song and let's get started.'

Breathing deeply, she sat straight and squared her shoulders. 'Rita Ora's "Let You Love Me".'

From the first beat, Carol lost herself in the music, the meaning of the words welling up in her heart and spilling from her mouth. Two hours later, exhausted, she nearly cried as Jex worked magic on her muscles.

'I can tell why you have so many clients. I'll feel like a new person by the time you're done.'

He pressed on a knot in her shoulder. 'Hopefully in more ways than one.'

Getting her to shift, pull one leg up and twist gently, he hummed his approval when her back cracked. After finishing with some stretches, Jex covered her back and shoulders with a towel. 'Lie there for a bit, okay.'

'Don't think I can move anyway.'

She closed her eyes and floated, her muscles relaxed and her mind blissfully empty. When it began to wander, she let it.

Memories she usually shied away from sat with her. How she'd danced around the kitchen while Gran watched, her eyes crinkling at the corners as she laughed. How Gran would catch her in a hug so big and warm she'd wanted to stay in it forever. How she'd watched Pop pull Gran in for a slow dance countless times, and he'd always whisper how much he loved her.

But then Gran had died, and even though Carol had told her grandfather how much she loved and needed him, and had done everything she could to make up for the emptiness her grandmother's absence left in their lives, she'd lost him, too. And with his death, her main source of warmth and love disappeared, leaving her world cold and colourless.

Now, Blake was pulling her to a place where colour and light shifted, as if she were looking at her life through a kaleidoscope. He warmed the parts of her she'd let freeze with neglect. He poked holes in the lies she'd believed for too long, made her no longer want to deny herself the simple joy of friendship and making memories with her friends.

Blake was a part of her life now, whether she wanted him to be or not, but as she lay there, with thoughts of him filling her head, she couldn't think of the reasons he shouldn't be.

CHAPTER 10

Standing on the side verandah, with his hip and shoulder leaning against the upright Carol had painted deep purple, Blake sipped his beer and took it all in. Pride for what he and Carol had achieved during the last week, both around the house and in their friendship, bubbled in his chest.

Music from his Milwaukee radio threaded through the conversations being held in his yard. Love flowed between the people crunching on chips and swigging from bottles. It saturated the air, sank into the ground and touched everything that now meant the world to him. They'd accepted him into their circle, and Drew as well if the animated conversation he now held with Ethan and Mark was anything to go by. And, when Carol had started an online conversation with her friends three days ago, inviting them to Blake's house-warming barbeque, Mark, the group's unofficial leader, had added both Blake and Drew to the chat. It had surprised Blake not only to have been added to the group's virtual hangout but to know they were enthusiastic about welcoming him to the community. Even more surprising was that they'd each taken on responsibility for planning the party; all he'd had to do was haul arse and get the place ready.

Of course, with Carol and Drew spending every free minute they had on painting, fixing, weeding and planting, he'd had time to work in his shed. And while he'd blasted rock from the radio in his shed, Carol's voice had filled his home. She'd sung everything, from current hits to commercials and even a few obscure songs he'd never heard before.

She hummed along to the radio now as she came up the steps and tapped her bottle of cider against his beer. 'Congratulations on hosting your first party here. I don't think this place has ever held so many people.'

143

He ran a thumb across her cheek and got a smile instead of a frown. 'It would have taken me months to get around to organising this, so thank you. And now that I can see how this place comes alive, I'm hoping to have everyone over for barbeques regularly.' Just like he hoped she'd come over regularly, even though she'd almost finished the painting.

'I finally set up the master bedroom today.'

She smiled up at him. 'Yeah? You like the colours?'

'I do.' She'd made his kitchen into a sunrise and his bedroom feature wall into a dusky sunset of purples, blues and pinks. 'And I know your grandmother would love what you've done.'

Her whole body softened. 'You think? I hope so. But I mainly hope you love it.'

He let his fingers linger on her face and, fascinated when she leaned into his touch, moved closer. 'I do. I was going for normal flat colours, but you've created something so much more. It makes the house breathe. It makes it a home.'

Carol rested her head against his shoulder. 'You suit the place, and it suits you. You're making a life here, Blake. You should start your own wall in the shed.'

He slid an arm around her waist and his hand rested easily against her hip. 'I wasn't sure if that would be going a step too far in making my mark on this place.'

She frowned up at him. 'No. I think it would be perfect.'

His mouth on hers would be perfect, but she hadn't let him know yet that she was ready. He'd promised her he'd wait, so although he craved a taste of her, when or if they took things further would be up to her. She'd said nothing in the last few days about Paul or receiving phone calls, and the bruises of fatigue she'd carried had faded—but still, something dragged at her. So until she could be with him without thinking of Paul, he'd give her these pockets of comfort.

She pressed a hand to his cheek. 'You should know that I tend to forget the rest of the world when I'm out here with you.' Lightly, she touched her lips to his and stole his breath. 'We better get the barbeque going before it rains.'

With his mind still on her and the way her lips barely touching his had sparked everything inside him, sending heat rushing around his body so that everything tingled, he pressed his forehead to hers.

'What barbeque?'

She laughed, without reservation or self-derision, and his heart took a tumble. He'd been heading towards the cliff's edge since that first night; now, he dived and rolled, tucking his limbs close as he slid to a stop at her feet. His galloping heart belonged to her.

'Hey.' Framing his face with her hands, she frowned up at him. 'You okay?'

'Yeah.' He found a smile and hoped it wouldn't tremble as the new sensation rushed through him. 'You'll sing later?'

'Jex brought his guitar, so between him, Kelsey, Lilli and me, you'll have a night full of entertainment.'

Except, he only needed her.

'Sounds like a night to remember.' Making himself move back a step, he took her hand. 'Everyone's gone.'

'They'll be poking around inside.' She turned them towards the door. 'You promised food and they'd happily renovate the whole house to get it.'

Still feeling lost, he followed her inside. 'I need to rethink my strategy then.'

Her friends *oohed* and *aahed* over the colour scheme and the quality of work she'd put in, but it was Kelsey who hung back with him in the kitchen when everyone moved on to the next room.

'I'm not being nosey,' she told him.

'Not yet.' He glanced at her as he took the sausages, sliced onions and salads from the fridge. When the silence stretched between them, he said, 'That wasn't a dig.'

'No, but whatever's going on between you and Carol is private. I understand that.' She stacked the paper towels on top of the paper plates he'd put on the table. 'I just wanted you to know that I've never seen her come alive with anyone the way she does when she's with you. Not before I left, and not since I got back.'

'If it makes you feel better, I've never had a connection like this with anyone, either.'

She tilted her head as she studied him. 'You haven't?'

'Never.' He crossed his heart, still jerking in his chest with new-found love. 'I'm as vulnerable as she is in this.'

'I know how that feels.' She smiled. 'I'm happy for you both.'

Ethan came in with the rest of the group, grabbed Kelsey around the waist and kissed her. 'I think you're right. We should redo our room.'

'Really?' Kelsey beamed. 'And the nursery?'

At that, everyone stopped talking and stared at Kelsey, their mouths hanging open. In the next moment, it was chaos as hugs and congratulations warmed the room.

Jex held up a hand. 'We have to organise a baby shower.'

A collective cheer went up as Blake gave Kelsey a congratulatory hug and shook Ethan's hand. Stepping back so Zoe could get to Kelsey, he reached for Carol. She stood, just outside the group, the sadness in her eyes like ice to the heat still surfing his veins.

'What's wrong?'

The smile she gave might have fooled some. 'I should have thought of that, throwing a baby shower. I've known for a few weeks but didn't even think of it.'

I'm a shitty friend.

She'd told him that twice, but how could she believe it when the people around her loved her so much? Did she even realise the impact she had on their lives, the joy and light she gave?

He kept an eye on her as she and everyone pitched in with the food prep and kitchen clean-up. She talked and laughed while they all made plans for the baby shower, though her dimple never popped.

When they moved outside, Drew set about lighting a fire in a halved forty-four–gallon drum and, as he did everywhere, joined in the fun by telling stories about his grandfather. Blake never tired of his friend's tales. He took it as a sign of Drew's honesty that the stories never changed, never grew beyond the truth.

146

By the time the roaring fire had settled into a bed of shimmering coals, the night sky was a cloud-framed patchwork of stars. The still air, scented with rain yet to fall, was cold enough to make them all billow like dragons with each breath.

Drew was the first to raid the wood pile for a log to sit on, and everyone else followed until they circled the fire. Blake sat his stump close enough to Carol's that their hips touched. Worried that her eyes stayed haunted though she joined in the merriment, he smoothed a hand up and down her back.

Sitting on her other side with his guitar, Jex stood and held a set of keys out to Carol. 'Before I forget, you better take these.'

'Oh, yeah. Another hot date.' She fished her keys out of her pocket. 'Let me know when you want me to drop your car off.'

'Sure. And maybe we can record another song.' He winked at her, then grinned at Blake. 'Did she tell you we started?'

A hint of a smile touched his lips as he met her gaze. 'No.'

She shrugged. 'I just ... wanted to get a few more songs done first.'

He rubbed his thumb across her nape. 'I'm glad you've started.'

Ethan, the smartest one of all because he'd brought a camp chair from home, snuggled Kelsey on his lap. 'I heard you were recording some songs. If you're selling, I'll buy.'

On Blake's other side, Drew leaned forward. 'You sing, Carol? I don't think I know anyone who sings. Decently, that is.' He shot Blake a look.

'Hey, I never claimed I could sing.'

For the first time in two hours, Carol's smile bloomed. 'I've never heard you sing. Can you?'

'No,' both he and Drew said together.

'No,' Blake said again. 'I've been compared to a drowning cat.'

'Oh.' Carol rubbed a hand over her mouth.

'Yeah, sure, laugh it up.' He glared at Drew when he chuckled. 'You, too. But at least I don't sink like a rock as soon as I dip a foot in the ocean.'

Drew crossed one tribal-tattooed arm over the other. 'That wasn't my fault.'

Blake settled in to tell the tale. 'He wanted to come surfing with me one day. Beautiful swell, glorious weather'—he grinned at Drew—'and this big

147

lug falls off the board before we've even paddled past the breakers. We were right over a sandbar, but no, he sinks, and I have to save him.'

Drew raised his drink in a salute. 'You impressed the bikini-clad tourist.'

'Yeah, who insisted on giving you mouth to mouth before following you everywhere.'

'We had fun for a few weeks.' Drew grinned and tapped his chest. 'My heart still flutters when I think about her.'

Carol laughed. 'How long ago was this?'

Drew grinned back. 'What's time but a societal construct when the heart is involved.'

'You should be on stage,' Blake cut in, then, taking Carol's hand, refocused her attention. 'You'll sing?'

She shrugged, then glanced at Jex when she got nods from the others. 'You know Taylor Swift's "The Archer"?'

Jex settled his guitar on his knee and strummed a few chords, the sound bending and bouncing around the fire, but as everyone settled in, their shoulders pressing together, Blake turned his focus on Carol. She took his hand in hers, and the cold night fell away when she started singing, as if readying for battle. All that existed was her voice, her fingers entwined with his, and the reflection of the glowing embers in her eyes.

He could ease her fears about being invisible by telling her he'd fallen for her, that he wanted to be with her no matter what secrets she still kept from him, but he knew it was too soon for her to believe him. So, while she tapped her heel to keep time and her friends supported her with their voices, as they cheered when the last note died away, he made a vow to show her every day that he was the one who'd help her hold on. He'd be the one who'd stay.

#

Carol held the rubbish bag open for Mark. The others had hugged and laughed and left in a convoy of cars with Jex on her motorbike protected in the middle of the line. He'd joked about dodging the kangaroos and returning her bike in one piece, and the rush of fear that had coursed through her had made her hug him tighter.

'I don't care about the bike,' she'd said, 'but I'd be royally pissed if you got hurt.'

When she was young, she'd wished for a big brother, one who would lead her on adventures, encourage her to do stupid stuff that they'd whisper about later and wonder how they'd survived. One who would protect her against bullies and tell boys they weren't good enough for her.

Jex, Ethan and Mark had taken on those roles in her life to an extent, except they were the ones who judged the stupid stuff she'd done and wondered how she'd survived. They would most likely disown her if they knew the rest. Now, Mark was taking it upon himself to be the big brother who questioned her choices about her relationships.

Had they drawn straws? Played paper, scissors, rock? Or worse, had they grouped together to talk about her and Blake?

Well, she'd set Mark straight and he could spread the word to the others.

'You're waiting for me to leave,' she said, 'but I'm not going to.'

He glanced at her as he bent to pick up a paper plate. 'Are you telling me to go?'

'No.' She put her hands on her hips and cocked her head. 'I'm making sure you know you don't have to hang around.'

He straightened and crossed his arms over his chest. 'And if I want to?'

She sighed. 'Then be my guest.'

'You'll be his guest?' He nodded to where Blake stood with Drew at the door to his shed, their hands talking as much as their mouths.

She could let Mark's question burrow into her skin, like a grass seed under a fingernail, but like the seed it would only fester until shame filled her. But why should she be ashamed? Her relationship with Blake was her business, and she wouldn't feel guilty for spending time with him. And if she slept with him? It would be her decision and not for anyone else to judge.

'For a while longer. You have a problem with me staying?'

He reached out and pulled up the hood of her jacket as the wind kicked up and whipped her hair into her eyes. 'I have no problem with you staying, but I need to talk to you at some point.'

Her blood spiked, prickling her skin. Had Paul been busy cultivating more lies during the last five days? Had he laid a trap while she'd been slowly relaxing?

'Is it you who needs to speak with me, or Officer Jones?'

Mark frowned. 'Me, for a start. Depending on what truths you tell me, I may need to speak with you in an official capacity later.'

Four years ago, she'd been terrified of being arrested for a crime she hadn't committed, and she'd tried to tell him the truth. But he'd been fresh out of the academy, his gaze sharper, his posture straighter, and his disappointment when he'd witnessed her being led into the station by a senior officer had been clear.

No one had deemed her innocent. 'How do I trust you to believe me this time?'

He rested his hands on her shoulders. 'I know you didn't steal from the bakery.'

'Only because nothing was missing. You still think I broke in.'

Frowning, he shook his head slowly. 'You were fun and happy before all that painful stuff happened, and I'm ashamed to admit that, yes, I believed you had broken in, on a dare or because you were acting out or wanting attention. Looking back, with experience and maturity behind me and seeing you struggle and worry yourself sick these past few weeks since Paul came back, I can see that there was more going on than I knew about.'

'You think he put me up to it.' She could guess where his suspicions lay now.

His hands tightened on her shoulders. 'For a while, yes, I did think that. But it doesn't add up. You've always been a hell-raiser. If there was trouble, you were never far away. But the distinction is, you never did anything to hurt someone intentionally. Breaking into the bakery and causing that mess of grief? That's not you. And the way the Todds stepped in ...' He shook his head. 'I never really liked Paul, and the more I learn about him, the more I think my gut instinct was right.'

Carol stared at the missing button on his jacket. Emotions tangled and mixed inside her. Anger muddied her relief, the oozing wound of grief warred with hope, and all of it sped her heart.

Stepping out of his reach, she picked up the garbage bag. 'It's in the past now.'

Shoving his hands in his pockets, Mark swore. 'I don't think it is. Not from what I'm hearing. And not when I have a report of a vicious dog.'

Her heart jumped. 'He's trying to have Snow taken away?'

Mark only stared at her.

'He wants Snow destroyed.'

'I can't tell you anything, and I haven't told you anything.' He waited a beat. 'I am saying, though, that without evidence, all I can do is advise the person making the complaint to go to the council, but without evidence, they won't do anything either. A dog protecting its owner would never be held accountable.'

Carol shook her head. 'Snow did nothing wrong.'

Mark sighed. 'You need to come and see me, Carol. Talk to me. I can help.'

Like he'd helped last time, letting her be interrogated by the hard-eyed cop every teenager loathed? But she swallowed the pain-filled retort. He'd only been doing his job, and still was, so she couldn't blame him for thinking her guilty back then. But her friend, her substitute brother, should have seen more, believed more, and she was still trying to come to terms with that.

She shook her head. 'There's nothing you can do at the moment.'

Blake walked over, his gaze cutting between them, and held his hand out to Mark. 'Thanks for the help.'

Mark kept his gaze on Carol a moment longer before he shook Blake's hand, then Drew's. 'You've all done a great job out here. We'll have to do this more often.'

Carol said nothing as they walked Mark to his car and fisted her hands against the need to wave as he drove away.

Blake slipped an arm around her waist and steered her towards the house. 'Let's stoke the fire inside, because I don't know about you, but my toes froze about an hour ago.'

'I'll put the kettle on.' Drew strode ahead of them, rubbing his hands together before blowing into them. 'It's so freaking cold down here that I can't feel *any* of my extremities.'

The blood rushing through Carol's veins meant she felt everything, and if she stayed in her own head, she'd either burst or slowly sink back into the darkness. She forced herself back to the present.

'You can tell the two of you have been friends a long time.'

'Seventeen years.' He stopped on the verandah to toe off his boots. 'Why does that make me feel old?'

Striving for levity, she reached up and ran a hand through his hair. 'Yeah, twenty-seven is ancient. Oh look, I think I see some grey.'

Catching her elbows, Blake slowly ran his palms down her arms, her sides, and let them rest on her hips. She curled her fingers in his hair.

This helped. He helped to pull her back and anchored her in the now. The past couldn't be changed, and whatever Mark had thought back then, he didn't now. She would hold onto that. And Blake.

She'd draw him like this, with his eyes so serious, his lips forming the smile that made her heart thud. If he asked her now, she had the answer.

His fingers flexed against her hips. 'Do you want me to kiss you?'

Not a tangled and humiliating demand but sweet concern.

'Yes.' And even though she'd had a hint of his lips against hers and the chance this time to brace herself for the explosion, she still fell as he drew her in, softly, slowly, and enveloped her.

He kissed her as she'd never been kissed. Emotions, the likes of which she'd given up on ever feeling, shot through her. Swamped, drowning, she tightened her grip in his hair and begged for more.

And he gave it to her. Still, as though the speed of time was altered, he slowed her rush and took her on an exciting journey of taste and texture that planted itself in her core.

Sliding her hands down to frame his face, she drew away an inch. 'How do you do that? How do you take my expectations and smash them into a thousand pieces? How do you put it all back together into something that rips me open?'

He touched her face. 'Sometimes we have to rip out the weeds to get the rest to grow. But I'd rather not hurt you as I do it.'

She pressed her lips to his again. 'I think it's going to hurt regardless, and maybe it needs to. But it feels better already.'

Blake's smile helped to soothe the last of her anger and pain. Should she continue fighting the hold he had on her, push away the pleasure and ease he offered? Could she?

He pressed his lips to her forehead. 'Will you stay a while? You might need to feel better again.'

As she leaned into him, her answer came easy. 'I wasn't planning on going home yet.'

'Good.' With his arm around her shoulders, he walked her inside where the kettle boiled, the smell of onions lingered and the warmth made them shed layers.

At home already, Drew had three cups lined up on the bench. He turned as Carol draped her jacket over a chair. 'Hey, Blake has a Mothman jumper like that.'

Blake traced the neckline, his smile smug. 'I wondered where it had gone.'

Carol lifted her chin and an eyebrow. 'I just figured I should wash it before giving it back.' Or wash it again, seeing as she'd taken to sleeping in it.

'No rush.' He ran a knuckle up her throat to her chin, lifting it. A question she answered by meeting his mouth with her own.

'Just 'cos a guy is single, you don't have to rub it in.' Drew shook his head when she smiled over at him. 'You two can make your own drinks. I'm gonna sprawl out on the couch so you have to sit separately.'

'Plenty of room on the floor in front of the fire.' Blake gave a shrug. 'More romantic, too.'

'More romantic,' Drew mimicked, then shook his head and laughed. 'Give me twenty-four hours and she'll forget you for me.'

'Yeah, right.' Blake strolled to the kettle. 'You walk out of the room and she'll forget you for me.'

'*She*'—Carol shot them both a look—'will decide for herself who she remembers and forgets. And who she sits with and who she kisses.' She held a hand up as both men opened their mouths. 'I know you were joking, but being told who you're going to be with, like you're a dog on a leash, isn't really all that funny.'

Both men frowned.

'I'm sorry,' said Drew. 'I never thought of it like that.'

153

She shrugged. 'Hard to when you're the one bantering.'

'Easier now it's been pointed out.' He came to stand in front of her and held out his hand. 'Friends?'

She rolled her eyes and took his hand. 'Blake wouldn't have you in his life if you were an idiot, so yeah, we're friends.'

He cleared his throat and stepped back. 'Good. But I'm still taking the couch.' He turned and walked into the lounge room.

Blake handed her a steaming cup of coffee. 'I'm sorry too. Joking or not, it was insensitive.'

But to her, it was more than that. 'I don't like the idea of not being able to choose who I'm with.'

Frowning, he sipped his drink. 'We never meant for it to sound like that, but it did. It won't happen again. And not because I like you being here with me but because it's offensive.'

They made their way to the lounge room where Drew sat on a swag in front of the roaring fire, admiring Jex's guitar.

'Figured I might as well stoke the fire, set up my bed and'—he smiled—'hog the heat, seeing as you two are creating enough of your own.'

As though to prove him right, Blake sat on the couch, swung up one leg and pulled her down to sit between his thighs, with her back against his chest and his hand comfortable against her stomach.

Carol nodded to the guitar. 'Do you play?'

'Not as good as Jex. He has magic fingers.' He twirled the guitar, laid his fingers over the strings. 'And he has excellent taste. I saved up for a Maton once.'

Ready for one of his stories, Carol relaxed against Blake. 'But?'

'I bought a shitbox car instead.' He grinned. 'We loved that Cortina, didn't we?'

Blake's laugh vibrated through her. 'He pulled the front seat out so he could fit the surfboard in, then put the seat back in when he found out surfing wasn't his thing.'

Grinning, Drew shook his head. 'You aren't ever going to drop that, are you.'

Carol yawned. Blake's body cradling hers, the easy banter and the long day were all taking their toll. And when Blake took her hand and entwining their fingers, rested his wrist over her heart, she took a deep breath, let it out and closed her eyes.

As much as she wanted to stay, she'd have to go home soon. Snow would want a run before her lunch shift at the pub. She thought about bringing him out to Blake's for a romp through the paddocks while she had Jex's car.

Pressing a kiss to her temple, Blake nuzzled her hair. 'I'm glad you're here with me.'

Smiling as sleep pulled her under, she mumbled, 'Me too.' And she meant it.

CHAPTER 11

Carol ran into the Mckinley Hotel with one minute to spare before her shift started. The rush from Blake's place after sleeping twelve hours straight had been worth it, especially when he'd kissed her good morning, then again before she'd driven away. She'd waved out the window until she couldn't see him anymore.

Behind the bar already, Zoe glared at her. 'Glad you could make it.'

Unwilling to let Zoe burst her happy bubble, Carol smiled. 'It was a rush, but yeah, I did.' She tied the short black apron around her waist. 'You didn't talk much last night. Is everything okay?'

Zoe's lips lifted in a sneer. 'Sure, why wouldn't it be?'

Carol had no time to enquire further as the early lunchtime crowd chatted while they lined up waiting to order.

Mr Arden, the third in line, smiled. 'What a lovely day it is outside! Have you had time to enjoy it yet?'

Carol nodded. 'I took Snow for a run around the block before work. You can almost feel spring in the sunshine today.' Or was that just her happiness? Either way, it was a good day. A great day.

Mr Arden's beard twitched with his smile. 'And it seems to agree with you. Will you join us on the weekend for the Wattle Yard Art Group meeting? I'm hoping the new young man, Blake, will join us too.'

She'd have to find a different subject if she went, though even if Blake did join them, she was pretty sure her hand would automatically draw him. What would he think of seeing himself staring out from a large sheet of paper?

Maybe it was time to find out.

'I'll make sure he comes.'

156

Once Carol had taken the order from the last in line, she helped Zoe with the drink orders. Sullen as well as silent, Zoe snapped glasses of soft drinks onto a tray and stalked out to the dining area.

After her second trip, Carol put her hand on the tray. 'What's going on?'

Zoe's nostrils flared as she glared at Carol. '*You.* You're what's going on,' she hissed. 'All this woe is me shit mixed with the I'm here for you crap makes one big steaming pile of you're so fucking selfish.'

Her words knocked Carol back a step. 'I don't understand. What have I done to make you so angry with me?'

Zoe bared her teeth. 'What have you done? Oh, I don't know, maybe playing games with one guy while acting like a dog in heat with another. And you think *I'm* the slut.'

Grabbing hold of Zoe's arm, Carol pulled her into the gap between the fridges. 'What the hell are you on about? Who am I playing games with?'

Zoe snorted. 'You're really going to play dumb? Fine! Paul. You're playing games with Paul, leading him on, then ignoring him. He tried to be nice to you, and what do you do? Start saying some really ugly shit about him. But we all know what you are, Carol. You're a lying bitch.'

How had she missed this? How had she missed Zoe's venomous anger? She'd been too wrapped up in her own world. Still, it didn't make sense, unless …

She pressed a hand to her stomach. 'Who told you I was playing games with Paul?'

'Who do you think? You're all he talks about, all he thinks about, even when …'

Nausea sped up Carol's throat. 'Even when, what?'

'What do you care?' Snatching up her tray, Zoe stalked away and stomped to the kitchen.

For three hours, they each did their job and avoided the other. When Paul walked into the pub, Carol nearly slid to the floor behind the bar, wanting nothing more than to curl up, cover her ears and wait out the rest of her life. But that wouldn't fix anything.

Neither would screaming.

He sat at the bar in front of her, even though Zoe stood a metre away. 'You should get your front door fixed. I told Dad I'd dropped in and that the mechanism must be faulty, to open like that when I knocked.'

The regular customer sitting further down the bar turned towards them. 'I had a door like that once. Only had to sneeze and it opened. Bloody dangerous.' He pointed at Carol. 'Especially for a woman living on her own.'

Paul tapped his thumb on the bar. 'That's what I tried to tell her. She needs to be smarter or she'll end up getting hurt.'

Carol's lungs burned with every breath. 'Statistics show a woman is more at risk from a male known to her than from a random attack.'

Paul stared her down. 'From the stories I've heard, women who push men to the edge complain when they push back.'

The regular raised his beer. 'Amen to that.'

Carol glanced at Zoe, who stood mute, her cheeks crimson and fists trembling at her sides. A kernel of pity wedged into Carol's seething anger and ever-present fear. Paul had obviously lied to Zoe, made her believe the same things he'd once made Carol believe. Now he was using Zoe against her, and her against Zoe. It had to stop. He had to stop chipping away at everything and everyone that meant anything to her.

Before her emotions erupted from her in a spew of shouted accusations that would only prove his claim true, she pointed at the regular. 'That's a shitty attitude to have. And I have better things to do than stand here and listen to you advocate violence against women.'

Paul reached out and grabbed her wrist. 'And what about violence against men?'

She lifted her chin and glared at him. 'I don't advocate violence against *any*one.'

His eyes went comically wide, but she saw the flash of glee in them. 'Really? Were you opposed to violence when your hand connected with my face as I was apologising to you? Does Blake know about that side of you yet? Or doesn't it matter because you're only with him to make me jealous.'

Everyone who'd turned their way was listening. No matter what she did or said now, he'd won the game he'd come to play. And everyone was waiting for her to snap, to give them a show of smashing glass and screaming. But they could keep waiting, because she wasn't going to give Paul or anyone the satisfaction of seeing her break like that.

Especially now that Paul had publicly involved Blake.

'You don't know me. You never did.' She lifted the wrist he still held. 'Let me go.'

With his jaw twitching and smile tight, he squeezed her wrist, sending a sharp pain up her arm before he released her.

Escaping to the secondary dining room on the pretence of finding something, she whirled when a hand grabbed her shoulder.

Still in full view of the diners, Paul lifted his hands. 'Don't hit me. I'm here to apologise.'

Oily nausea slid around her belly as she edged away from him, and he followed her step for step until her back hit the wall. No one could see them now; no one would hear her unless she screamed. How could she beat him? How could she cut him from her life when he'd made sure everyone believed she couldn't live without him?

Her avoidance tactics had led to this, she realised. But her fear of people finding out the truth no longer outweighed the lies he spread to make her miserable, because those lies now affected people she loved.

Gritting her teeth against the need to throw up, she stared up at him. 'Leave Zoe alone. Leave Blake alone, or I'll tell everyone what really happened between us.'

He shook his head and fished his phone from his pocket, his shark smile growing even as his eyes narrowed. 'No. You won't. Because what would Mark think if he heard this? What would your boyfriend think, I wonder, if he knew exactly what you'd asked of me?' He tapped his phone and held it up to her ear.

She heard her own voice, crying, pleading, begging for him to fuck her, to go harder, to come.

'Now, what evidence do *you* have?'

None. And they both knew it. Her head thumped in time with her heart, each pound threatening to push bile up her throat and out of her mouth.

'Why are you doing this?'

Lifting a hand to touch her face, he laughed when she moved away. 'You've had all this time to tell people that I'm a—what did you call me after slapping me?—a narcissistic bastard that you'd never let touch you again?' He held up his phone. 'I'm happy to let everyone know exactly what *you* are.' He stood straight and held his arms wide. 'And do you know who'll win? Me! Because everyone loves me, no matter what girls like you say. Everyone will always love me, and they'll always see you as the desperate, hysterical little girl that you are.'

With a wink, he ruffled his hair, pulled his shirt from the waistband of his trousers and slapped a hand against one of his cheeks. Backing away until he was once more in the line of sight of those in the main dining room, he raised his hands. 'I never wanted it to come to this, but if you don't stop, I'll have to go to the police. I don't want to do that, Carol. Please don't make me.'

If there was a window to crawl through, she'd escape and run to Jex's car. She'd drive away and keep driving until the scenery around her no longer held memories. Until the people who saw her no longer recognised her. Instead, she made her shaking legs take her back into the main dining room where everyone stared at her as though she'd just committed a murder.

Afraid to make eye contact with anyone, she began clearing tables. Mr Arden still sat at his and held out his empty plate to her. 'You look pale. Are you okay?'

Words locked in her throat.

'I'm fine,' she managed.

She balanced his plate on top of the pile, and as she reached for his glass, Mr Arden leaned closer.

'You know I'm always here if you need to talk. It's not good to bottle things up. Especially things that might make you do something you'll regret.'

Her heart didn't break, and she knew it would keep beating as a reminder that for a little while she'd been fully alive. That for a moment she'd believed she could have a relationship and a future with Blake. A man who'd treated her as though she deserved those things.

He wouldn't now. Not once the rumour mill filled him in and made him think he didn't really know her at all. She could tell him the truth first; let him believe her or not. At least then she would have told one person.

But when Blake walked in with Drew towards the end of her shift and gave her the smile she'd come to crave, all conversation around the bar stopped. Blake would want to talk, to flirt, but with Paul's performance still fresh in everyone's minds and the ghost of his touch still on her skin, she couldn't let him do either of those things. Besides, if he tried to touch her now, she'd fall apart.

He sat on the same stool Paul had occupied earlier and patted the one beside him. 'We thought we'd drop in and say hi, see if you wanted to follow us out to my place.' His smile dimmed and he cocked his head. 'Are you okay?'

Each time she opened her mouth, sick heat surged up her throat, threatening to overflow. 'Long day.'

He reached for her hand. 'We can wait.'

'You don't need to.' She shifted back, hating the puzzled frown he gave her.

Drew sat on a stool and rested his elbows on the bar. 'Why don't we get a drink while we're here?'

Blake's gaze followed her as she served them both a Coke. Drew kept up a mostly one-sided conversation about the work he was doing on Blake's garden, old times and the future. Carol said nothing, not even goodbye when they left minutes before she handed over to the next shift.

It was for the best. She needed to eject the sickly heat sliding around in her belly before facing him, before telling him what she'd hoped never to tell anyone.

But when she got home, Blake's ute sat in her driveway. He waited until she'd parked and locked her car before getting out, then, hands jammed in his pockets, he walked around to stand between her and the front door of her house.

When Drew got behind the wheel, Carol glanced at Blake. 'You're staying?'

His jaw twitched. 'You don't want me to?'

She did. More than anything, she wanted his warmth, his comfort. But Paul had touched her and tainted her skin. Would she ever be able to scrub him from her body, her mind, her life? Would Blake still want to stay once he knew about the hold Paul had on her?

There was only one way to find out, so she nodded. The ute's engine rumbled to life. Drew sat behind the wheel, his eyebrows lifted in question. Because she couldn't smile, she lifted a hand in a half-hearted wave.

With a nod to both of them, Drew reversed out of her driveway and drove away.

She moved past Blake, opened the door and waited while he toed off his boots, then closed it behind him. Though she'd rather the gloom, she flicked lights on. 'Would you like a cuppa?'

'I'd like you to tell me what happened.'

Straight into it then.

'Paul came in while I was working.' Surprised she could get the words out, she gave him the rundown about everything that had happened from the time she'd walked into work to when she'd left. Minus the details about the recording. She couldn't tell him about that yet. Or ever.

Blake paced as he listened, alternating between shoving his hands in his pockets and running them through his hair. 'He's a bastard.' He stopped and looked at her. 'He scared you, made you sick. He made you hide what you needed, what you felt. You couldn't even talk to me.'

'No, I couldn't.'

All she wanted now was for him to hold her while everything fell apart.

She hiccupped a sob as he sat next to her on the couch and pulled her onto his lap.

'This is why I couldn't let you touch me,' she said, 'because I would have broken down in front of everyone.' Words roiled up inside her even as she fisted his shirt against her mouth. But when his arms tightened around her, she gave in. 'I want this, even though I swore I never would. I want you even though I tell myself I shouldn't.'

He pressed cool lips to her forehead. 'It seems we both failed on that front, and I'm glad we did.'

162

'You came here instead of going home and forgetting about me.' Her stomach clenched. 'And after I throw up, I'll tell you the reasons you might want to rethink that decision.'

Saliva pooled in her mouth as she scrambled from his lap and ran to the bathroom. And when she felt his hand on her back, soothing her, she was grateful for the connection. Embarrassment could come later.

Silently, he filled the cup on the sink and handed it to her. She rinsed her mouth, splashed more water on her face and took the ratty towel he held out. Her stomach was raw and her head pounded to a tribal beat as she hung the towel back on its hook.

'I want to say you shouldn't have been in here for that, but it helped, so thanks.'

He slipped his arm around her waist. 'Are you ready to tell me now?'

She rested a hand on his chest. 'I'm not avoiding, but I need a shower. I need to get clean before I can sit and talk about other things I'll need to wash off.'

He glanced at her outdated shower cubicle. 'I can make those cuppas while you do if you like.'

She tried a smile. 'That would be nice, thanks.'

But when he turned for the door, she grabbed his shirt. 'Actually, I don't want to be alone. Can you stay for a bit and just close your eyes?'

In answer, he sat on the closed toilet seat, hooked his hands behind his head and shut his eyes. She stood, struck that she trusted him to stay like that until she said otherwise.

As she undressed, she started at the beginning. 'It was about a month between Gran getting the diagnosis and her dying.' The memory of that time still had the power to grab her lungs, but she ran the water and stepped under the spray. 'You can open your eyes now.'

#

Blake kept them closed a moment longer. The toilet seat offered no comfort, but then, neither did the words coming from Carol as she stood under the steaming shower stream.

163

His rage ran deep. He'd never been the reckless type, but the idea of finding Paul and showing him what it was like to be cornered and scared burned bright.

'I'm sorry about your gran.'

'Me too. I loved Pop and he loved me, but Gran got me. Do you know what I mean?'

'I do,' he said, rubbing his temples. She'd started with heartache; perhaps it was the easiest of her burdens to share.

Suds splashed against the frosted glass as she washed her hair.

'She went from vibrant and happy to sick so quickly that I worried about touching her. The day she died, she held her hands out to me. Pop said she wanted a hug, but I couldn't. I was terrified of breaking her.'

Her voice cracked, along with his heart.

'What can I do?' he said. 'How can I make this easier for you?'

'I just want you to hold me. Please? Just until the shaking stops?'

He grabbed the towel hanging on the back of the door, held it open and closed his eyes. 'I'm ready when you are.'

The hiss of the shower stopped, the door creaked open and her body pressed against his. Wrapping the towel around her, he held her tight.

Her breath shuddered against his neck. 'You'll get wet.'

He opened his eyes and stared down at her. 'I don't care.'

She was already pale, already exhausted and she'd barely begun. He wanted to shield her but couldn't; she needed to purge what had grown deep and dark inside her. Needed to slash the lies that had tangled among her truths and choked them.

'Come on, let's get you warm.'

Her teeth chattered. 'The fire isn't lit.'

Taking her weight, he walked her out of the bathroom. 'Your room, then.'

She shuffled down the hallway beside him. 'You'll stay?'

'Do I look like I'm leaving?'

She lifted her gaze to his, searching. 'No.'

He kept her tight against his side as they walked into her room, then, leaving her to stand on her own, he grabbed the worn but soft blanket from her bed, held it out and closed his eyes. 'Drop the towel.'

The towel made a soft thud on the floor, and Carol stepped into him. He wrapped the blanket around her and opened his eyes.

Carol was studying him. 'You're angry with me.'

He took a slow, deep breath and rubbed her shoulders. 'No, I'm not. I'm so pissed off, though, that I can hardly think let alone talk. I'm pissed off that anyone has the power to make you so upset that you throw up.' He pointed to the bed. 'Sit down before you fall down.'

She stared up at him. 'You don't know everything, Blake.'

The anguish in her voice broke his heart. He had to make her see he was in this for the long haul. 'When you sang that song last night, it was as if you were asking me to help you hold on, asking if I'd stay, so I'm staying, and I'm holding on.'

He sat on her bed, rested his back against the headboard and reached for her. When she stepped to him, he gathered her up and pulled her against him.

'If you don't want me to stay,' he said, 'then you just need to tell me.' Silence throbbed along with his heart. 'You're not telling me you don't want me here.'

'Because I can't lie to you.'

Relieved, he picked up the story for her. 'You couldn't hug your gran because you were afraid to hurt her.'

She rubbed her cheek against his chest. 'Gran was frail and so small. Just bones and clinging skin. I kissed her and told her I loved her, then I walked out. Pop came out half an hour later and he couldn't talk, couldn't look at me. It was the nurse who told me she'd died.'

Aching for her, he pressed his lips to her temple. 'You think he was angry at you?'

She shrugged against him. 'How could he not be?'

Because he loved you. 'Did you talk to him, sort it out?'

She shook her head. 'No. He stopped living that day. He came home, but it wasn't him. Not all of him. He died a month after gran. I nearly didn't go in to wake him before I went to school.'

He closed his eyes. 'You found him?'

'Yeah.' She burrowed closer, her shivers vibrating through the blanket between them. 'I can feel your heat, but I'm freezing. Would it be okay if we
shared the blanket?'

Automatically, he closed his eyes.

'It's okay. You don't need to do that.' She wriggled until the overlap of
blanket came free. 'I felt too tainted, too raw for you to see me before. But
you closed your eyes because I asked you to, and you made me feel better. So
thank you.' She kissed his chin as he wrapped them both in the blanket.

He could get lost in her scent, her warmth, but there were still things she
needed to say and hear. 'You can't keep carrying all this guilt around, you
know that don't you?' In her silence, he pushed on. 'Think about it. If you'd
given her that last hug, would you be tearing yourself apart for killing her?'

She stilled. 'I don't know. Maybe. Probably. I don't know how that makes
me feel.'

She fit snugly against him, her shoulder against his chest, her hand over
his heart, her legs curled so her knees rested against his side. At that moment,
though, she wasn't the woman he loved, but the heartbroken teenager who'd
lost her grandparents.

He linked his hands on her bare hip. 'And your parents didn't come
home, for either of them? For you?'

Her laugh held no humour. 'They were in the middle of a Canadian tour.
The passengers and crew needed them.'

'Their daughter needed them.'

Carol sighed. 'She did. I did, but I've learned to live without them.'

Blake's parents had been around his whole life. Distance hadn't stopped
Annie from mothering him or being an involved parent. And yet, he knew
the ache of it not being enough.

'Doesn't take the pain away,' he said.

She pressed her lips to his throat. 'No. But it helps to talk to someone
who understands, so thank you.' She took a deep breath. 'I'm not sure you'll
be so forgiving when you hear the rest though, but I need you to let me just
get it out, okay? If you comment, I'll stall, and I'll never get it all out.'

Taking care not to dislodge the blanket, he brought a hand to his chest and crossed his heart. 'Take your time, we have plenty. And if you stall, I'll be here to give you whatever you need.'

She took his hand and gripped it. 'I was nearly seventeen by the time Gran and Pop died. Pop had been teaching me to drive, to save money, to be independent, and my parents sent me extra money after they told me they were selling the property, so I found a room to rent in town. Paul was my housemate, and for the first month, he lived up to his good guy reputation. But then he started making little digs. "You'd look better with darker hair. Curves are good, but a man likes long legs. It's okay, I'm sure there's some guy out there who'll want you."'

He understood why she avoided his gaze, but she needed to know the truth. 'He had no right to say any of those things to you. You know that, don't you?'

She shrugged against him. 'I know he manipulated me, but he was the first guy who I didn't consider a brother to take notice of me. So when he sometimes borrowed money or left me to pay the rent, I didn't mind. But then he started picking on my friends and telling me I'd eventually find someone who'd want me. Three months after I moved in, I was miserable, and every time I tried to lift myself up, he'd drag me back down by saying if I was prettier, kinder, sexier, then people would like me. He'd grimace at my drawings, cover his ears when I sang.'

She pressed their joined hands to her forehead. 'The first time he kissed me I was shocked, but then he didn't talk to me for two weeks. Didn't even look at me. So when he came into my room and lay down next to me, started kissing me and touching me, all I thought was, finally, someone wants me.'

Blake let her silence stretch. If she needed time, he'd give it to her.

She cleared her throat. 'I didn't know what to do when he rolled on top of me. I wasn't ready for sex, but before I could tell him that, he was inside me and the pain was enormous. I looked it up afterwards, and it's not supposed to hurt that much, if at all. But every time, it hurt, because he always went ahead before I was ready.'

He kissed her temple, banking his rage for now. 'He never made you orgasm?'

167

She pressed her face against his shoulder. 'I can't believe I'm talking to you about this, but no, he didn't even try to make it good for me. We fell into a pattern. He'd ignore me for days or weeks until I was on tenterhooks. Then he'd walk in with this certain look and everything inside me would jump. It took me a while to realise it was a mix of fear and a disturbed kind of excitement because he kept coming back. He was the only one who ever came back.'

'He knew you were vulnerable and used it to manipulate you. But you know it's not your fault, don't you? He preyed on you.'

A shudder ripped through her. 'That's not all. He started asking me what I wanted him to do, but he wouldn't do it until I begged him. Before long, he wouldn't do anything until what I begged for was so twisted that I'd throw up afterwards. He'd sit there and laugh at me, because I was pathetic and that's why no one else would ever stick around. Meanwhile, he'd tell people he bought me things. Jewellery, tickets to concerts or shows or equestrian exhibitions. They'd gush over how lucky I was to have such a thoughtful and loving boyfriend. Whenever I tried to stand up to him, he'd tell people I'd sold the jewellery or refused to go out because I was being petulant. The one time I tried to tell someone the truth, I nearly got arrested.'

'How?'

She fiddled with the button of his shirt. 'Someone broke into the bakery. They left one of my earrings behind.'

Blake had to unclench his jaw before he spoke. 'Paul set you up. Did the coward break in himself or get someone else to do it?'

She shook her head. 'His parents are realtors and have keys to nearly every commercial property in town. Those they don't have access to, he'd find a way to get. That's what he told me anyway, after he came in and played the white knight. They let me go. He made sure people kept talking about the break-in, and about me and my need to grow up. After that, if I ever hinted to anyone that he wasn't a nice guy like everyone thought, they'd shake their head and sigh, as if they were saying, *there she goes, being an immature brat again.*'

He glanced at her ears. 'So you stopped wearing earrings. Stopped trying to tell people what was really going on.'

168

She snuggled closer and hugged his hand to her chest. 'I did. I stopped doing a lot of things. No one seemed to care that I didn't go out to parties anymore, didn't go riding, didn't do anything except scrape together a pass in my exams. My whole world revolved around him. His was the only company I kept, when he took notice of me. The only person I had contact with was him. The only human touch I felt was his. I hated it, hated him, but where else could I go? It made it so much harder when I came home to find him in my bed with someone else. I really did snap then. I burnt that bed the next day. Gave the fire brigade an impromptu exercise, and Mark gave me a talking to.'

As though she'd been held up by her secrets and lies and could now rest, her body grew heavy against his.

Holding her close while he rubbed a hand over her back, he kissed the top of her head. 'You didn't tell Mark the truth?'

'No, I'd seen the disappointment on his face the day the bakery was broken into.'

'Will you tell him now?'

'I can't. Not while Paul is still here. Not when he has evidence and I have none.'

'What evidence could he have?'

'A recording. Of me. Begging.'

Blake sighed. 'He abused you, baby. Heart, mind and body. No matter what he thinks he has against you, he's in the wrong. He needs to be exposed.'

'I just want to forget it all and for him to leave me alone.' She lifted her head to stare up at him. 'You know it all now. You know what I did, what he made me do, and you're staying.'

It wasn't quite a statement, so he pressed his lips between her eyebrows. 'I'm staying.'

'Then he can't hurt us. Can we lie down for a bit? I don't think I can take us out to your place yet.'

He slid his phone from his pocket. 'The morning is soon enough. I'll let Drew know.' He typed one handed. *Staying here the night. Make yourself at home.*

Good, and already have. You need milk, and nearly everything else. You have the appetite of a five-year-old.

He huffed a laugh and tossed his phone onto the pile of clothes in the corner of the room. 'You need to sleep. Get into bed, I can take the couch.'

She moved off his lap, taking the blanket with her. 'Would you mind staying in here with me?'

'No problem. Get into bed, snuggle down, and I'll lie next to you.' He stood and flipped the blankets back so she could get in.

Instead of crawling into bed, she stood in front of him, her eyes clear. 'Stay with me, Blake.'

His gut clenched. 'I am. I will.'

In answer, she reached for his jeans and unzipped them. Pushing them down his hips, she traced a finger around the waistband of his boxers. 'Kiss me. Please?'

Desperate to show her what she'd never been given, he cupped her face and kissed her until she shuddered against him. It would be easy to go further, to show her everything, but when she let the blanket fall away, he nudged her to the bed.

'Crawl in. We'll get some sleep and see what the morning brings.'

'I don't want to sleep.' She pushed at his jumper until, giving in, he grabbed it and yanked it over his head with the shirt still inside. Tracing cold fingers across his chest, she licked her lips. 'I got you mostly right when I drew you.'

Her touch was sweet torture, but he'd bear it. 'I need to know what you want, Carol.'

'I want to make love with you. I want to have you touch me, kiss me. I want you inside me. I want you to show me what it's like to have an orgasm.' She ran her tongue over his nipple. 'Does that cover it?'

'You've jumped from exhausted to aroused so quickly. I need you to be sure, because this isn't going to be one-sided. You're going to be right there with me the whole time.'

'Yes. I'm sure.' She sucked on his other nipple and made his eyes roll back.

'It's not going to be quick, either.' Grabbing her hips, he pulled her close so that he throbbed against her. 'This doesn't come into it until well down the track. Think you can handle that?'

Her smile made her dimple pop and burned the fatigue from her eyes. 'I'm willing to find out.'

Picking her up, he tumbled with her onto the bed and started with a kiss that he hoped would show her everything she meant to him. But would it be enough to convince her that before, during and after, he'd be the one to hold her, the one to stay? Would she believe him if he told her he loved her?

CHAPTER 12

With one kiss, Blake destroyed every false notion Carol had about what should happen between two people.

It sprinted through her—the fear, the joy, the excitement of touching him, his weight holding her down. He'd move if she asked. He'd slow down if that's what she needed.

'You're thinking.' He nipped along her jaw. 'You need to be feeling.'

Running her fingers over his ribs, his muscles bunching under her palms as she pressed them flat against his chest, she lifted her chin. 'I know that you'd stop if I asked. You'd let me explore you as much as you do me. You won't hold anything back, and it's terrifying.'

He lifted his head to stare down at her. 'It's not supposed to be.'

She smiled as he braced his hands either side of her head, his eyes dark, his breath fast and uneven. 'You're magnificent, you know that?' She traced the line of muscles down his sides to his hips. 'I've never touched anyone like this.' With her eyes on his, she trailed her hands over the boxers he still wore. 'You make me feel powerful.'

'That's because you are.' He groaned and dropped his forehead to hers as she continued to memorise his body with her hands. 'And beautiful.' But he didn't touch her, just hung above her, shaking.

'Will you touch me, Blake? Please?'

As though she'd flipped a switch, he moved. With his hands, his mouth, he found places she never knew could make her groan, make her insides shake. Heat gathered low in her belly, intensified beyond any pleasure she'd ever been able to give herself.

Fear plunged back. What if it was too much? What if he gave her so much that she couldn't let go?

His mouth came back to hers while his fingers kept her high up on that edge. 'Stay with me. Hold onto me.'

Close to tears, she threw her arms around his neck and hung on. Lost in him, in his kiss that demanded she answer with everything she had, she let go, giving him all and trusting him to catch her. It flashed through her, bowed her against him and left her shaking.

'I've got you.' Kissing her throat, he hummed, his fingers gently stroking. 'I love the taste of you, the feel of you.'

'I can't think.' She could only feel the low edge he kept her on as his mouth cruised down her body, stopping at places that made her gasp. And when his mouth replaced his fingers, she bowed up. 'I don't know if I can again.'

'Do you want to?'

'I want you.'

He nipped her thigh. 'You'll get me, but I want to give you this. Do you want it?'

'With you, I want everything.'

'Good.' His movements achingly slow, he brought her back to that peak.

And this time, she took the jump running and flew even as he slid up her body to wrap around her.

'I want to taste you,' she said. 'I want to know I can make you forget everything.'

He brushed the damp hair from her face. 'You do. I can hardly think around you at the best of times. It's taking everything I have not to kick these boxers off and be inside you.'

'But you won't?'

'No, I won't, because I want more with you. I want this to last as long as it can.'

Which meant she wouldn't get to touch him as she craved. 'You can only do it once a night?'

His eyebrow rose. 'A challenge? Okay. I'm all yours.' He rolled onto his back and pillowed his hands behind his head.

He'd expect her to go straight for the prize, but she'd learned from him already. Following his lead, she straddled him, pressed her mouth to his and deepened the kiss when his lips parted. Emboldened with the power he gave her, she tested muscle and flesh with teeth and tongue, soothed with fingers and lips until his skin turned salty.

By the time she reached his boxers, he was panting, his breath rasping harshly. Holding his gaze, she cupped him through the material. 'You make me want so much.'

He sat up and captured her face in his hands. 'Anything I can give you, I will. I never thought I'd find what I have with you.'

'And anything *I* can give *you*, I will.' She kissed him as she stroked him. Swallowed his groan when she slipped her hand under his boxers. Shivered when his fingers found her again. Matching her movements to the roll of his hips, she let instinct take over.

'I need you to come.' His teeth found her shoulder.

She bowed against him, squeezed him on the final downward stroke. Then his arms were around her, holding her tighter than anyone ever had, his face pressed between her breasts. Wrapping her arms around his head, she rocked them both, crooned to him as she pressed kisses to the top of his head.

She swallowed the words on the tip of her tongue. She loved very few people. Had spoken those words to fewer still. Did speaking them count in the afterglow of an experience like this? When the sun rose and a new day began, would they mean less? Could she risk saying them if there was a chance that she'd receive silence as an answer?

'Let me grab the blanket before we both freeze.' Blake nudged her back a bit, then looked down at himself. 'Do you have any tissues?'

Glad for the distraction, she used his shoulder for balance as she moved off him, stood for a moment to make sure her legs would hold her, then passed him the tissue box. 'Here. I'm going to get some water, if you want some.'

'I do.' He balled up the tissues and threw them into the bin in the corner. 'Hey,' he caught her hand as she turned away, 'was I too rough?'

She smiled. 'No. I just need to get my breath back.'

174

He leaned over the edge of the bed for the blanket. 'Okay. You know we're not finished yet, don't you?' Then he stopped. 'Shit.'

'What? What's wrong?'

'It's okay. It's just that I brought condoms but left them in the glove box of the ute.' He glanced at the alarm clock on her bedside table. 'It's nearly nine. The supermarket might still be open.'

'Not in winter it won't be, but I have some. That was one thing I won an argument about. Babies before marriage would have been more of a scandal than even he could handle.'

'He better hope I don't see him for a while.' But he cupped her chin and kissed her. 'Here.' He picked up his jumper and, tugging the shirt free, slipped it over her head. 'I figure you might as well add another one to your collection.'

'I've been sleeping in your Mothman jumper.'

His grin grew as he flicked the blanket over the bed and got in. 'Really? And have you been dreaming about me?'

She had to bite her lip. 'You'll never know.'

'Carol,' he called when she got to the door. 'I dream about you, but being with you is better. I want to stay with you, though I doubt I'll stop dreaming about you.'

Glancing at him over her shoulder, she nodded. 'I doubt I'll stop, either.'

His chuckle followed her down the hallway to the kitchen where she drank the first glass of water in one go. The second she drank slower, then filled the cup again. In the bathroom, she found the box of condoms she'd jammed behind her pink hair dye. Taking them back to the bedroom, she stopped short when she saw the sketchbook Blake had in his lap.

'I haven't opened it yet and that alone should get me on Santa's nice list again.' He took the glass she handed him and gulped its contents down. 'Do you mind if I do?'

She could say no or give him a sketchbook that didn't feature him on nearly every page, but she shook her head. 'Just ...'

What? Don't laugh? Don't judge? He wouldn't anyway.

'I haven't shown anyone else.' She sat the box of condoms on the bedside table, and the indecision on his face as he eyed them made her want to smile.

But he patted the bed beside him. 'Are you just going to stand there or get in here with me?'

In answer, she pulled the jumper over her head. This time it was impossible to hide her grin at the conflict she'd stirred in him.

'Hmm. We'll get to that.' He opened the sketchbook to Snow's laughing face.

Leaving him to it, Carol crawled into bed and snuggled her back against his hip. The need in her belly settled as her body relaxed and Blake's voice floated around her. When she woke, the room was dark, and Blake held her close against his chest, his leg between hers and his breath on her nape. How many firsts could she experience in one night?

And how good, how right did it feel to have him plastered against her back, his warmth and scent imprinted on her. Blake had taken pleasure in her body, but he'd made sure she was right there with him and that they were together at the end. The wonder of it hit her as she replayed the way his voice had vibrated with effort and need. The way his teeth had found the exact spot to push her over the edge. The way he hadn't wanted to leap over until she had.

Heat dropped from her belly to her core. Squeezing her thighs together only made it worse, so she closed her eyes again and tried to relax.

Would things change when they both woke? Would they share such an emotional connection the next time they had sex? Would he always be as considerate as he had been earlier? He'd said they weren't finished, but was that because she hadn't satisfied him? Or was it because they both wanted more? That thought sent a quick thrill through her.

Blake's arm tightened around her. 'You think too loud for someone so small.'

The urge to wiggle against him, to share the need that built up with each breath he feathered against her neck, became almost impossible to control. 'Sorry.'

He nuzzled her shoulder. 'You know it's not begging if you ask for what you want, don't you? I'd like to know you want me as much as I want you.'

'I do want you.' She blurted the words before she could swallow them. 'I went to sleep wanting you, and I woke wrapped in you, wanting you.'

176

He pressed his pelvis against her, the hot throb of him stoking her need to burning. 'No, don't move.'

Cold washed over her as he reached back and grabbed the box of condoms, wrestled with it one-handed, his other arm snug under her head.

'I just want one,' he muttered, making her laugh.

'Do you need a hand?'

'Not yet.' He tipped the condoms on the bed beside her and threw the empty box on the floor.

'Ambitious?'

'Let's find out.' He ran his hand down her side to her hip and along her thigh. Nudging her leg with his knee, he guided it up and back to drape over his hip, opening her, then trailed his fingers up her leg once more and brushed them over her.

Her breath rushed out, then hitched when he began to stroke her. Dip and stroke until she panted his name as she freefell.

'I want you.' She patted the blankets until she found a condom, then rolling to her back, she ripped it open with her teeth. She watched him as she rolled it on, then stroked him as he had her, long and slow. Tortuously.

Still gripping him, she pushed him to his back and straddled him. 'Tell me you want me.'

'More than life.' He gripped her hips but didn't thrust, just balanced her above him as she slowly sank onto him.

If there was a heaven, this was what it would feel like. The glorious slide of him filling her, radiating the need and euphoria to her fingertips and toes until she was nearly bursting with it. She pulled back, sank again.

His whole body arched, then he held her still and breathed deep. 'Give me a second. You feel incredible.'

'So do you.' She leaned forward and kissed his chin, his mouth, and sank deeper onto him, into him.

They started slow, their hips undulating, almost lazily, their breaths hitching as need pushed their movements into a rush of hands over damp skin, of mouths tasting and teeth scraping. When he scissored up and took her breast in his mouth, she threw her head back and groaned his name.

'Again.' He pushed a hand between them. 'Again.'

She had no choice but didn't care; her whole body flashed with the heat of her orgasm. Still, she craved, needed him.

'More.' She hooked an arm around his neck and pulled him with her onto the bed.

With a grunt, and some finessing, he settled between her thighs, his mouth on her shoulders, her breasts, her neck. And still he moved, slid a hand under her and hitched her hips higher.

She hooked her legs around him, meeting him thrust for thrust, and unbelievably, the heat gathered again. This time, she clamped her teeth on his neck, sending them both over.

She swallowed the tears that burned her throat. Everything she'd believed about sex, intimacy, even her body, had been a lie. How did she reconcile that? And how could she tell herself she'd rather be alone when the weight of him comforted, and the stroke of his hand along her side spun wishes of waking like this with him every morning. And not just for the sex, but for the way he looked down at her, for that slow smile that made her answer in kind. For the ease with which she talked to him about her darkest fears and secrets. For the temper that burst through him in defence of her. And for all that she could give him in return.

Swamped with emotions, she pressed her hands to his face. 'It scares me that you make me feel things I didn't want to feel.'

Blake kissed her. 'You make me feel things I didn't think I'd find in this lifetime. I think, for now, feeling them is enough.'

Digging deep for levity, she smiled. 'Want to know what else I feel?'

He cocked an eyebrow, let his gaze skim down her body. 'You might have to give me a minute.'

It made her laugh, loosened the weight on her chest enough for her to push at his until he flopped to his back.

'Hungry,' she said. 'I feel hungry, and I bet Snow is going to tell me off when I get out there.'

'I can fix us some breakfast while you appease the dog.'

'There are some eggs in the fridge, bacon in the freezer.'

There wasn't much else, though, because she'd been taking ingredients out to his place to cook. She was amazed that she still felt so at home out

178

there, even now that it was Blake's. She'd lived in *this* house for the past four and a half years, but it had never felt like hers, even with her things, her memories scattered around. It had always been a temporary place to live until she could buy Gran's home. The future she'd been preparing for, striving for since Paul had broken her, stretched long and lonely. She'd accepted that she'd grow old alone with only a succession of pets to gauge the passing of time.

Now, that vision wasn't enough. And Blake was to blame.

#

Blake held Carol's hand as they walked the aisles and filled a basket with food.

'I think we made the late breakfast up to Snow.' He grinned at the jam she added to the mostly healthy load he carried. 'He finally figured out the fetch thing.'

Her dimples popped. 'Having you race him for the ball helped.'

And it had made her laugh, so he'd played with the dog until they'd both fallen at her feet. She'd rewarded the dog with a belly rub, and when he'd complained about being left out, she'd straddled him, right there in the back-yard with the sun blinking between the clouds, and had kissed him until he'd forgotten his own name.

'It was worth it.' He slipped a box of Coco Pops into the basket and shrugged at her look. 'You don't have to eat them.'

She shook her head but grinned. 'I bet Drew fights you for them.'

'No chance. I'll hide them.'

'Hmm.' She nodded to a woman pushing a trolley with a sleeping baby in the carrier as they turned for the next aisle. 'Do you have tissues?'

'Good question.' He let go of her hand and grabbed a box of extra-large tissues. Then, pausing, he glanced at her and grabbed another box.

Her eyes were bright as she bit her lip. 'Ambitious?'

He pulled her against him, loved it when her arms went around his waist. 'I've got a taste for you now, and I know you've got a taste for me.'

Rising up onto her toes, Carol kissed his cheek. 'I do.'

He nuzzled the side of her neck. 'Then we'll be indulging in each other. And there's nothing wrong with being decadent in the clean-up.'

Someone cleared their throat nearby. Carol jolted and slipped her hand into Blake's, gripping his tightly as she turned to see who had made the sound.

Blake gave her fingers a reassuring squeeze, then relaxed when he recognised the man. Biker Beard, who still looked more like a character out of a Mad Max movie rather than an art teacher, gazed down at their joined hands and then back to Carol.

Blake stuck out his free hand. 'I'm a bit embarrassed. I never thought to ask your name the other night,' he said to fill Carol's silence. 'I've been meaning to catch up with you, I just haven't had the time.'

Biker Beard shook Blake's hand and smiled at them both, though he mostly kept his eye on an oddly silent Carol, who didn't quite meet his gaze. 'My students know me as Mr Arden. But as I keep telling Carol, though she can't seem to bring herself to do it, you can call me Marley.' He threaded his fingers through his beard. 'And as for other things I've told you, Carol, my wife pointed out that the attempted words of wisdom I offered you yesterday could be taken two ways. And now that I'm talking to you, I think that maybe you misinterpreted my meaning.'

Blake glanced at Carol and wondered what had been said. Whatever it was, it now made Carol duck her head and rub her chest.

Marley cleared his throat. 'I meant it when I said I'm always here if you need to talk, but when I warned you about bottling things up and doing something you might regret, I was imagining you punching that little jerk and getting yourself arrested for assault.'

Carol's mouth dropped open. 'You don't like Paul?'

Marley dipped his head and raised bushy eyebrows. 'I was his teacher for four years and yours for longer. I didn't like the way he talked to you yesterday, and I'll be telling his parents as much at our Lions meeting tonight.'

Carol's hand jerked in Blake's. He raised it to his mouth and pressed a kiss to her knuckles.

She glanced at him, a mixture of relief and embarrassment twisting her lips before she faced Marley again. 'It's reassuring to know that not everyone thinks he's a saint.'

Marley rumbled a laugh. 'He might think he's fooled us all, but let me tell you, not everyone believes he's the thoughtful, selfless, loving person he tries to convince us he is.' He tapped his nose. 'You can't make a silk purse out of a sow's ear.'

At Carol's blank stare, Marley laughed again. 'He can talk and dress as fancy as he wants, but he'll never live up to the Todd name. He's slick and selfish. Always has been, always will be. But he is a Todd, and unfortunately, the name affords him a status he doesn't deserve, so as much as you might want to punch him, I'd advise you against it, because he would no doubt find a way to make you even more miserable than he already has.'

Blake rubbed Carol's back. It must be a double blow, to have someone she looked up to confirm that Paul Todd was a selfish bastard but, in the same breath, tell her she couldn't stop him. Blake was tempted to set the record straight and tell Marley exactly what Paul had done, but as much as he wanted to, it wasn't his place.

Carol pushed her hair off her face. 'I'm just glad you don't think I'm the sow's ear.'

When Marley's laugh tumbled out, Carol smiled. It wasn't the carefree one that popped her dimple, or the lopsided one she often gave Blake in answer to one of his jokes, but a small self-conscious one that made him wrap his arms around her shoulder and hold her close.

Marley wiped his eyes and pointed at Blake. 'Now that's sorted, I need to change the subject. Will we see you on the weekend? The Wattle Yard Art Group would be excited to have you join us.'

Carol hissed a breath. 'I forgot to tell him.'

Marley clucked his tongue. 'You were rattled yesterday, and I'm sorry I added to it. I hope you can forgive my fumbled attempt to comfort you.'

Carol shook her head. 'Of course I can.' She tipped her face up to Blake, her dimple flashing. 'You'll enjoy the art group. Mr Arden and the others tell your kind of jokes. They think they're hilarious too.'

Blake smiled and dropped a quick kiss on her mouth, smothering her feigned irritation before turning back to Marley. 'I'd love to join you all.'

Marley's beard twitched with his grin. 'Excellent. I look forward to seeing you both.' With another chuckle, he walked away, whistling Katy Perry's 'Roar'.

Carol stared after her former teacher. 'He'll check every week whether we plan on going to the meeting. And that I'm not thinking about punching Paul.'

Blake kept her hand in his as they made their way along the aisle. 'He cares about you. And as for not thinking about punching Paul, he'd better start checking in with me, too.'

Her disbelieving huff made him tug her to a stop. 'You don't believe Marley cares about you, or that I may have a hankering for punching Paul?'

If she couldn't believe either of those truths, what hope did he have of convincing her that he loved her?

Before she could chew up the words she obviously wanted to spit out, his phone buzzed in his pocket. Pulling it out, he kept his gaze on hers. 'This is Blake.'

'Blake. Mark Jones. There's no emergency, but I need you to come into town as soon as you can.'

Instinct had him walking to the shop's windows. Over the road and half-way down the next block, a crowd gathered between the bakery and the town hall. 'What's happened? Is my mum okay?'

'As far as I know, she's fine. I'd like you to come to the town hall. There's been an incident with your displayed artwork, and I'd like to ask you some questions.'

An incident? 'What happened? How bad is it?'

'I'll fill you in when you get here.'

Blake sighed. 'Okay. I'm in Foodworks with Carol. I can be there in a couple of minutes.'

A pause. 'Okay. Can I speak to her?'

Hating the dread that chased the light from her eyes, Blake handed Carol the phone. 'It's Mark.'

After saying hello, she listened, her confused frown deepening until she said goodbye, then she hung up and handed him his phone. 'He wants me to wait for you in Ethan's office. There's the usual whispering crowd gathering along the street, and he doesn't want me caught up in it before he can talk to me.'

Blake reached for her hand. 'Caught up in it? What's that supposed to mean? And why does he want to talk to you?'

She curled her hair behind her ears. 'I don't wear earrings anymore.'

He frowned. 'You don't …? Shit.' Panic spiked when she took a step back. 'You didn't do anything, I know that. Even if I hadn't been with you all night, I'd know it wasn't you.'

She stared through him, her arms stiff at her sides and her shoulders slumped. 'It doesn't matter.' Woodenly, she took the basket from him, then stepped out of reach. 'I hope the damage isn't as bad as you think.'

It already was, but it had nothing to do with his artwork and everything to do with the woman about to walk away from him.

Terrified that if he didn't try, he'd lose her, he grabbed the basket to stop her. 'This probably isn't the time to tell you, but I'm falling for you. Hard.'

He held his breath as she closed her eyes.

When she opened them, she looked at him. 'You need to go and deal with Mark so you can get your artwork home and fix it.'

What he needed to fix, he couldn't. All he could do was let her go, for now, and hope that she believed him. 'Don't let *this*, whatever you're thinking and feeling right now, get between us. Please.'

Stepping up to him, she kissed him. 'I can't name what I'm feeling for you. I only know that it terrifies me, especially when it could be ripped away before I can get it under control.'

He threaded his fingers through her hair. 'Don't control it. Trust it. Trust me.'

Her struggle flickered in her eyes and cut him at the knees.

'I'll wait for you,' he said. 'Once I've talked to Mark, I'll wait for you.'

She shook her head. 'I've done this before. You'll need to get home before half the town wants to interview you.' She patted his chest, her smile little more than a sad twitch. 'Call Drew. Don't worry about me.'

But all he did was worry as he strode down the road to the town hall. How couldn't he? Whatever damage had been done to his artwork could be fixed, but his relationship with Carol? It felt as if they were right back at the start, and just when he'd begun to convince her to trust what they could be together.

Now, she expected him to what? Walk away? Think she'd done something wrong? Abandon her to the lies that would spread?

Instead of losing his mind over it all, he pulled out his phone and called Drew. Listening to his friend hiss a litany of creative curses should have lifted some of the weight, but Blake's boots dragged as he approached the crowd speculating on the closure of the town hall.

Ignoring the whispers and people calling his name, he made his way up the steps to the wide glass doors. Inside, someone had pulled concertina partitions across, blocking the crowd's view of the crime scene. Conscious of the dozen or so people watching for any sort of reaction, he raised a hand and knocked lightly, keeping his face neutral while he waited.

Mark opened the door and locked it again behind Blake. 'This way.'

Bracing for the chaos of a break-in, Blake followed Mark around the partition, then shoved his hands in his pockets when he surveyed the damage. 'He only vandalised one?'

It was still one too many, but of the eight works on display, all of them large and intricate, the one he'd called *Home* would be easiest to fix. And now, through morbid curiosity, it would probably fetch a higher price at the auction. Glad that the money would go to charity, Blake stepped as close as he dared to the ruined piece.

Mark took out a pen and a little black notebook. 'Why did you say *he*? Who do you think did this?'

Blake shot him a glare. The rips and dents in the art piece were obviously deliberate but also had a desperate, chilling edge—and if Mark didn't see that, he wasn't much of a cop.

'We both know who did this,' said Blake. 'And he'll spread rumours that it was her. He'll lie and make up some bullshit story like he did with the bakery break-in.'

Mark's carefully controlled cop face cracked, showing he was also a worried friend. 'She told you about that?'

Blake rubbed the back of his neck. 'She told me everything last night. But now I'm going to struggle to get her to listen to me, let alone say anything back. And you're keeping something from me, because I know he left something behind to incriminate her.'

Mark said nothing.

Blake paced. 'Fine. How long until I can take that back home?' He jabbed a finger at the piece lying on the floor.

Mark pointed to a couple of seats off to the side. 'Soon. I still need to ask you some questions.'

Not wanting to sit, Blake crossed his arms over his chest. 'Ask away.'

With a shake of his head, Mark stood at ease, his pen poised over his notebook. 'I'm officially asking you, who would have something against you and why?'

Blake raised an eyebrow. 'Just one person. Paul Todd. He wants Carol. She's with me.'

As though he didn't know already, Mark noted it down. 'Has he threatened you?'

How much did he say without stepping over a line that Carol couldn't forgive?

'Not me, no,' he said carefully. 'He went to see Carol at work yesterday, but it's not for me to tell you about that. She needs to. She needs to decide to tell you.'

Again, Mark said nothing. His frown, though, spoke volumes.

Blake rubbed at the headache forming. 'She's waiting for you to question her.'

But she hadn't wanted Blake to wait for her. As angry as he was at the senseless vandalism, the bone-chilling fear he felt that she might use this incident as a reason to stay away nearly choked him.

His phone buzzed with a text, though not from Carol. He turned his phone for Mark to see. 'Drew's out front.'

Mark slid his pen and notebook away and walked to the partition. 'I'll keep everyone clear until you're loaded up. And Blake, let me know if you hear anything else.'

Blake stayed where he was until Drew walked in.

'Well, shit.' Crossing his arms and planting his feet, Drew surveyed the damaged piece. He tilted his head at Blake. 'You don't seem too upset.'

Blake stood beside him. 'I'm livid, for more reasons than you can imagine. But I can't make a big deal out of this or the bastard wins.'

Drew turned to stare at him. 'You know who did this?'

Blake gritted his teeth. 'Yeah, I do. It was done to get at Carol more than it was me. And it's worked.'

'Sounds like whoever did it is an arsehole.'

Shoving a hand through his hair, Blake puffed out a breath. 'He's that and more. But this isn't the time or place to get into it. Let's get this loaded and head home.'

And if Carol didn't come to him, he'd go to her, because he refused to let her carry the blame, or the shame, for something she didn't do. And no way was he letting her sacrifice what she could have, just because his artwork had been damaged. Because that's what she would do. What she'd been doing for most of her life.

Now, though, she had him and he had her. Together, they'd face Paul and his scare tactics. And Blake was determined to win.

CHAPTER 13

Carol took her time walking to the town hall. Maybe she'd built up drama where there was none. Maybe someone else had broken into the building and made a mess of everything, and Blake's artwork had just been in the wrong place at the wrong time. But after the second person to walk towards Carol gave her a wide berth after she'd smiled at them, she couldn't hold onto the fantasy. She'd lived through this before after the bakery break-in. Parents had hugged their children closer, as though she might have snatched them away. Women had clamped their handbags under their arms, their hands tight on the straps. Men had winked and called her light fingers. Her skin might be thicker now, but her heart ached just the same.

Still, she lifted her chin as she reached the crowd of people standing in groups of three and four outside the town hall. Mark had told her to go straight to Ethan's office, but she had nothing to hide, nothing to be ashamed of, even if her pulse said otherwise. She had proof that she didn't destroy Blake's artwork and that the break-in didn't have anything to do with her. Except it did, because Paul had done this to hurt her. And he'd hurt Blake as well. It had to stop; she'd put up with his phone calls, the photos, his unwelcome visits and his hands on her, but to bring Blake into it like this? She couldn't stand by and let him do it again.

Blake was falling for her. She'd told him the truth, that she didn't know what she felt for him; saying it aloud was brilliantly freeing and terrifyingly suffocating at the same time. He let her breathe, but how could she catch her breath when he took it so easily? He gave her room and space to be herself, but she wanted him close, wanted his smile, his laughter, the intense stare he

187

levelled her with when she spoke. She wanted his thoughts, his dreams and for his future to mingle with hers …

She was falling for him. *Had* fallen. During that first horse ride? Or while they'd painted the house that was now his home? Did it matter? She put a hand to her chest. Her heart beat a steady rhythm. Where was the gallop? Her fear?

She needed to tell Blake. He deserved to know how she felt and that she wouldn't let Paul's attempt to control her come between them.

But as she made her way through the crowd, a woman to whom Carol had served Sunday roast at the pub for the last four years turned to her.

'How can you even show your face here?' the woman sneered. 'And a tip? If you're going to get revenge, don't leave behind hair that incriminates you.'

Carol lifted a shaking hand to her head. 'I didn't do this. I didn't do anything.'

Ethan strode towards her from the ugly brown building that held his office. 'Don't say anything else.'

Gaping at him, Carol let him lead her away. Only when they were back in his office did she close her mouth and swallow. 'Do you realise how guilty you just made me look?'

He sat behind his desk and pointed to the seat opposite. 'About as guilty as you already look?'

Her legs gave way, and she collapsed into the chair. 'To you? I look guilty to you?'

He said nothing, just sat with his fingers clasped against his stomach, waiting. Waiting for her to incriminate herself?

'Why am I here?'

But before he could answer, Kelsey burst into the room, her face flushed and her hair wild. Her eyes, though, sharp green fired with gold, were what had Carol standing and holding out her hands.

Kelsey pointed a shaking finger at her. 'I don't know what happened between you and Blake, but this wasn't the answer. Why didn't you come to me if something was wrong? How could you be so reckless and so uncaring of someone else's property?'

188

Carol sank back onto the chair. Afraid it wouldn't hold her weight now, she braced her elbows on the desk and rested her forehead in her hands. 'Do you really think I could do this?'

Ethan and Kelsey stayed silent, which suited her. How could they think this of her?

'Am I really such a bad person that you'd believe I could hurt him like this?' She lifted her head to stare at Ethan, then Kelsey. 'How could you even think that?'

Kelsey took a step towards her. 'I've avoided Paul because he hurt you, but all I hear from him is that he's worried about your mental health and wants to help you. Everyone is talking about you stalking Paul, how you hit him and have been using Blake to make Paul jealous.'

Her words ripped Carol's heart out. 'And you believe them? You believe him?'

'You aren't telling me any different. In fact, you're showing me that it's true. You've been erratic, forgetful, angry. And worst of all, you've been keeping secrets.' Kelsey knelt in front of Carol and took her hand. 'I've been worried about you too, and I want to help. I just need to know the truth.'

Carol was sitting in Ethan's office losing her best friend because she'd threatened Paul. What would he do if she told Ethan and Kelsey everything? Because he'd find out she told the truth. If Ethan knew, he'd dig until he discovered all of Paul Todd's secrets. He'd confront him and whatever happened afterwards would be on her head.

She shuddered. 'How long before Mark gets here?'

Kelsey's shoulders sagged. Standing, she crossed to Ethan and leaned against him.

Ethan put an arm around her waist. 'I don't know,' he told Carol. 'He only asked if he could talk to you in here.'

Carol nodded, her fingers and jaw refusing to work, just like on the mornings she jogged with Snow through the frost.

Detached from the pain rocketing through her, she leaned back in the chair and rested her fists on her thighs. 'Do you trust me not to run?'

Ethan frowned. 'Where would you go?'

She huffed a laugh. 'Exactly.'

If she went anywhere, she'd go to Blake's, but would she be welcome there now? He'd spent the night with her, but had they formed a connection strong enough for him to believe her? Or would he, after listening to everyone else's version of events, think she'd played him? Before this moment, she hadn't been worried, but if two of the people who knew her best believed she could carry out such a low act, anything was possible.

'I'd rather wait alone,' she said. 'If you trust me, I'll go to the tearoom.'

When Ethan only nodded, she pushed to her feet and walked to the door.

'Carol?' Kelsey came to stand beside her. 'If you tell me you didn't do this, I'll believe you. Because even though you're keeping secrets, I know you wouldn't lie to me about this.'

Holding Kelsey's gaze, Carol held back tears that would drown her. 'I didn't do it.'

'Okay,' said Kelsey, then took a deep breath. 'I have kinder duty this morning, but I'd like it if you came out this afternoon so we can talk.'

Carol could say no, but she'd do more damage to their friendship than she already had, and Kelsey didn't deserve that any more than Carol deserved being blamed for something she didn't do. 'Okay.'

Kelsey drew her in for a hug. 'I'll drop your shopping off for you.'

Though Carol searched for it, she couldn't find the warmth Kelsey's embrace usually held, so she stepped back. 'It's Blake's.'

'Then I'll take them home,' said Kelsey, picking up the bags. 'You can collect them from there.'

Silence hung over the tearoom as Carol sat alone. Living in her own space, she'd become used to talking to Snow, and over the last few weeks, she'd adjusted and enjoyed talking to Blake. She'd even looked forward to Drew's teasing. But now she had nothing to give and no one to listen, even if she did have anything to say. So she sat and dog-eared every page of the magazine that had been left on the table.

By the time Mark walked in, she'd smoothed them all out again, had paced a dozen laps of the table and convinced herself not to throw up until she got home. Her stomach lurched as Mark pointed to a seat.

She stood her ground. 'Are you arresting me?'

He hooked his thumbs in his vest. 'No, I'm just here to talk.'

There was a knock on the door, then Mrs Glade stepped in. 'I'd like to sit with Carol. She didn't have proper representation last time, so I'd like to make sure she does now.'

Carol closed her eyes. Did everyone think she was guilty? 'I don't need representation because I did nothing wrong.'

Mark sat and pulled out his little black notebook. 'You don't need representation because I'm not interviewing you, but if you'd like support and company, then you're welcome to have Mrs Glade stay.'

What support could someone offer if they already thought she was guilty? 'I don't care either way.'

Obviously taking that as an invitation, Mrs Glade sat at the table, her back straight and hands folded in front of her.

'Now, Senior Constable Jones, I'd like to say something first.' She turned to Carol. 'I hope you don't think I'm invading your privacy, but I saw Blake's friend drop him off last night and you and Blake in the backyard this morning.'

Carol opened her mouth, then closed it again. She wouldn't be ashamed of the night she'd spent with Blake—she had no reason to be—but discussing it with Mark and Mrs Glade would make it seem cheap and dirty. It had been neither, and she wanted to keep the memory of it crisp and clean, full of colour and texture, and the scents and sounds just between her and Blake.

'He stayed the night, yes.' It was all she was prepared to admit.

Mark merely nodded. 'And you didn't go out at all?'

It was his job to ask questions, but the cut sliced deep. She had to put it away, roll it up like a rug and store it somewhere so she could defend her innocence.

'No, I didn't,' she said, lifting her chin. 'I didn't do this, Mark. I couldn't do that to Blake, or to myself. I don't lash out to hurt people, I'd rather ignore them.'

Mark held her gaze for a long moment. 'Who are you ignoring?'

He'd offered her an opening. Should she take it? Could she afford not to? Paul had already set up his gauntlet of lies against her. She had to tell someone the truth. Mark believed her about the bakery now, so could he see past the latest rumours?

'Paul,' she admitted. 'I have no proof, but he's been stalking me.'

Mark's face blanked. 'Stalking you?'

The urge to fidget or squirm under his cold stare overrode any shame she felt. 'I've been getting prank calls since he came back. And texts. And pictures.'

Mark raised an eyebrow and held out his hand.

Carol gritted her teeth but pulled out her phone and scrolled to the conversation. 'They've been coming from a private number, and there's nothing in the calls or pictures that could be considered harassment or incriminating, so I couldn't report it.'

He flicked her a glare as he scrolled through the one-sided stream of texts and pictures. 'And when I asked you to come and talk to me, after I told you I could help, you didn't think to tell me about this?'

She squirmed. 'At the time, no.'

His sigh hurt her heart. Whatever she did, she disappointed him.

'I'm sorry.'

He handed her phone back. 'Send me screen shots of everything. And consider what else you should be telling me so I can do my job.'

What did Mark know? Had Blake said something to him? Had he betrayed her confidence? A spark of anger flared, but she couldn't hold on to the feeling. Sick of hiding the lies that should be Paul's shame, she glanced at Mrs Glade before turning back to Mark.

'He's spoken to me a few times and said nasty things. He gripped the back of my neck one night.' She put her hand to the spot. 'That's why Snow barked at him.'

Mark held her gaze but stayed silent. She hated how he could do that, just sit calmly and wait her out. But two could play at that game, so she set her jaw and stared back at him. And only lasted until the count of twenty.

'Okay, fine. He came into work yesterday and harassed me.' She told him about how Paul had followed her into the empty dining room at the pub.

Slowly, Mark leaned close. 'Let me get this straight. Over the past three weeks, you've suspected that Paul Todd has been prank-calling you and sending you photos of yourself. But not only that, he cornered you in a room by yourself, effectively holding you against your will, and harassed you verbally and physically, and you've said nothing?'

She hung her head. 'It sounds worse when you say it like that.'

Mark shoved to his feet. 'Sounds worse? Worse than what? Why the hell didn't you mention it when we talked about this? Did you think there was nothing wrong with what's been happening to you? Did you think I wouldn't do something to stop it?' He dropped back into the seat beside hers. 'Or didn't you trust me to help you?'

Carol stared at the name badge on his chest. 'I didn't have evidence that it was him.'

Mark swore. 'So you didn't trust me.'

She lifted her gaze to his, unable to voice the words.

'Is there anything else you need to tell me?'

Carol fisted her hands. Her friends were unsure of her innocence because she'd tried to defy Paul. And he still had the recording to use against her. The truth sat like a hot coal in her throat. Two scenarios lay before her. She could tell Mark and hope he believed her enough to stop Paul, or she could tell Mark only to have Paul turn everyone against her. In that version of the future, she'd have no chance of redemption.

And what about Blake? Paul had plans for him now too. She didn't doubt that for a second.

'There's nothing more I can say right now,' she said.

Mark's shoulders sagged. 'Which means there is more but you won't tell me about it.'

Unable to hold his gaze, she pulled the magazine closer again and dog-eared more pages. 'So what happens now?'

He tapped the table until she looked at him. 'I need to look at some CCTV footage and talk to people. Then I keep investigating until I find out who broke in and vandalised the artwork.'

It was more information than she'd expected from the man who never gave anything away about his work. And though his transparency smoothed away some of the hurt, the rest dragged behind her as she walked home.

Jex was waiting in her driveway, her motorbike parked next to his car. He held his arms open, and on a sob, she walked into them.

He held on while he rocked her and murmured in her ear. 'It'll be okay. You'll see, it'll be okay.'

#

Blake's stomach grumbled, but nothing in his fridge appealed, so he snapped the door closed. He wouldn't find what he wanted in there. And he wouldn't find the person he wanted sitting at his table or stealing one of his jumpers, making him smile because she knew he needed it.

He'd come out of the town hall to whispers and bold questions. Mark had been wise to ask Carol to go to Ethan's office; at least she wouldn't have experienced the animosity and finger-pointing.

Drew dropped the magazine he was reading onto the table. 'If you open that fridge one more time, I'm taking the door off its hinges.'

Fisting his hand an inch from the handle, Blake sighed. 'What am I supposed to do?'

Drew pushed away from the table and put his empty mug in the sink. 'Do what you usually do.'

When Blake turned to stare at him, Drew shrugged. 'Work. You always worked harder when something was bothering you. Hence why you were always employee of the month.'

Blake scowled. 'Not every month.'

But Drew was right. Waiting for Carol to come over or to contact him was driving him crazy. He needed to do something to distract himself from the gut-clenching rage that gripped him. Leaving Drew to his own devises, Blake rugged up, stomped down to the shed and blasted AC/DC so loudly that it competed with the scream of the grinder.

The chaotic sound of music and power tools helped him order his thoughts and calmed the need to break something just to see it shatter. For Blake, violence rarely raised its hand as a solution, but as his hammer reshaped crumpled metal and his grinder shot red-hot sparks around his legs, he imagined what he'd do the next time Paul's smug face came within striking distance.

194

He knew it wouldn't help, that it would only jeopardise what he'd been building with Carol. Still, he could dismember the bastard in his mind without hurting anyone, least of all Carol. She'd been the one targeted, even though it was his work that'd been damaged, and he'd be damned if he added to the pain she was experiencing right now.

So he pummelled rebar into curves over the anvil, gloved up and welded thinner wire to the piece, making veins that threaded through the wings he was forming. He propped the first on the bench and imagined her sitting there, her legs swinging and her dimple popping, making him want to kiss her.

Would she come out here once she'd finished in town with Mark? Would she go into his room and change out of her leathers and the lycra leggings she wore under them? Would she raid his shirts, find another jumper to borrow?

Bracing his hands on the bench, he hung his head. He should have waited. He should have been there when she finished talking to Mark. She'd had Ethan there for support, but still, it should have been him. He could kick himself now for wanting to get out of there just to avoid people speculating whether he'd spent the night in town with her. But that had been more for her benefit than his; it didn't worry him what people thought. He'd happily tell anyone and everyone how he felt about her and that he planned on spending as many nights with her as he could. As many nights as she'd have him.

When the rumble of her motorbike echoed in the valley, he let out a breath and strode to the front of the house. He found her standing beside her bike with her helmet tucked under her arm, her brow creased in a pensive frown.

If she was undecided about staying, he'd give her plenty of reasons not to leave.

'I thought you were an impish fae the first time I heard you sing,' he said, 'and I thought if ever I was to have a muse it would be you.'

She'd swung around at his voice, her eyes wide and red-rimmed, and it crushed him to know that she'd been crying without his arms around her. Would she take his comfort now?

Her eyebrows shot up but her uncertainty stayed. 'If I were a fae, I would have found a way to resist you. Besides, you don't need a muse. Your talent is your drive.'

He walked to her and rested his hands on her shoulders. 'That's the best compliment I've ever received. And you've been crying.'

Her shoulders shifted under his hands. 'It's been a morning.'

'You talked to Mark?'

Resting her forehead against his chest, she let out a deep breath. 'I'm sick of having to convince everyone I'm innocent.'

'Who are you still convincing?'

She lifted her chin to stare up at him, tears filling her eyes as she told him of Ethan's and Kelsey's doubt. 'What have I ever done to make them think that? I just don't get it.' Her voice broke.

'I'm sorry that I don't have answers for you,' he said and wiped a thumb across her cheeks. 'I can only offer you this. *I* believe you. Even if I hadn't spent the night with you, I couldn't believe you'd do it.'

She dropped her helmet to the ground as she wrapped her arms around him.

Holding her close, he pressed his face to her hair. 'Do you want to go for a ride?' Her low laugh lifted most of the morning's worry from his shoulders and made him smile. 'We can do that as well, if you like.'

She snuggled closer. 'Can we just do this for now?'

Forever and always.

'Sure.' He kissed her temple, and when she turned and took his mouth in a slow sweet kiss, it rocked him to his core.

'Why do I always feel like the kid walking in on his parents having sex when I'm around you two?' Drew said as he came around the corner of the house. 'Don't get me wrong, I'm happy for you both. I just don't know if this perpetual blush is going to do me permanent damage.' He pointed to his cheeks.

Carol chuckled. 'Somehow, I don't think it's us making you blush.'

Drew rolled his eyes. 'I'm going to put the kettle on. Feel free to get all the kissy stuff out of your system before you come inside.'

196

With his arms still around Carol, Blake raised his eyebrows at Drew's back. 'Am I missing something?'

Carol huffed a laugh that still held sadness. 'I think he's wondering if the single life is what he wants right now.'

'As in, he wants a relationship? But he's never been interested in commitment.'

Carol kissed his chin. 'I didn't even want a friendship with you when we met but look at us now. People can change their minds when circumstances show them it's possible to have more.'

Her words warmed him. 'You needed to believe you deserved more, that's all.' Bending, he picked up her helmet and walked them to the house. 'But I'm glad that I'm the one who helped you figure it out.'

She stopped on the verandah. 'It helped that you weren't pretending to be someone you weren't. You said to me once that with you, you get what you see. I still disagree, because there is so much more to you that sets you apart from the likes of Paul.'

Now that she'd opened the door to the topic, he stepped in. 'Paul conditioned you to expect the worst and take the blame. I don't work that way and it terrified you. Still does.' He touched her cheek. 'But I worry about what he'll do next. Where will it stop, Carol? Unless you tell Mark everything, Paul has the upper hand. I want to protect you. *Us*. And if that means exposing all that Paul's done, then too bad for him.'

She stood at the threshold of his house, on the brink of fully trusting and believing him, but she shook her head and, leaning against the verandah railing, hugged herself. 'I told you everything because I trust you like I trust no one else. But there will always be someone who doesn't believe me, or who'll ask what I'm after this time. Those same people will lump you in with me.'

'Do you think I care if they do?'

'You will when they drag you down whenever they feel like it.' She shook her head. 'I grew up convinced that I don't need or want someone to love me, so to have such intense feelings for you terrifies me, because then shit like this happens and I ruin it.'

'First of all, and I need you to hear me when I say this'—he cupped her face in his hands so she had to look up at him—'you don't ruin it. And you don't have to take the blame for this, okay? Don't take the blame from him and keep it for yourself.'

Her jaw twitched against his hand as she fought the truth. When she didn't argue, he kissed the tip of her nose. 'You'll get there. And while you are, take this in too. I didn't think I'd ever find what I have with you either. And, to be honest, I didn't want it. I'd just gotten back on speaking terms with Tish and didn't want to jump into another relationship while I had to work on this place, build my business and get my life in order. But then there you were, tipping my world upside down without even trying.'

Her sigh could have been pleasure or pain.

'You did the same to me.'

How could he not love her when even at her lowest she made him smile.

'Well, I guess we're stuck with each other then.'

Leaning into him, she rested her hands on his chest. 'If this is being stuck with someone, then I think I'm one very lucky woman.'

Smiling, he kissed her. She smelled of leather and wild weather, tasted of tears and hope, and he could have stood there with her forever. But she pushed his chest, holding him back, her eyes serious as they searched his.

He held his breath. 'What's wrong?'

Cupping his face, she frowned up at him. 'I think I'm falling for you.'

And with that, his world righted. 'How about you go raid my wardrobe for a jumper and we'll explore that revelation a bit more over a cup of coffee.'

CHAPTER 14

Carol took her time in Blake's bedroom. When she'd painted the walls, she'd had Gran's love of colour and a sense of mischief in mind. And she'd known that Blake would want something more than ordinary. Not that he'd put that desire into words, but the whimsy and wistfulness of his art spoke for him. So she'd taken his grey walls and had turned them into a turbulent wash of atmospheric power—one wall now featured a sunset, with the sky on the verge of breaking into storm. Against the centre of the wall, the bed was like the eye of the storm, the pillows and linen in calming deep blues and dark greys, and the four redgum posts surrounding it giving the space a pop of colour. It was a room that invited the occupant to either relax and fall asleep or gather energy and go wild. For Carol, the idea of letting go with Blake didn't scare her anymore.

Holding on to the tingle that raced down her back, she rummaged through his clothes and pulled on a stained and ripped Jaws shirt and a jumper that shouted *I'm A Cereal Killer!*

Now dressed and warm in Blake's clothes, Carol stood at the bedroom window and stared out at the garden and paddocks beyond. She rubbed at the ache in her heart. Hindsight prodded her until she closed her eyes and rested her forehead against the cold glass.

She'd tried ignoring Paul and letting him win, but it had changed nothing. She'd tried standing up to him, but it had only made things worse. Everything she'd done so far, she'd done alone, partly because it shamed her to have been so weak and pitiful and partly because Paul had made her believe no one would help her. He'd been right to an extent—some people had no interest in helping—but her true friends had always been there for her; she just hadn't given them a chance to truly help.

She knew now that she'd kept her silence for too long. Paul was the one who was guilty, and it was time for him to be pointed at and whispered about. She refused to feel shame any longer, and though she'd probably continue carrying guilt for her own weakness, the time for hiding behind Paul's lies had to end. It was time to open up, to tell her friends the truth and let them help put a stop to Paul's manipulative stranglehold on her. And she'd start by coming clean to her best friend.

Before she could lose the spark of confidence, she pulled out her phone and texted Kelsey.

At Blake's. Will come to yours later so we can talk. About everything. Need Ethan there too. Kelsey would need him there to support her.

Carol jolted when her phone vibrated with Kelsey's reply.

Good. He'll be here and I'll have the kettle on.

Accepting that her stomach would always tremble at the thought of telling her story, she headed for the kitchen and joined Blake and Drew at the table.

Blake handed her a mug of hot coffee. 'You look determined.'

Taking a sip, she closed her eyes and sighed. 'I'm *feeling* determined. It's an odd heat here'—she tapped her chest—'but I think I like it.'

'Well, it suits you.' Drew saluted her with his mug. 'And while you're feeling things, how about giving me a hand in the garden?'

Carol glanced out the window. Sunlight sparked off wet leaves so it looked as if they were covered in jewels, while a rainbow of birds darted from tree branch to grass and back again.

'I'd love to.' She smiled at Drew. 'You know, if you ever decide to move here and set up shop, I'd put my hand up for a job.'

Drew pointed at her. 'Funny you should say that.'

Blake choked on his coffee. 'You're thinking of moving here?'

Drew shrugged. 'Why not? You love it here and we always talked about going into business together. Now that you've found your niche, adding a gardening and landscaping service seems like a good next step. Besides,' he leaned over and lightly punched Blake's shoulder, 'I miss you.'

'What about your business?'

'Storm's ready to take over. They've been running things for the last couple of months and are excelling, so I think it's time to expand.'

Carol raised her hand. 'They?'

'Storm's non-binary,' Drew explained, then turned back to Blake. 'Tell me you don't think it's a great idea.'

Blake scratched his chin and glanced at Carol, his eyebrow raised in question. 'What do you think?'

'Me? It's up to you two.'

Blake reached across the table and took her hand. 'You're a part of my life, so it's a question about our future, our plans, not just mine.'

How did his words not terrify her? He talked of togetherness and permanence, but though her heart raced, it wasn't from fear. He'd given her the parachute she'd always been missing, and it was a thrill to finally take that leap. Still, there were things that might make him hesitate.

'Kelsey loves being pregnant,' she said, 'and it suits her.'

He raised an eyebrow. 'I don't think gardening induces pregnancy.'

She shook her head, refusing to be swayed by his crooked smile. 'I'm saying that I don't know about having kids. What do I know about parenting? What if I've inherited my parents' lacklustre attitude towards offspring?'

'Well, first of all, having kids is something we'd need to talk about more, because I don't know if I'm ready yet, either. And secondly, I'm mad about you, Carol, so I can wait for the rest.'

Not caring if Drew fainted from blushing, Carol climbed into Blake's lap. Taking his face in her hands, she stared into his eyes. 'No one else has ever, or will ever, make me want the things I want with you.'

She kissed him, slow and deep, and almost purred when he clamped his arms around her and held her close.

By the time Blake shifted her from his knee, Drew had left the kitchen.

Carol straightened the shirt that skewed under her jumper and licked her lips. 'Do you think he'll still offer me a job?'

Blake cleared his throat. 'Give me a minute to remember my name before you ask me questions.'

Carol laughed. 'I was wondering what sort of energy we'll bring to your bedroom.'

He groaned. 'Are you trying to kill me?'

She leaned forward and kissed the back of his neck. 'What good would that do me?'

The prospect of being free of Paul and of starting an exciting stage of her life with a man who encouraged her to be playful, to take control and to trust, made her giddy with energy. It burst through her and had her dancing around the kitchen. Raising her arms high, she pirouetted in front of Blake's new stove and gave the movements rhythm with the song that burst from her heart. She grinned when Blake sang along with her version of Welshy Arms' 'Sanctuary'.

When she flourished a bow, he applauded. 'I love it when you laugh like that. Your dimple pops, and I feel like a king for playing my part in making it appear.'

Pulling him up for a slow dance, she pressed her ear against the beat of his heart. 'I know what you mean. Every time I make you smile and your eyes go that gunmetal grey, I feel like I could touch the moon.'

He moaned her name, but Drew was working just outside, so she curbed the need to bite Blake's neck, just to hear the sound again.

'I better find Drew,' she said, 'and you better go and get some work done.'

He stared down at her, his eyes darkening with desire, but he shook his head and blew out a breath. 'Okay. You'll stay tonight?'

'I want to,' she sighed, 'but I can't, not until I sort something out with Snow. I don't like leaving him alone.'

Blake rested his forehead on hers. 'I can pick him up tomorrow. He'd love it out here. But'—he lifted his head and caught her gaze—'that doesn't mean you have to stay if you aren't ready for that yet.'

To have him read her and accommodate her fears, however irrational, made her tumble further in love.

'I have to work tomorrow night, so if you don't mind a midnight visitor, I can come out afterwards.'

'Maybe I should come in and have a meal.'

'So you can watch over me?'

'So I can make sure Paul keeps his hands and his lies to himself.'

Resting a palm against one of his cheeks, she kissed the other. 'You've helped me begin to cut the ties he had me tangled in. He's tried to hurt me, hurt us, but for the most part, he's failed. And I'm not scared of him anymore.'

At least, not as much. Maybe. But if she kept telling herself he didn't scare her, it had to come true at some point, didn't it?

One side of Blake's mouth lifted. 'No, you're still frightened, but that's not a failing on your part. Can you see why he chose you? Why he still tries to break you?'

'I know why. He saw a weak girl, desperate for attention, and swooped.'

Blake shook his head. 'No. That's one of the biggest lies you believe. It'll be a hard one to let go, but listen to me, because I'm telling you the truth. Manipulators don't target people who are weak. What sort of challenge would it be to break someone who caves easily? They choose the strong ones, because they get a buzz when they can finally break them and keep them in line. And the fact that you aren't letting him do either anymore must really chap his arse.'

She smiled, though the truth of just how strong she'd been last year ate at her. 'You just wanted to say *chap his arse* in a sentence.'

'That was a bonus.' He rubbed his hands up and down her arms. 'There's something else, isn't there? Something you think will make me change my mind.'

How did he know her so well?

'Just one more thing. He stayed in the house with me for a month after I'd burned the bed. He tried everything to convince me to have sex with him again. The ignoring, the looks, the promises, the gaslighting came in such quick succession that it literally made me sick. I couldn't eat or sleep, I had panic attacks walking through the door, and I started behaving like the crying, screaming, unhinged person he told everyone I was. I just wanted it to end. I wanted *my life* to end.'

She gulped in air, her chest tightening, her stomach rolling.

Blake slid his arms around her so gently that it made her lean in and snuggle closer. He pressed his lips to her temple. 'So you slept with him to stop it all? To save yourself?'

'Part of me wishes that's what happened. But no, he asked me to marry him. Told me he was the only one who could handle my erratic emotions, my sullen silences and my perverted sexual needs. I didn't love him, but if he was the only person who'd ever put up with me, maybe I could make it work.'

She tipped her face up. If his showed disgust, she could take it. She'd carried it for so long it was like a second skin.

But he kissed her, breathing warmth and hope into her soul. 'You think I'd be what? Disillusioned? Repulsed?'

She put a hand on his chest. 'You might be once I finish.'

'Okay, let's do this then.' He pulled a chair out and sat, tugging her onto his lap. 'Finish it, get it all out, and then there'll be nothing between us but what we build together.'

'What if my foundations are too shaky?'

'We'll strengthen them. You aren't in this alone anymore, Carol. Your friends will all support and help you. And I'm here, backing you and loving you because I can't imagine doing anything else. You're in every plan, every vision I have of the future. I'm not going to let you go unless you tell me you can't stand to be with me anymore.'

Wrapping her arms around his neck, so their hearts were pressed together, she hugged him tight. 'I can't imagine anything else either. And for so long, I didn't want to plan anything with anyone, because Paul had conditioned me to respond to him, even when I didn't want to. He proposed to humiliate me one last time, then he packed up and left the next day, telling everyone I was too immature to move to the city. For a year, I worked hard to get over everything he'd done, everything he'd made me. I was so confident that I'd be able to look him in the eyes and tell him to get fucked. Then he turned up before the Crazy Hat Night fundraiser last year, and I was back to being the girl who had nothing and no one. He laughed when he realised that I hadn't been with anyone else.'

She buried her face against Blake's shoulder. 'I was supposed to sing that night, but I couldn't stand up there in front of everyone covered in the bruises he'd left on me. I was ashamed that I'd been so desperate for someone to want me that I let him do that to me.'

'And he turned up again this year expecting the same.' He smoothed a hand over her back. 'But guess what, baby, you got up and sang. He tried to beat you down, but you stood your ground.'

She shook her head. 'I clam up every time he comes close. I shut down as a defence. I'm not as strong as you think.'

He cupped her face. 'Are you with me just to fill that need for touch and belonging?'

'How can you even ask that?' She struggled to shift off his lap, but he held her still.

'Exactly.' He kissed her again. 'You're stronger than you give yourself credit for. Being here with me is proof of that. You're mine, Carol, and I'm yours, equally. We both have regrets and ghosts, but we'll deal with them together. Okay?'

He was handing her the world along with his heart.

She took it and offered the same. 'Together. I don't want anything but to be together with you.'

#

Carol stood and stretched. The sky had gone from being a vast stretch of blue that hinted of spring to an ominous expanse of mottled grey and purple, reminding her that winter still held on. It would be dark soon, and though she'd exercised Snow that morning, she needed to take him for a run before bed or he'd wiggle and groan all night.

Drew grinned at her as he spread the last bit of mulch on the once weed-choked muddy garden. 'Job well done.'

Carol nodded. 'Come spring, these beds will be a riot of colour again. And with the herbs you'll plant, the smell wafting through to the kitchen will be fantastic.'

Drew stood and wiped his hands on his jeans. 'This will be a garden to envy once we're finished.' He angled his head. 'If you're serious about a job, that is.'

She didn't even try to hide her smile. 'I am. A new start, a new outlook, is what I want.'

205

Drew held his hand out. 'Welcome to the family.'

It felt right, freeing and terrifying all at once.

'I can't remember the last time I made a decision based on my own happiness and needs.' She pursed her lips. 'Other than letting Blake into my life, of course.'

That had been her decision and had brought her happiness—although that hardly even began to describe the emotions that still hummed inside her.

Drew bumped her shoulder. 'I'm not asking for nitty-gritty details, but this Paul guy is doing some shitty things, isn't he?'

'He is and he was, but he's not going to anymore because I'm done playing his games.' Lifting her arms to the darkening sky, she spun in a circle.

Drew's laugh rumbled across the yard. 'One thing's for sure, it won't be boring working with you. Between the singing and the dancing, it'll be like watching one big show.'

Carol shrugged and picked up the shovels. 'Gran always said, why be silent and still when you can sing and dance.'

'Words to live by.' He hefted two bags of mulch and followed her to the shed.

Blake flicked off his radio and smiled as he removed his earmuffs. 'You two look like you've had fun.'

Carol wriggled her dirt-stained hands. 'We have. Though I'd be happy to have a little more before heading home.'

Blake's grin deepened as he stowed his tools away. 'What do you have in mind?'

'And that's my cue.' Drew turned and walked out.

Familiar heat coiled in her belly as she sat on one of the benches. Now eye level with Blake, she draped her arms around his neck.

'Whatever we do, we better be quick. I want to leave sooner rather than later. The weather is about to turn, and I need to take Snow for a run.'

'Well, then.' He nipped at her jaw, her neck, then took her mouth in a hot kiss that made her wrap her body around his and hang on.

Easing back, he lifted her from the bench and let her slide down his body. 'That'll have to hold us both for now. Or I could follow you back into town and cook us some dinner while you take Snow for a run.'

Tempting as it was, especially after that kiss, she shook her head. 'I don't want our time together to be all about sex. It's been a turbulent twenty-four hours and spending most of it with you has been an experience I want to repeat. A lot. But I also need to know that I can be fine without you. I'll miss you. I already do, but I need to do this, for me.'

Blake took her hand and, raising an eyebrow at the dirt, pushed up her sleeve and kissed her wrist. 'You'll let me know when you get home?'

Staring at the spot his lips had touched while heat and need rocketed through her, she fought to push words out that were on the tip of her tongue.

Dipping his head so they were at eye level, Blake frowned. 'What is it?'

She swallowed past the lump in her throat. 'Paul always told me that no one else would ever be able to turn me on, and I believed him. He convinced me I was too perverted, too cold. But you … you wake everything in me and make me believe I can be more, have more. And you make me forget, so many things.'

She rubbed her forehead when something niggled her brain. 'Shit, I'm supposed to call in on Kelsey. And she has your groceries.'

'Don't worry about the groceries. I can get them in the morning.'

The sunset made the world outside the shed door glow like dying embers. Getting home before dark wouldn't happen, but she'd promised Kelsey. Snow would have to wait a bit longer for his run.

She took Blake's hand and pulled him with her to the house. He leaned against the bedroom doorjamb as she changed into her underclothes and leathers, and when she was dressed, he pulled her against him and kissed her. Before he let her go, he rubbed his cheek against hers, the heat of his scratchy stubble staying with her as she raced out the door. Waving to him, she straddled the bike and kicked it to life.

Kangaroos were scattered on the side of the road; some of them jumped away into the falling night as she drove past, others stayed put as her headlight crossed them and cast long shadows over the landscape. Already travelling at a crawl on the dirt road, she changed to a lower gear when the rain started.

Her thoughts turned to the conversation she was about to have with Kelsey. A chill settled in her bones, but they'd work it out. They had to. Life without Kelsey to talk and laugh with would be cold and dull. Much like it had been for the five years she'd been gone. They'd started to get that back, had begun to rediscover their friendship, and Carol would willingly bare her soul to Kelsey to show her that she trusted her, and that she could be trusted.

Her chest loosened when she turned onto the main road and her tyres gripped the bitumen. She opened the throttle as she drove along the five hundred–metre stretch to the Ryders' turn-off.

She lowered her gears as she approached the turn but had to squint against the flash of bright headlights. When they didn't dip, she threw up a hand. Blind, she hit the brakes, locking her tyres so the stench of rubber filled her nostrils as her bike jerked. The scream of metal scraping against the road clashed with those ripped from her throat.

Her leathers saved her skin, but she felt bone crunch. Her helmet hit something hard, and when everything greyed, it dampened the pain ricocheting through her body, and she let the darkness take her under.

CHAPTER 15

Gran laughed as she sat on the verandah, the warmth of the sound curling around Carol as she ran through the grass, a spring lamb at her heels, the sun a too-bright ball in the near-white sky. Someone called her name, and though she twirled like a puppy chasing its tail, she could see no one other than Gran around.

Gran, who was healthy, happy and alive.

Carol had named the lamb Harry fifteen years ago and had buried him the year before Gran. He bleated and skipped beside her.

'Carol?' Pop walked towards her with his arms held wide.

Carol ran to him and buried her face in his chest. The familiar scent of grease and sweat tumbled her heart, but the cloying smell of fuel made her gag.

'What's happened, Pop? Why are you doused in fuel?'

'I'm not.' He held her at arms-length and stared down at her. 'It's you. You need to wake up.'

Carol sniffed at her arm. He was right. It soaked and burned her skin. She swiped at her arm with the hem of her shirt but only smeared more fuel over it.

'Help me, Pop. Help me stop it.'

He stepped backwards, smiling sadly. 'I can't, honey. You need to wake up and make it right. Open your eyes.'

She tried. Hard. But her eyelids weighed too much.

'Carol, wake up!' Hands gripped her shoulders, sending lightning down her arm.

She groaned, tried to push words out. 'Hurt.'

'You fell off your motorbike. I nearly hit you. God, I nearly ran over you!'

Sleep pulled at her, but shivers woke other pains. She tried to curl up, to hug herself, but the hands stopped her.

'No! You have to stay still. An ambulance is coming.'

The left side of her body flamed and throbbed, while her right side was icy emptiness. Each breath gripped her ribs, making her shiver and ache, and each ache pushed her closer to tears.

She forced her eyes open and blinked at Paul as he hovered over her.

'Not you.' She tried to shake her head but stopped when nausea swirled in her gut.

Paul smoothed a hand over her cheek, his eyes bright in the glare of light. 'Just lie still, okay? Lie still and keep talking. An ambulance is coming. You skidded and hit your head. And your bike ...' He leaned down. 'You were on the wrong side of the road. I flashed you. You swerved and skidded, then you were sliding across the road towards me.' He pressed a hand to his mouth. 'I could have killed you.'

Everything jumbled, his words, their meaning. Her ears rang, sounds falling and rising until her head throbbed. Carol tried to focus, to remember what had happened.

Red and blue lights flashed in time with the thump in her head. Paul gripped her hand in his and moved over as an ambulance officer squatted beside her.

The paramedic gave her a quick once-over as he pulled on a pair of gloves. 'Can you tell me your name?'

Paul squeezed her hand. 'She fell off her motorbike. Maybe she was going too fast, I don't know, but she hit her head.'

The ambo nodded. 'We'll get to that.' He held a finger in front of her face. 'Right now, I need you to follow my finger with only your eyes and tell me your name.'

She watched his finger but it blurred in and out. 'Carol.'

'Good.' He stopped torturing her eyes. 'Last name?'

Her teeth chattered. 'Mc ... McGrath.'

He shifted, pressed fingers to her wrist and lifted his other hand, his watch flashing in the brightness. 'Can you tell me what day it is?'

'Um. Tuesday?'

He smiled. 'And the date?'

She stared at him. His face was familiar. 'I know you.'

'You should.' His gaze connected with hers. 'What's the date, Carol?'

Her brain ached, along with everything else. Why was it so hard to capture the words, get them from her head to her mouth? 'Um, it's August, twentieth.'

He smiled. 'Good. And for the bonus prize, who's our current Prime Minister?'

Paul's laugh jolted her. 'Carol isn't one to follow politics. Ask her who's on *Farmer Wants a Wife*.'

The ambo flicked a glance at Paul. 'I'm going to need you to give us some room.'

Keeping his grip on her hand, Paul shuffled over a little more. 'She needs me. I'm all she has.'

It flashed through her—Blake's face, his smile, his laughter. He was who she needed, who she wanted.

'Blake.'

Paul let go of her hand and moved to her other side. 'No, baby, it's me. Remember? We're going to work things out, because you're right, we're meant to be. We'll work everything out and get you better, you'll see.'

Work things out? When had that happened? Had she lost time? Lost her mind? She loved Blake, didn't she? Nothing made sense. But although nothing lined up enough for her to argue with Paul, she didn't have to stay near him. She rocked, wanting to get to her hands and knees so she could get away from him and his lies, but she cried out when pain exploded.

Hands held her down, held her still. 'No moving.'

The ambo leaned down, forcing her to look at him. 'You took a savage tumble, and I'm going to be honest with you, a neck or back injury is high on my list of concerns. We're going to stabilise you, and I don't want you to move unless I say so. Okay?

The tears she'd been holding back now ran and dripped into her ears. 'But I'm okay. I can feel everything. It all hurts.' In more places than she could name.

He nodded. 'Which is why I need to assess you.'

She answered his questions about pain, about her medical history, about the accident she couldn't quite piece together. Filling in the gaps, Paul answered what she couldn't. He kept telling her she'd be okay, that he was there. And when they cut off her leathers because it hurt to breathe, he took them, and her phone and her wallet, and told her he'd get her keys and organise for her bike to be picked up.

The ambo braced her neck, constantly asking about head and back pain until she gritted her teeth to stop them chattering.

Then she gripped the ambo's sleeve. 'My phone. I need my phone.' She needed to call Blake, to hear his voice, to have him tell her everything would be okay.

Paul held up her phone. 'I've got it. I've got everything.' He touched her temple. 'I nearly lost you. And I know that I kept hurting you by turning you away, but I understand now that I need you just as much as you need me.'

Trapped in the neck brace, in her pain, with the words locked in her head, Carol could only stare through the strobing lights that masked the stars and clouds as Paul told the ambulance officer how lucky he was to realise his mistake before it was too late.

Carol fought to swallow the overflowing agony that every touch, every movement caused, and each time she would whimper or groan, Paul would touch her, reassure her, until the contents of her stomach rushed up her throat.

'Sick.' Gasping for breath, with her chest a volcano of heat and rippling pain, she gagged.

And for once, Paul kept his distance while the ambulance officers cleaned her up, reassured her and set a pain management plan.

By the time they loaded her into the ambulance, she was floating on a vibrating cloud that kept her just out of sleep's reach. Voices overlapped as Paul joked with the ambo about having to baby patients who weren't capable of cleaning up after themselves.

A silent movie played, of Blake lying beside her, his smile slow and sweet as he leaned in to kiss her. It flipped to a rush of cold and noise that jerked her into blinding light.

'Where?' Her tongue stuck to the roof of her mouth. 'Where are we?'

The ambulance officer smiled down at her, his face upside down. 'We've bought you to Hamilton Base Hospital, remember?' He talked to the nurses as he parked her in a narrow, curtained cubicle. The words they used were alien, though some she caught made her tremble.

A hand took hers and squeezed.

'Don't worry, I'm here.' Paul leaned into her line of sight.

'I don't want you here.' Pain spiralled from her shoulder to her wrist as she tried to pull her hand from his.

Glancing away, Paul gestured to someone. 'She's asking for water.'

He turned back to her, his jaw tight. 'I'm all you've got, so you're going to be a good girl, lie there and do what I tell you.'

She gritted her teeth. 'And if I don't?'

His smile chilled her. 'Try me and find out.'

#

Blake missed Carol. During their time together, they'd fallen into an easy routine of talking while they ate, saddling up to ride the property or explore the surrounding bush and pine plantations, then laughing while they sanded and prepared surfaces for paint or moved furniture around to fit the new pieces he'd bought.

And when he went to work in the shed, his creativity flowed as hot and bright as the blowtorch that helped bite open and bend the steel he reformed, because when he came out, with his back tight and muscles aching, she was there. But once the work was done and she left for the night, even Drew's good humour and company didn't fill the void she left. So he missed her. And he would for a while yet while they navigated the newness of their relationship.

Drew walked into the lounge room and handed Blake a cup of coffee. 'Are you going to sit and stare at the fire while it dies, or are you going stoke it up so that your friend and guest doesn't freeze in the night?'

'I'm sure my friend and guest can stoke the fire himself if he gets cold.'

Drew raised his cup. 'I knew it. You're brooding.'

213

'Not brooding. Contemplating.'

Putting a log on the fire, Drew quirked an eyebrow. 'Contemplating what?'

Blake sighed and sipped his coffee. 'Life.'

'The universe.'

He grinned at Drew. 'Everything.'

Sitting on the couch, Drew kicked his legs out and slung an arm around Blake's shoulders. 'It's quieter without her energy, isn't it?'

'It is.' In more ways than just the absence of her voice. 'I think the house misses her as much as I do.'

'She'll be back tomorrow. And then you can get those puppy dog eyes doing their thing and get her to stay.'

Blake shook his head. 'Staying will be up to her. But I'll pick Snow up in the morning and bring him out.'

'Sounds like a plan. Speaking of which, it's your turn to cook dinner.'

Blake turned to stare at Drew. 'I cooked last night.'

Drew grinned. 'I'm the guest.'

'Brother, you have never been a guest in any of my houses.'

With a sigh, Drew stood. 'Well, it was worth a try.'

And while Drew rattled pots and pans in the kitchen and filled the house with the spicy aroma of his famous curried sausages, Blake closed his eyes, breathed out and smiled. Two horses were enjoying the early spring grass in his paddock, his house had become a home that welcomed him after a hard day's work, his business was taking off and he'd see Carol tomorrow.

Yes, he missed her, but in that moment, life couldn't get much better.

#

Pale blue curtains surrounded Carol's world. Beyond them, on one side, someone groaned in varying pitch and volume, while on the other, someone sobbed. Carol did neither. It took all her strength to open her eyes and stare at the white ceiling tiles.

She lay shivering under the heated hospital blanket, with her arms at her sides and her head and neck held in uncomfortable straightness, causing both

214

to throb. Of course, that could be the concussion, too. Nausea sat deep in her belly, just below the cold ball of dread that weighed her down.

The bed might as well have been made of rocks with the way pain jabbed and burned every inch of her skin. And every measured breath she took pushed shards of glass deeper into her lungs and crushed her ribs. All because of an accident she couldn't remember.

'You were on the wrong side of the road,' Paul had told her while the nurses checked her vitals. *'Riding too fast in the rain. If it hadn't been for me, you might have been killed.'*

With his threat still echoing in her head, she'd done what he'd told her to do, which was to say nothing. Besides, what could she say? The accident was a black hole in her memory, so even if her mind revolted at the notion of being so irresponsible, she had no proof to argue against Paul's version of events.

Now, as her head thumped, all she wanted was to go home, get into a warm bed and seek oblivion until she could move her head without her stomach threatening to eject its contents, something it had almost done half-way through a CT scan. But she'd swallowed the queasiness and had kept still, as she'd been told.

The X-rays, though, with all the shifting of arms and the propping of her torso to get the right angle, had reduced her to tears. The *just a moment more* comments from the radiographer had lasted hours—days, maybe—until he'd patted her hand and told her she'd done so well and was so brave.

But that bravery leaked away with every beep of the monitor she was connected to, because no one would listen to her. The nurses stroked her forehead or her hand and told her to rest, that everything would be okay because Paul would take care of her and everything else.

The beep of the monitor beside her picked up speed. The groaning beyond the curtain reached a pitch that grated, the sobbing on the other side matching its volume. Without thinking, she reached up to clamp her hands to her ears, and her silent scream cracked her jaw and added another layer of agony to the volcano already erupting in her chest.

Fighting for breath, she begged for the void to swallow her. And when a warm hand took hers, she gripped it, sniffed back tears and opened her eyes.

'Hey.' Paul smirked down at her.

Relaxing her hand so it hung limply in his, she stared at the ceiling. 'You're telling everyone that I'm reckless, that I swerved in front of you on purpose.'

His fingers tightened on hers. 'Is this what I'm going to have to put up with now? I've been outside in the freezing cold and rain making phone calls for you. I've found someone to pick your bike up off the road and scrap it, and this is the thanks I get?'

Could her breaking world take much more?

'You can't scrap my bike.'

'I can, because *you* totalled it. Besides, you nearly killed yourself tonight, so riding it is out of the question now.' He tugged at her hair. 'And as my fiancée, you're going to have to make some other changes.'

Touching an electric fence would have given her less of a jolt. 'Fiancée?'

The familiar, exaggerated sigh he gave made her shiver. And even though the nurse walking in with a smile would only see Carol's worry, her stomach jittered with the fear of what Paul would do to keep her in line this time.

Standing, he waggled her phone where she could see it. 'I saw you were supposed to drop in to talk to Kelsey, so I sent her a message to let her know you couldn't make it. Apparently, they're having trouble with foxes at the moment. Ethan said something about his chooks being mauled, so I might kill two birds with one stone and take the rifle around, see if I can get the culprit and make sure Kelsey knows why you won't be around.'

Carol stared at him as the cold ball in her belly grew larger.

Finishing up her notes, the nurse patted Carol's arm and nodded at Paul. 'You've got a keeper there, honey. I'll leave you in his capable hands for a minute while I grab the trolley to do your obs.'

Once the nurse had tugged the curtains closed, Paul picked up the cup of water on Carol's hospital table and downed it in one go. 'Maybe one day you'll realise just how lucky you are.'

Carol licked her dry lips. 'I do.'

That made him smile down at her. 'There's my girl. I knew it was the pain making you cranky. Oh, and on that note, I talked to the doctor. She said nothing's broken, just some bruising, so they'll keep you in until morning, then I'll take you home.'

Just bruising? How could her body be full of knives with her ribs getting stabbed every time she breathed if it was *just* bruising? And as for him coming back in the morning ...

'I'll get a lift home with someone. Save you the trouble.'

He stopped scrolling through his phone and raised an eyebrow at her. 'The only trouble is that you're not listening to me. I'll be back in the morning, unless someone calls me beforehand to say that you aren't following orders. You know, doing things like getting out of bed when you're supposed to be resting. I'll have my phone on me and reception is good out at the Ryder place.' He glanced at the hospital phone beside the bed. 'I wouldn't trust that either if I were you. You never know who's listening.'

Whether he lied about bugging the hospital phone or not didn't matter; his threat was clear. Do anything, talk to anyone and he'd hurt Kelsey. Calling his bluff would mean Carol would be risking the life of her best friend and her unborn child, and she wasn't prepared to do that. And even if she was, if she could get out of bed and find a pay phone, she didn't have any money. He had everything—her phone, her ID, her keys.

When he leaned close to kiss her cheek, she froze, and his low chuckle turned her stomach.

'You're wondering if you can warn her before I get there. You can't, because although I'm forty-five minutes away, I have a friend camping out in the bush a minute away from her front door. Once I've told the nurse I'm worried about your mental health and need to know about any move you make, I'll find out if you attempt to get hold of a phone. And if you do, it'll be seconds before your best friend's blood is on your hands. Understand?'

Shaking, Carol licked her lips. 'Yes.'

'Good.' He pressed his lips to her forehead, then straightened and glanced at the nurse as she came back in. 'Can I speak to you a moment?'

The curtains hissed along the metal poles as Paul shoved them aside and walked out into the corridor, the nurse's shoes squeaking on the floor as she followed him.

The murmur of their voices reached Carol—Paul's low and full of concern, the nurse's sympathetic. Whatever Paul told her, the nurse would believe him, especially as he was choking back a sob.

After a moment, the nurse's footsteps squeaked away, while the sound of Paul's confident stride moved in the opposite direction.

Holding her breath against tears, panic and hopelessness, Carol squeezed her eyes closed. She'd let Paul create this disturbed reality, and now, once again, he had her trapped. If she'd been stronger and had fought against him two years ago, or even four years ago, Blake wouldn't have had his work ruined, Zoe wouldn't hate her, and Kelsey wouldn't be in danger. But she *had* let him, and now he owned her again—she couldn't let Kelsey pay the price for this nightmare of her own making.

#

Blake woke at dawn after dreaming he was surfing. Carol had swum alongside him, with her mermaid tail in hues of magenta and amethyst and her smile knowing as she'd tumbled him into the sea with her.

With the salty taste of her lingering on his lips, he got up and layered on items of clothing before the chill air could nip the warmth from his skin. After pulling on a pair of thick woollen socks, he padded out to the kitchen and made his first cup of coffee in near darkness.

A month ago, this kitchen had been strange and unfamiliar, its cupboards always an inch closer than he remembered, its benches narrower. Now, he could reach for a cup, boil the kettle and get the milk from the fridge, all with muscle memory serving him better than the dull morning light.

Adding a coat to the layers he already wore, he stepped out into the crisp icy air. The clouds had cleared since it'd last rained, which was just after Carol had left last night, and the dew on his newly revitalised lawn sparkled in the light of dawn.

Stepping out from under the verandah, he swore and shivered as his breath billowed white steam. How did Carol go for a run in this? Would she expect him to join her when she stayed over? Did he want to?

218

Maybe. They'd spent a lot of time together as friends; now, as they took the next step in their relationship as lovers, he wanted to do it right. They'd both come from relationships that had left scars. His might have been partially self-inflicted, but the wounds still needed to heal. And Carol's? Well, she still dealt with an ex who wanted to control her every move, every choice. And why would she not expect the same from him after living it for years?

His hand paused in lifting his cup. It was just as she'd been telling him all along. She had to go through an unlearning, as she'd called it, of all she'd been conditioned to expect. And she'd chosen him to unlearn with. She trusted him to take her as she was, trusted him not to change her, belittle her or use her as Paul had.

If he'd known of her past that first night, would he have acted the same? And if he hadn't, would they have arrived where they were now? It didn't bear thinking about. He'd been himself—no acting, no over thinking, no guarding—and it had been enough for Carol. And she'd been enough for him.

He'd tell her as much when he went into town.

Actually, no. He'd show her.

So, as the sun rose and painted his part of the world in colours only nature could conjure, he formulated a plan and hoped that he would once more be enough.

CHAPTER 16

Carol sat up in the hospital bed with a breakfast tray of cereal, a piece of toast and a cup of juice before her. Every shift of her body or wiggle of her knee woke her aches and pains into a roaring howl, but her bladder was currently causing her the most discomfort.

Too afraid to get up in the night in case the nurse contacted Paul, she'd held on. And even though her tongue stuck to the roof of her mouth with each swallow, she didn't touch the juice. Just looking at it caused her bladder to tremble.

Whether Paul had gone to Kelsey's or not didn't matter, because his threat had been real. Carol knew her movements were being watched—Paul's chat to the nurse had no doubt ensured that—and the knowledge of it had tied her to the bed with an invisible rope from which she feared she'd never cut herself free.

When he walked in, he was whistling, and, grinning smugly at seeing her so uncomfortable and desperate, he glanced at her breakfast tray. 'Not hungry? I'm starving. We bagged three foxes and a deer last night. Nearly shot a horse this morning, but I realised in time that it was being ridden. Big black thing too. Would have gotten a fair amount of meat off it.' He took the piece of toast, bit in and screwed his nose up. 'How was your night?'

Carol gritted her teeth. 'Fine. I have to pee.'

He leaned forward under the pretence of helping her out of bed. 'You didn't hold it in all night, did you? Afraid the nurse would tell on you?' He chuckled. 'What a silly girl you are.'

It would do her no good to cry. He'd just belittle her for that, too. Already, he'd achieved in one night what it had taken him two years to do last

220

time—reduced her to an emotional mess too scared to move in case he did something.

As she hobbled through the curtain with her knees clamped together, even though it sent sharp jabs into her hip and ankle, she held her breath until she lowered herself onto the toilet.

She didn't risk taking the time to wash her face or rinse her mouth but limped back with one hand pressed to the wall and the other to her head in an attempt to hold in the disjointed thoughts punching through the fog in her brain. She imagined running through the hospital screaming that Paul was a monster, but that image was replaced with one of Kelsey and Snotty lying dead on a trail, a bullet hole in each of them.

She walked back into the small cubicle to find the nurse and Paul chatting like old friends.

Paul held out a hand to her. 'I was beginning to think you'd gotten lost.'

Cringing on the inside, she let him help her onto the bed. 'Walking takes longer at the moment.'

She stayed quiet as he and the nurse discussed her pain management plan, her injuries, her discharge, and booking a follow-up appointment with her local doctor.

Picking up the juice cup and peeling back the lid, Paul smiled at the nurse. 'I'll take care of everything and make sure she follows doctor's orders.'

The nurse's cheeks pinked. 'She's lucky to have someone like you in her life.'

Paul glanced at Carol. 'I keep telling you that, don't I?'

The nurse left, and Paul cocked his head until the squeak of her shoes died away, then he saluted Carol with the juice cup and downed the contents in one swallow.

'Let's get you home so you can shower. You stink of hospital. Oh, and just so you know, I came straight here, so all of my hunting gear is still in the car. I hope your dog behaves, because I'd hate to have to shoot him in self-defence.'

#

221

Carol sat in the car, staring at her house while Paul rummaged in the boot.

'Just grabbing some gear,' he'd said with that shark smile, so although Snow needed exercise and feeding, she'd have to leave him in his cage, because no way would she give Paul any excuse to hurt her dog.

Still, when he opened the passenger door and hooked an arm under her elbow to pull her out, she froze.

In answer, Paul propped the rifle bag against the car. 'Seeing as you're hurt, I'll get the dog while you have a shower.'

She lifted her hands. 'I'm not refusing. You jolted me and it hurt.' At his glare, she swallowed. 'You didn't, I did. I jolted and it hurt.'

Paul pursed his lips. 'Then you better be more careful.'

This time, when he clamped a hand on her elbow, she let him pull her from the car, then he marched her to the house. Forcing herself to ignore the pain, she hurried to her room and found clothes, then stopped at the bathroom door when Paul swore. He was pacing the lounge room, and every few moments, he passed the hallway with his phone pressed to his ear.

Even if she could sneak out the back and get Snow, he'd find them. To punish her, and to stop her from trying to escape again, he might do more than just hurt her dog. So she did as she was told; she got in the shower and skimmed soap over her bruised skin. Ignoring her hair, she stepped out before the room had even had a chance to fill with steam.

Exhausted, and with sickening pain rolling through her body, she left her clothes where they lay, wrapped a towel around herself and headed back to her room, one step at a time. She let the towel fall and eased into bed. Maybe if she rested, she'd have more energy to think straight. Then she could come up with a plan that wouldn't get her friends or her dog hurt. Or worse.

As she fell into oblivion, she hoped that when she woke she'd realise she'd been having a nightmare, and that she was, in fact, living the life she'd begun to believe she could have. And so, when she woke naked, with an arm curled around her and an aroused body at her back, she smiled. It *had* been a nightmare. One she wouldn't hang onto or think about ever again.

But the deep breath she took seared her lungs and jerked her limbs, sending a chaos of pain and horror through her.

'Mmm,' Paul's sleepy voice hummed against her neck.

Icy panic shot through her, freezing her lungs and causing her heart to gallop, as all that had happened with Paul that morning flooded back. And now he was sleeping in her bed, curled against her as if they'd spent the night making love.

Pressing one hand to her mouth to stop the sudden rise of bile, she slid the other between her thighs. She'd know if he'd raped her, wouldn't she? He'd have been as rough as always, would have left her sore and sticky, so she'd know, right?

She had to get away from him before the need to scream, claw and beat at him overtook common sense. Shifting to the edge of the bed, she clutched the blankets to her chest as she sat up and swung her legs to the floor.

'You just took all the blankets.' He wasn't sleepy now, and his voice held a familiar edge as he yanked the bedding back over him, leaving her shivering and naked.

Covering herself as best she could with trembling hands, she stood and rummaged for something, anything, to stop him from looking at her.

'What are you doing?'

'Getting dressed.'

The bed squeaked as he sat up. 'Are you pissed at me? Did you expect me to sleep on your couch like an unwanted guest?'

Carol pulled on the Mothman jumper, feeling guilty that she wanted Blake close to her even as Paul glared at her from her bed—the bed where she and Blake had made love.

'I didn't say anything.'

'No, you're just looking at me like I raped you, so thanks for making me feel like utter shit.' He threw the blankets off and stomped into his boxers, then jeans, and shoved his arms through the sleeves of his shirt and jumper. 'I'm going out of my way to help you, Carol, so you better get over being so fucking dramatic or you're going to find out what being married to a monster is really like.'

He left the room and slammed the door behind him.

Hobbling as fast as her seized hip would let her, Carol made her way to the lounge room. She wouldn't let Snow take the brunt of Paul's ire. He was angry at her, so that's where she'd keep his focus.

223

Her usually hyperactive dog was curled in front of the fire, with his nose tucked to his tail. His eyes followed her as she walked to the couch and sat down. Her heart broke, and with it came rage. She'd never forgive Paul for dampening Snow's spark—and she'd always feel guilty for letting him.

But the fight in her disappeared when Paul walked out of the kitchen with a shopping bag in one hand and a steaming mug in the other. Ignoring her presence, he upended the bag's contents on the coffee table. Picking up a box of hair colour stripper, he clicked his fingers and pointed at the floor in front of him.

She eased down at his feet.

Without a word, he sat on the coffee table behind her and ran a hand through her hair, fisted it, then pulled her head back so she stared at his up-side-down face. 'Just in case you're confused again, I'm not going anywhere. All of this is your own fault. If you hadn't overreacted two years ago, we wouldn't be in this situation. You hurt me, then twisted things to suit yourself and make people feel sorry for you. But it didn't work, did it. Want to know why?'

Every bruised muscle screamed, but her heart screamed louder. 'Why?'

He shoved her head forward and ripped open the box. 'Because you're pathetic, and no one cares about you. Unlike your friend. She's been hard to get alone, which is why I was out on the road last night. That bastard Ryder has been spreading lies about me, asking questions that don't need to be asked. But what would he do, do you think, if his new wife had an accident? Especially now that she's pregnant.'

The icy zip that pulsed through her veins froze her heart. 'But you have me now. You don't need to hurt her or anyone else. I'll do whatever you want, you know I will.'

He cocked his head. 'Don't tell me what I can and can't do. And I know you'll do what I want. Girls like you always do, because if they don't, well ...' He leaned close to her ear. 'I know how to deal with them.'

#

224

As the morning sunshine thawed the grass outside his shed, Blake took progress photos of his current commission. With spring on the way, he'd have to think about stocking up on supplies, especially if he went into business with Drew. Haggling prices at garage sales around town with Carol at his side would be an experience. Would she laugh and tease him? Or would she flash that smile and show him just how it was done in a small country town?

As he walked back to the house, he smiled when the scent of pancakes hit him. At the side door, he kicked off his shoes and shrugged out of his coat, and as soon as he stepped into the warmth of the kitchen, his nose ran. Rubbing it, he flicked the kettle on.

'I'll be heading into town soon to pick Snow up and see Carol before she starts work. Let me know if you want anything.'

Drew flipped a pancake into the air, caught it with the frying pan and grinned. 'I'd say lunch, but I have a feeling you'll find a way to have yours at the pub.'

Blake shrugged. 'I figure that if I time it right, she'll just shake her head and give me that *I know exactly what you're doing* smile.'

It would pop her dimple and make his heart thud. Eager to see it, and her, he slipped his phone from his pocket and messaged her.

Heading in soon. I can drop you at work if you want. :)

She'd say no, but he'd keep offering, and one day she might take the chance to rely on him and say yes.

His phone dinged, and Drew's voice faded out as Blake read the message, twice. The words didn't make sense, and he checked to make sure it was Carol who'd sent it.

Don't bother. I don't want to see you anymore. Don't contact me, I won't answer.

He rang her anyway.

She answered. 'You said that if I ever asked, you'd leave me alone, Blake. I'm asking you to leave me alone.'

'I don't understand what's happening.'

'I told you I'm a shitty friend, but I've realised I'm not the only one who is. We're all better off without each other.' She sniffed. 'Goodbye, Blake.'

In the silence, his ears rang. Was he dreaming? Having a frighteningly real nightmare?

Drew moved in front of him, took his shoulders and gave him a light shake. 'Breathe, man! You're scaring me.' He shook harder when Blake just stared at him. 'What's wrong? Is it your mum?'

He shook his head. 'Carol.'

Drew frowned. 'Carol? Is she okay?'

Reality punched him in the gut. 'No.' He tipped his phone so Drew could see the message. 'She doesn't want to see me anymore.'

Drew mouthed *what the fuck*, which would have been comical under other circumstances, but Blake only felt twisted shards of the grief and dread he'd thought finally behind him. They lurched through him, doubling him over.

He was a little boy again, hearing his father's regret at having had children, facing the bullies in primary school, trying to fit in where he never belonged during his teenage years, then, as an adult, he was standing on the wrong side of the line to his peers. But none of those experiences had crushed his soul like Carol just had.

He couldn't grasp why she would deliberately hurt him. If she'd changed her mind and didn't want to be with him, she only had to say so, but to be so dismissive and cruel?

He stood straight again. 'Something's going on. This isn't how she does things.'

Drew turned the stove off. 'You'll go and see her?'

Blake thought about it. He could, but that might push her even further away. 'Not without finding out what's happened first.'

Drew glanced at him as he flipped the pancakes onto a plate. 'Do you think Mark talked to her again? She isn't being charged or something, is she?'

The smell that had moments before invigorated him now churned his stomach. Would he ever be able to smell pancakes without being pulled back to this moment?

'I don't know,' he said, 'but I know who to ask.'

Grabbing his keys and wallet, he strode towards the front door, but Drew hurried past him and put a hand out to stop him opening it.

226

'Give me three minutes. I'll get changed and come with you.'

'I don't have time to wait.'

'Bullshit. You drive in like this and you'll either get pulled over for speeding or run off the road, then where will you be?'

Blake waited while Drew got ready in record time.

He held his hand out for Blake's keys. 'She went to Kelsey's last night, didn't she? Did they fight?'

Blake closed his eyes, his head thumping as Drew negotiated the driveway. 'I messaged her last night. She said she got home and crashed but didn't mention Kelsey.'

Once on the road, he stared out of the window with one fist clenched in his lap, the other jammed under his chin and his elbow propped against the cold glass. What could he do but sit and stew until he knew where to direct the fire that flamed his blood.

'Want me to come in?' Drew asked as he pulled up in front of the red brick police station. Blake shook his head. 'I don't know how long I'll be.' Besides, Carol hadn't told Drew much about Paul, and Blake would rather be able to talk freely with Mark.

When Blake walked in, Mark stood at the front desk. He held a hand up before Blake could open his mouth. 'I'm only just hearing about the accident now, so I doubt I can tell you more than you already know.'

Blake stilled. 'What accident?'

Mark's usually guarded expression disappeared as he gaped at Blake. 'You weren't there?'

Bracing his hands on the counter, Blake contained the burst of dizziness. 'She told me she'd gone home and crashed.' He lifted his head. 'Paul's involved, isn't he?'

Before Mark could answer, the door opened and Kelsey strode in. 'Blake, I saw your car out front. Is Carol with you? She didn't turn up last night, and when I messaged her, she said she left your place too late and went home and crashed.'

Blake eyed Mark. 'Why is she lying to everyone?' He let his head fall back and swore at the ceiling. 'She's not. *He* is.'

Kelsey touched his arm. 'Who is?'

227

Carol deserved her privacy, but this wasn't the time for secrets. He'd keep as many of them as he could, but if Paul was behind her sudden change of heart, then he would do anything he could to free her. If she really did want him to leave her alone, he would, but the words had to come directly from her.

'Paul is making Carol lie to us,' he told Kelsey.

Kelsey frowned and shook her head. 'What? Why? How?'

Blake glanced at Mark. 'I don't know, but I'm going to find out.'

Mark cleared his throat. 'I'd advise you to take this to Ethan's office, and stay away from both Paul and Carol until I have more information.'

'You think I'm just going to stand back and do nothing?'

Mark raised an eyebrow. 'I'm telling you to wait. There's more at play here. Carol's dealt with Paul for four years now. I trust her to do it for a few more hours, and if all goes to plan, she won't have to for much longer.'

Blake jammed his balled fists into his pockets. 'What exactly is going on?'

'I can't tell you about an ongoing investigation.'

Mark's thinly disguised hint stopped Blake from getting arrested for assaulting a uniformed officer.

'Ongoing …' Questions jumbled and bunched, but he couldn't ask any of them.

'Sounds like you both know more than I do.' Kelsey pulled her phone out. 'Why has she deleted herself from our group chat? Why do you both think Paul has such a hold on her? What aren't you telling me?' Resting a hand on her baby bump, she stepped towards Mark. 'You know what she was going to tell me last night, don't you, and why she thought I'd need Ethan there to hear it.' She pointed at Blake. 'And you know too. Why don't I? Why hasn't she trusted me with it?'

Blake's mind was humming. 'I'll tell you what I can, but Mark is right. We need to talk somewhere without worrying about who's listening.' He gestured to the door. 'Drew's in my ute. Do me a favour and let him drive you around to Ethan's office, and I'll bring your car.'

Her chin lifted. 'I'm not going to break.'

'No,' he said, attempting a smile, 'but Carol would kick my arse if she knew I'd let you drive while you were upset.'

Kelsey burst into tears.

Mark grabbed a box of tissues and, coming around the counter, rubbed a hand up and down her back. 'It'll be okay.'

Kelsey shook her head as she pressed a handful of tissues to her face. 'What sort of friend am I that I couldn't be there for her? That she couldn't tell me what was going on in her life?'

'She didn't want to upset you,' said Blake, 'or remind you about everything you've been through. And if it makes you feel any better, she keeps saying she's a shitty friend because she thinks she hasn't been there for you.'

When Kelsey turned to Mark and buried her face against his chest, Blake stood helpless, his stomach a twisted ball of tortured dread. How was he going to stay away from Carol when Paul had clearly threatened her enough to make her step away from everyone she loved?

The phone rang, and Mark eased Kelsey back. 'I need to get that. If it's who I think it is, we're going to be one step closer to ending this.' He met Blake's gaze. 'Let me do my job so this ends the way we want it to, okay?' He didn't wait for an answer, just let himself back into the office area to answer the phone.

Kelsey wiped the last of her tears away. 'Okay. Let's get everyone together and get this sorted. I want my best friend back, and you want your girlfriend back.'

He did, because she *was* his girlfriend—though the word didn't properly convey what she actually meant to him. Regardless, she was his girlfriend until she looked him in the eye and told him otherwise.

CHAPTER 17

Carol stared at her reflection in the bathroom mirror. Her face lacked contour, life, as if he'd stripped the colour from her soul as well as her hair. A caricature of herself now, she turned her head, touched a finger to the mousy brown hair she hadn't had in two years.

Maybe she could shave it off. If she had clippers, she would, just to see what Paul would do. He couldn't hurt her anymore. He'd taken everything, left her life hollow, her heart vacant. And to keep those she loved safe she'd continue living the lie until she died.

As she dressed, layering clothes to keep Paul's touch as dull as possible, she embraced the pain that rippled through her with each movement. Her physical aches kept the emotional pain at bay. What she would do once she healed, she didn't know, but by the way Paul talked, she knew they wouldn't be in White Wattle Creek much longer.

Before that reality could take hold, she tidied the bathroom so that Paul didn't haul her back to do it, then closed the door behind her. In the kitchen, she boiled the kettle, set two cups out and wiped the circle of spilled coffee Paul had left on the bench.

After taking a moment to ready herself for whatever Paul had planned for her next, she took their drinks to the lounge room. And froze.

'What are you doing?'

Paul glanced up, with the sketchbook on his lap opened to pictures of Blake. 'These aren't me.'

Carol swallowed. 'No.'

He ripped a page out and held it up. 'If I had pictures of other women hidden under the bed, how would you feel?'

He'd had sex with another woman *in* her bed. Not that it mattered now. He could have sex with anyone he wanted, but he'd never touch her like that again.

She kept her thoughts to herself, though, and her face blank as he ripped the page in two.

He could destroy her relationship with Blake and erase every trace of him from her life, but he'd never be able to take Blake's face from her mind or the love she had for him from her heart. Those she would keep forever.

Paul held out the sketchbook. 'Rip it up and burn it.'

If she hesitated, he'd somehow make the demand worse, so she sat the mugs on the coffee table, but as she took the book from Paul, she caught the glint she'd sketched in Blake's eye. How had she convinced herself that she could live this life Paul had forced on her? How could she ignore the love that flowed through her just by looking at a sketch? How could she live her life never having Blake trace his fingers over her face, his lips under hers, his laughter dancing through her heart? She couldn't. Wouldn't. Burning the pictures she'd drawn while she'd been falling in love with Blake wouldn't kill her, but losing him forever because of a lie she'd told would, and that lie had to have carved out his heart.

Even if he never spoke to her again, she'd make sure he understood that he'd been everything good and right in her life. But to tell him that, she had to stop Paul from making good on his threats against Kelsey and Ethan—she had to find a way to expose him for the monster he was.

For now, she sat and carefully removed page after page from the book, her chest aching with each rip. She tore each sheet of paper until pieces of Blake lay scattered around her. They were only pictures but burning them was like cremating fragments of her heart.

Paul picked up his coffee, took a sip and grimaced. 'What else do you have that belongs to him?'

She resisted hugging the Mothman jumper closer to her skin. 'Nothing.'

Snapping his fingers, Paul pointed to the seat beside him on the couch. 'I don't know why you need to lie to me. I forgive you for trying to make me jealous with the artist, but I won't have reminders of him everywhere. Tell me what else is his.'

231

She pointed to the mantelpiece where a heart-shaped rock sat. She'd found it in his garden one day and had sat it on the step. She'd forgotten about it until he'd given it back to her. He'd wrapped it in wire after working the raw shape into a smooth heart that had melted hers.

Paul stood and picked up the rock, testing its weight in his palm. 'You surprise me. It's not like you to fall for sappy tokens.'

Carol kept her gaze on her hands. 'You don't know me.'

Dropping the rock on her coffee table, Paul sat on the couch once more. 'I know you better than you think, better than you know yourself. I know this is what you thrive on, what you secretly crave. You can't love and can't *be* loved. You were born to be alone, and without me, you will be. Once we're married, you won't talk about him or any of your so-called friends. The sooner we move away from here the better. Maybe then you'll remember everything I've done for you.'

Ice shot through Carol's veins. She couldn't marry him. She could move wherever he wanted and slowly die until she'd made sure her friends would be safe. But take his name? Legally be his to rule and use?

'You're going back to Adelaide?'

He glared at her. '*We* can't go back to Adelaide. Not yet anyway.'

She needed distance to make sure Kelsey was safe, only then could she escape and warn everyone what Paul had planned. 'But why not? It's where your friends are, your job.'

He curled a hand around her neck and pulled her face close to his. 'Because girls like you exist. Always talking, always complaining. Always wanting shit that they don't deserve, then crying foul when I give them what they do.'

Carol held her breath as she stared at Paul. Had that cold fury always lurked in his eyes? Had that tickle she'd felt in her throat the first time she met him been fear instead of misdirected attraction? Or, like her, had he changed and settled into a skin that cloaked who and what he was now.

Either way, she could never marry him and survive. Of course, he could demand anything, because he knew she'd do whatever it took to protect Kelsey and the rest of her friends.

In the pulsating silence, a phone buzzed.

Swearing, Paul stood and, pulling his phone from his pocket, frowned at the readout. He bared his teeth as it vibrated in his hand with another incoming call.

'Start packing,' he said. 'And my parents will want the house cleaned before we leave. I want to be out of this town by tomorrow and married by next week. I need you by my side. I need a family. Because who would people believe? Me, a soon-to-be doting father and a newlywed who's desperately in love with his wife? Or vindictive little girls out to destroy a man's image for money and fame?'

Carol blinked. It was all a ruse. She'd known that from the start, of course, but now it made sense. So how could she stop him?

'I can't leave yet.'

He raised an eyebrow at her. 'Pardon?'

She swallowed and closed her mouth.

Turning away, Paul tapped his phone and pressed it to his ear. 'You told me you'd sorted out this stupid charge,' he said by way of a greeting. 'Yeah, then why are they still calling me, trying to arrest me?' He paced away. 'They left me a message. I haven't listened to it yet.' Tipping his head back, he said, 'Fine.' Then he hung up, tapped his phone and pressed it to his ear again. And swore.

The glare he threw Carol evaporated the bubble of hope she'd nurtured from among her misery. Her plans of escape crumbled, and the future she'd begun to imagine with Blake once more now spun into a chaos of desolated horror that collapsed her soul—and her knees.

Paul squatted in front of her, gripped her chin and tilted it up. 'No use crying. Life's a bitch. And then you marry one.'

Though her back cramped, she didn't move. 'I have to ring work,' she said, her mind spinning. 'I'm supposed to start at midday.'

Paul snorted. 'And have your boss spread lies about why you're quitting? I don't think so. I'll take you down there, and you can tell him to his face that you're leaving with me. You'll tell anyone who asks that I saved you last night, that you've been trying to get me back, and that when I nearly lost you, I realised that what we had was everything.'

'I don't want to talk to anyone or even see anyone.'

He let her go and sat back, a lazy smile bending his lips. 'You know, I have some of the oddest friends. I know someone who knows someone who works with pyrotechnics in the movie industry. Do you know what happens when they rig a car to blow with dummies inside?' He leaned forward again. 'Beautiful chaos. Just imagine if someone was actually inside.'

In Carol's mind, Kelsey sat in the car, her face bloodied, her mouth open in a perpetual scream as the car erupted and tore her apart.

'I'll tell him,' she said. 'I'll tell anyone who asks.'

Paul tilted his head. 'Tell them what?'

Nausea burned her throat. 'That you saved me. That we're together.'

'And if they ask about the artist?'

Please, no one ask. 'I used him.'

He stood, picked up the heart rock, tossed it in the air and caught it. 'Good girl. Now, get changed and fix your face. Anyone would think you don't care how you look.'

He rolled his eyes at the jeans and Mothman jumper she'd struggled into earlier. She could waste time now by putting on clothes he wouldn't like, but every small movement felt like a sledgehammer to the ribs, so she pulled out the long forest green skirt shoved to the back of her wardrobe and topped it with a baby-blue knitted top. She hated it.

Paul chewed on the last apple from the dish on her bench and circled his finger in the air. When she'd completed a slow spin and faced him again, he pursed his lips. 'It's a start, I guess. One more thing, though.' He tapped a finger to her eyebrow piercing. 'This isn't my Carol.'

No matter how much he changed her on the outside, inside she'd never be his. She removed the silver bar and handed it to him. He threw it into the empty fruit bowl, where it clinked against the glazed bottom. Most of her body throbbed; the parts that didn't stung like a white-hot needle sat under her skin.

'I need to take some pain meds.'

Paul took her arm. 'You don't need them. Let's get this done so I can get out of here.'

Panicked, she glanced around for something, anything to stop him. 'Don't you want me to clean the house?' If it meant she could stay another day, she'd do it. Because surely then someone would come looking for her. Wouldn't they?

As though he'd read her mind, he sneered down at her. 'So you can escape? I don't think so. I'll pay someone to do it and you can owe me.'

Carol shivered all the way to the pub—walking into the warmth of the dining room didn't stop the tremors—and when Paul announced their farce of an engagement to the first person they saw, the ice around her heart thickened.

To escape the congratulations and hugs, Carol stepped away from Paul and found her boss in the kitchen. He was getting ready for the lunch hour.

He glanced at her over his shoulder, gave her a once-over, then went back to checking off his list. 'You got my message then.'

Carol gritted her teeth. 'No. My phone is flat.'

He pursed his lips and glanced at her again. 'I guess that's why you never got back to me.'

'I'm sorry.'

He put his hands on his hips and sighed. 'You aren't one for leaving me hanging as far as shifts go, so I'll look past it this time, but next time I won't be so lenient.'

Carol hugged herself. 'There won't be a next time. I'm leaving.'

His expression flickered from stern to surprised and finally settled on confused. 'I think there's been some miscommunication. Taking you off the roster until the complaint has been looked into isn't meant to be a punishment, just a precaution. When it comes to sexual harassment, I need to do things by the book.'

Carol blinked. 'I didn't make a complaint.'

Setting his list aside, he came to stand in front of her. 'Paul made the complaint. He said that when he tried to talk to you, you tried to kiss him, and when he refused, you slapped him.'

If she laughed now, she wouldn't stop until she passed out. Besides, her ribs couldn't take it.

'I don't know what to say,' she said, 'other than that's not what happened.'

'Then what did happen? Because I didn't think that sounded like you.'

235

'There you are.' Paul gripped her shoulder. 'Everyone wants to say congratulations.'

Her boss glanced from her to Paul. 'Congratulations?'

Paul smiled. 'She wore me down, so we're moving and getting married.'

Her boss ran through his confused-surprised-stern cycle once more. 'Married?' he said to Paul. 'We were just talking about the complaint you made, and now you're saying you're together?'

Paul's grip tightened on her shoulder, but he smiled. 'What can I say, the world's a crazy place. Come on,' he said to Carol, 'people who care about you want to talk to you.' Tugging her away, he leaned down and ran his lips over her ear. 'Just remember, you don't have that many more people to lose, so I'd hate to see anything happen to the few you pretend to care about.'

Carol stayed silent through each hug that squeezed her already abused ribs. She'd given up telling people it hurt to be touched, that she'd been in hospital overnight because of the accident. And each time Paul told the tale of how he'd saved her, it distorted and grew until it sounded as if Carol had deliberately tried to get herself run over and that he had singlehandedly saved her from the fiery crash that had nearly killed her.

People patted her hand and told her she was lucky. Told her that with Paul, she'd have nothing to be depressed about and everything to live for. Everyone was sympathetic, except for Mr Arden, Annie and Alex—they listened to Paul with raised eyebrows and exchanged glances.

Mr Arden pulled her aside first. 'This seems sudden, Carol. And it's not exactly in keeping with what you were saying and clearly feeling yesterday.'

She kept her gaze on the *Love is Love* button Mr Arden had pinned to his lapel. 'It's all a lie.'

'What you were saying yesterday, or the story he's telling today?'

Keeping the truth from him, from everyone, became harder every time she opened her mouth, so she kept it shut. Mr Arden rested a hand on her shoulder and made her wince.

He lifted his hand a fraction. 'Are you hurt?'

Carol nodded and dropped her gaze to the floor. Paul could tell the tale and change it to his liking. It didn't matter anymore.

As if he'd heard her thoughts, Paul came over and wound a possessive arm around her waist. 'What stories are we telling now, Carol?' He smiled at Mr Arden. 'I keep warning her that making things up will only come back to bite her.'

Mr Arden stroked his beard. 'I agree with the sentiment, but to my knowledge, Miss McGrath isn't one for being dishonest. I can't say the same about you, Mr Todd.'

Carol jerked her gaze up to Paul. Would he blame her for Mr Arden's words and strike out at Kelsey, Snow or someone else she loved?

Too hot now, she tugged at the neckline of her top. The room began to spin, the floor to tilt. Carol knew she had three options: she could give in and let oblivion take her, she could hide away in the dark and hope that when she woke the nightmare would be over, or she could grit out a smile and keep it together until her friends were safe.

Taking a deep breath, she met Mr Arden's gaze but couldn't manage the smile. 'I'm not above telling a lie to keep the peace.'

Mr Arden frowned as he searched her face. 'I've found that telling the truth is better in the long run. At least then everyone knows exactly what's going on.'

With a laugh, Paul tightened his hold on her, his fingers digging into her bruised muscles. 'People living in small towns think they know everything anyway, don't they? But you can tell him, babe. Tell him the truth about us.'

Holding Mr Arden's gaze, she gritted her teeth. 'Yesterday was yesterday, today is today, and this is where I have to be.'

Paul snorted. 'She's always been about as elegant with words as she is with clothes. That'll change soon.' Turning away, he tugged her with him. 'Come on, people want to congratulate us.'

Though her pain made her lightheaded, Carol glanced back at Mr Arden and hoped that he'd understood.

#

Blake gathered with everyone in the tearoom of P B & R Solicitors, and though he sat at the head of the table, the six people sitting with him had just as much at stake in losing Carol as he did. Only they didn't know it yet, because he hadn't found the words to tell them. But if they were going to get her back, there were things they needed to know.

He cleared his throat and everyone turned towards him.

'There's a lot I won't tell you,' he said, 'because it's Carol's story to keep or share, but I will say that Paul isn't who you think he is. He didn't break her heart when he left town, he broke her spirit and her trust well before that.'

Jex sat his mug down with a snap. 'The bastard stripped her bare emotionally and used us to keep her in line. He made her believe that no one cared about her, that she was worth nothing.'

Kelsey frowned. 'Why didn't I know about this?'

Ethan put a hand on her shoulder. 'You aren't the only one.'

Blake sighed and rubbed his hands over his face. 'Whenever she tried to tell anyone, he made life hell for her. He'd convinced everyone that she was an unhinged wild child, while he was her saviour. Or at least that he'd tried to be. She didn't break into the bakery or destroy my artwork. She's not that sort of person. And she's not the sort of person to stay away from her friends or break up with someone via text message unless something else is going on.'

Lilli sat forward. 'She broke up with you?'

He took a deep breath. 'I don't believe she did. I think Paul either sent the message himself or made her do it.' He told them what he could and hoped she'd forgive him for telling her secrets. When he finished, they all sat staring at him. 'My theory is that Paul was somehow involved in the accident last night. Either that or he heard about it and took the opportunity to get close to her so he could control her again. Most likely by threatening to harm one of us.'

Ethan pushed up from the table to pace. 'I've been digging, asking questions. He's not a squeaky-clean golden boy like everyone thinks. In fact, the only reason he's not behind bars for harassment and rape is because he has money and a slick lawyer.'

Kelsey turned to stare at her husband. 'You didn't tell me any of that.'

'Most of it I only found out this morning. It worried me that she wanted me there when she talked to you. I knew it had to be about more than Paul being an arsehole. I should have realised when she said she was worried about triggering you, but I honestly didn't think she was hiding anything so serious.'

Kelsey sighed. 'I should have seen it too. I should have known. But she should have told me, regardless.'

Lilli raised a hand. 'Sometimes we hurt the ones we love when we're trying to protect them.'

Zoe snorted a laugh. 'That's why it's better to look out for yourself. Less trouble and less pain.'

Lilli shook her head. 'I'll never understand you.'

Zoe merely shrugged. 'You don't need to.'

Frowning, Drew leaned forward. 'So, in short, this Paul dude is manipulating her to do what he wants, and has been for four years but only occasionally during the last two?'

Blake could only nod. 'That's the crux of it.'

'So, what are we going to do about it?' In his calming way, Jex reached out to stop Lilli chewing her thumb nail. 'There are seven of us, eight counting Carol, and only one of him. We make sure she's safe with one of us until he leaves.'

'Except she's been with me most days,' said Blake, 'and he's still getting to her. Besides, she won't agree to being babysat twenty-four seven.'

'And she shouldn't have to.' Kelsey blew out a breath. 'I know what it's like to be stalked. It takes every bit of energy to act normally, which is probably why she's stayed away from everyone. Except you.' She gave Blake a smile.

Blake flipped his phone over as it vibrated on the table. Alex was calling him, but he ignored it. 'Mark wants me, us, to stay away for now. He mentioned an ongoing investigation, which I think was his way of saying Paul's about to get what's coming to him, but it's killing me to know she's having to bend to his will, for whatever reason.'

His phone vibrated again, so he picked it up and answered the call. 'I'm in the middle of something, Alex. Can this wait?'

'Depends,' Alex drawled. 'I'm at the pub with mum for a going away lunch, and I wanted to invite you.'

Blake rubbed at his temple. 'Where's Mum going?'

239

'No, I'm the one who's leaving. I start a job up north next week.'

'Look, I don't have time for this right now. Carol might be in trouble, and I need to sort out what to do.'

'Well, that's the other reason I'm calling. She's here, with Paul, and he's announced to everyone that they're engaged and moving, probably overseas. Jex mentioned that you and Carol had grown pretty close, so I thought you might like to know.'

Blake's world stopped. He heard nothing other than the thud of blood in his ears. His focus narrowed to the next breath, the next heartbeat. When someone took the phone from his hand, he let them.

Cold hands pressed to his cheeks and turned his head. Kelsey held his gaze, her mouth moving, but all he could hear was Carol's laughter, her voice as she sang. Did Paul think he could take her away? Did he think no one would step in to make sure Carol chose who she wanted to be with, where she wanted to go, what she wanted to do?

Of course he did, because he had control. And unless her friends believed the truth, Paul would continue to drive a wedge between them and Carol.

'You believe she didn't break in to the bakery and the town hall, don't you?' Blake asked Kelsey.

She frowned, then closed her eyes. 'Paul did.'

He nodded. 'She couldn't prove it. Just like she can't prove anything else he's done. He always gets in and spreads his lies before she has a chance to tell the truth.'

Kelsey sank into her seat. 'And we believed whatever he said. No wonder she didn't trust us with the truth.'

'She wanted to.' Blake glanced around the table, where everyone sat looking at him.

Jex had Blake's phone, his usual smile a flat line as he talked to Alex.

'Are Paul and Carol still at the pub?' Blake asked.

Jex nodded. 'Paul's parading her around like she's a goat he's made into a goddess. Alex's words, not mine.'

Blake sat straight and squared his shoulders. He had to make sure Carol was free to make her own choices. 'Tell him I'll be there soon.'

Ethan stood and offered a hand to Kelsey. 'Tell him we'll all be there soon.'

CHAPTER 18

Paul pulled a chair out at one of the dining tables, squeezed Carol's shoulder until she sat, then bent and kissed her cheek.

'Do people still hunt witches?' he asked her. 'It'd be sad if Annie Sender met the same fate as her ancestors.'

Her pulse jumped. 'She hasn't done anything to you.'

'She put her hands on you and gave me the evil eye. I have every right to protect what's mine. And you are mine, aren't you?'

Her throat closed on the word, but she pushed it out. 'Yes.'

With a smile, he patted her on the head. 'Good girl. Now sit there and don't cause any trouble.'

While Paul stood beside her talking and laughing with his friends, Carol sat and tore a paper serviette into confetti, which she let float to the floor around her. The throb in her temple had reduced to a pinpoint when the chair beside her shifted away from the table and Mrs Glade sat next to her.

She touched Carol's hair. 'This is such a big change that I hardly recognised you.'

Paul turned and put a hand on Carol's shoulder. 'It makes her look like an adult now, don't you think?'

Mrs Glade held Carol's gaze. 'I heard you're leaving?'

Hearing those words spoken by someone else, Carol's situation became real. She stared intently at Mrs Glade. 'Can I ask you a favour?'

Paul bent and braced his hands on the table. 'She's your neighbour, not your fairy godmother.'

'*She* is the cat's mother.' Mrs Glade took Carol's hand. 'Ask me anything.'

Take me home, away, anywhere but here. Take me to Blake, even if he won't talk to me or doesn't want me anymore.

She wanted to tell him the truth about everything, wanted him to know that he inspired hope when he took what was broken and discarded and made it new again. He deserved to know that she hadn't rejected him, that when she'd said she was falling for him, she'd meant it. But to keep him safe those words would stay locked in her heart.

'Will you look after Snow for me?' she asked instead. 'I'd be happy if Blake took him, but if he doesn't want him'—she took a shaky breath—'will you find him a good home?'

With tears in her eyes, Mrs Glade picked up a serviette and handed it to Carol. 'If that's what you want, I'll make sure that he's happy and loved.'

Carol nodded. She wouldn't cry, though she gripped the serviette tightly. She had nothing left to give. Paul had stripped her of everything. She'd be his plaything. His dog on a leash. His alibi. And though keeping her distance from her friends might make them safer, Paul would always have enough power over her to keep that leash chokingly short.

As more people arrived to congratulate them, Carol sipped the water Alex had given her and tried to blank her mind. But she could not escape the chatter and laughter as the dining room, which maxed out at seventy diners on the busiest of days, became standing room only.

How could it be that among so many people she drowned in silence? How could no one hear her screaming? Why had no one noticed that she was slowly dying? She sat alone, crumbling from the inside while people laughed and toasted to their happiness.

Someone patted her shoulder. 'Will you sing one last time before you go?'

Carol kept her head down. 'I can't.'

Like a shark smelling blood, Paul turned around. 'Of course you can.' He grinned at the woman who'd asked. 'Are all creatives like this? Needing their ego stroked every five minutes?' Holding his hand out to Carol, he pulled her close when she stood. 'Sing me a song, babe.'

Hiding her limp, she made her way through the crowd, blindly acknowledging the congratulations and pats on the back she received as if she'd won some big prize.

243

In the room behind the bar, where Jex stored a couple of guitars and a small sound system, Carol leaned against the wall and closed her eyes. This couldn't work. Sacrificing herself for her friends was not only stupid but worthless. If they found out that she'd gone with Paul to protect them—instead of trusting them, banding together and taking him down—they'd be insulted, offended and angry. How could they not? It's how she'd felt when Kelsey had first returned. And though she now understood what Kelsey had tried to do, Carol had at first resented her for not confiding in her friends.

So why hadn't she told Kelsey the truth about Paul? The excuse of protecting her didn't hold; Kelsey was one of the strongest people Carol knew. She wouldn't have belittled Carol's pain. She would have hugged her and stroked her back the way she did with Pipa. Then right after she'd told Carol everything would be okay, she would have sat her down so they could work out how to make it so. And if Carol had explained everything to Ethan and Mark, if she'd given them the chance, they would have done the same.

She should have trusted her friends, then maybe they would have trusted her and believed her without question. Instead, she'd let them down. Let herself down. It was time to stop that now so she could stop Paul. Whether her friends forgave her or not, it was time to tell the truth, to everyone. She had to warn those closest to her that Paul was not just an arsehole but a dangerous one.

She lifted a hand and waited for the shaking to start. Nothing. She put that same hand to her chest, where her heart beat a steady rhythm. This was right. Telling her truth and standing against the lies Paul had been spreading for too long wouldn't destroy her. People would think and say what they wanted whether she stood up to Paul or not. What mattered was what her friends thought. And that she prevented Paul from breaking more girls in the future. What she saw in the mirror each day and the way she moved through the world mattered. Living her life in the skin she wore, in the skin that fit instead of suffocated, mattered. Being the person Paul wanted her to be would kill her. The version of herself who loved Blake, Kelsey and all her friends was the person she wanted to be.

It was time.

Taking a guitar, she stepped from the room and made her way to the cleared space where someone had put out a chair for her. People were crammed around each table while others leaned against the walls and bar.

Paul raised his drink in a salute as she sat and tried to find a comfortable way to hold the guitar.

'Sorry, everyone,' she said, speaking into the mic. 'As you might have heard, I was in an accident last night.' She strummed the guitar and glanced at Paul. 'Apparently, I have Paul to thank for surviving it.'

The door jangled as more people came in. Not just anyone, though, but those who mattered most. Blake, his eyes bleak, met her gaze. She held it, cleared her throat and started strumming Ed Sheeran's 'Thinking out Loud'.

'I don't remember much about the accident,' she said, 'just bright lights and the scream of metal on bitumen. But I do remember how I spent the hours before that. Maybe because they were filled with love. So, remembering that and knowing what I know'—she shifted her gaze to Paul as she started strumming something new—'I want to dedicate this song to Paul, the man who changed my life and made me understand where I fit in the world and what I want.'

Glad that his smile faltered when she hummed a few bars, she started singing Sex Pistols' 'Whatcha Gonna Do About It', a classic hate song.

The room erupted. Some cheered, some stood with confused frowns frozen on their faces. Others whispered, pointed.

Paul was the first to her side and held his hands up to the crowd. 'What Carol didn't tell you is that she's unwell, not just from the concussion but from her ongoing mental health problems.' He grabbed her arm and leaned down, making it look as if he were helping her stand. 'What the fuck!'

Carol shoved him away and, groaning, pushed to her feet. 'I'm sorry, everyone. That was wrong of me. I should have just told you all straight up that I haven't agreed to marry Paul and I don't want to go anywhere with him. The only reason he wants me by his side is so he can protect his image and save himself from the accusations of other girls he's abused.'

Paul stepped in front of her. 'Like I said, she's unstable. I've been trying to get her the help she needs for years now, but she refuses to admit she has a problem.'

Mr Arden crossed his arms. 'How about you move out of the way and let her speak?'

Paul laughed. 'You can't believe anything she says. She's a compulsive liar.'

Mr Arden lifted his chin. 'That hasn't been my experience.'

A rumble of agreement travelled the room. Bolstered, Carol sidestepped Paul. 'The truth is, I'm not the weak, reckless, immature and unworthy small-minded girl he's tried to tell you I am. I'm not mentally unstable, either. But I have been foolish in thinking that if I go along with his games my friends would be safe, because he threatened to harm them to keep me quiet. He manipulated me, stalked me and made me do things that I'll forever be ashamed of doing. But it all stops now.'

She faced Paul. 'I'm taking back the power I gave you out of fear and shame. I'm not letting you hurt my friends or anyone else. I'll be telling the police that you threatened Kelsey's life last night and, not even half an hour ago, Annie's.'

'Really? And when they hear this?' He pulled out his phone and tapped the screen. Her voice echoed loud in the silence. 'Now what will they believe?'

Fighting the urge to run, Carol blocked out the sound. 'I was seventeen. You were twenty-two. What's your excuse?'

Alex stepped forward. 'Yeah, you know that's statutory rape, don't you?'

Not even Paul's fake tan could keep the colour on his face. 'I didn't do anything. *She* seduced *me*. What was I supposed to do?'

Alex snorted. 'Even if that were true, it's on you. You were the adult, so it's safe to say you're in a shit ton of trouble.'

Paul grabbed her arm. 'Tell them the truth!'

Zoe pushed through the crowd at the back. 'I can tell them the truth.' Her cheeks were bright on her pale face as she lifted a finger and pointed at Paul. 'He's a sick, manipulating bastard. He bragged to me about setting Carol up for both the bakery and town hall break-ins, and he threatened to tell everyone things about me if I didn't help him stalk her. I'm sorry, Carol. I'm so sorry.'

Carol didn't know what to say. It wasn't okay—it crushed her to know that Zoe had hurt her like that—but she'd experienced Paul's controlling tactics firsthand. And although she'd like to believe that she wouldn't have deliberately hurt anyone else, especially not her friends, could she fully blame Zoe? Only time would tell. Right now, she had more important things to deal with.

When another person stepped forward, Paul swore under his breath. The girl, a teenager, hugged herself. 'He threatened to … hurt my brother if I didn't sleep with him. He was rough, and I didn't want to, but I didn't know what else to do.'

Paul tried another laugh. 'It wasn't like that. She's remembering it wrong because she was drunk. She wanted it.'

The girl wiped at the tears running down her cheeks. 'No, I wasn't, and I didn't want anything to do with you.'

Wanting to go to the girl and wrap her arms around her, to tell her everything would be okay and that it wasn't her fault, Carol twisted out of Paul's grip but jolted to a stop when he grabbed her again.

Carol glared at his hand on her arm. 'Let me go. I have witnesses now when I say I don't want you anywhere near me ever again. I don't want you to touch me ever again.' She bent his hand back. 'You don't scare me anymore, but you better be afraid of me because I'm owning my truth from now on.'

Blake burst through the crowd just as Paul grabbed for her again. He knocked Paul back a step and stood in front of Carol, a human barrier between her and the man who would do her harm. 'You better listen to her, because not only will she kick your pathetic arse but so will plenty of others.'

A few people in the crowd had their phones out, either snapping pictures or filming the unfolding drama or talking rapid-fire to those missing out. The girl who'd stepped forward cried in her mother's arms, while Annie had an arm around Zoe, who, though she stood dry-eyed, trembled visibly.

Wishing that Blake would gather her in and hold her, Carol gritted her teeth. Would she have that with him now? Too afraid to ask, she rested her hand on the small of his back as she moved to stand beside him.

Lifting her chin, she held Paul's cold gaze. 'I suggest you leave and find a lawyer, because you're going to need one.'

Paul jabbed a finger at her face. 'Fuck that. Fuck this. Fuck her and fuck you.' He turned to the crowd. 'And fuck all of you. You think you're all so righteous, so wholesome. But I know things about each of you, just remember that.' He turned to stalk away, but the crowd refused to part for him, so he swore and shoved his way through.

The pub door opened before Paul could reach it, and when Mark walked in, fully kitted up, everyone in the room seemed to hold their breath.

Paul stopped. Held by the crowd at his back, he glanced left and right as if looking for a way out.

Carol slipped her hand into Blake's, and when he gave hers a squeeze, she had to swallow back her tears. Things had shifted between them. How could they not? She'd hurt him, had ripped their connection to shreds, even though it had been right and true. She didn't have the words to tell him what she needed to right then, so she took comfort in the feel of his hand in hers as Paul and Mark each stood with their feet planted, the air around them electric.

Mark hooked his thumbs in his vest. 'Paul Todd, can I talk to you outside?'

'You can't touch me.' Paul waved his phone in the air. 'I've talked to my lawyer, and you can't fucking touch me.'

Mark stepped forward. 'Let's talk outside. Don't make this worse than it already is.'

Paul turned to glare at Carol. 'This is your fault. You did this. Remember that.'

She shook her head. 'No. It's all on you.'

Paul jutted his chin and stalked towards the doors as if he'd decided to cooperate, but he pushed past Mark at the last second.

Mark had him pinned to the carpet within seconds, then two more officers rushed in and cuffed him.

Carol wondered whether she should have felt something in that moment. Or maybe when Paul, sullen and silent, was frogmarched from the room filled with people who would forever whisper about him. But as she sank into a chair with her knees shaking, the thing she hung onto, the thing that mattered most, was the warmth of Blake's hand in hers.

#

Carol took the painkillers and the bottle of water Mark held out to her, then grimaced as she swallowed the pills. Even doing that hurt her ribs now. Beside her, in the mostly empty pub, Mrs Glade put her phone on silent and placed it face down on the table.

Willing the painkillers to work, Carol closed her eyes. 'When you told me to be careful about who I spoke to, it wasn't because you didn't want me to smear Paul's reputation, was it?'

Mrs Glade's breath hitched. 'That's what you thought?'

Carol opened her eyes. 'At the time, I thought the town would riot if I said anything against him. To me, it seemed as if everyone loved him and thought he could do no wrong.'

Mrs Glade shifted forward in her seat and took Carol's face in her hands. 'I'll be honest, I did think you were carrying some resentment, maybe even bitterness, towards Paul because of the way he left you, but I believed you when you said you wanted to move on. I was worried that, with the influence he had around town, if you said something he didn't like, he might have had you charged with slander, and then things would have gotten even worse for you. When I talked to Mr Glade about it, he agreed that Paul Todd is an entitled little prick.'

Carol blinked. 'Are you drunk?'

Mrs Glade's laughter bounced around the walls. 'No, but maybe I can talk Mr Glade into pouring me a few later.'

Carol screwed up her face at the images Mrs Glade's words conjured. 'Why do you always tell me stuff like that?'

Patting Carol's cheeks, Mrs Glade sat back. 'We were never able to have children, but if we'd had a daughter, I'd like to think she would have been just like you.'

249

Mrs Glade's smile held the same glow of love and affection Gran's often had, and Carol had to press a hand to her chest to keep her heart in place. 'I thought you just liked teasing me.'

'Why else do people have kids?' Mrs Glade winked, then softened her smile. 'I couldn't say this while you were my student, but I want you to know that your parents don't deserve you. You deserve so much more than they've ever given you.' She leaned over and pressed a kiss to Carol's cheek. 'Just know that I'm here if you need me.' With a pat on Carol's shoulder, she got up and made her way to the bar where her husband waited.

Carol sniffed and took the tissue Mark offered her. He'd been quiet throughout the exchange, his face passive.

'I know you're angry with me,' she told him, 'and I'm sorry I didn't tell you the truth when you asked, but at the time, I didn't think I had much choice.'

He kept his steady gaze on her. 'And now?'

'You did what you could with what you knew. I know you'd be there for me.'

He shook his head. 'I *am* here for you. And I'm not angry. Not at you anyway. I should have seen, even back then, that something was going on. I'm sorry I didn't.' He rubbed at his chin. 'I guess that's the common thread. He's so good at lying and finding ways to manipulate people that even his victims' families are unaware until their daughters break down and confess.'

Carol slumped forward and hugged herself. 'I could have stopped him. If I'd said something sooner, I could have stopped him from hurting anyone else. But I didn't.'

He rested a hand on her shoulder. 'Do you blame them for not coming forward?'

'That's different.'

'Because you're somehow better than them?'

Her chin shot up. 'No.'

Mark nodded. 'No. You didn't say anything because you didn't have the support you needed at the time. You can't blame the kid you were through the filter of knowledge you have now.'

She frowned, because although she'd carry the guilt of her silence for a while at least, his words made sense. 'What do I do now?'

Mark stood and helped her up. 'The detectives will be in touch. They'll need you to make a statement. Until then, go home, rest and let everyone mollycoddle you for a bit. They're going to need to.'

She wasn't so sure about that, but she let him lead her to the door. 'No one says mollycoddle anymore.'

He shrugged. 'My mum does.'

Carol gave him a smile. 'I'll make sure I use it too, then.'

He opened the door for her, and when she stepped out into sunshine, she blinked. Then blinked again when everything blurred, because everyone had waited for her. Blake, Alex and Drew leaned against Blake's ute, and Ethan, Kelsey and Lilli stood with them. Zoe sat alone on the park bench across the road, but she got up and walked over as everyone crowded around Carol.

Carol clasped her hands together so that she didn't reach for Blake. What right did she have to touch him or seek the warmth and strength he'd always offered?

'Mark says I'm free to go,' she told everyone awkwardly.

Blake held a hand out to her. Almost too afraid to take it, she held her breath when his fingers closed gently around hers. He tilted his head to his ute, and with her heart already wobbling, she turned to see Snow sitting in the front seat, his nose pressed to the partially open window.

Blake tugged her forward. 'I just wanted you to know that he's safe.'

Turning her face to his chest, Carol finally let her tears fall. Blake's arms, tender and warm, came around her and broke the last of her resistance. She wanted this, *him*, for the rest of her life. She wanted to accept whatever he gave her. She wanted to make him smile and laugh, to give him the same joy she'd found in being with him. But if she'd fractured that, even a little, she'd have to find a way to live with it.

He pressed warm lips to her temple. 'What can I do? Where can I take you?'

'Home,' she said, turning her face to his. 'Take me home with you?'

His smile loosened her chest. 'Home it is, then.'

#

Although Blake wiped sweat from his forehead, Carol still shivered, so he turned the ute's heat up to maximum.

Behind them, Drew drove Zoe's car, while the twins followed in Lilli's. Jex and Alex followed in Alex's car, and Kelsey and Ethan brought up the rear of their convoy.

Carol had said nothing on the way out of town and the silence was killing him.

'Do you have any follow-up doctor's appointments?' he asked, just for something to say.

She shook her head. 'Not yet. I have to make one.'

'I'm sorry I wasn't there for you, Carol.'

She rolled her head and pinned him with a miserable stare. 'I'm sorry for hurting you.'

The fear of losing her to self-recrimination ran a cold finger down his back, so he rested his elbow on the console between their seats and offered his hand. She flexed her fingers, then slowly, gently, put her hand in his. It was a small step forward, and he wouldn't take her trust for granted.

When they passed the Ryder's turn-off, Carol's grip tightened.

Blake glanced at her, his heart jumping when he saw how pale she'd become. 'What's wrong?'

'Lights.' She held up her free hand as though shading her eyes. 'It happened here, along this stretch of road. The lights were so bright. I'd slowed down to turn into Kelsey's, but I couldn't see. I panicked, hit the brakes and came off my bike.' Clearly haunted, she turned to him, her eyes slowly focusing. 'I wasn't speeding or on the wrong side of the road. The lights blinded me. And Paul didn't just happen to find me. He told me he'd been waiting for Kelsey because Ethan had been poking around.'

'It's okay. You'll tell Mark, and Paul will be held accountable for everything he's done.'

She sighed, releasing tension and fear, and her shoulders sagged. 'Will you sit with me when they take my statement?'

He lifted their joined hands and kissed her knuckles. 'I'll sit with you anywhere, for anything.'

Her lips curved, just a little. 'Very smooth.' But then her frown returned. 'I didn't mean anything I said to you on the phone. You know that, don't you?'

Turning onto McGrath Lane, Blake took a moment to choose his words carefully. 'It killed me at the time, to hear you say those things. I couldn't understand what had changed between us. But it didn't take me long to figure out it was him making you push me away. So yes, I know you didn't mean any of it.' Her fingers flexed in his grip, but he held on. 'Carol, you need to understand that it was his intention to hurt you just as much as me when he forced you to call me. And as long as you blame yourself for hurting me, it'll keep hurting us.'

She held her silence as he drove along the dirt road, the other five cars following like a lazy snake down his driveway before parking side by side in his front yard.

Blake was at Carol's door before she could open it, and offering her an arm, he helped ease her down. Each time she grimaced or held her breath he wanted to swear. Now that she was safe and he had her back, the reality of nearly losing her almost buckled his knees. He needed some time, just a minute or two, to sit in the quiet with her before they dove into a conversation that would be devastating and exhausting for all of them.

'Do you want to get changed?'

Carol ran a hand over her skirt. 'I don't have any other clothes.'

He put a fingertip to her cheek and her gaze lifted to his. 'You know you can wear anything of mine.'

'Thank you,' she said and walked ahead of him to the house.

Blake followed her to his room, but when she went to stand at his window, staring out at the paddocks beyond instead of rifling through his cupboards, he stood awkwardly by the door.

'I'm … I'm not sure what to do now, what to say,' he said.

She turned to face him. 'If you've changed your mind about us, if I've hurt you too badly to fix things, tell me now. I'd rather know before I go out there and bare my soul so everyone can get their answers and go home.'

253

'Whoa, hey.' Going to her, he put his hands on her shoulders but lifted them when she winced. 'Do you know why everyone is here? They're here because they want to support you, not hammer you for answers. If you tell them nothing more than what they already know, they won't push, because they love and respect you. They want to know what's happened so they can help you, in any way they can.'

She hugged herself. 'I don't know why they'd want to.'

Dipping his head, he gave her a pointed look. 'Carol, that's not you talking.'

Her eyes fell closed, and she lifted a shaking hand to her mouth. 'No, it's not. But right now, I don't really know who I am.'

He gathered her close as her tears fell, and when her arms went around his waist and she held on, relief flooded through him.

'It'll be okay,' he said. 'You'll see. You were well on your way to finding yourself before he came back to town, and you'll do it again. But this time, you have all of us to lean on.'

She sniffed and rubbed her face on his jumper. 'You didn't say whether I hurt you too badly.'

'Don't take the blame for that. It was his fault, not yours. And I promise you, my feelings for you haven't changed.' Framing her face with his hands, he kissed her nose. 'Do you know how strong you were to stand up there and tell everyone what he did to you?'

'I couldn't give you up.'

Blake rested his chin on the top of her head and rocked them both. They would be okay. It would take some time for Carol to heal, for the two of them to get back to where they'd been, but he had plenty of that. He had her, she had him, and that was all that mattered.

After he'd helped her change, Carol sighed. 'I guess we better go out and get this done.'

He smiled. 'I like it when you say *we*.'

'I was scared I'd lost the right to say it, but I'm so thankful I haven't.' She pressed her palms to his cheeks. 'I love you, Blake. I knew it before, but I want everyone else to know it now. And I want you to know it too, beyond a doubt.'

'I have no doubts. Because I love you too.'

Pressing her lips to his in the sweetest kiss, she sighed against his mouth.

CHAPTER 19

At the head of the scarred dining table, Alex tapped a finger against his mug. 'So this all started back when we were in high school?'

Carol had shared the bones of the story with everyone, but some details she kept between her and Blake—he was the only person she wanted to share everything with.

'Yeah,' she said, answering Alex's question. 'At the time I didn't realise he was controlling me, only that I was miserable and alone. Everyone was dealing with their own shit and seemed to be surviving okay, so why couldn't I? I felt like the weakest one of our group, and Paul homed in on that. It was like a game to him.'

Lilli shook her head. 'You weren't weak then, and you definitely aren't now.'

Kelsey leaned across the table and took Carol's hand. 'I'll second that.'

'I'm sorry I didn't tell you the truth,' Carol told her. 'It wasn't that I didn't trust you, or any of you.' She glanced at each of her friends before focusing again on Kelsey. 'I was worried about you, about how you'd react when you were still dealing with your own trauma. I didn't want to add to your problems or remind you about your own.'

'I understand that, but I've been going to counselling the last few months, which is helping. When you're ready, I can help you find someone to talk to. I'll even go with you and hold your hand if you want, because as cathartic as it is, it's bloody hard.'

'It is hard,' said Drew, nodding, 'but if you find someone you feel comfortable talking to, it can really help.'

Carol raised her brows. 'You've been?'

He shrugged. 'Sure. You've got to get shit like that out somehow and talking is better than picking fights or self-destructing in other ways.'

He was so laid back that Carol couldn't see him picking fights, but maybe that was because he'd found someone to talk to.

'Thanks, both of you.' She let go of Kelsey's hand and, shifting in her chair, tried to hide her wince. When everyone frowned at her, she smiled. 'It's okay. I'm just sore.'

'See, don't do that,' Jex said, pointing at her. 'We're all sitting here because we love you and we're worried about you, but you're downplaying what you've been through. Don't shut us out anymore.'

Carol thought about it, then nodded. 'You're right, it's a habit I need to break. But I'm not the only one.' She looked around the table. 'We all do it, so one in, all in. No keeping secrets anymore. None that can pull us apart, anyway.'

'To no secrets.' Kelsey raised her mug, saluting everyone with it, then drank. Everyone but Zoe joined in the chorus. Sitting at the end of the table, she hesitated before lifting her cup and taking a tiny sip.

Carol would mourn the damage done to their friendship and could only hope that one day they'd be able to mend the wound Paul had stabbed between them. Although they'd hurt each other, they'd also each stepped forward to stop Paul. That had to mean something, didn't it?

As talk turned to other things and laughter returned, Carol pushed all her stray thoughts aside, rested her head on Blake's shoulder, and when his arm came around her, she snuggled in and closed her eyes.

#

When she woke, everything ached, and only her and Blake remained in the kitchen.

He helped her sit up, and his hands, which wrought metal and wrangled tools, were so gentle on her body that she had to sniff back more tears.

'I don't know what's wrong with me,' she told him. 'I don't usually cry so much.'

Getting up to fill the kettle, he glanced at her over his shoulder. 'You don't think you've got a good reason to cry? You've been through hell in the last twenty-four hours, not to mention the last month. And that's not counting everything you went through in the last four years. Like Drew says, you've got to get it all out somehow.'

But it was more than that; she still had things to tell him.

He sat a mug of hot chocolate in front of her. 'I know that face. You're thinking that whatever you're about to say will upset me and make me feel differently about you.'

'It still scares me that you know me better than anyone ever has.'

He gave her a lopsided grin, which made her smile, but then she chewed on her bottom lip. 'He made me burn all the pictures I drew of you. When he asked if I had anything else of yours, I kept your Mothman jumper a secret. Burning that would've been like cutting out a part of my heart.'

'I could have bought another one.'

She shook her head. 'I slept in it because it smelt like you. When I dreamed of you, it was like I had part of you wrapped around me for real.' She had to close her eyes for the next part. 'This morning, though, after I got home from the hospital, I went to bed naked and woke up with him next to me. He was naked too. I don't think anything happened, but he had his hand on me.'

Blake's gentle hands cupped her face, and he pressed his lips to her forehead. 'Do you really think I'd hold that against you?'

She opened her eyes, determined not to cry again. Blake shouldn't have to deal with her old insecurities, just as she didn't deserve to live with them.

'No, you wouldn't,' she said. 'You wouldn't because you're a good guy, Blake. And you love me.'

'I do.' He peppered her face with kisses. 'And you love me.'

The thick block of ice that had been weighing her down melted. Warmth curled through her as she rested her cheek against his. 'I really do.'

EPILOGUE

On either side of the garden path, bright yellow daffodils nodded next to purple pansies while bees trekked from flower to flower, their legs heavy with pollen. Carol set a shallow bowl filled with marbles and water in a clump of alyssum.

Pipa leaned over Carol's shoulder for a closer look. 'So they not die?'

She absently ran her hand through Carol's hair, which glowed pink once more. Lilli and Kelsey had dyed it after scouring the shops for every shade they could find. Carol loved it; it looked even better than it had before.

'Yeah,' she said, 'so they don't die. My grandmother always put out a bowl of water for the bees and small birds. One year, there was a blue tongue lizard living under the verandah. I called him Speedy, and he'd waddle out whenever I tipped water into the bowl gran had left out.'

'Daddy screamed at a lizard.' Pipa giggled. 'He thought it was a snake.'

'I bet he did.' Grinning, Carol stood and held out a hand to Pipa. 'There are plenty of flowers here now for you to pick.'

'Mummy said to ask you first, 'cos it's your gran's garden and you might not want me to take them.'

'She would have wanted you to take some and enjoy them.'

They walked around the house to the side verandah, where Kelsey sat in the shade talking to Drew, her baby bump now clearly visible.

'Are you excited to be a big sister, Pip?' Carol asked.

'So excited.' She lifted their joined hands and twirled. 'But Mummy says I have to wait until after my birthday next year.'

'Yeah, it takes a while to cook a baby.' She took Pipa's other hand and walked her through the steps to the Pride of Erin. 'You've been practising.'

259

'Uh-huh. Daddy and Mummy have been dancing too.'

'I bet they have.' She grinned over at Kelsey, who blushed.

Pipa did a quick boogie between twirls. 'Does Drew dance?'

'I'm sure he would if you asked him.'

Already up and coming down the steps, Drew opened his arms as Pipa took a running leap at him. He spun on the spot and dipped her, and her deep belly laugh was answered by a kookaburra.

'Lilli's here.' Drew arrowed towards the car as it pulled up. 'Ask Lilli to dance.'

Lilli took Pipa to dance her around the car, while Drew came back and pulled Carol into a waltz. 'Your turn now.'

Giggling, Carol twirled. 'Last time I did this, my dance partner told me her husband liked to spank her.'

Drew grinned down at her. 'Ooh, really? Who?'

'Mrs Glade.'

'Oh man! I could have done without having the image of old people sex planted in my head.'

'You asked.'

'You could have warned me.'

She changed things up by spinning him out and pulling him back in. 'Why would I do that when I can share and spread the suffering? Besides, I figure I owe you. You're keeping me occupied because Blake is up to something. Isn't he?'

'I'm doing nothing of the sort.' He jutted his chin. 'If you don't want to spend time with me, just say so.'

She smirked at him. 'He and Ethan have been locked in that shed most of the morning.'

'They're doing boy stuff.'

She raised an eyebrow. 'Boy stuff?'

'Okay, okay, I know, define boy stuff. They're just doing stuff, then. Stuff he'll share with you when he's ready.'

'That's what I thought.' She spun him out again, then grabbed Kelsey as she came onto the grass. 'Do you know?'

'I know they're up to something, but I don't know what.'

'Okay.' As Carol slow danced with Kelsey, she began humming Snow Patrol's 'Chasing Cars', then sang the first line.

Lilli joined in, swaying in time with Pipa. And when Mark drove up with Jex right behind him, Carol handed Kelsey to Mark and wrapped her arms around Jex.

'Are we celebrating or commiserating?'

He grinned at her. 'Guess.'

'Celebrating?' It jumped inside her, the flare of hope she'd tried to bury. 'They'll stock it? A music shop will stock our CD?'

'They will!' He lifted her off her feet and swung her around.

When her feet hit the ground, hands closed over her hips and turned her.

'Told you so,' said Blake, his grin wide and eyes bright as he lifted her high. 'Congratulations.'

'Thank you.' She kissed him. 'I would have done it eventually, but you helped me get there quicker.'

'Don't mention it,' he said and grinned. 'Now, come on, I have something to show you.' He took her hand, led her into the house and stopped at the door to the spare room.

She couldn't help smiling. 'What have you done?'

He took her hand and placed it on the doorknob. 'It's not what I've done, but what you'll do.'

She turned the handle and pushed the door open. For a moment, no words came, but then she pressed a hand to her heart. 'You've made me an art studio?'

He'd thought of everything—the light from the windows, the shiny wood floor, the shelves of papers, inks, brushes, pencils, pens, everything. Even the cushions on the floor. She stepped inside and turned a slow circle.

'It's ...' Holding her hand out to him, she linked their fingers. 'It's beyond anything I've ever dreamed. Thank you.'

'If you want to change anything, let me know.'

'No, nothing gets changed. I love it because you made it for me.' She rose onto her toes and took his mouth with hers as heat and love pulsed through her.

'Save some of that,' he said, pulling away after kissing her long and deep. 'I have something else to show you.' He led her outside to the shed, past gardens that were a riot of colour and showcased his metal artworks. 'Close your eyes.'

She did, her heart leaping as his hands on her hips propelled her forward. He'd already surprised her with her bike, which he, Drew, Mark and Jex had rescued and restored.

'Is everyone else here?' she asked.

'They are.'

'So I shouldn't tell you what a turn-on this is?'

He chuckled. 'I don't mind.'

'We do,' Mark said from somewhere on her right.

'I think it's cute.' Jex's voice came from the left.

'Okay.' Blake turned her slightly. 'Open your eyes.'

She did, blinked and sucked in a breath. 'Oh, Blake.'

Above her grandfather's timeline, he'd framed another strip along the wall. Two dates in Blake's bold script documented the start of their journey.

'The day we met.' She traced a finger over the first date, then the second. 'And when I moved in.'

'Yes.' He handed her a permanent marker. 'And today's date.'

She eyed the marker and then him. 'Oh no, you don't get to give all the surprises today. Stay there.'

Heading to the shelf stacked with toolboxes, she slid hers out and rummaged in it until she found the open-ended spanner. Carrying it in her shaking hand, she went to stand before him.

'Okay. During the last month, you've worked to turn this place into the home of my dreams, and you've worked to make your business a success too. You've been there for me through police interviews, while people who still believe Paul pointed fingers, and when I just wanted to rage at the world. You level me. You make me fly. You make me want to reach for things I never believed I could have. You love me when I have trouble loving myself. I love you, so much that it's still a pressure here'—she tapped her chest—'and I don't always know what to do with it. There is no one else and never will be.

262

It's you, Blake. You're the one I want to fight these battles with. And even though I'll never surf with you, I'll always be there with you.'

She held the spanner out.

He took it but frowned. 'It's ...'

She rolled her eyes. 'Turn it over.'

'Oh.' He flipped it and stared down at the two words etched in the metal. *MARRY ME.*

'Only you could wreck my well-laid plans with something better.' He wound his arms around her and rocked her where they stood. 'I was going to get you to write today's date, and you'd ask why, and I'd say because I love you ...' He turned his head to their audience. 'Come on, guys, that was your cue!'

'Oh shit, yeah.' Drew started tapping a beat on the workbench.

Jex cleared his throat and, grinning at her, started singing Savage Garden's 'Truly Madly Deeply'. Carol held Blake close and rocked with him as their friends sang, and when they finished the song, everyone was grinning.

Blake held up the tool she'd given him. 'You've thrown a spanner in my works.' He traced a finger over the engraved words. 'I want you to know, Carol, that you've been there for me just as much as I have been for you. I can work my arse off because I know that when I'm done you're there. You push me to be my best, do my best, and you don't even realise it.' He ran a hand through her hair and pulled her close for a kiss. 'Marry me?'

Throwing her arms around his neck and her legs around his waist, she hugged him tight. 'Yes, Blake, I'll marry you. I'll stand beside you through the good and bad, and I'll always be ready to throw a spanner in your works because I love you.'

'I wouldn't have it any other way,' he said, then kissed her.

She lifted his hand that held the spanner. 'Does that mean you'll marry me?'

Blake grinned at her. 'You betcha.'

The pressure in her chest swelled, squeezed her heart, then freed it.

She pulled her friends into a group hug and, encircled by love and family, she slid her arms around Blake and kissed him.

'Now,' she said, glancing around the group, 'let's get this party started! The sooner we do, the sooner I can take my fiancé to bed.'

When everyone but Blake groaned and fled, she laughed, then pulled the permanent marker from Blake's pocket. 'We mark this day together, because from now on it's us, facing everything together.'

'Together.' He closed his hand over hers.

It might not have been the neatest date on the wall, but Carol loved it. 'There's room for so much more.' She turned her head and captured his lips. 'Let's fill it with as many memories as we can.'

'Let's.'

Taking his hand, she led him out into the love and laughter that filled their yard and home, into the gardens they'd created from the old and the new, into the future they would create together.

Author Note

I became an avid reader at a young age, picking up my first Mills and Boon at fourteen years old. In those days, I read to escape my life and it saved me. That, along with my horse, Dusty, who kept all my secrets, witnessed all my tears, and was my biggest reason for staying on this earth.

But, by escaping into books and the love lives of others, I experienced something I never believed I would. For me, as a survivor of child sex abuse, trusting someone enough to have that kind of intimacy *was* the stuff of fairytales.

As I grew older, I realised that the heroines in the books I read were never like me. I was different, and therefore, more alone. Did no one else think like me? Have the same story as me?

I want to tell stories that people can connect to. Stories other survivors can read and see themselves in. I want to show that life after trauma is not only possible, but deserved. And that if we want it, love can be woven out of the frayed beliefs we carry.

The *White Wattle Creek* series comes after nineteen years of writing and finding my way through the world of words to finally create something I hope inspires and touches the hearts of readers.

Facebook: @vikkiholsteinwriter
Twitter: @VikkiHolstein
Website: vikkiholstein.wordpress.com

ACKNOWLEDGEMENTS

To all my supporters, both online and in person, I thank you.

To the Melbourne Romance Writer's Guild, thank you for accepting me as one of your own so quickly, and for all your encouragement.

To Deb Portch, for giving all when you have nothing. For keeping me on track, for not letting me fall down the hole of imposter syndrome.

To Caroline Angel, for your friendship and championing me every chance you get.

To my dad, who never loses faith in me.

To my kids, who give me the oddest inspirations.

To my editor, Libby Iriks, without whose support I would never have grown, or would keep growing, as a writer.

Last, but never the least, to Craig, for everything.